**LOVE BETRAYED HER ONCE.
NOW IT'S OPENING THE DOOR
TO DANGER AGAIN.**

*Floy and Max. They were enemies at the start. But
now they are running from the Nazis, running for
their lives.*

*He is a man who gambles in a deadly game of
violence and intrigue, but he is her only hope for
safety. She is willing to pay his price. But now as
passion draws her into Max's arms, Floy wonders
if she has made a fatal mistake in trusting her life—
and her heart—to a man whose loyalty may be for
sale to the highest bidder. For in this war-torn
land, both have become part of a game of power
and passion . . . where all appearances are
calculated to deceive . . . and only peril is
undeniably real. . . .*

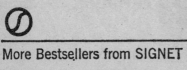

Souvenir

David A. Kaufelt

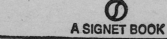
A SIGNET BOOK

NEW AMERICAN LIBRARY

NAL BOOKS ARE AVAILABLE AT QUANTITY DISCOUNTS
WHEN USED TO PROMOTE PRODUCTS OR SERVICES. FOR
INFORMATION PLEASE WRITE TO PREMIUM MARKETING
DIVISION, NEW AMERICAN LIBRARY, 1633 BROADWAY,
NEW YORK, NEW YORK 10019.

Copyright © 1983 by David A. Kaufelt

 SIGNET TRADEMARK REG. U.S. PAT. OFF. AND FOREIGN COUNTRIES
REGISTERED TRADEMARK—MARCA REGISTRADA
HECHO EN CHICAGO, U.S.A.

SIGNET, SIGNET CLASSIC, MENTOR, PLUME, MERIDIAN AND NAL
BOOKS are published by New American Library,
1633 Broadway, New York, New York 10019

First Signet Printing, January, 1985

1 2 3 4 5 6 7 8 9

PRINTED IN THE UNITED STATES OF AMERICA

For my friend,

Joan Tyor Carlson

Paris, 1942

Chapter One

She woke with a terrible taste in her mouth and a queasy, seasick feeling in her stomach. It was as if she had been eating ashes. But Floy knew she wasn't ill, only scared.

The maid—the Last of the Maids, Louisianne had dubbed her—placed the enamel breakfast tray squarely on the Italian desk, still managing to spill the tan ersatz coffee on the sour gray bread.

She had an absurd music-hall name—Minuette—and the black uniform was too tight across her farm-girl buttocks, so that the seams showed, threatening to split. The other maids had gone home to the country or been taken away to Germany to work in factories. Somehow, Minuette had stayed on.

"Mademoiselle," Minuette said, as she did every morning, but this morning her voice broke, and Floy realized that she too was scared. Floy had a momentary impulse to go to her, put her arms around the girl, give and receive comfort.

The big girl made an awkward curtsy and left. Floy got out of bed, decided she couldn't face the coffee, and went to the French windows, which had been painted blue under the direction of the neighborhood's air raid warden. She opened them, letting the September sunshine into the room, and stared out into the empty courtyard.

He only wants to have lunch, Floy said to herself, reverting in her mind to English, which she invariably did when she was ill or nervous or frightened. It is only a luncheon. Not a beheading.

And then, because she didn't want to think of beheadings, she went into Curry's room, purposely forgetting that he too had left for the country. A pair of his shoes, badly scuffed, stood on his bureau. They had been forgotten in the rush to get him off. She touched them and then, vowing not to cry, not today, she went in search of her aunt Louisianne.

But when Floy looked into the darkened salon at the opposite end of the circle that made up her aunt's apartment, she saw that Louisianne and Sacha were just entering the tiny room Louisianne chose to call her office. They were having one of their increasingly private discussions, but turned politely when they sensed her presence.

They said, "Good morning," and Floy said, "Good morning," and then she went back to her suite and into the old-fashioned, high-ceilinged bathroom. She brushed her teeth with enthusiasm, as she had been taught—as if the metallic-tasting toothpowder could override the bitter taste of fear and cowardice.

She dressed carefully in a dark-gray suit, a hat, gloves, leather shoes that needed new heels and wouldn't get them, and quietly left the apartment.

She made her way down the unlit stairs. The tiny gilded birdcage of an elevator had stopped running soon after the war, and there were no mechanics to fix it. Now, of course, the Germans gave Paris so little electricity that it wouldn't have been much use even if it had worked.

She crossed the cobblestoned courtyard, passing the loge in which Mme. DeFarge sat knitting. Short, ancient, moving with difficulty, she had been given that Dickensian name so long ago that no one knew her real name. A black oilcloth shopping bag containing her knitting, her lunch, and—according to Louisianne—all her worldly goods stood next to her, as always, on the table that took up most of the loge.

"Bonjour, mademoiselle," Mme. DeFarge said in her croak of a voice, and Floy found herself able to smile, to say, *"Bonjour, madame,"* though what she really wanted to say was Help. Help me.

Floy hadn't told her aunt about the invitation to lunch. Louisianne had, it seemed, her own private worries and fears.

She walked quickly down Avenue Niel's little hill to the metro station at Avenue de Villiers. She didn't look behind her to see if anyone was following her; she didn't have to. She took the number 2 line six stops to Place d'Anvers and thought that her route would probably go into the report. Dutifully she sat in the second-class carriage; first class was reserved for Germans and "important French officials"—which Floy read as "collaborationists." She studied the Wanted signs above the windows opposite her: "Pierre Paul Bernard, 23, blond hair, brown eyes, wanted for questioning"; the patriotic signs: "France, Germany, the New Europe"; the signs exhorting Frenchmen to volunteer to work in German factories.

It was in the metro, Floy thought, that the German occupation was really brought home to one. She looked at the watch the man sitting next to her was wearing. She had nearly three hours to kill until it was time to turn up for that lunch date at the Ritz.

Reluctantly surfacing from the metro at Place d'Anvers —there was something reassuring, womblike about the metro—she walked across the trafficless street to the Gaieté Rochechouart (Pigalle's premier cinema, the marquee proclaimed).

Once, before that other war, it had been a music hall, and there was a plaster girl dating from that time standing over the marquee, lifting her skirt, smiling down at the Gaieté's customers with mock innocence. A naughty Pigalle plaster girl. Floy smiled back at her as she paid her money and entered the theater.

She wasn't surprised that it was nearly filled at ten o'clock on a Monday morning in September. A great many people living in Paris under the German occupation went to the movies at odd times of day.

Early on, in 1940, after the shameful armistice, the movies had taken the place of churches. They had become a refuge, a safe, dark place where the hunted and the despairing could sit quietly for a time without being disturbed.

That security hadn't lasted, Floy thought, finding a place in the mezzanine, tipping the usherette, thinking of the gray-uniformed men who would be standing at each exit at the end of the presentation to demand identity cards and "recruit" for French workers in Germany.

Floy looked around the cavernous auditorium. In the dim half-light she could identify half a dozen men, women, and pathetic children, all with the thinnest clothes, accents, identities. They were the ones the men in the gray uniforms would be waiting for.

This film would be their last resort, their last pleasure, their last money spent.

"The theaters," Billy had said, "have become giant mousetraps; the movies, the cheese."

Floy felt that she herself had joined the ranks of the helpless mice, no longer in charge of her life, frightened by all the cats in the world, one of whom had demanded she have lunch with him.

It's only a meal, she told herself for the tenth time that morning, relieved when the news film began and she wouldn't have to think.

It was being shown in the half-light, in accordance with an official regulation, so that booers and hissers could be identified. The UFA cameramen utilized every trick to glorify the might of the Nazi panzer divisions moving across the screen.

The obligatory arms parade over, the film segued into a segment portraying a group of French men and women working happily in an unidentified German factory. Munitions, Floy thought.

Those workers were so well dressed, so well fed, so beautifully cared for, it was a wonder that half France didn't get up and go to Germany. Perhaps, Floy thought, watching the French Workers in Germany cavort around a swimming pool in a Bavarian resort, I should become a French Worker in Germany.

But she wasn't French, and Chambertin wasn't going to let her off that easily. That much was clear. She had come to the Gaieté Rouchechouart to forget that fact, but it wouldn't stay submerged. Her imagination continually betrayed her.

The news film not providing the diversion she wanted, Floy looked around her. Besides the sad, diminished families, there were a few single women like herself and German soldiers. But for the most part the audience was made up of old people.

A middle-aged man in a faded blue suit sat next to her, his hands folded in his lap. Once, Floy thought, if she had gone to the cinema alone, she would have had to worry about unsolicited hands on her knees. No longer. Frenchmen seemed to have lost that characteristic acquisitive sexual instinct.

Or perhaps, Floy thought, as the news film finally came to an end and the advertisements came up, I've lost my attraction for the sort of men who haunt movie theaters. Fear rarely heightened one's magnetism, Billy had told her early on, when she had been frightened.

"But I'm scared," she had shouted at him in the dressing room he had taken her to, slamming the door.

"Everyone's scared," he had shouted back. "You're an actress. It's your job to disguise that fact."

Well, she hadn't been much of an actress. Billy hadn't

7

wanted to believe that. She thought of his smile—sour, as if he were chewing on a lemon rind, but amused all the same—and decided she didn't want to think of Billy either.

She only wanted the film to come on, so that she wouldn't have to think at all.

But the advertisements went on, and rather than Billy she thought of Chambertin, who was waiting for her at the Ritz. She closed her eyes, saw him too clearly, and opened them again. She knew what he was going to say, the offers, the ultimatums he was going to make.

A milliner's display was on the screen. Mme. Leonard, 6 Rue St. Honoré. Custom-made hats, despite the shortage of silk, cotton, straw, linen. "Wonderful," the Germans said, "what the French can do with paper."

Paper hats and wooden shoes and acorn coffee. The French were such imaginative children. She wondered if she should have worn a paper hat. The one she had put on was felt and old and black. She had put her hair up into it and pulled the mannish brim down over her eyes—to look inconspicuous. She wanted to look so inconspicuous that she vanished.

If only the fear would vanish. If only she could stop feeling like a vampire's victim, empty and bloodless. Just as she decided that she couldn't sit still a moment longer, that those Technicolor images she was keeping at bay couldn't be held off, the lights went down and the film came on.

Floy nearly laughed aloud. She had chosen the Gaieté because it was a big, dark, middle-class theater on a convenient metropolitan line. She hadn't thought to find out what film would be playing.

It was called *Infidel* in its first incarnation and was one of her early films. Billy had directed it, but Sacha's name was on it because Billy was English and had fought in the war in Spain against the Fascists, and the French

8

government even then wasn't taking any chances on insulting the Germans. Billy had been officially proscribed: a non-resident, a non-director, a non-person.

Billy would have been amused, Floy thought, to see *Infidel* resurrected under a new, non-ironic title, *The Hero*. It was the sort of film Billy had done easily. Powerful, a bit old-fashioned, a melodrama set against the background of an earlier war.

They're getting desperate, Floy thought, if they're showing a pro-French war film several years old.

But there weren't enough new French films, and the people wouldn't watch the German movies. They went to the Italian offerings only to laugh, to throw rolled-up newspapers at the screen.

She felt embarrassed during that first scene, watching herself. She had a bit part, the standard French clothes-horse idea of a rich American girl. She wore a black sequinned evening dress that weighed ten pounds and left little red scars on her skin. She watched herself walk across what was supposed to be a grand hotel's ballroom through half-closed eyes. The script had called for her to lead on the young hero. Not my finest twenty minutes, she thought, looking away.

She was relieved when Arletty—who had a very different sort of style—came on screen, taking over the film and the hero, relegating Floy's character to a life of empty luxury on the Côte d'Azur.

It was the battle scenes that moved the audience. The irony of French soldiers being slaughtered by an unspecified enemy wasn't lost on the Monday morning audience in the Gaieté Rochechouart in September, 1942.

In the dark Floy saw pinpoints of white as the women —and many of the men—wept into their handkerchiefs. They wept with fear and they wept with anger and they wept with a terrible ache for their dead. But most of all they wept with shame. Their leaders had given their

9

country to Germany with only a token resistance, and they had stood by and watched.

As Louisianne had said in that characteristic dry, understated way of hers, *"La belle France* didn't put up much of a fight."

"They gave France to Hitler on a silver platter," Billy had agreed. "And then they told him to keep the platter. The Maginot Line," Billy had said in despair, shaking his head, referring to that supposedly invincible line of fortifications the French government had claimed would keep the Germans out.

"The Imaginot Line," Sacha had said.

And suddenly, before she was at all ready, *The Hero* came to an end, and people were putting away their handkerchiefs, getting out their identity cards and their papers. The house lights came half up as the closing credits appeared on the screen.

Billy had liked to reserve the cast for the end "so they will know who to blame," and Sacha had followed suit.

They were simple credits, black names on gray backgrounds, and Floy sat still for them. She rarely enjoyed seeing herself on the screen, but she got a certain satisfaction when she saw her name. It gave her, she felt, credibility. She could say with a fair degree of confidence that she was a film actress.

Arletty had a card to herself, as did Robert Grillet. The supporting actors were spread over several cards. Every five lines or so a name was blacked over with heavy ink. The idea, of course, was to eliminate the names of Jews and anti-Fascists.

Floy waited for her own name. Another card appeared, with still more blacked-out names. She marveled at the thoroughness of the Censorship Bureau, at the time it must have taken to black out those offending names laboriously by hand.

And then suddenly she realized as the credits ended that her own name had been blacked out as well.

She sat in her seat, a little breathless, feeling diminished. It was as if the censor's pen had scratched out not only her name but her being as well.

She wanted to protest, to have them stop the reel from coming to an end, to have them rewind it. She wanted them to put her name back.

But that most final of all words, FINIS, came at her with its terrible cheap irony, and the house lights came all the way up and the exit doors opened and the audience began to move out. They were silent, their papers in their unsteady hands, sheep passing before the gray-uniformed wolves who stood at each door.

Floy waited, as several others did. She tried to tell herself that she had merely missed her name, that she had been so anxious to see it that she had overlooked it. She didn't believe that, but she tried.

A family stood near her. The father and the mother were in their early thirties, and the boy might have been Curry's age, about five. They were pale and scrupulously clean, as if they had been washed and pressed for this occasion.

They seemed unnaturally calm. They stood by their seats, their hands held firmly together in front of them, and waited long after they should have joined the exiting queue. Once, giving herself away, the woman turned and looked at the entrance, as if hoping they could escape through it, but two soldiers stood in the entry arch, smoking, talking, barring the way.

Finally Floy stood up and went to the nearest exit, handing her papers to the big, anonymous, square soldier, thinking she might be able to face death but not torture.

The thought of torture left her queasy and ill, nearly paralyzed. There had been too much talk of torture. Too many stories, descriptions, eyewitness reports.

She heard another soldier shout at the family who had remained standing by their seats, but she found she had little to spare for them. Her entire being was concentrated

11

on this soldier studiously examining her papers—those poor, tawdry, tattered, and essential papers.

This was the ultimate German method of debasement: making the conquered doubt their existence.

Abruptly he handed them back to her, and with a polite, perfunctory *"Merci, mademoiselle,"* he stood aside. She moved past him into the alley, which smelled of urine and something else, something sweet and indefinable. Fear, Floy decided as she walked up the alley to the Boulevard Rochechouart.

Regard for her own safety dictated she should not turn around. She had become zealous in keeping herself safe of late. But the thought of that family, standing at their seats, was too much for her and she turned once. The soldiers had left their posts, joining their comrades inside the theater. There was no sign of the family and no sound of them either. It might have been more bearable if there had been a scream, a muffled shout. It was the absence of sound that so chilled Floy, that made her think the family had disappeared in the same way her name had disappeared: scratched out, inked over, as if they had never been.

A velo-taxi was discharging a passenger in front of the theater, and Floy got into its rickshaw-like cab, exhausted, fatalistic. She had seen Rivet. His appearance had driven the sad, doomed family out of her mind.

He was small, thin, and dark, working a toothpick in and out of his little sharp teeth. He wore a toothbrush mustache, yellow and brown, and a soiled white suit. He was smiling to himself.

"My Parisian water rat," Chambertin had called him.

"Why do you keep him about?" Floy had asked, revolted.

"He reminds me of what I might have been," Chambertin had answered. "Besides, he is intensely loyal. He is not the sort of rat who bites the hand that feeds him."

She sat back in the velo-taxi and took a long deep breath as the woman driver pedaled through the light traffic. Billy had taught her that trick, to be used before difficult scenes. "A Hindu exercise, my dear," he had explained, smiling that sweet-and-sour smile of his. He had been no taller than Rivet, but he had had such strength, such purpose in his little body. She thought that if he had wanted to, he could have been anything.

She gazed at the checked cap of the velo driver and decided that for once Billy's Hindu breath trick wasn't working. She couldn't concentrate. She could only wonder if Rivet was in a velo-taxi behind her. Or if the driver in the checked cap was a spy.

She marveled at the manpower Chambertin had at his command. She wondered how many spies were assigned to real enemies of the Reich, to those who might be genuinely dangerous.

She wished, as the velo-taxi moved into the Rue Cambon and stopped at the rear entrance—the French entrance—to the Ritz, that she were genuinely dangerous.

Chapter Two

She hadn't been to the Ritz since the spring and she wondered where the blond Ritz ladies with their white fox muffs and tiny brown lapdogs had gone. The Germans had taken over the Place Vendôme Ritz buildings. The French—Coco Chanel, Mme. Ritz, her son, and the others—were allowed to live in the Rue Cambon buildings. Perhaps the blonds were still there, tucked away in unobtrusive comfort on the fourth floor.

Claude, the little *sous-directeur*, saw Floy and bowed sadly, looking at her with his long, doggy eyes. She tried to smile at him. He had wanted to close the Ritz when the Germans came, but Madame was having none of that. The Ritz was above war and occupation. The Ritz was in business.

It's a rather melancholy business, Floy thought, deciding that the Ritz warmth and *joie de vivre* had left with the Ritz blonds—or had been stored away in camphor until the occupation came to an end.

That didn't seem likely in the very near future, not if the news films were to be even partially believed. Floy wondered if the war would go on forever, for her entire life and more, like the Hundred Years' War. I'm young at the wrong time, she said to herself. But she didn't feel young. Her mouth was dry and her palms were sweaty and she wondered, as she walked across the black and white marble passageway that connected the Rue Cambon with the Place Vendôme, if she looked as ill and used as she felt.

"Try to put that fear aside," Billy had told her repeatedly. Then she had been so nervous that she was hardly able to speak her lines and she would ruin scene after scene. "Get out of yourself, you selfish little girl," Billy would say to her in that closet of a room from which he directed Sacha directing the actors. "You must stop thinking about yourself, Floy, my dear. Become someone else, preferably the woman you are trying to play."

It was an actor's trick that came with experience, but she wasn't all that experienced. She would have stopped if Billy hadn't continued to yell at her, to advise her, to support her.

She caught sight of herself in one of the ancient Ritz mirrors. It needed refinishing, but the Ritz blonds had liked that aspect of the corridor mirrors. They presented faded images, softer lines, illusions of what was and what might have been. The Ritz blonds had insisted the mirrors remain as they were, and Madame had happily complied.

Floy looked at herself in the not quite clear mirror and thought that for once she looked like a film actress.

She had dark hair, the color of the expensive furs for German consumption artistically draped in the corridor shops. No Frenchman could afford them now.

She had green eyes that had the color and depth of the Colombian emeralds displayed in M. Boutan's jewelry boutique. She had good shoulders and nice legs, and in the tarnished mirror she might have been a model for those boutiques or an elegant salesgirl. Or someone's mistress, not quite certain about the emeralds or the furs.

The expensive shops had earned the passageway the name Temptation Walk. The only temptation Floy felt was to retreat, to go home to her aunt's apartment and to sleep.

She closed her eyes again and put out a hand, touching the cool surface of the mirror, and then, taking a deep

Hindu breath à la Billy, she entered the Place Vendôme section of the Ritz and walked steadily, bravely to the dining salon, where Maurice—charming, patient, removed—greeted her at the door.

There were the usual complications. The French who continued to dine at the Ritz were seated at the right of the salon. Their German occupiers had chosen the left.

"Monsieur Chambertin?" Maurice asked, knowing whom Floy was meeting, giving her a moment to get used to the room with its rich odor, its expensive atmosphere, its delicate seating arrangements.

Nearly imperceptibly Maurice gestured with his beautifully shaven chin to the left, warning her. Before, because she had asked him to, Chambertin had sat at the right when she lunched with him. It had seemed important at the time, a valid gesture.

Now it seemed a purposeless fancy, what Louisianne would call hogwash. She agreed with Maurice that she was to sit at M. Chambertin's table, at the left.

The French turned their eyes away as she followed Maurice, refusing to look. But the Germans, operatic in their uniforms—black and silver, death's-head medallions, dazzling boots, jodhpurs, tightly fitting tunics—an entire light-opera company—deliberately turned to watch.

She moved, she knew, nicely. Her film career, such as it was, might have been based on that one fact. And now, of course, they knew who she was. With the scarcity of actors—so many had left for Hollywood only days before the Germans came—she had been given bigger and more important roles.

Sacha billed her as the new Garbo, remote and unavailable. Quickly she had become another precious French commodity to be bought up and shipped home. Her films, she was told, did very well in Germany.

Chambertin stood up as she approached his table. She was always, even now, surprised at his beauty. When she was away from him, she never thought of his somewhat delicate good looks. But now, after not seeing him for some time, she was again surprised by them. The blond hair, the highly colored cheeks, the perfect symmetry of his nose, his wide and noble forehead. He looked like an impossibly fine French schoolboy, aristocratic, his skin so thin, so lightly colored that it gave him an unwanted porcelainlike fragility.

Though he looked as if he had been brought up in aristocratic seclusion in a chateau on the Loire, he had been born and reared in a Paris suburb, the son of a grocery-shop keeper and a peasant's daughter.

Floy had met them once, on a late Sunday afternoon, coming out of his *pied-à-terre*. They had been shy, and Chambertin's angry embarrassment had made her awkward. The meeting had not been a success.

As a boy, he had a gift for languages. An Austro-Hungarian count, a remittance man and one of his father's customers, had taken to him and sent him to school. The count's remittances had long stopped by the time he was ready for college, but Chambertin had already formed alliances. He joined the government as assistant to a minister of finance and later, after that minister had been publicly denounced as a Stavisky partner, Chambertin switched his allegiance to Laval.

The minister had had his finger, Chambertin said, in Stavisky's make-believe financial empire. Laval had his entire hand in a shady Fascist pie and made no bones about it.

Early on, Chambertin had married the disgraced minister's daughter, who had kept his money when he went to prison and died. A staunch Catholic who couldn't have children, she remained in her father's country house after the trial, spending most of her time with the sympathetic village priest. She gave Chambertin an allowance and her father's Hispano-Suiza and retired from the marriage.

17

"When I was a boy," Chambertin had told Floy, "I would spend every afternoon at the movies. I would come home from school in my blue uniform, leave my books, and go to the cinema. I couldn't bear that apartment over the shop with its smells of disinfectant and sawdust and overripe vegetables. My schoolmates were picked up in limousines and taken home to mansions in the Faubourg St. Germain. But we had one thing in common. We all loved the film stars. Only I was privileged to go to the movies at will. In those days the films did not have sound, and I saw mostly American films. Clara Bow. Theda Bara. Mary Miles Minter. They seemed to me, in my innocence, more beautiful, more unattainable than any of my schoolmates' well-born sisters. I would sit in those late-matinee audiences, surrounded by housewives and prostitutes and their attendant aromas, hypnotized. I told myself I would have my own film star one day and I would never share her with anyone. She would be all for me."

He had stared at her with his pale-blue eyes, the irises nearly white; his long, thin hands inched toward hers. She had thought he looked like a man born blind, trying to fathom what it would be like to see.

He had frightened her with his intensity then.

He frightened her more now with his cordiality, several years after that conversation, as he stood behind his chair in the Ritz dining salon, waiting for her.

He would have kissed her hand—he indulged in all the passé continental absurdities—but she had kept her gloves on. The Last of the Gloves—like the Last of the Maids—to be treasured, cared for.

Seated, gloves removed, Floy looked at him and tried to smile. He wore round rimless blue smoked glasses in imitation of his long-dead Austro-Hungarian sponsor. He thought they gave him an eccentric, aristocratic air, but they only succeeded in making him seem cryptic and more fragile, an out-of-sorts invalid whose demands could never be satisfied.

"You're pale," Chambertin said, beginning as usual in the middle of a conversation. "He's not making you happy, that's clear."

"There is no he, Chambertin." But even through the blue smoked lenses she could see the peculiar set of his child's blue eyes, the nearly white irises contracting, and she knew he still didn't believe her. He still thought he had a kind of option on her body and that one day she would allow him to exercise it. He was an obsessed collector, and she was the prize porcelain. One day, when the price was right for both of them, he would own her. He was certain of that.

He had ordered. A fish soup and an escalope and that pale yellow wine he never told anyone the name of, as if it had been laid down by Chambertin forebears decades before.

She was, surprisingly, famished. She ate everything, while he stared at her just as he had that first day: the frustrated collector again, examining a new and rare piece he couldn't afford at the moment. She had realized early on that he had never seen her as she really was. She was his own celluloid fantasy, and still he didn't want to let go.

"You need a rest," he told her, when the sweet came. "You need a vacation, Floy, perhaps a few weeks in the Vosges."

The sweet was very small, no bigger than a child's pincushion. It was a creme caramel, and she pushed it away untasted. She knew she would regret it later, that creme caramels were not to be had so easily; but she suddenly felt nauseous, helpless. And angry.

"Why am I having lunch with you, Chambertin?"

He smiled his thin-lipped smile. It made him seem less beautiful and less human. He grasped the sides of the linen-covered table with both of his thin, long hands and spoke slowly, with infinite care, watching her. "You are to be picked up by the Gestapo within twenty-four hours. I tell you this because I want to give you an opportunity to wind up your affairs. A few last hours with your lover, perhaps."

She stared at him, thinking she was going to be ill. He shook his head, misunderstanding.

"No. It is not me, Floy. All American women in Occupied France are to be taken to a hotel in the Vosges and kept there for the duration of the war. It is not unreasonable, is it? We are at war with your country. It would be peculiar, would it not, if we did not take some action?"

He waited for her to react, seemingly poised. But his hands gave him away. They were grasping the table so hard that they had turned nearly as blue as his smoked lenses.

She had often thought of those long, perfectly formed hands. They weren't feminine, but they weren't particularly masculine either. At those weekly luncheons he would use them to touch her whenever he could, brushing against her own hands, gripping her elbow to help her up, letting them rest on her shoulders too long when he helped her on with her coat. She shuddered at the thought of that touch and said in a voice that sounded artificially bright, "Do you think I might have a brandy, Chambertin?"

He smiled, relaxing his grip on the table. "Good, Floy. Very good. Your serenity would fool most anyone. But I know you so well. You are frightened. Allow me to re-assure you: It will not be unbearable in Vittel. The food and the sanitary conditions, of course, will be a problem. Not up to Ritz standards. And your guards will be men without many distractions. You will learn soon enough that the more cooperative you are, the easier it will be for you. You should be exceedingly popular. They will all want the cinema star, *n'est-ce pas*? I understand your last film, *Les Filles du Jour* is a favorite with that class of men."

She drank the brandy slowly, letting it burn her throat. Her fat cousin Gloria used to pinch her arm when she had toothache. "Makes it hurt less," Gloria said in grown-up tones. Gloria, like Chambertin, had seemed a child disguised as an adult.

Floy looked at Chambertin staring at her. Nutty as a fruitcake, Auntie Ida would have said. That, of course, was obvious—in his obsession with her, at least. But he seemed to handle everything else, especially his career, with a clear rationality. She wondered in that isolated moment as they stared at each other how nutty, how neurotic his obsession with her was, how far beyond the range of normality it lay. In the beginning she had thought it would dissolve with time, go away. But it had only strengthened and become hard, like a jungle vine that thrived on darkness, on unfriendly conditions.

He smiled and stood. He bowed. She turned. It was the first time since she had entered the dining salon that his attention, his examiner's stare, was off her, and she wanted to see what brought the relief.

It was Göring, all of him. He had stepped into the dining room for a brief conference with Maurice about his evening meal. He wore a sky-blue uniform of his own invention and smiled across the room at a monocled general, at a lovely woman in a red dress, at Chambertin, who bowed.

"You mustn't think of escape, Floy," Chambertin, reseated, went on, his eyes turning back on her like a powerful blue-white beam. "You mustn't allow yourself to dream of trying to cross over into the Free Zone. It would be so very dangerous. You are not yet a star of the first magnitude. But after *Les Filles du Jour* you are well known. And then, of course, you would have what they call in England an implacable bloodhound following you. I wouldn't let you escape, Floy."

"I couldn't be that important," she said, reaching for a conversational tone, nearly achieving it.

"If you try to escape, Floy," he said after a moment, "I would find you. I promise you I would find you." His voice had risen a level and sounded thin, artificial. "And when I found you, Floy, you would not end up in *résidence forcée* in a hotel in the Vosges. I have learned a great deal from the Germans, Floy. I would not hesitate to employ my knowledge on you."

Without warning, he reached across the table and wrapped his long, narrow fingers around her wrist. His nails were perfect pale half-moons, beautifully manicured. Floy looked down and watched his fingers for a moment as if a snake were wrapped around her wrist.

"No," he said, releasing her, rubbing his palms together, placing his hands flat on the tablecloth. "Better do as you are told, Floy. Be a little quiet and a little obliging, and nothing too terrible will happen to you."

Georges the waiter brought her another brandy when he took the empty wine bottle away. She drank the brandy, grateful to Georges. She wondered again what the yellow wine was called and decided that it was probably too late to ask. Much too late.

"There is another option, Floy."

She had known that from the moment she had entered the room and felt his eyes on her. She almost laughed. There had always been that option. She had been waiting for him to put it into words again.

But he didn't. He merely turned his hands, palms up, on the linen cloth. She looked at those soft white palms and turned away. "You would be safe," she heard him whisper. "Safe."

She looked up at him, but it was his turn to look away, as if he were in pain. She knew he wished he were free of her, that he didn't need her so badly, that he didn't have to make this embarrassing offer. "You would be safe," he said again, as if he were—in another time—offering her an expensive, tempting present.

Miserably, because she so much wanted to be safe, she shook her head, no.

He put the serviette to his lips, crumpled it in his hands, and threw it aside as he stood up, now avoiding looking at her.

It was her turn to stare at him as he signed the bill and pushed his chair away. His jacket doesn't fit nearly as well as it should, she thought. And then she caught sight of his pistol, a steel-blue Schmeisser, lodged in a holster under his arm and she knew why his jacket didn't fit. It was illegal to carry sidearms in the Ritz. The German officers were required to check all weapons in a special room off the Vendôme entrance.

But perhaps Chambertin doesn't think of himself as a German officer, she thought. And then he hesitated for a moment and took off his smoked glasses. He looked at her as if he were trying to memorize her face. There was too much passion in those pale, one-dimensional blue eyes. They were filled with lust and hate and, Floy decided, insanity. They frightened her more than *résidence forcée* in the Vosges or any of the other threats, real and imagined, he had offered her.

"I wish," he said, still looking at her, "I had never known you. I wish I didn't need you." He put on his glasses and left her sitting with the Germans and the collaborationists on the wrong side of the Ritz dining salon.

Absurdly, she found herself a victim of social fears. She was afraid that she wasn't going to be able to move, that she was, as Billy's writer would put it, paralyzed with fear. She was afraid that she might conceivably do what she had done only once before, and that was faint in a public place.

She nearly laughed. I'm still my aunties' niece, she thought, and tried to gather her hat, her purse, the last, worn gloves. But she still heard those desperate final words of Chambertin. She saw his pale-blue eyes behind the smoked glasses and her hands shook and she knew the fear wasn't going to go away. That it was as relentless as Chambertin's need for her.

"I'll live with it," she said aloud in English. Because she knew she was not going to allow herself to be rounded up with the other American women left in Paris and "detained in a little hotel in the Vosges."

Even if she wanted to, she couldn't go along peacefully to the Vosges. She had an obligation, one Chambertin knew nothing about.

That thought gave her the energy she needed to steady her hands, to walk out of the Ritz dining salon, the Germans watching, the French looking away.

Chapter Three

Floy left the Ritz by the Rue Cambon and found a velo-taxi and directed the driver to take her to the Collioure, a large, middling café on the Champs, within walking distance of the Rue Balny d'Avricourt.

She waited a moment before entering the café, but Rivet—Chambertin's Parisian sewer rat—didn't appear. Perhaps he's been called off, Floy thought. Chambertin was no longer interested in her phantom lover. She was to be arrested and sent away, and her case would be closed. Rivet could be diverted to more important game.

She sat at one of the round outdoor tables under the green canopy and ordered a white vermouth, knowing she wouldn't get drunk. She was too anxious. She sat with her back against the Collioure's mammoth plate-glass window, sipping her vermouth, watching men in dark suits and women with upswept hairdos walk up and down the once noisy Champs with purpose.

The cars for the most part were gone, and so were the street vendors and the thin man with the little monkey who used to grind an organ on the Rond Point, playing "Auprès de ma Blonde" over and over again. German flags flew from several of the buildings, indicating their occupants, and she wondered how many of those efficient people walking up and down the Champs were on their way to the Rue des Saussaies, to Gestapo headquarters, that solid limestone building, to report on their friends, relatives, neighbors.

Perhaps I am drunk, she thought. But she knew better. It was the fear—the memory of Chambertin's fingers wrapped around her wrist—that kept her from thinking clearly. And it was the knowledge that all she had to do was say yes, and she would be safe, protected. A Woman's Virtue, she thought, but didn't smile. The thought of Chambertin, of his cool, blue-white body—that boy's body—made her feel queasy and ill. She had had her moments of ecstasy, she thought bitterly. And in true melodrama fashion, she had learned her lesson. She had paid. That part of her, her sexuality, had been left behind when she came to France. Certainly Chambertin wouldn't be able to bring it to life. He was as sexual as a pretty castrato, as attractive as a snake.

When she felt she could, Floy stood up and moved through the maze of tables where men were reading what passed for newspapers in Paris, Germany. She bought a *jeton* from the cashier and, aware that she could be overheard in that crowded café, made her call.

Louisianne answered, uncharacteristically, after just one ring. "I am afraid," she said, in the voice she reserved for Strangers Who Don't Measure Up, "that it is difficult to talk now. Do not bother coming round as I am too occupied to see you." There was just the slightest emphasis on the words "occupied," "afraid." "Perhaps," Louisianne went on, in that odd, distant voice, "we might have a drink one night at *the* café. *Au revoir, mon lapin.* And *courage.*"

Floy forced her hand not to tremble as she replaced the receiver. Either they were already there or Louisianne thought the phone was tapped. That was one of the facts Floy had such difficulty in taking in. That telephone conversations could be overheard. Quiet talks in private homes could be listened to. Old friends were not to be trusted.

She returned to her table and paid her bill. She

26

thought of Louisianne's cold voice, those slightly emphasized words. "Afraid." "Occupied." *"Courage."* It was obvious she wasn't to go home. That scared and depressed her as much as anything Chambertin had said.

She didn't know what to do. If she couldn't go home, where could she go? And then she remembered Louisianne had said they might have a drink one night at "the" café. It was clear she should go to Chez Anya.

She seized on that fact as if it were a lifesaver and she were drowning. On her first trip to Paris, when she was thirteen, Billy had taken her for an aperitif to Chez Anya, and Louisianne had been furious. She had referred to it as "the" café and implied that women of ill repute took their meals there.

Billy had told her later that Anya had once been a rival of Louisianne's, and when Floy had charged Louisianne with this, Louisianne had insisted on taking dinner at "the" café once a week to refute it, to show how magnanimous she could be to "poor little Anya."

Chez Anya faced the Trocadero, and Anya, a plump, tough hen of a woman, had once been someone important's mistress and had received the café as a parting gift. Anya, wearing a white, classically draped dress wildly inappropriate for her figure and the time of day and year, welcomed Floy at the door, putting her arm around her, clucking.

As she led Floy into the restaurant, Anya complained. It was three in the afternoon, "German time." The Germans had insisted the French put back their clocks to match theirs. The chef was already busily preparing dinner. The Germans were giving Paris only a half-hour of electricity at night, and while candles were fine for dinner, Jean-Claude's provincial cooking required electricity.

"I am meeting my aunt," Floy said, not knowing what else to say.

27

Anya looked up at the younger woman for a moment and put her thick arm around her shoulder. "You may have to wait awhile," she said, leading Floy to a table in the rear of the long, dark, quintessentially Parisian room. There were mirrors, of course, and a dark-green velvet ceiling and black-carpeted floors. It was expensive and dim, and Anya, in that white dress, looked as if she had wandered in from a neighborhood bistro.

She brought Floy a tiny cup of precious genuine coffee and a genuine madeleine and disappeared into the kitchen to watch Jean-Claude warily.

It occurred to Floy that she might have misheard or misread Louisianne's message. Now, an hour after the call, she wasn't quite as certain about those underlined words, about Louisianne's message. She thought she would wait a little longer and perhaps call again. She wondered quite suddenly if the Germans considered Louisianne an American. She had been born in Philadelphia but she had lived in Paris most of her life and had married a Pole.

She wondered if Chambertin knew about Louisianne; she wondered just what Chambertin knew and thought that as always he had lied a little.

It was clear she didn't have a day to "wind up her affairs." Someone was waiting for her in the courtyard or perhaps in Louisianne's salon, sitting on the striped sofa, his legs crossed, a warrant for her arrest in his pocket. Did they have warrants for arrest, or was that an American custom, a nicety the Germans did without?

Certainly Rivet, with his yellow toothbrush mustache, the soiled suit, and the overworked toothpick, wouldn't wait for a warrant.

"I should have gone home when I could have," she said to herself aloud in English. "I should have forced Louisianne to come back."

And then, because she couldn't stand the guilt—of course she should have gone home when she could have

28

—and because she couldn't listen to her thoughts any longer, she closed her remarkable green eyes, rested her head against the green velvet plusli of Anya's most important banquette, and allowed herself to remember.

Philadelphia, 1937

Chapter Four

In the spring of 1937 Floy Devon wore organdy dresses
with hats to match to the teas and weddings and tennis
parties she was invited to. They didn't suit her. The
organdy made her look thinner than she was, and the
pale pastels had nothing to do with her dark hair and
luminous green eyes. She was not considered beautiful or
even particularly good-looking, blonds, just a little plump,
being à la mode on the Main Line in those days.

She was a day student at Bryn Mawr College and as
such a little removed from the girls who boarded there.

She had wanted to go to school in France, but her
father's sisters Ida and Rose had said that that was
absurd, just the sort of ridiculous idea Franklyn's
daughter would have.

Franklyn Vaughn Drexel Devon had died in 1935 of
an instantly fatal heart attack in his Chestnut Street law
office in downtown Philadelphia. Not that he had practiced all that much law, but he wasn't able to play golf
at the Germantown Cricket Club or dine at the Union
Club every hour of the day, so he had an office.

It was a smart, comfortable office, all dark wood and
unread leather-bound books. It smelled of rich tobacco,
manly, and Floy had enjoyed visiting him there, reading
the somewhat racy magazines he subscribed to, talking
to his secretary, Miss Holtz, who was pretty in a leftover
way and had a lover who was both married and alcoholic
and about whom she liked to talk.

Floy had suspected Miss Holtz was really in love with

her father, but so many women seemed to be in love with him. He had been a handsome, kind, and infinitely patient man who had never let anyone get in the way of his pleasure—least of all his wife, the somewhat hazy Charlotte.

"I married a girl named Charlotte," he liked to say. "Even though she was a harlot. Now I laugh all life with glee. For what others paid for, I get free."

"Oh, Franklyn," Charlotte would say, as if it were the first time she had heard that limerick, as if she were capable of being shocked an infinite number of times. And perhaps, Floy thought, she was.

In that depressing spring of 1937 Floy missed her irreverent father more than she would have thought possible. He would never have allowed Ida and Rose to put her into pale organdies. He would have had her in rich greens and translucent blues, in silk and linen. He understood women's clothes.

When Floy complained about the organdies, about Ida and Rose, Charlotte sighed. She was a big, amorphous sort of woman, not unlike Miss Holtz, with a faded beauty and a mind filled with unclear ideas all having to do with her own comfort. She was an admiral's daughter, brought up in naval compounds around the world. She was naive and pliable, but she knew who she was: Franklyn Devon's wife. When he died, she became, easily, Ida and Rose Devon's sister-in-law.

She's never been, Floy thought with some bitterness, Floy Devon's mother. Brought up by foreign nurses—amahs, nannies, tutors—Charlotte didn't know how to play the role of mother.

After Franklyn's death Ida and Rose ran Charlotte's and Floy's lives with a clean, despotic, according-to-the-old-rules touch that Charlotte rather liked. They were, after all, not that different from the amahs and the nannies and the tutors.

They all agreed about Floy and her future. She wasn't

really pretty, not in a Philadelphia/Main Line acceptable way. Franklyn hadn't really left much money. She would have to marry early and not brilliantly.

There was a young Drexel connection, Harris. He was a law student at Penn, who wore glasses and was earnest and would do.

Ida and Rose talked to his parents and then to Charlotte and as an afterthought to Floy, who didn't seem to have much choice.

"How does Harris feel about it?" she asked, thinking of the years of birthday parties in which she and Harris had been lumped together, the poor cousins.

"He's all for it," Rose said.

"Hot to trot," Ida put in.

There didn't seem to be anything else to say. She and Harris would be married when he finished law school.

Ida and Rose had another sister, Louisianne, the bad hat of the family. She lived in Paris, which was suspect enough. Franklyn, the only one who had kept up with her, took Floy to Europe for her thirteenth birthday and parked her with the disreputable Louisianne while he went off on what he chose to call his little adventures.

Paris, he told Floy, was a city of little adventures.

But Louisianne was the first large adventure of Floy's life. She was beautiful whereas her other aunts were pretty. She stood straighter than they did, dressed far better (though they wouldn't have recognized that), and seemed, despite her reputation and their airs, infinitely more aristocratic.

She had left the Devon family house in Haverford, Pennsylvania, in 1898 with Mario, the Italian chauffeur, who had taken most of her father's suits and her mother's sterling. The sterling got them as far as Paris, where he deserted her to return to his wife and five children, who were patiently waiting for him in Ravenna.

"I was poor and hungry," Louisianne told Floy, "and

35

someone suggested I become a prostitute. The idea, I must say, appealed to me, but I was living in a lice-infested hotel on the Rue de Schomberg, surrounded by prostitutes, and they all led the worst possible lives.

"Instead I went into a revue." She had sung American songs and paraded around "on a stage no larger than a soldier's tin drum, showing rather a lot of my body." She had gone on to be happily notorious, appearing in the Folies in feathers and little more.

"I adored it when visitors from Philadelphia turned up. They were invariably seated stage center, and for them I would bare all." They promptly returned to Philadelphia and told all.

During that first meeting, while Franklyn was engaged in one of his little adventures, Floy grew to know and love her aunt. Louisianne had a lot of showy jewelry and a collection of furs and that apartment house at 33 Rue Balny d'Avricourt and a great many odd decorations. Sterling silver cigarette tables and lamps made of elephant tusks. Floy, wise about certain things, doubted aloud whether her aunt's career in the Folies could have paid for all the extravagances with which she surrounded herself—including little Lord Billy, who had the upstairs apartment and seemed to spend most of his time on the telephone, discussing politics in execrable French while draped across Louisianne's leopardskin-upholstered chaise.

Floy looked into Louisianne's slate-gray and infinitely pragmatic eyes, and Louisianne looked into Floy's thirteen-year-old emerald-green ones and decided it was time her niece stepped up a rung of the ladder of worldly sophistication.

She led her out of the salon and into the room she called her office. She had a maid bring her a brandy and Floy a hot chocolate, and crossed her still-beautiful legs.

"I have had," Louisianne said, sipping her brandy, "a series of protectors, Floy. I call them, for a variety of reasons—some you are now too young to know—*mes lapins*. My rabbits. The first, when *I* was very young, was a French count's son, and the last was a poor Polish prince with an impossible-to-pronounce name, whom I married. When he died of dissolute living, he left me this apartment house and not much else except the decision to never have another rabbit in my bed." She upended the brandy glass and rang for another. "You do understand, don't you?"

Though Floy wasn't certain that she did, she nodded her head agreeably. Her aunt was the only woman she knew who spoke like a character in a Michael Arlen novel.

The day before Floy was to return to Philadelphia with her father, at Billy's urging ("they won't tell her in Philadelphia until she's twenty-one"), Louisianne sat Floy down in her office for another chat. Carefully, unemotionally, she explained the mechanics of the sex act.

"Is it fun?" Floy asked doubtfully.

"Rarely. But it can be diverting when the circumstances are right."

Louisianne handed Floy a velvet box, and when Floy opened it she found her first serious jewel, a tiny but perfect fire-green emerald suspended from a worn, thin gold chain.

"I thought you were hard up," Floy said, using one of her father's phrases, studying herself and the emerald in the *faux* Louis Quinze mirror in the salon. The emerald was the same color as her eyes.

"I am not hard up," Louisianne said, adjusting the clasp. "I have the rents from this building and I have a tiny bit of capital. In 1933 this is considered filthy rich.

"Besides, I did not buy that emerald. It came from one of the *lapins*, a Turkish gentleman of great mystery and dash. He was a boy, actually, attached to the embassy, and I think it nearly ruined him to purchase that bauble. The Turks didn't overpay their second secretaries in those days. It didn't suit me. I am more ruby than emerald, but he didn't know that, poor Mustapha. You, my dear child, must never wear anything but emeralds."

"And diamonds," Billy said, his round eyes half opened, his small, elegant body stretched out on the leopardskin chaise.

He was nearly thirty then but seemed far younger. He crossed his small, neat arms, resting his child's hands on his chest. "Diamonds," he said again.

"Diamonds," Louisianne reproved him, "are vulgar."

"Floy," he had replied in his odd French, "would elevate them to elegance. She is going to be that kind of a beauty, believe me."

When Floy asked Louisianne if Billy were one of her *lapins*, Louisianne laughed that musical, hard laugh so reminiscent of the aunties and said no, Lord Billy was nobody's *lapin*.

"That sounds very sad."

"It is and it isn't. His father was one of the great *lapins*. He died during the war, leaving Billy to his mother, a miserable specimen of English ladyhood. Luckily, when he was of age, Billy came to Paris and looked up his father's old acquaintances. He's never left, and we've been great friends ever since."

"What does he do for a living?"

"What a question. Sometimes you are Ida's niece, after all."

Lord Billy told her. "I make films. Nothing too serious. Charming films that would never play in Hollywood. They all have middle-aged heroes."

He had taken to Floy immediately, and since Louisianne never ate lunch, he treated Floy to all the best restaurants in Paris. He taught her to drink wine and corrected her French, though his was execrable.

When Floy found the nerve to point this out, he said that a doctor could cure a heart attack without having one.

He was the first person—and the last for some time—
to tell Floy she was beautiful. And when he said it, she
believed him.

"It's an odd sort of beauty," he warned her. "Not
everyone is going to be aware of it. Not immediately.
But when you're thirty-five, you'll be the most ravishing
woman in Europe."

"Do I have to wait till I'm thirty-five?"

"Think of the women who have to wait all their lives,"
he said, kissing her.

At home, in gray and white Philadelphia, Floy had a
recurrent fantasy in which she married Lord Billy in
tricolored Paris.

There was no one like Billy or Louisianne at home, and
after her father died of his massive coronary ("It would
be massive with Franklyn," Ida had said at the funeral),
she felt there was no one in her life at all.

Louisianne wrote monthly, charming letters filled with
suggestions for "broadening your spectrum of interests,"
which the aunts told Charlotte to censor. Luckily
Charlotte was too slow and lazy.

Lord Billy, Louisianne wrote, had gone to Spain to
fight against Franco and the Fascists. He had been
wounded, and the French didn't want to let him back
into France because the Germans—it was complicated—
had told the French not to let anyone who had fought
against Franco live and work in France.

The French equivocated ("It's what they do best,"
Louisianne wrote) and finally allowed Billy to live in
France, in his apartment above Louisianne's. But he was
no longer allowed to work in France.

It was difficult to imagine little Lord Billy fighting
against the Fascists and more difficult to think that the
French should care where he lived or what he worked at.
It all seemed—in that lovely boring spring of 1937, on
Philadelphia's Main Line—unreal and far away.

Floy was to marry Harris Drexel in June. They were going to go to the Adirondacks on their honeymoon. They were going to live in a house the aunties owned in Lower Marion, on the fringe of the Main Line. Harris and the aunties were in seventh heaven.

And then Harris made a fatal error. He introduced Floy to Curry Greene.

He was in the same class as Harris in the University of Pennsylvania's law school and looked like a cross between Gary Cooper and Franchot Tone except that he had dark hair.

He had been to Paris when his father still had zillions, before the Crash, and he talked to Floy about the Champs and Sacré Coeur and Chez Anya at a dance at her cousin Gloria's house. Harris wasn't able to come, because he had toothache. Gloria was busy with her guests and her mother. Floy and Curry Greene sat on the enormous back porch, which Gloria's mother called a veranda, while servants raced about with trays of champagne and Curry Greene said in French, "You are the most beautiful woman I've ever met."

"That's not supposed to happen till I'm thirty-five," Floy told him.

He took her home from cousin Gloria's dance in the white Cord he had managed to hide from his father's creditors. He parked under the ancient weeping willow that obscured her house from the road and kissed her with his mouth open. His hands found ways to touch her body under all that organdy as no other boy had done. Floy felt, for the first time, like a woman. She touched him back.

"Can I see you tomorrow?" he asked, holding her to him, and she could feel his hot whiskey breath on her neck and knew she should say no.

"Tomorrow night?" she asked, and he said, no, tomorrow morning, and she could feel how hard and hot

40

his body was under his dinner jacket and she said yes, tomorrow morning.

In the morning, driving in the Cord into Philadelphia, he didn't say much and neither did she. He took her to his apartment, which was located in a building called the Wallingford Arms on Walnut and Thirty-ninth streets. It looked to Floy like a place where men kept their mistresses.

"I'd better not," she said, when he stopped the car.

He got out and held open the door. "I think you had better."

"What about Harris?" she asked, playing her last card.

"He'll thank me."

His bedroom smelled of sweat and tobacco and talcum. He undid the organdy skirt before she thought to stop him, while his arms were still around her and his tongue was exploring hers. She pushed him away, breathless, but he had already unbuttoned her blouse.

"You've done this before," she said, trying to make him smile, wondering if she really wanted him to stop, but he had undone his trousers by then and was taking off his shirt, exposing all of his finely muscled body, reaching for her again.

His trousers fell to the floor with a little collapsing sound. She reached down tentatively. "You don't wear underwear" was all she could think to say as one of his square, thick hands caressed her breasts and the other moved between her legs.

"Gets in the way," he told her. Slowly he led her to the bed and drew her down on top of him. Expertly he rolled over on top of her. He looked at her, all of her, for a long moment before he let his mouth find the secret places of her body. "You don't have to wait till you're thirty-five," he told her, and she closed her eyes, giving in, thinking that both Billy and Louisianne would approve of her first *lapin*.

* * *

41

He made love to her every day for the entire month of April. Harris was cramming for exams, law boards. The aunties had taken Charlotte, cousin Gloria, and her mother on a cruise to Cuba. There was no one to say no.

In early May he told Floy he couldn't see her as often as he wished. Exams, he said. He had been neglecting his work. "I'll have to earn money eventually," Curry Greene told her, but it was hard to believe him.

"I'm going to have my period anyway," she lied to him on that last Thursday when he explained he had to cram all weekend.

"That's never stopped me," Curry said, and looked at her with regret. "You're so beautiful," he said, kissing her. "I'd like to be around when you're thirty-five." He didn't smile, as he usually did, when he drove the Cord under the weeping-willow tree and onto the road. He looked back once, but he didn't smile.

She called him on Sunday to see if she could bring him lunch, but there was no answer in that apartment in the Wallingford Arms.

She called all night and there was still no answer. Charlotte, several days home from Havana, wondered if she might not be "coming down with something." Floy laughed, became a little hysterical, and then cried. Charlotte was bewildered until Floy said it was that time of the month. It was supposed to be that time of the month.

On Monday Auntie Ida sailed into the house, her little pilot ship, Rose, in her wake. Their thin, shapely Devon lips were set in the stern, repressive smiles that indicated they had choice gossip.

"You'd better sit down," Ida told Floy, who was gathering up books for a class she hadn't attended in over a month.

"This isn't going to be pretty," Rose said, lifting her chin, setting her bottom on the arm of the chintz-covered chair her sister had chosen.

Charlotte, unnerved, stood up. "Perhaps," she said, not looking at her sisters-in-law but sensing something discomfiting was in the air, "we'd better have tea."

Routed for the moment, Ida and Rose followed Charlotte and Floy into the octagonal parlor and sat down on painted wicker furniture. Annie brought in the large teapot.

They all sat silently for the moment, doing things to their Lipton's, balancing the Spode, waiting for Annie to get out of the room.

"Haven't you been seeing that New York boy Curry Greene?" Ida at last opened, and Floy put down her teacup. She thought, at the least, he was in a hospital.

"Yes," Floy admitted, and she didn't like the way her stomach flip-flopped. "I've been seeing quite a bit of him," she went on, hoping the aunties might be kind.

"What about Harris?"

"He's been cramming."

"Well," Rose said, "you won't be seeing Curry Greene anymore."

"He's dead," Floy said, standing up.

"He's married," Ida told her, coming in with the punch line, waiting for Floy to sit down, then delivering the one-two. "You'll never guess to whom."

"Cousin Gloria," Rose said, taking over.

Gloria and Curry had been courting for over a year and he had asked her to marry him and she had said yes, but Irene, her mother, had said no, and so they had all gone to Havana together to give the romance time to cool off.

"But it was still sizzling when she got back," Ida said. "They eloped over the weekend. Gloria was supposed to have gone up to Yale to see that Jimmy McClernan boy but . . ."

"I don't believe it," Floy said, standing up again, spilling tea on the organdy skirt. "I don't believe it."

"He was only seeing you," Rose said, "to fill in the

43

time, to keep busy. He's as poor as a church mouse, and Gloria is disgustingly rich. You didn't think you'd have a chance against Gloria, did you? Now you had better go and call Harris. He's heard rumors, of course, but he's willing to give you another opportunity."

She ran from the octagonal parlor, but she could hear Ida's voice cutting through the house. "Of course, Irene is pretending to be distraught, but it is a good match. He has the name and she has the money. I suppose Irene wants an enormous vulgar reception. Irene says Morgan's giving them the townhouse and a car and driver. Can't live on bread and kisses, you know."

"It's not true," Floy said later, when Charlotte came to her, a concerned expression on her big, faded, pretty face. "It's not true. Curry wouldn't do that. It's not true, Mother." She cried helplessly, hopelessly, while Charlotte stood at the door, her hands flailing a bit, not knowing what to do.

Irene was not to have a big, vulgar reception. Morgan had put his tiny foot down. If Curry and Gloria had chosen the way they were to marry, he would choose the way that marriage was to be celebrated. There was to be a reception at the Germantown Cricket Club. Only the immediate family, Ida reported. And the closest friends. Two hundred or so.

"Floy should not attend," Rose said.

"She says she's going," Charlotte told her.

"She'll create a scandal that will do no one, least of all Floy, any good," Ida said, looking genuinely concerned.

"She's been in her room all week. She won't eat." Charlotte hesitated, but the situation was too much for her. "She tries to call him."

"No," Rose said.

"Yes. But he won't come to the phone. I don't know what to do."

"Keep her home, Charlotte," Ida counseled. "Do try to keep her home." Quiet, mousey little Floy was becoming, suddenly, an unanticipated problem. She had always listened to reason before.

Floy wore the pale organdy skirt Curry Greene had so deftly unzipped on their first date. She wore a hat of the same material and gloves and pale shoes, and she didn't look very different from the other young women attending that Sunday morning reception.

There was a moment of if not silence at least hushed voices as Floy and her mother walked into that room at the Germantown Cricket Club filled with people they had always known.

They know, Charlotte thought. People talk, Ida had said, and she had been right. Floy didn't seem to care.

An orchestra played "It Was on the Isle of Capri That I Found You," and a fat tenor in a white dinner jacket sang while several couples danced.

Harris Drexel looked at Floy from across the room, but Floy didn't see him.

"You'd better go over there and congratulate Gloria," Ida told Floy. "You'd better kiss her. You'd better pretend you're as happy as a clam."

"Why?"

"Because if you're not very, very careful, you'll end up being known as the girl Curry Greene jilted. Whenever you walk into a room, wherever you go, no matter who you marry—Harris or anyone else—people will say, 'That's the girl Curry Greene jilted.'

"Now, march across that dance floor and smile and kiss the air around both of Gloria's fat little cheeks and say, 'I'm so happy for you, dear.'"

"I can't, Aunt Ida."

"Your mother's always talking about what a swell little actress you are. So act. Go ahead."

She knew Auntie Ida was right and she also knew she

didn't care. But she wasn't so far gone that she couldn't foresee the day when she might care. So she walked across the dance floor and took her cousin's plump blond hand and had started to congratulate her when Craig, Gloria's skinny brother, came in through the French doors looking even more emaciated than usual.

"There's been an awful accident," Craig said, much too loudly, so that Tony Lyle's Society Orchestra stopped playing and everyone shut up and looked at Craig in his pale-blue seersucker suit. "Curry's dead. A bus smashed into the Cord up on Market Street. Curry's dead."

Everyone turned to look at Gloria, who stood very still, one chubby hand to her mouth, wondering what to do with that news.

But before she could decide, Floy took a few steps toward Craig and let out a terrible scream. It was a scream filled with unbearable pain, a scream of such anguish that no one in that banquet room at the Germantown Cricket Club would ever quite forget it.

And then Floy fainted.

Paris, 1937–1942

Chapter Five

Auntie Rose gave her the money to go abroad. Auntie Ida gave her a check for five thousand dollars. "Some swell little actress," Auntie Ida said.

They were sitting in Floy's stateroom on a ship the owner had called the *Continental* in a vain hope that the name would add an air of romance to its undistinguished lines. Still, it was a first-class suite on A Deck on a transatlantic liner. Floy was satisfied.

Rose wasn't. "The *Normandy* it ain't," she said. After all, she had paid for the ticket. Ida remained silent for once, looking at her niece's pale face, while Rose moved her bulk around the stateroom, opening closet doors, picking up ashtrays.

Charlotte sat in an upholstered chair, drinking tepid champagne. She held the glass in one hand, a huge pink clutch purse in the other. She looked like a race runner waiting for the starting signal.

Finally the purser put his neat little head into the stateroom and told them they had better leave; the final call was just being given.

"Send Louisianne our regards," Rose said, kissing Floy, moving out into the corridor. After some consultation Louisianne had been deemed the only member of the family equipped to deal with the situation. Her living in Paris, France, suddenly seemed a godsend.

Ida stood looking down at Floy until Rose came back and jiggled her elbow. "I'd go with you if I could," Ida said. "You're the only one in this family I give a damn for, Floy. Louisianne will be better at this kind of thing. I'd only be a big pain in the can in Paris. You take care of yourself, Floy." For the first time Floy could remember, Ida bent over and kissed her and held her, and though Floy was impatient for them all to be gone, she found there were tears in her eyes too.

The aunties, she thought, kissing Ida's dried leaf of a cheek, had come through.

"Bring me a nice souvenir, Floy," Charlotte said, not knowing what else to say, kissing her daughter awkwardly, clutching her pink envelope of a purse, moving out into the gray corridor.

"That's the single most fatuous remark I have heard in my life," Ida said to Charlotte as the three women made their way across A Deck to the exit ramp.

Floy, unable to find a handkerchief, wiped her tears away with her hand as she laughed and wondered if she were going to be ill for the entire crossing.

It was September, 1937, certainly not an auspicious year to be going to France. She lay in her bed thinking about the bed in the apartment in the Wallingford Arms —about Curry Greene. She remembered the ridge of muscles that extended across his stomach like a washboard, and the way he would curl up and go to sleep after he had made love to her.

She remembered Auntie Rose sitting in the parlor saying, "Well, you won't be seeing Curry Greene anymore," and herself replying, "He's dead," and she wondered if she was psychic or just overly prescient.

Floy thought about Curry's lovemaking, his jilting her, that marriage for money with poor round blond Gloria. She thought about that final treason, his death.

But most of all she thought that the aunties, Ida and Rose, had been right. Such a terrible cheap irony. She had disregarded their sound advice. She had transgressed that dearly held Protestant code. She had "gone too far" with a man—much too far—without being married, and everything they said would happen had happened. She had lost him. ("The man's not going to buy the cow if he gets the milk free," Auntie Rose had said on more than one occasion.) First to cousin Gloria and then to Death. She was being punished for going so far. She thought that probably she would never go even a little way again. "I'm my aunties' niece," she said to herself. The thought of Curry's long, lean body made her want to throw up. She literally could not bear the thought of that bed and what they had done in it. She put it out of her mind forever.

Then she rang for the purser and asked him to send around the ship's doctor, because she thought, she knew, she was going to be ill.

The aunties' most dire prediction for girls who went too far had come true. "I've gone so far," Floy thought, "I can never go back again."

She was just six weeks pregnant, and Ida's check was supposed to cover the abortion she was being sent to Paris to have.

Lord Billy was waiting for her at Bordeaux. He introduced her with pride of ownership and love to a young man named Sacha. Whereas Billy had a small body and a big head and was oddly dressed in worn British tweeds —his "baggy bags"—Sacha was perfect.

He was six feet tall with chestnut-brown hair and melancholy brown eyes. He wore a beautifully tailored suit that fitted his athletic body as only a good French suit could. If Billy was the embodiment of the eccentric British peer, Sacha was the apogee of the affable Parisian aristocrat.

"Gorgeous, ain't he?" Billy asked, as they drove at top speed up to Paris in a low-slung yellow Renault.

"Lovely," Floy said, putting her arm in Billy's. She sat between them and felt safe. The top was down, her

51

luggage was securely tied to a rack on the trunk, and Sacha drove expertly.

"He makes your poor old Sacha drive everywhere," Sacha said, smiling at her. It was an unexpectedly sweet smile. He spoke half a dozen languages, Billy said, extolling Sacha's acomplishments.

"He says his father's in the diplomatic corps. He says he grew up in half the capitals of the world. I don't believe a word of it. He's just another salon spy sent by my enemies to report on me."

"Really, Billy," Sacha said, giving him a genuinely hurt, reproachful look.

Billy leaned across Floy and kissed Sacha on the cheek. "Still, he is pretty. I don't mind confessing that I'm wildly in love with him."

"Billy, you're making your poor old Sacha blush," Sacha said, turning a little red.

"He just tolerates me. We make lovely movies together. Only *his* name goes on the film."

"He directs," Sacha explained to Floy in careful English. "They do not let him put his name on the picture because he fought in Spain, and the Germans have asked . . ."

". . . oh, the Germans haven't asked, dear boy. The Germans have demanded . . ."

". . . so we have a marriage of convenience."

Billy laughed. "It's a bit more than that, Floy. But you know continental perverts. Ashamed of 'the love that dares not speak its name.'"

They stopped at a roadside restaurant for lunch. They were the only customers, but the patron busied himself as if the little inn were overflowing. "One of those," Billy said. "We might as well enjoy ourselves." He ordered a bottle of wine and put their meal in the hands of the patron.

Sacha excused himself, saying he had to make a call, and then Billy looked at her and took her hands in his.

52

She broke down then, and while the patron put on his chef's hat and set about broiling their hen, while Sacha sat outside in the car talking to the patron's wife, Floy told Billy what had happened.

He handed her his handkerchief. She never seemed to have one at hand. Then he put his arms around her and held her to him and said, "You poor thing."

It had never occurred to her before that she was to be pitied, that she wasn't the villain. She had, after all, broken one of her society's strongest taboos, and without a second thought. Now, in true Protestant fashion, she was paying for it.

"Don't be an ass. It was your boyfriend who should have known enough to take precautions. Selfish bastard. He got what was coming to him." Billy certainly held a novel view of the situation. "You're not going to have an abortion, are you?"

"I can't have a baby."

"Why not?"

"My mother . . . The aunties . . ."

"They'll never know."

"When I go back . . ."

"Who says you're going back?"

And she suddenly realized how much she did want that baby, how nice it felt to be pregnant, to feel life within her. "I want my baby," she said, grabbing for Billy's handkerchief.

"Then you're going to have it."

After that memorable meal, as they drove through the green and gold countryside, past entire fields of dandelions, through ancient villages of red-tile-roofed houses, Floy felt lighter and happier than she had since the moment when Auntie Rose had announced Curry's marriage to Gloria. She was going to live, after all. She wasn't going to die with some abortionist's needles sticking into her, which was how she saw that particular operation. She was going to be able to smile and laugh

53

and eat. She was going to have a baby, Curry's baby, to take care of and love. She—they—were going to live in Paris and be taken care of by Billy and Louisianne.

She felt hungry and nauseous at the same time, but she managed to be sick only once in the thirteen hours it took them to reach Paris.

Louisianne didn't say anything. She was standing in the center of her salon in that apartment that circled the courtyard at 33 Rue Balny d'Avricourt and she simply put out her arms and Floy ran into them.

She took Floy to the little suite she had set aside for her, her arms still protectively around her. Billy and Sacha were left to make their own drinks, find their own food. "Your poor old Sacha's famished," Sacha said, leading the way to the kitchen.

"I could tell you." Louisianne said in the cream and gold sitting room off Floy's bedroom, "that he wasn't worth it, but you wouldn't believe me, and I might be wrong. At least he understood your attraction and the fact that sexual magnetism doesn't always make for a good marriage, especially when there's no money. Cry. It's good for you. Pretend, if you have to, that he was noble and self-sacrificing and . . ."

"He was a rat, Auntie. A sexy, sexy rat." Floy looked up at her aunt, relieved to see Louisianne was the same woman she had left in Paris seven years before: aristocratic, tough, genuine. "I loved him. I don't anymore."

"In time, my dear, you'll discover that he wasn't a rat. Only a frightened rabbit, marrying for money. In short, your first *lapin*."

Louisianne stood up and sat next to Floy on the silk sofa. "You don't have to have this abortion, you know."

"So Billy said."

"Has he told you his big idea? Not yet? He is going to propose to you. It might be easier if you were married."

"I like the idea of being Lady Floy. But I think I'll

remain a spinster mother. It somehow seems more honest."

"More honest for who?"

"My baby." And Louisianne had to grant her that.

Floy stopped breathing for a moment and held her hands to her stomach. Then, gently, she took Louisianne's hand and placed it on her stomach.

"Dear Lord, they really do kick, don't they? Are you going to tell Ida and Rose?"

"That would be too honest. And besides, I don't think they'd want to know."

"What will you call him?" Louisianne asked, her hands still on Floy's stomach.

"If it is a him, I'll name him after his father. Curry Devon. Has a nice sound, don't you think?"

"Like an Anglo-Indian dish served up in Rangoon to keep colonialists from feeling homesick. Still, it's your choice. And if it's a girl?"

"Louisianne Ida Rose Devon."

"Oh, dear. We must all get down on our knees and pray for a boy."

Curry Devon was born at home, at 33 Rue Balny d'Avricourt, on a peculiarly warm January morning in 1938. He had dark-brown hair, emerald-green eyes, and a dimple in his chin. Floy suffered through eight hours of labor, with Billy holding one hand and Louisianne the other, while a series of doctors and midwives alternately propped her feet up and put them down. At the appropriate moment Curry put his head out into the world and then his arms and then the rest of him, and the midwife had looked at Billy, the putative father, and asked him if he wanted to cut the umbilical cord.

"Indeed I do," he said, performing that operation. Then he helped to bathe the boy in warm water.

"Does he have all his toes and fingers?" Floy asked weakly.

"And more," Billy said, putting Curry to his mother's breast, where he fed, looking up at her looking down at him with tears in her eyes.

Billy, passing his handkerchief to Louisianne, said, "I finally know what they mean by the miracle of birth."

And then the doctor, filled with excuses for his lateness, arrived, and chased everyone save the nurses out of the room.

"Are you all right?" Louisianne asked, before she allowed herself to be sent out.

"I'm in love again," Floy said.

"We'll spoil him madly," Lord Billy announced the following morning, when he was allowed back into the room. "We'll give him every single thing he wants. I'm a great believer in spoiling children, especially godsons."

Floy waited for Louisianne to say they certainly would not give him every single thing he wanted. But Louisianne was holding Curry, and his perfect pink little hand was grasping her thumb. "We certainly will not," she said, too late, and Billy laughed.

Floy spent the next few months fighting with the wet nurse Louisianna had insisted upon. "You'll lose your figure forever," Louisianne had warned, when Floy protested.

"I don't care."

"You will."

She had given in, but then Minuette's sister, Alouette, was imported from the village where her family lived to devote her entire life to Baby Curry. She took him for walks in the Rolls-Royce of a baby carriage Billy had given him and she changed his diapers and she comforted him in the middle of the night, sleeping in a narrow bed in a little room off the nursery. She was big and red and white and stubborn and good, and though it was clear Curry loved his mother, it was also clear he relied on Alouette.

"Such a ridiculous name," Floy said, sitting on the long zebra-skin sofa in the salon some months after Curry was born. She looked out the French windows on another perfect Parisian spring day.

"You're jealous," Louisianne said, pouring tea.

"Your poor old Sacha thinks she's bored," Sacha said from his usual post at the pale-pink marble mantel.

"She needs employment," put in Lord Billy, sipping tea on the edge of the leopardskin chaise. Louisianne's upholstery had been provided by a big-game-hunter *lapin.*

"I do need a job," Floy said. Auntie Ida's five thousand dollars was disappearing quickly. Louisianne couldn't afford to keep Curry indefinitely. Nor did Floy want her to.

And she was bored. Her days were spent in waiting for Alouette to bring Curry home, to bring him into her room, to let her hold him.

Billy and Sacha were busy turning out the films the French, always insatiable moviegoers, demanded. "He's working your poor old Sacha to the bone," Sacha complained. With the threat of war drifting west from Germany, the French movie appetite was even more insatiable. It was easy to disregard what was going on in the world while at the cinema.

And Louisianne wasn't as much company as Floy had thought she would be. She was oddly occupied, spending hours with Billy and Sacha and a strange group of ill-dressed people in the little room off the salon that she called, importantly, her office. Its glass doors suddenly sported new, opaque curtains, and the maids were told to keep out, that she would tidy it herself.

Once, when Floy was looking for Louisianne, she had tried those doors and found them locked. She was a little shocked. Louisianne never locked anything.

"What sort of employment?" Floy asked, setting her

57

cup on the silver table. She realized the subject had already been discussed between them and she wasn't at all certain she liked that.

"You're to be an actress," Louisianne said.

Billy, irrepressible, jumped up and began to pace around the room, skirting the orange-and-green pottery Buddha and the pair of carved dragons that guarded the entryway. "Not a great actress. But an actress. You move so nicely. Doesn't she move nicely, Sacha?" Not waiting for an answer, he took her arm and made her walk up and down the room with him. "And of course she's even more ravishing now that she's a mother, isn't she? A sort of poor boy's dream of what a rich girl should look like. Those shoulders. Those eyes."

"You mean I don't have to wait until I'm thirty-five?"

"What do you say, Sacha?"

"You would be marvelous, Floy," Sacha said, watching Billy lead her up and down and around the room with that amused, slightly removed look in his big eyes. "Working with you would make life so much more easy for your poor old Sacha."

"It will get you out in the world," Billy went on. "That's what you need. You've had a baby but you've been mourning a lost lover. The wound is deeper than you think. It's time you stopped picking at it and let it heal. What do you say?"

"Auntie?" Floy said, appealing to Louisianne.

"I'm all for it. When I was a girl one was launched at the Folies. Now, of course, it's the films. If you let yourself, you'll have some fun and make some money. What more could you want?"

"Your poor old Sacha will be there to watch over you."

"Fat lot of good that will do," Lord Billy said, staring at Sacha with an excruciatingly vulnerable look of love that reminded Floy of the way she had once looked at her baby's father.

"Now what should be her first role, do you think?"

Billy said, sitting down, releasing Floy's hand, and discussing her as if she were no longer in the room. "Something that will make a bit of a stir, *n'est-ce pas?*"

Floy looked down at herself over Billy's head in the *faux* Louis Quinze mirror. She saw a girl with regular, plain features and odd-colored eyes. She didn't feel pretty, much less beautiful. She had felt beautiful only when Curry Greene was making love to her, and he had, after all, rejected her. She thought Billy and Sacha were being kind, that this proposed film career would consist of standing in crowds and handing letters to the heroine. She thought that would at least be diverting. She was quite prepared to be an extra.

Chapter Six

Billy wanted to make another war movie. But it was 1938, and the French government was tiptoeing around, being even more careful not to tread on the sensitive toes of its neighbor to the east. A tight rein was being kept on all filming by the Department of the Censor, which said no more war films.

So they decided on a comedy, *Ma Tante*, and Billy sat in a little room fitted out with a peephole and a buzzer attached to a wire that ran to Sacha's chair. Billy would buzz when he didn't like something. And Sacha would have to go into the little room, once a closet, and get directions so that he could direct. All of which he did with rueful good humor.

"Poor old Sacha," he said.

The studio was out on the Boulevard Richard Lenoir, a massive old warehouse in which carriages were once manufactured. On the first day on the set Floy, not cast as an extra and exceedingly nervous, asked Sacha if it really was necessary for Billy to stay cooped up in that closet.

"Billy says it is," Sacha told her, fixing the paste diamond pin that held her dress together. "Billy says there are spies everywhere."

"But what are they spying on?"

"Your poor old Sacha would tell you if he knew." He gave her his sweet smile and turned to talk to the cameraman, who thought the set—the receiving room in a Marseille bordello—was overlit.

Floy stood at the edge of the set and wondered if the other actors could hear her teeth rattling. Her legs felt weak, but she was afraid to sit down in case she couldn't get up. Even the thought of Curry—her baby, her son— holding out his chubby hands to her couldn't distract her.

She watched as Sacha calmed the cameraman and spread his own particular ease around the set, discussing the scene with the star, Robert LeVignan, as if it were Shakespeare and not what Billy dismissed as "a provincial housewife-pleaser."

She was cast as an American girl who thought it would be an adventure to work in a bordello, a rich girl bored with her life. LeVignan was to fall momentarily in love with her before being happily reunited with his childhood sweetheart, the madam's pristine daughter.

Floy had little dialogue that first day. She paced quietly, feeling thirteen years old and infinitely awkward, going over and over again in her mind the scene she was to be in, hoping the time would never arrive when she would have to perform.

Perhaps, she thought, they won't get to me until tomorrow. I'll be so much better tomorrow. But then Sacha looked at her, and so did the cameraman and the assistant director and the producer's mistress who was the script girl. They were waiting for her.

It had all been rehearsed the evening before, but her mind was a blank.

She stepped out under the hot lights, onto the set, and wondered if she could faint, black out the entire experience. I'm not an actress, she wanted to say to everyone watching her. Let me go home to my baby. Let me be quiet and in the background.

Sacha called a break at that moment. He stood up and went into the little room and returned and said to Floy, "Your poor old Sacha has been sent to tell you that he wants to talk to you."

Floy went into the little room, wondering why Billy

hid in it when everyone knew he was there. He looked at her as she stepped in and closed the door, and shook his head.

"You're a self-centered, selfish girl, Floy. And some actresses can get away with that, but not on my set. I could see even from here you were only thinking of yourself and I knew the scene would never play. Now, I want you to go back to that set and take your acting hat off and get out of yourself and think and move as you did at last night's rehearsal. Without conscious thought. Stop intellectualizing and stop, please, I beg you, feeling sorry for yourself. You'll make fools of both Sacha and me. Now go back to that set and be an actress. And don't forget to take a deep breath."

She returned to the set, closed her eyes for a moment, took a very deep breath, and indicated to Sacha that she was ready. LeVignan took his place at the center of the set, hands behind back, a worried look on his face as he waited for the woman he thought he loved to make her entrance.

Floy, on the other side of a wallpapered cardboard wall, was given her cue by the assistant director.

She tried to put herself out of her mind as she opened the door and walked onto the set. She was a rich girl, she told herself, seeing how the other half lived. She wore a green sheath held together by the paste pin. She walked to where LeVignan was standing and looked at him with that practical, sultry stare the Montparnasse prostitutes had perfected into an art. Billy had made her watch them from a café for one entire evening. The look was meant to indicate enormous depths of sexuality aligned with a certain degree of business acumen.

"I want a close-up," Sacha said as the camera moved in and LeVignan reached out to touch her.

"You are still a client," Floy said, pulling back, her dress coming off on schedule and revealing a great deal of black lingerie. "You still have to pay the going rate."

LeVignan touched her breast; she pulled the dress out of his hand. "Pig," she said, moving off the set.

"Cut," Sacha shouted, and the camera stopped and the lights dimmed.

"You are marvelous," LeVignan said to her with a certain invitation, but Sacha came to her and took her hand.

"All right?" she asked.

"You were fine," Sacha told her. "But poor old Sacha will have to talk to LeVignan. He's supposed to be a naif. Instead, he was acting like an ancient roué confronting a nubile virgin. Now, come. You have to be nice to someone important."

"Important to whom?"

"All of us. Without him we wouldn't have a license and we wouldn't have government approval and we couldn't make a five-minute cartoon much less this great feature upon which we are embarked. He's asked to meet you."

She hadn't noticed the two men come into the studio. One she knew. He was the familiar little alcoholic from Censorship. The other was introduced as an assistant to Laval and in charge of French film production. She hadn't heard his name before—Chambertin—but there were so many people in charge of French film production.

He wore his smoked glasses and a Stavisky hat, which he removed and held in his too-long blue-white hands as Sacha led her to him. He had a beautiful boy's face and a pinched, deprived look, like a child wanting ice cream. "You are very beautiful, mademoiselle," he said, much too seriously.

Sacha dealt with the cameraman while Chambertin stared at Floy through those smoked glasses with a concentration that was more disconcerting than flattering.

Floy felt repelled but interested. He so obviously wanted her in a sexual way. She hadn't thought of a man in that way since she had come to Paris. She knew why she felt so safe, living with Louisianne, working with Billy and Sacha, focusing all of her love on Curry. No one made any real demands on her, certainly not sexual demands.

Billy had been right, of course. She was still too hurt by Curry Greene's rejection, confirmed in her belief in spite of all evidence to the contrary, that she was a plain Philadelphia girl in an organdy dress.

But she had learned the aunties' lesson well. She, of all people, knew what happened to women who found men attractive and she had deliberately closed that part of herself, much as Rose and Ida had. She thought of herself now as a spinster, and the irony of a born old maid playing a bordello girl didn't for a moment stop her.

But Chambertin obviously didn't think she was plain. She decided in that first moment that he didn't look so much like a child yearning for ice cream as like a prisoner catching sight of freedom. His intensity was frightening but convincing.

She thought he was as wounded as she, though he seemed in command of the situation, of himself. He continued to stare at her in that hungry way as a girl handed Floy her robe and Sacha and the little alcoholic went to find LeVignan.

"Will you have lunch with me tomorrow?" Chambertin asked, and the formal way in which he spoke made her feel more sympathetic toward him. Still, she said no, she had to work.

"Perhaps another time," Chambertin said, and moved off to LeVignan's dressing room while Floy went to hers.

Billy was sitting in front of the makeup mirror, waiting for her. "What did he want?" Billy asked.

"Lunch."

"And you were to be the entrée?"

"I declined."

"I don't like the way he ravaged you with his little

blue eyes. He may insist, and you may have to go. At lunch you could explain that you suffer from some terrible contagious disease and put an end to it."

"Does Monsieur Chambertin always act this way with your actresses?"

"He's a dangerous man, my dear. I didn't think until that little scene that he liked women—or men. I thought he only liked himself. Now, as to your being an actress, you must learn to keep your eyes open—I know it's bloody difficult under those lights—and to resist the temptation to purse your lips. You look especially unattractive when you purse your lips, not unlike a discontented goldfish. What's more, you must move more abruptly, quicker, like a woman who is used to having men stand up for her."

"What else?"

He looked at her for a moment and gave her his sweet-and-sour smile. "Other than that, you did a pretty fair job, considering."

"Really?"

"I'll know more when I see the rushes," he said, retreating a bit. Then he put his arms around her and kissed her on both cheeks. "I think you'll do, Floy. I think you'll do nicely."

"No Oscar, though?" she asked, wanting more.

"Not for this bit of fluff," Billy said, not giving it to her.

He left, and Floy sat down at the dressing table and began to remove her makeup, thinking how tired she was suddenly. There was a knock on the door, and she said it was open.

The man with the blue glasses, Chambertin, put his head in. "The director says the film will be finished at the end of the week. So you can have lunch with me on Monday. Will the Ritz suit you? One o'clock? I will see you then." He bowed formally and shut the door.

"Do I have to go?" she asked Sacha later.

"I am afraid you do. If only for your poor old Sacha."

But in the end, Billy insisted on three more days of reshooting, and she had to cancel after all.

"Did he believe you?" Sacha asked.

"He didn't ask for another date," Floy said. "Besides, it doesn't really matter, does it?"

"No," Sacha said. "Not really."

Chapter Seven

When Floy saw the rushes in that claustrophobic screening room, she had to push past Sacha and Billy and get out into the air. She had seemed ridiculous in that black corset, snatching her dress away from LeVignan. But Billy, restrainedly, had said he was pleased.

"Your poor old Sacha is in seventh heaven. He's discovered a star." Sacha was somewhat less restrained.

As the filming went on, she found that she had more confidence, that she had almost begun to enjoy it. When her part was over, she was disappointed.

"You are a natural," Sacha said. "A new Garbo." Still, she didn't have anything to do and she felt let down.

"What next?" she asked.

Billy laughed. "You've been bitten. I can see that." Sacha told her they would be starting a new film soon. She was going to play a rich, beautiful woman who falls in love with an iconoclast waiter. "Perfect for you," Billy said.

While she was working, she had insisted that Curry be kept up until she came home, no matter what time that was. Alouette, shocked, had threatened to quit, but Floy had been adamant. "I'm not going to spend a day without seeing my baby." In the end Alouette had given in.

Now, with Billy and Sacha at the studio, editing *Ma Tante*, and with Louisianne making strange, unexplained day trips around France, Floy had nothing to do but tag along with Alouette and Curry on their walks in the Bois.

Alouette wasn't pleased. She could hardly gossip with the other nurses with Floy walking beside her.

Occasionally Floy had lunch with Maude Hamilton. A friend of Billy's, she had played the madam in *Ma Tante*. "Not that she needs the money," Billy had said. "The husband is rich."

"Filthy rich," Maude had amended, overhearing him. "Filthy, filthy rich. I love it."

"Then why do you work?" Billy had asked.

"Oh, I like to keep my hand in."

"Yes, that's what they say about you."

"You should hear what they say about you, ducks."

Maude was the only person, always excepting Louisianne, who had the last word with Billy. Floy liked all that blatant honesty. But Maude wasn't always free. "One has to lunch with one's husband occasionally, dear. That's the time of day most married men get big ideas about their sex life and start sending girls flowers from Klemée."

The day after the opening of *Ma Tante*, in that bright, sweet spring of 1939, Floy herself received an elaborately wrapped box from Klemée. Inside were half a dozen white orchids. Louisianne, who had arrived home that morning from "seeing friends you don't know in Brittany," read the card as if it were an invitation to an execution.

"He wants to take me to lunch," Floy said, not liking the way Louisianne handed Billy the card and he in turn passed it on to Sacha.

"Perhaps," Sacha said after a long silence, "she should have dinner with him."

"Lunch," Billy said.

"You only run my career," Floy said, taking the card from Sacha and the flowers from Louisianne. "Not my life."

"Lunch," Billy said, putting his arm around her, kissing

68

her absentmindedly. "Yes. She'd better have lunch with him."

They were to lunch late in the day at the Ritz. It had turned cool, and Floy had borrowed Louisianne's dusty yellow summer furs. She met him there. He had already ordered, simply. An elaborate meal would have been a mistake. The yellow wine—the same pale shade as the borrowed furs—and the hushed, respectful room, made her feel easy, protected.

Chambertin was courteous, pretty, distant behind his smoked glasses. He spoke to her of European politics, which she didn't understand, and of his one visit to America, which he admitted he didn't understand. She felt all the time that other things were being said, that his distance was only a cover for his uneasiness. She felt touched by him, sorry for him. He seemed the sort of person who could never under any circumstances be happy.

There was a silence before the brandy was served. He touched her hand twice as if by accident. She didn't know whether it would be more offensive to put it in her lap or to leave it there on the linen cloth. She moved her hand eventually. She didn't want him to touch it again.

The brandy came. The waiter retired. There was no one anywhere near them.

"I am married," Chambertin said, moving the brandy about in his glass. He made the statement abruptly, as if he were about to begin a scholarly dissertation. "My wife lives in the country. She cannot have children. She is wealthy and religious, not a good combination. I see her only on formal holidays, but I will always be married to her. You understand?"

Though Floy didn't, she said she did.

"When I was a boy I spent a great deal of my time in

the movie houses. I made up fantasies about the stars. Not about any one film star, you understand. My dream actress was always an amalgam. Theda Bara's eyes. Mary Pickford's nose. Fifi D'Orsay's figure. That first day when I met you, I nearly blacked out. You are my fantasy film star. You look exactly like her. You even speak like her." He moved his thin white hand across the table as a starved look came into his face. Floy looked away. He scared her, but at the same time he touched her. He was so very much in need.

"I want you to be my mistress," he said, his hand stretched across the table toward her. "There isn't anything I wouldn't do to have you."

"It's not possible."

"You have a lover." He said it as if it were a fact. He pulled his hand back and lifted his brandy glass. His face assumed that bland, threatening, distant look.

"No," Floy said too loudly. She wanted him to understand. "I am not interested in men."

"You're not interested in women," he said, with such distaste that she thought he would be ill.

'No. Nor in children, animals, and leather boots. I am not a sexual person. That part of me is dead."

"It's sleeping. You could not look the way you do if it were dead."

"Then it's in a very deep sleep. I am sorry," Floy said, and she genuinely was. She would honestly have liked to alleviate his misery, his extraordinary need. He would have been disappointed, she knew. People with such great expectations invariably were. She touched him, but now it was his turn to pull his hand away, as if he had been burned.

He drove her home. His car, an old, hand-crafted Hispano-Suiza, was waiting for them. The driver, so closed in and so far away from the passenger compartment that he might have been in a different car, held the door open for them, and Floy was surprised to see his less than clean white suit and a toothpick projecting from his ferret-like mouth.

But he drove expertly. It was clear that the car was another come-to-life fantasy for Chambertin, one long line of sculpted metal from its low nose to its swooping tail. It's like some fantastic bird, Floy thought, ready to take flight. Appropriately, a silver stork with drooping wings was poised on the radiator cap.

Curtains covered the windows in the pigskin-upholstered passenger compartment. A dim light came from recessed niches.

"You could sleep a family of ten," Floy said, but he didn't smile.

Instead, he looked at her for the first time since they had left the Ritz. "You're not a virgin," he said, not asking a question.

"I don't want to discuss my sexual life anymore, if you don't mind."

Abruptly he put his arm around her, and she could feel the coolness of his touch through Louisianne's dusty old yellow summer furs. "I need you." He kissed her with his thin lips, and Floy felt nothing, not even distaste. He moved away after a moment.

"I'm sorry. I had to try, you understand."

She didn't say anything. She took her compact out of her purse and reapplied lipstick.

"You will allow me to take you to lunch again?" he said as they pulled up to number 33. "You must allow me that."

"Not if you continue to maul me."

"I shan't touch you again until you ask me to. I promise." He looked so sad, so young, so desperate.

"Yes. You may take me to lunch again."

"Tomorrow?"

"Next week."

She didn't hold out her hand as the chauffeur, Rivet, opened the door to let her out.

"You look all done up," Louisianne said. She was waiting for Floy on the leopard chaise longue.

"It was a long lunch." Avoiding the Louis Quinze mirror, she sat next to Billy on the zebra-upholstered sofa.

"Did he make love to you?" Billy asked.

"He tried. I wasn't interested, and he seemed to accept that."

"Chambertin never accepts anything," Louisianne said. "He's a dangerous man, Floy."

"He's a wounded man, Auntie."

"You're going to see him again?"

"He wants to take me to lunch."

Louisianne looked at Billy, who looked at Sacha.

"He doesn't want to torture me. He only wants to take me to lunch."

"Try to keep it non-political," Billy said, and Floy laughed. "He's a Fascist and, as Louisianne says, dangerous."

"Political? I'm as political as Jean Harlow. You all worry too much about me."

A pattern was set. Her life took on form and shape if not meaning. Despite Alouette, Floy spent her early mornings and evenings with Curry, who stopped being an infant and became a boy overnight. His first word, *mama*, was distinctly French. She realized with a little jolt that his first language would be French. She tried to speak English to him, but Alouette discouraged that and Floy found herself repeatedly slipping into French.

She began a new film, and her days were spent in the studio on the Boulevard Richard Lenoir, where she appeared as the rich, spoiled, and misguided heroine in a series of comedies Sacha and Billy turned out right up until the war.

At night, after she tucked Curry in and gave him his last kiss, she would have supper with Louisianne and Billy and Sacha when they were home. Often as not, they weren't, and she found herself alone in the little sitting room, eating soup and toast, reading, ready for bed by ten.

Once a week she lunched with Chambertin at the Ritz. Over lunch he would speak to her of the government, of the crises that seemed to come three a week in those grim summer days of 1939. He never asked about her personal life. She never spoke of Curry, of Louisianne, of her life in the Rue Balny d'Avricourt. They spoke only of general topics. For Chambertin, Floy's life began and ended on the striped satin chairs in the Ritz dining room.

They were oddly soothing, those lunches. The food, rich and subtle, perfectly prepared, made her feel nourished, pampered. The pale yellow wine went down effortlessly.

Chambertin, always restrained, nevertheless managed to let her know he still found her infinitely desirable. Once he said to her, "When you were merely a fantasy I could take you out and put you away at will. Now that you have become a reality of sorts I am obsessed by you all the time."

But usually he contented himself with touching her surreptitiously once or twice as he helped her into her chair or into the car, with pleasantries about how well she looked, about her latest performance. They were like old friends who did not have too much in common and enjoyed the ritual of their meetings more than the meetings themselves.

"He flatters me," Floy said to Louisianne, once.

"You of all people need to be flattered?"

"You have no idea."

"Oh, I have a little idea."

Despite her success in Sacha's and Billy's films, unless

she was staring in a mirror or aware of Chambertin feverishly staring at her when he thought she wasn't looking, she continued to think of herself as that depressed, plain Philadelphia girl in organdy, cousin Gloria's poor relation.

"In some ways," Floy said, "I need those lunches with Chambertin as much as he does."

"Someday," Chambertin said, "after the war, you will change your mind."

"About what?" she asked, knowing what he meant.

"Everything."

"I thought there wasn't going to be a war. That the cannons in the Place de la Concorde were a kind of joke, a phony war ploy."

He explained about the approaching war, that it was a war for a new Europe, a greater France, a pure France without Jews and other disrupting foreign elements.

"I'm a foreign element."

He didn't hear her. He spoke of Hitler's economic miracle in Germany, of the Rothschilds' stranglehold on the finances of France.

Despite Chambertin's warnings, the war with Germany surprised her. "You're the only person in Paris who is surprised," Maude Hamilton told her over lunch at Fouquette's.

"Imagine being raped by hordes of big blond German boys. Are you going to finish that artichoke?"

Curry and Alouette were sent south to Alouette's parents' farm near Joigny on the Yonne River. Minuette refused to go. She said she loved Paris and Louisianne. She wasn't afraid of the Germans.

They were issued gas masks and told to use blue dye or paint to darken the windows against German air raids. All filming, of course, was halted. Even if it hadn't been, Billy and Sacha would have been too occupied with Louisianne in her little office to make movies.

Floy spent her days moving between the little sitting

room and the salon and having lunch with Maude or with Chambertin, though twice he had to cancel, the government being in a permanent state of *crise*.

She missed Curry, her baby, constantly. That sweaty little-boy's smell, that grabby touch, that smile so reminiscent of his father. They hadn't been separated before. She felt a deep emptiness each time she looked into the nursery and saw his crib under a dust cover.

"I feel as if I'm separated from a lover," Floy told a preoccupied Louisianne. "The Freudians would probably have my ego or my id or whatever it is they go on about for breakfast, but there it is. I love him so totally."

"I miss him too," Louisianne said, surprising Floy. She had thought Louisianne too involved to notice Curry's absence.

"You're as near to my having a child as I shall ever come," Louisianne said, again displaying a surprising emotion on the night of the black rain. Pieces of soot fell on Paris for hours and the Germans, unbelievably, were half a day's march away.

Sacha said a munitions plant had been blown up, but Mme. DeFarge said the black rain came from a disappointed God.

They stood at the blued windows, watching the black rain fall and cover everything. Louisianne, uncharacteristically, put her arms around Floy and held her close. Floy could smell her perfume, Molyneux Number 5. Since her childhood it had made her think of luxurious comfort, fantastic riches, female mysteries.

"I love you," Louisianne said. "I love Curry."

"Are you afraid of what the Germans may do?"

"Terrified."

"Why don't we try to escape?"

"Too late for that." Louisianne went back to the little office, where an anxious Lord Billy waited for her.

Later, Billy and Louisianne called her in. It was a dark room, especially now that the window was blued. A new,

75

odd piece of equipment stood to one side; it looked like a military medical case. They wanted her to leave, they said. They were going to arrange for her to rendezvous with Curry and Alouette and be taken to Brittany. A boat would take them to England. "Before it's too late," Billy said.

"I won't go. I won't leave without both of you, and you won't leave."

"She's not in such danger," Sacha said, reasonably enough. "After all, Germany isn't at war with America."

They talked for an hour, and still Floy refused to leave without Louisianne at least.

Chambertin kept their lunch date a week later in a half-empty Ritz. He was exultant. His "new Europe" was nearly a fact. A constant stream of people was making its way through Paris, taking trains, buses, carts, automobiles, bicycles, running south, away from the Germans, who still hadn't marched on Paris. They were, Chambertin said, waiting for the perfect moment.

"Curry," Floy thought and finally said to Louisianne.

"Someone is watching both him and Alouette. If the Germans march in, they will go further south."

"And if the Germans march to the Mediterranean?"

"They will sail to England and then to America."

"He's only a child," Sacha said. "They would hardly harm . . ."

"They are capable of anything. I want him safe," Louisianne said, and Sacha looked at her with his big brown eyes, reprimanded. The subject was closed.

Chapter Eight

On the day France surrendered to the Germans, Chambertin was in the south at Bordeaux with Laval and other members of the government, "making plans."

"Yes," Billy said. "Deciding on the most efficient way to appease their new masters, to capitulate in the most expeditious way possible."

Floy had never seen him quite so still before. He sat in the depths of a monkey-fur chair in a corner of Louisianne's salon, the blued windows behind him making him seem deathly ill. "What an absurd, scandalous lot those bastards are." They had surrendered to the Germans after thirty days. They hadn't let Billy fight, and Sacha had been sent back after he arrived at the front.

"They didn't want your poor old Sacha," he said sadly. "They don't want homosexuals."

"Sanctimonious cowards," Billy said, getting up, joining Sacha at the pink mantel, taking his hand.

"Billy won't leave," Sacha told them. They were all worried and looked it. Only Sacha seemed the same poor old Sacha in his beautifully cut lounge suit. "Billy refuses to leave," he said again.

"Damned tooting," Lord Billy said, using one of his deliberate Americanisms. Dropping Sacha's hand, he moved about the room with his old insouciance and nervous energy, ending up on the arm of Floy's chair, draping his arm around her shoulder before he stood up and began pacing again. 'Why the bloody hell should I?"

"You're a British alien enemy who fought in the Spanish war against the Germans and you are counted, at the very least, as dangerous," Louisianne told him.

"I am an artist first, an enemy second."

"Germans do not make those fine distinctions. They'll put you away in a prison camp—not the Germans but the French. They are anxious to show the Germans that their new, convenient conversion to Fascism is serious. If you stay, Billy," Louisianne said, looking at him with her earnest slate-gray eyes, "they will eventually take you away and they will kill you."

In the end, after what Floy thought was too much talk, he stood still, agreed to think about leaving, and quite formally kissed them all good-bye, Louisianne last.

"You will be careful," he said, holding on to her for a moment. She said she would. "Remember," he told her, "you're the only woman I ever really loved."

When he had left, when he had gone to his apartment above Louisianne's, the room seemed somehow darker, less alive. There was a long silence before Louisianne said, "What is there to be careful of? We've given ourselves to the Germans totally. They should be careful of us. We are in their care. And it's true they are behaving like perfect gents, looting in the politest way possible.

"A truck pulls up. A sergeant gets out and requisitions all your sheets. There are no sheets in Germany, you understand. The looms have been too busy making uniforms and such. You get a receipt. The sergeant and his men go on to the next house. *Danke schön, madame.* No rape. No blood. Only systematic, bureaucratic looting." She suddenly stopped talking and covered her eyes with her hands. "I'm so ashamed. I became French years ago because I thought we were brave and good and civilized, and now I find we are only civilized."

Sacha came over and kissed her because he knew she had been talking out of concern for Billy.

"Your poor old Sacha had better go to Billy," he said, smiling that sweet, surprising smile.

78

An hour later, while Louisianne was in the office with the doors shut and Floy was on the leopard chaise with her eyes closed, they heard the cars pull up. Louisianne came out into the salon and stood very still, her hand clutching Floy's, as they listened to the sound of jackboots reverberate up the stairs and throughout 33 Rue Balny d'Avricourt.

Minuette came out of the servants' quarters, her face very pale, and Louisianne motioned to her to be quiet. Floy started to go to the door, but Louisianne held her back.

And then, in that eerie stillness, in that blue-shadowed room, they heard the sound of the jackboots overhead. In Billy's apartment. In his salon. And then, nothing. Floy nearly screamed when the door to the salon opened and Sacha stood there without saying anything, tears in his huge brown eyes.

"He made his poor old Sacha leave the back way," Sacha said. "He said he wouldn't run, and even if he did, they would find him. He said he was going to show the world there was one brave Frenchman, and I told him he wasn't a Frenchman at all, and he looked at me and said that in his heart he was."

The jackboots going down the stairs made less noise than the jackboots going up. Car doors opened and shut, and then they heard that curious whining noise Gestapo cars always made when pulling away from what Louisianne called the scene of the crime.

They all looked at Sacha, who said, "Now what is your poor old Sacha going to do?" Louisianne went to him and put her arms around him. It was an affecting sight, that ramrod-straight elderly woman with the faded yellow-white hair and that tall, handsome young man holding on to each other as if their lives depended upon it.

Later Louisianne said, "You're going to continue with your work, Sacha. We're going to continue with our work, as Billy planned."

"Perhaps," Floy said, looking down through the blued-out window into the courtyard where DeFarge was sweeping, "they'll let him out soon."

And then she saw DeFarge run into her loge, and a few moments later the bell from the loge rang. It was the Gestapo. But a different branch. Their boots didn't make very much noise at all. They were coming to take an inventory of the apartment, coming for the sheets.

Chapter Nine

By the beginning of 1940, France had settled down to become a province of the Third Reich, undergoing a curious occupation. The northern three-fifths of the country was officially under German control.

A French government under the aged Marshal Pétain, a World War I hero, supposedly controlled and administered the south as well as French North Africa, which were lumped together under the designation *Zone Libre*. The new capital of this truncated, unoccupied France was located in the old spa town of Vichy.

"Veni, Vidi, Vichy," Louisianne said when she heard.

Lord Billy had not come back to number 33. They had no idea where he was, nor could anyone find out. Curry and Alouette had returned. Sacha had received permission from the Department of the Censor (with Chambertin's approval, now necessary for all film productions) to begin a new comedy. Floy was to star. She continued to lunch at the Ritz with Chambertin one afternoon each week. His Hispano-Suiza—one of the few gasoline-powered cars permitted by the Germans on the streets of Paris (gasoline was in very short supply)—continued to take her home.

A silver swastika had replaced the stork on the Hispano's hood.

"You should leave," a sadder, thinner Louisianne repeatedly told Floy.

"I couldn't leave without you, Auntie, and you know it."

"Once America is in the war, neither you nor Curry will be able to get out. Prison would be a possibility." There was a rumor, unsubstantiated, that Lord Billy was in a prison in Cologne. "A distinct possibility."

"Do you really believe America will come in?"

"She has to. Europe hasn't a hope without her."

Louisianne continued to spend most of her days in her office. The diplomats and businessmen who had formerly resided at number 33 had left and been replaced by a melange of nationalities.

After Pearl Harbor all American women were forced to register at the Chambre des Députés, where an enemy alien bureau had been set up. Floy arranged to go with Maude Hamilton.

As an actress, Maude had peaked in the twenties, playing frizzy, dizzy blonds. She spoke French with an alarmingly accurate street accent and enjoyed shocking French taxi drivers. "My first French boyfriend," Maude explained, "was a pimp. He had bow legs and a snaggle tooth, but there was something about him that drove me wild."

Her husband, Peter, had been taken off to the concentration camp at Compiègne, along with the other American men who had been trapped in Paris after Pearl Harbor.

"Don't you love it?" Maude asked as she filled out the lengthy registration form in the big, dark-green room at the Chambre des Députés. They were required to answer such questions as "How many horses do you own?"

"The alien invaders," Maude went on in English, scratching away with the dry pen, "have set up an enemy alien bureau. The Krauts, poor dears, have no sense of irony. But why are you here? I thought lover-boy was a big shot."

Floy laughed. Maude could usually make her laugh, even now, under the sullen eyes of the conscripted

French petty bureaucrats. "My weekly luncheon partner? He advised me to do everything according to the rules of the game."

"I daresay. Well, ducky, this slightly overweight enemy alien is leaving Paris and the Occupied Zone as soon as she can—*tout de suite*." Maude adjusted her silver foxes and, taking Floy's arm, led her to the nearest café. Maude ordered her usual—pink gin, dearie—but was told she would have to take weak beer or nothing.

"What the hell are the Krauts doing with our gin?" Maude wanted to know, shifting her heart-shaped bottom around in the cane-seated chair. "I can't help it about Peter," she went on, following her own thoughts. "I'm not about to rot here until they throw me into a cage and send me off to white slavery in Dresden. I rather fancy German boys, but I loathe and detest German men. Anyway, it's Peter's fault we're still in France. We have that perfectly safe and marvelous house in Monte. Peter's pater left it to him. But look at us. He's in prison camp, and I'm leaving. You'd better come with me, Floy."

"I can't, Maude."

"Bring baby with you. It's all very easy, they tell me. You get yourself a guide, some little Frog who, for eight thousand francs—not free, but luckily one has it—supplies you with tons of papers and guarantees. Mine swore on his mother's desiccated prune of a heart that he would get me at least to Lyon, and from there it's duck soup. Once you're in the Free Zone . . ."

"How did you find him?"

"There are thousands all over Paris. They wear those black jackets and bright white aprons and walk like penguins. Your basic café waiter, my dear dope. Ever since the occupation, they've been doing a thriving business getting people into the Free Zone. You simply stroll up to the first one who looks at all savvy and you say,

'*Connaissez-vous un passage?*' and you're home free. We'll tell them you're my little sister with her baby boy . . ."

"I can't, Maude. Not without Louisianne, and she won't go. Not now. Not until we hear something decisive about Billy."

"Well, dearie, if you change your mind, there's a tiny flat at the top of the house, and you and baby and Louisianne and anyone else you care to bring along can always bunk there. Personally I'd love the company. Thank God Monaco is a neutral country. Country? It makes New Jersey look like Russia, but it won't be a bad place to sit out the war, *n'est-ce pas?*"

She wrapped her big arms around Floy for a moment and held her close. "Kiss that baby for me. I'll take him with me if you'd like. Give him the best care. He'd be safe with me, Floy. No one mothers kids like a big, fat childless mama on the windy side of forty."

Floy shook her head. Maude kissed her and was gone, leaving behind her a little cloud of Coty's most expensive perfume.

Floy walked home slowly along the Seine. It was late spring, and if it hadn't been for the Nazi flags draped over occasional buildings as if they were coffins in a military burial, if it hadn't been for the *motards*—soldiers in gray riding black motorcycles—one might have thought nothing had changed.

Schiaparelli was still designing gowns, albeit with last year's fabric. Chevalier was being relentlessly cheerful at the Odéon. The food rations were annoying; the lack of electricity, now that the cold was over, more a matter of boredom than hardship. But the Eiffel Tower was still the Eiffel Tower, and on a spring day in Paris nothing seemed so wrong it couldn't be righted.

Floy crossed the Seine and walked lazily up the Champs and then down the more austere Avenue de

Wagram to Rue Balny d'Avricourt. DeFarge was short-sightedly knitting in her loge, her black oilcloth shopping bag in its place by her elbow. She looked up, frowned, and put her finger to her lips.

Curry was asleep in the army cot DeFarge and Alouette had somehow gotten their hands on. It had been set up in the patch of cobblestoned courtyard that caught the afternoon sun. Alouette sat next to the cot on a green kitchen chair, her thick arms folded, her milk-white ankles crossed: a sentry on guard.

And Curry, the young prince, slept peacefully, one hand wrapped around a tattered black toy bear Billy had given him early on.

Floy didn't want to think about Billy. She found she couldn't think about Billy. Better to think about the spring day, about Curry looking like an illustration of angelic childhood, than to think of Billy.

She went up the tiled steps and heard the sound of jackboots in her mind. She let herself into the apartment and saw that the doors to the salon were open, that Louisianne was sitting perfectly still on the leopard chaise, holding a cup of tea in midair, as if she had been turned to stone.

Sacha was standing in front of the pink marble mantel, his hands stuffed into his trouser pockets, as still, as immobile, as Louisianne.

It was too silent in that large, pleasant room. Not peaceful. But so very, very quiet.

Floy entered; Louisianne looked up, put down the thin china teacup, and pointed to the silver table, where a newspaper lay.

Comically, the Germans published two versions of *Le Matin*. There was the morning *Le Matin* and the evening *Le Matin*. Someone, Floy supposed, had never told them that *le matin* was French for morning. Floy referred to the late edition as the German evening morning.

Floy picked up the thin, comical evening *Le Matin*, hypnotized by the grainy black-and-white photo taking up most of its front page. She would have liked to put it down, to drop it, but the thin, beastly pages seemed glued to her fingers. It felt hot with sickness, hate, filth. It stuck to her as if it had some life of its own, as if she had to pay for her easy life by having that photograph imprinted on her mind forever.

It was of Billy. Or what had been left of him. It had been taken in a windowless cement-block room. The wood-handled axe had been propped up for artistic effect in a corner, its edge dark with blood.

The Gestapo photographer had worked with the head as well. It lay unnaturally on its side, its eyes wide open, its mouth contorted as if in the middle of a scream. A little pool of black blood had formed at the base of the neck where once it had joined the body.

The body lay in a neglected heap a few feet away, indistinguishable except for one of Billy's custom-made black shoes. One small hand stuck out as if to protect itself—a pathetic, futile gesture.

Floy stared at Billy's head once more, knowing she shouldn't. And then, finally, she dropped the evening *Le Matin* with its headline warning other enemies of the Reich of the consequences of rebellion, pictured below.

She started to go to Louisianne, but suddenly felt an overwhelming, irrational fear. She ran down the steps to the courtyard. Despite Alouette and the shocked look on little Mme. DeFarge's face, she picked up Curry in her arms, waking him, holding him close.

The following day she met Chambertin for lunch. He was seated, as a special concession to her, on the right side of the dining room with the French. He wore a swastika in his lapel made of pink gold. She saw him watching her, as she entered, with those pale, nearly white, blue eyes, the blue smoked glasses in his thin

86

hand. He looked hungry, a starving man whose entire consciousness had been reduced to the one thought of eating.

It worried and sometimes flattered her that his need never diminished. It grew and fed on itself to a point where he would do anything to attend these weekly lunches at the Ritz.

Shivering slightly, avoiding those grasping, pale eyes, which were much too naked without the blue glasses, she approached the table.

He put on the glasses and stood up, touching her arm as the head waiter held her chair. She looked down and saw his anemic hand on her dress sleeve and pulled away.

She reached the ladies' room just in time to be ill.

It was only when Chambertin, concerned, waiting in the tiny lobby off the ladies' room, said he would call a doctor that she managed to stop, to come out of the ladies' room, to calm him.

Later, in the Hispano-Suiza, she put her head against the pigskin upholstery and closed her eyes.

"You don't look well, Floy," he said. "As if you've been having bad dreams."

In her mind's eye she saw Billy's head, his mouth a circle crying out a silent scream for help, and she opened her eyes.

"Nightmares," she said. "I'd like to talk to you alone, Chambertin." She indicated the open window, usually closed, which separated them from Rivet. He wore his soiled white jacket and kept his toothpick in his mouth as he drove. Floy thought again of Billy and wondered if his executioner had been as whimsical, as epicene as Rivet, and then she forced herself to put that thought away, to concentrate on the business at hand.

"We are alone," Chambertin said. The air in the Hispano-Suiza was redolent of the black and perfumed soap he used. His steel-blue Schmeisser lay on the open

87

bar—such a nuisance, he said, always to be carrying it around, and it ruins the cut of one's suit. On the bar in the back of that car, it looked like a thoughtfully displayed *objet d'art.*

"Talk," Chambertin said as he poured himself a brandy. "Do talk."

"I can't continue these lunches, Chambertin," she managed to say. "I can't see you again. I'm sorry." Even to Floy it sounded weak, childish. There didn't seem to be any adequate way to make her excuses, to tell him that when he touched her, when he looked at her with those dead eyes, she could only think of Billy's severed head. Just sitting next to him, in that car, suffocating in that perfumed atmosphere, she was using all of her control not to be ill.

He removed his glasses, looking at her with such naked hate that she nearly lost that control. But suddenly she was no longer just ill. She was ill and terrified.

"Who is he?" Chambertin asked, so quietly it took her a moment to understand. She grasped the door handle as if she would open the door and jump out onto the Place Vendôme. She wanted, at the least, to open a window, but that seemed such an irrelevant action.

"There is no he. I'm sorry, Chambertin. I can't lunch with you again. I can't see you again. I'm sorry." She wished she would stop saying she was sorry. She wasn't sorry at all. She was scared sick but she wasn't sorry.

Chambertin motioned with his head, a very slight movement. Rivet caught the gesture in the rearview mirror and stopped the car, smoothly, at the curb. Floy didn't wait for the little man in the dirty white suit to help her out.

She looked into the car once more before she shut the door. Chambertin sat still for that moment, his eyes closed behind the blue smoked glasses. Only his hands—too long, too thin, clasped together—showed emotion. Suddenly he raised them over his head and brought them down with terrible strength on the sheet of blue glass that made up the Hispano's bar. It shattered, leaving blood on his hands.

Turning, nearly running across the Place Vendôme, she felt free, liberated from that overwhelming menace that was so much a part of Chambertin's persona. She would never have to lunch with him again. She would never have to feel those eyes on her, those hands brushing against her. She was, she told herself, free. She wasn't going to torture herself with possible consequences.

"I'm not having lunch with Chambertin anymore," she told Louisianne and Sacha that night.

Sacha whistled through his teeth. "Your poor old Sacha's going to have to walk the line from now on. I wonder if he'll close the studio."

"How did he take it?" Louisianne asked, not interested in the studio, going to Floy, putting her arms around her. Yet it was Louisianne who needed comforting. She seemed to have aged a decade since the publication of that particular issue of the evening *Le Matin*.

"He wanted to know who the other man was. I was tempted to tell him it was Billy."

"How do you feel?"

"Relieved," Floy said after a moment. "As if the doctor has told me I don't have an incurable disease after all."

Soon after that, she realized she was being followed. Rivet, the tiny Parisian water rat with the filthy white suit and the yellow, toothbrush mustache, was always near her, working his toothpick, not bothering to hide his presence.

She didn't mind being followed as much as she disliked being reminded of those lunches at the Ritz.

"I was lunching with a monster," she told Louisianne. "A small monster. A few lunches. Not so very bad."

"You should have told me."

"You wouldn't have listened." She turned her honest gray eyes on Floy. "Put it out of your mind. In a short time we will get you and Curry out of France and back to America."

"Not without you." Louisianne made an impatient gesture. "Surely," Floy went on, "whatever you're doing in your locked office with those men who need to bathe can be done by someone else. You've done enough."

"The less you know about that, the better."

"Come home with us."

"I am home, Floy."

Chapter Ten

She became aware that someone was living in Billy's apartment when she heard the pacing. The Germans had taken Billy's Persian rugs, and she could distinctly hear the sound of someone continually walking back and forth on the floor above. It was a very different sort of pacing from Billy's, more rhythmic and steady.

"It's only temporary," Louisianne said, and for nights at a time Floy didn't hear him. And then quite suddenly the pacing would begin again, and she knew he—it couldn't have been a woman—was back.

"Your new tenant keeps irregular hours," Floy told Louisianne, but Louisianne refused to be drawn. "Another of your great unshaven unwashed?" Louisianne looked at her, and Floy gave it up. She was about to leave the dining room—they had just had a treat: fresh eggs Minuette had managed to come up with—when a thought struck her.

"You're not doing anything dangerous? That's ridiculously naive," Floy said in the next breath. "Of course you are. But I hope you're not doing anything too dangerous." Resolutely she forced herself not to think of that photograph taken in the prison in Cologne.

"Not that dangerous," Louisianne said, reading her mind, and Floy was reassured about Louisianne if not about the new upstairs neighbor.

She saw him the day Curry fell. It was the afternoon when Alouette went to queue up in the Rue Daumier with all their food coupons. She had heard fresh vegetables might be had. Minuette had taken five hundred francs and gone to the black market in the Rue Cunin-Gridaine for butter. The boy had to have better food.

Floy took Curry to the courtyard. He had dropped her hand and was attempting to show her how he could walk backwards down the stairs when he slipped down the last six steps. The cut below his knee looked dangerous, and Floy left him with DeFarge and burst into the office without thinking, to ask where the disinfectant and the bandages were.

He was standing against the room's one narrow and blued window. He wore a shabby suit, the collar turned up, and a shirt without a collar under it. Like all Louisi-anne's visitors, he needed a shave. He looked dangerous and not, as Auntie Rose would have said, either whole-some or clean-cut.

Sacha was sitting in a chair, for once, his hand to his jaw.

"This is Max Winterhagen," Sacha said, with ironic courtesy. "He's just this minute punched your poor old Sacha in the mouth. If you ever meet him on the stairs when it's dark, feel free to scream. Be certain to scream."

Floy said she needed bandages and explained why, and Sacha and Louisianne both ran down the steps ahead of her to the courtyard, where Curry was sitting on DeFarge's bony knee, his leg expertly bandaged, eating the stewed chicken DeFarge had brought for her lunch in her black oilcloth shopping bag.

In 1942 France had the most beautiful summer in years, as if in compensation for her troubles. Each time Louisianne brought up the possibility of Floy and Curry leaving, Floy countered with the suggestion that Louisi-anne should come with them. It didn't seem possible or even necessary during that lovely golden summer that they should leave.

Each day Alouette drove Curry on her bicycle to the

Bois, while Louisianne stayed in her office, interviewing her great unwashed, keeping the doors locked. Sacha and Floy made movies.

In that last film, *Les Filles du Jour*, she played a rebellious rich girl who accepts a job as a dancer at a second-rate hotel's *thé dansant*. In a key sequence she was to perform a torrid tango with the hotel gigolo. She spent that last warm August week rehearsing the dance with a man who specialized in such roles. He wore elevator heels and held her too close, asking her, through garlic breath, to have supper at a café he knew where they served genuine beefsteaks.

Still, he danced the tango well enough to disguise the fact that she did not, and she was upset when Sacha told her that Yves had been arrested.

"For what?"

"Do they tell your poor old Sacha anything? No. Who knows why they arrested Yves? Killing his father or poaching rabbits or spitting at the wrong time."

"Poor Yves."

Sacha had found a replacement. He didn't want to lose the day, and the new man supposedly danced as well as Yves.

Floy, with help from the dresser, managed to get into the tight and backless dress. The head-dress weighed several pounds and gave her a headache. She was supposed to be masquerading as an Argentinian.

The motheaten orchestra Sacha had inherited from Billy was already playing a tango when she appeared on the set. Sacha was talking to the new man, who wore Yves' bolero jacket. It was too narrow across the shoulders. His hair had been slicked back and was as shiny as his patent-leather shoes. He turned, and Floy recognized him instantly as the man Louisianne called Max Winterhagen, the upstairs neighbor who had punched Sacha in the jaw and who paced at odd hours in the apartment above her.

He looked at her apparently without recognition. He barely managed a smile when they were introduced by the assistant director. He had black eyes with long, curly lashes, the sort dolls in Rue Rivoli arcade shops sported. He had cupid's lips, like a spoiled angel's. He had broad shoulders and slim hips and looked so obviously what he was: a gigolo, an expensive one, the kind who once preyed on middle-aged American women who came to France for Romance and Adventure.

"You've met Winterhagen," Sacha said, coming onto the set.

"Twice," Floy said, and Winterhagen bowed his head ironically.

They rehearsed during the morning, saying little. Floy wasn't certain why she found it a difficult experience. He smelled better than Yves and he didn't hold her nearly as close. She could feel the strength in his arms, and once, when she missed a step, he held her to him to keep her from falling. For a split second she thought, for no reason at all, of that apartment in the Wallingford Arms in Philadelphia.

In the afternoon, after a scratch lunch, Sacha filmed the sequence, getting it in one take. "Not much passion," Sacha said, smiling, "but it will do. Floy, do you think you could run through tomorrow's scene with Monsieur Grasse just once more for your poor old Sacha? It's a bit tricky . . ."

That night she lay in her bed, awake. But it wasn't the fear of seeing that photograph of Billy's execution that kept her from falling asleep. She was listening to her dancing partner pace overhead.

And she remembered his catching her, the sense of his firm, muscular body against hers. He had made her aware of her body, and she didn't like him any the better for it. Though she was perfectly aware of the irony of her career: playing desirable women while she so assiduously protected herself from sexual feelings. With an effort she put Philadelphia, her upstairs neighbor, and little Lord Billy out of her head and went to sleep.

The following morning, after kissing Curry good-bye, she went down the tiled stairs into the courtyard on her way to film that difficult scene with the even more difficult M. Grasse, a veteran of silent movies who longed for their return because he had trouble memorizing dialogue.

DeFarge was in her loge, involved with her knitting, while Winterhagen, in his old dark suit, the collar up, no shirt at all under the jacket, was standing in the patch of sunshine usually reserved for Curry and Alouette.

He was talking to the sort of chic woman Paris had once been filled with. She was in her late thirties, with red hair pushed up and back in the new upsweep style. A small prewar hat with a blue veil sat perched on top of all that hair. She wore a Mainbocher suit and a sable jacket, the sort that demanded an orchid corsage.

She would have looked expensive and a little silly if it hadn't been for the expression on her too-white face and the solemn little boy in an Eton suit, holding her hand.

"You must," the woman said so desperately that Floy, embarrassed by her need, stepped back into the entryway. "You simply must." She had a thin voice, foreign, educated. The boy stood still and straight, a little soldier waiting for a command. "You are our only chance."

"I am too many people's only chance," Winterhagen said. He lit a Gitane and held the cigarette between his teeth as he blew smoke into the air. "A diamond cluster pin, madame, won't get me a decent meal, much less you and the boy out of the Occupied Zone." He talked around the cigarette. "I must have cash and a great deal of it."

She closed her brown-gloved hand around the diamond pin and turned, not letting go of the boy, walk-

95

ing with deliberation in high-heeled shoes that had once cost much too much money. Only the tears sliding from under the frail blue veil gave away her terrible distress.

She and the boy moved past DeFarge's loge, disappearing onto the Rue Balny d'Avricourt.

Floy stepped into the courtyard and looked at Winterhagen as he stood in the patch of sunshine and smoked his Gitane. He turned and saw her.

"*Bonjour, mademoiselle,*" he said.

She didn't answer. She followed the red-headed woman onto the street and walked as quickly as she could to the metropolitan station at Avenue de Villiers.

There are too many monsters loose in Paris, Floy thought. She preferred hers on the screen, in celluloid, fading out in the last reel.

It was in September, after *Les Filles du Jour* had been released and had become, for a time, very popular, that Louisianne came into her bedroom late at night. She said, standing in the dark, that she thought Curry and Alouette had better go south to that town on the Yonne for just a while.

"Something's going to happen," Floy said as she looked at her aunt and heard the sound of Winterhagen pacing overhead.

"Curry and Alouette will leave in one hour. There won't be any problem. It's all been arranged."

Floy reached for her aunt's hand and held it. "I'm frightened, Auntie."

"We're all frightened, Floy," Louisianne said, bending over her, kissing her, and leaving.

Floy got out of bed, lit a candle, and packed Curry's bag while a frightened, sleepy Alouette dressed him.

Floy answered all his questions, held his firm little body to her, willed herself not to cry, and reassured him as best she could. Alouette tied a kerchief around her head and took him off to meet the farmers, relatives of hers, who were going to take them into the Free Zone.

Minuette had stood in the dark courtyard with Floy to kiss her sister and Curry good-bye. Together the two women, so very different, turned and walked up the tiled stairs.

Louisianne was waiting for them at the top of the steps. "I wanted you to leave with them, Floy."

"I wouldn't have gone without you." Floy allowed Louisianne to take her arm, to lead her into the salon.

"They wouldn't have taken you," Louisianne said, pouring tea. "Now you're too great a risk."

A week later DeFarge handed Floy a thick, cream-colored envelope. Chambertin was requesting lunch at the Ritz again. After thinking about it, Floy decided it was not so much a request as a demand.

France, 1942

Chapter Eleven

Floy waited, sitting on the banquette at Chez Anya for over an hour, though it seemed longer, bored with her memories, her past.

She tried not to think of Chambertin and that luncheon at the Ritz. He hadn't eaten, she recalled. He had watched her with those pale-blue eyes, still hungry for her, for the fantasy he had of Floy.

It occurred to her that he wasn't sane. She remembered a children's book Billy had given Curry in which the world was turned upside down. Sitting on that green plush banquette, unable to go home, not knowing what would or could happen to her next, more frightened than she had ever been, she thought that perhaps the world had turned upside down. Chambertin and the Nazis were on top now.

When they had first started making threatening noises at France, Sacha had made a joke of them, calling them the Nasties. Billy, for once, hadn't laughed.

Billy. She always tried to think of him not as he had died, but as he had lived. It rarely proved possible. That photograph. Billy's head on one side, his mouth in that hideous O shape, the axe in the background, artfully arranged.

"They might have faked it," Sacha said. "They're very good at faking photographs."

But no one, not even poor old Sacha, believed that.

She forced Billy out of her mind and replaced him with Curry. She hoped Alouette would find enough milk for him. She supposed they would have plenty of milk on that farm. She tried to remember if it was a dairy farm and couldn't. She hoped Alouette wouldn't force him to eat carrots. He loathed carrots. She wondered how she would get to Joigny, to Curry. And when. She felt a terrible need for her son, her boy, overriding everything else: her fear, the terror, Chambertin.

The restaurant was still empty. She could hear Anya in the kitchen, arguing with the chef. She wished she were in the kitchen, occupied, thinking about food and customers and black-market cream.

She was about to telephone Louisianne again, even though she knew that was clearly not a good idea, when Anya came out of the kitchen. She held her arthritic finger to her lips, gesturing with her head to the far end of a corridor leading to the ladies' room.

Floy went quickly along the darkened corridor and stepped into the ladies' room, expecting Louisianne, finding Winterhagen.

In the half-light he seemed insolent, more remote than ever. He kept both hands in the pockets of his tight-fitting jacket as, a Gitane clamped between his teeth, he smoked and surveyed her through his blue-black eyes, through those dime-store lashes.

"Remove all your makeup," he said. "And your stockings. They're silk and too memorable. And put this on." It was an enormous, wide-brimmed summer straw hat, red, with white paper orchids pinned to its crown. It was a pre-war hat, the sort a foolish older woman would wear to look young, or a foolish young woman might put on to look older.

"I can't . . ." she began, feeling paralyzed.

"You have no choice. I won't wait very long for you."

"Louisianne sent you?"

"You have five minutes."

The door suddenly swung open, and he stepped quietly into a compartment.

"Everything all right?" Anya asked, looking about.

"Yes," Floy said, and Anya left. Winterhagen emerged and watched as Floy removed her makeup with the cream and pads he had brought. He continued to smoke as she stared at herself in the sharp, unfriendly mirror and wondered who the scared girl staring back at her was.

She took off the silk stockings. Like Minuette and the gloves, they were the last. The Last Silk Stockings. She put on the hat and saw his eyes watching her.

"A bit conspicuous, don't you think?" she asked, trying for insouciance, sounding frail.

"That is the idea," he said, putting out the cigarette, placing the remains in a silver case. "They will only see the hat. Not you."

He took her arm and led her out the rear door of Chez Anya, into a service alley, and onto the Avenue Gustave V. They walked quickly, silently across the Place Varsovie. It had become overcast, humid, the air too hot and heavy. He set the pace across the Pont d'Iléna, stopping at the Eiffel Tower to watch sturdy German tourists look up at it in wonderment.

He took a black wool beret from his pocket and put it on. It made him seem less sophisticated, more homespun —a clerk in a market, perhaps. He opened his jacket so that it hung about him, appearing not to fit well. They walked across the Champ de Mars, and a late-summer breeze cut through the heavy air for a moment, full of false promise.

She wondered where he was taking her but she wouldn't ask. He asked her if she smoked, and when she said she didn't, he said it was a pity. "It would give you something to do with your hands."

She was immediately conscious of them. She had been holding her purse between them, in front of her, as if she were praying.

He took one and held it. "We are lovers," he said, "with

103

a few hours to spend together. I work in a shop. You are up from the country in your sister's hat. When we have enough money we will be married, and you will make *gigot* for me on Sundays."

"Where are we going?" she asked finally, not letting herself be caught up in his scenario.

"We have three hours before we rendezvous with the others. Three hours to avoid your pal Chambertin and his pals, the Gestapo." He looked at her and went on. "They raided number 33 this afternoon, twenty minutes after your call. Louisianne and Sacha were slipping out the back door as the Gestapo were kicking in the front. They found a transmitter and a great many papers they'll have fun poring over."

"The transmitter . . ."

"It was hidden in that army-style medical case. She used it to send messages to De Gaulle in London. The Gestapo want to talk to her very badly." He looked at her again, incredulously. "Don't tell me you didn't know . . ."

"I knew she was involved in some resistance work . . ."

". . . some resistance work! She's the White Rose, one of the most important resistance leaders in France. She and Sacha—Colonel Violet—run the show. They call themselves Les Fleurs du Mal—Flowers of Evil. They've taken these lovely floral names. All an invention of the late Lord Billy."

"What is your name?"

"I am not a flower of evil. I am a paid employee." He hailed a velo-taxi. "The Dôme," he told the driver, who pedaled furiously in the direction of the Boulevard du Montparnasse.

"The Dôme?" Floy asked, as conversationally as she could for the driver's sake. "I thought we didn't want to see anyone."

"They all know, *chérie*. Why not tell the world?" He bent over and gave her a long, casual kiss. The velo driver looked over his shoulder in sympathy. When

Winterhagen moved away, sighing for the benefit of the velo driver winking at him, Floy caught her breath. She felt as if she had been under water a fraction of a second too long.

They sat outdoors at the Dôme. As the sky darkened, the humidity lifted. The chestnut trees overhead were in bloom. The Parisians, cut off from world news, concentrated on more immediate matters as they sat at their cafés, drinking whatever the Germans hadn't proscribed.

She sipped at her vermouth, but her hands weren't steady. There were too many questions in her mind. She made an awkward movement, spilling the vermouth, breaking the glass.

"You're an actress," Winterhagen told her, after paying for the vermouth and the glass, taking her arm, leading her out of the Dôme. "You'd better act."

On the street she stopped him. She had to know. "My baby. My son. Do you know if he . . . ?

He took her arm again and piloted her along the street. "He is safe in Joigny. The people in the village have been told he is Alouette's illegitimate child. They won't ask too many questions. As far as we know, Chambertin and the Gestapo are unaware of him. He's safe."

He handed her a clean but unpressed handkerchief. "You'd better stop crying," he said.

"I'm crying," she told him, "because I am so happy to be with my fiancé on the streets of Paris." She took his arm. She felt nearly gay. Curry was safe.

They went to the Flore, where he ordered a *fine* for himself, another vermouth for Floy. She said the Flore and the Dome seemed like odd hiding places.

He shrugged, and for the first time it seemed to her that he was genuinely French. There were many people in Paris in 1942 claiming French nationality, with perfect accents but without that authentic shrug.

He ordered another *fine*. A pair of gray-uniformed German soldiers walked by their table, went inside, made a circuit of the room, and left. "You are not bad-looking without makeup," he said to distract her.

"Certainly a gigolo can do better than that."

"I am a sometime gigolo. I sell my services only when the price is very high."

"That woman with the young boy in the courtyard. She couldn't pay your price?"

"She is a Jewess," he said, lighting a Gitane, cupping the match as if there were a high wind, clamping the cigarette between his teeth. "From Warsaw. Her husband has been arrested, and she is stranded. She wanted to be taken into the Free Zone, along with the boy. But she couldn't pay my price."

"But you are going to take me?"

"And your aunt and your Colonel Violet—Sacha—and a couple of others. This is my swan song as a *passeur*, my last excursion. I am charging a great deal. I will get you all into Spain. But this time I will not come back. I am *brûlé*, hot. And I have enough money now."

"Enough for what?"

"To get myself to Portugal and then, perhaps, to America."

"No pretenses? Politics, heroism, *la belle France*?"

"None. I do what I have to do for the money, to save my own skin."

She looked away from him at a group of men in dark suits, smoking pipes, talking earnestly about the "new cultural rejuvenation of France."

"And my baby?" she asked, her voice unsteady.

"You always think about him."

"Yes."

"Don't worry. He is included in the price."

When it was dark they strolled along St. Germain to the Odéon and then they moved more quickly through a series of back streets and finally up what appeared to be a cul-de-sac. They heard footsteps behind them, but he led her through a narrow space between two buildings which opened up at the University of Paris end of the Rue Monsieur le Prince.

She had taken off the hat, but now he signaled her to put it on as they went into a low, dark Chinese restaurant. A group of drunken German noncommissioned officers sat around a large table under a lantern garnished with paper dragons.

"More mishmash, *Fräulein*," the fattest called out, and a delicate waitress in a thin silk dress hurried behind a screen that hid the entrance to the kitchen.

Winterhagen, taking Floy's hand, followed the girl, going past her and an old Chinese man who wore a chef's hat at a rakish angle and through a door that led to a flight of stairs covered with ancient red linoleum.

The waitress and the old man ignored them, talking to each other in their own language, intimately, as if Floy and Winterhagen weren't racing across their kitchen, as if Floy and Winterhagen didn't exist.

They went up the red-linoleumed stairs and entered an apartment that seemed thick with Oriental cooking smells rising from the restaurant below.

Sacha sat on an old leather chair, his eyes closed, his hair rumpled. He looked tired, but he sprang up when they entered and embraced Floy. "Your poor old Sacha has been so worried. We had no idea when you would . . ."

"Where are the others?" Winterhagen asked, removing his jacket, folding it carefully, laying it on a painted cabinet. He whispered. They were all to whisper. He removed his shoes and motioned to Floy to do the same. "We don't want the *sales Boches* to hear us, to come up and investigate."

"They're too drunk."

"Colonel Violet," Winterhagen said, using his code name with irony, "you must not forget: you are no longer the director or De Gaulle's best pal or the little lord's favorite bedmate. Now, Colonel Violet, you must do as you are told. If that's not too polite, why, you and your friends can go out and find yourself another *passeur* you think will get you through. In the meanwhile, I am the boss, and you do as I say, and maybe, just maybe, Colonel Violet, I will get your precious person into Spain in one piece."

Standing in the center of that odd-smelling, smoky room, still wearing the beret, in his shirt-sleeves, Winterhagen looked young and angry and dangerous. While Sacha, in a brown plaid suit, an ascot protecting his neck, seemed effete, too malleable.

Winterhagen went to the door that led to another room. "Come," he said to Floy. "It is a short night, and we have a great deal to accomplish."

Floy touched Sacha's hand in sympathy as she followed Winterhagen.

There were two women in the bedroom with Louisianne. One was long and painfully thin, and the other was short and not fat but well padded, plump. They wore expensive, skin-colored, old-fashioned lingerie, and had too-bright red hair, too-red lips.

"The beautiful Weinberg sisters," Winterhagen said. "Ilone and Chantil."

They looked frightened but not without strength as they shook Floy's hand formally.

"We are from Holland," Chantil, the younger and plumper, said. "We came two days ago."

"With diamonds sewn into the hems of their skirts."

"They're not in our hems any longer," Ilone, the older and thinner sister said, looking at Winterhagen with some bitterness.

"We're to meet our parents in Lisbon," Chantil went on, talking to Floy. "They are waiting for us . . ."

"Are you finished?" Winterhagen asked Louisianne, cutting off Chantil. Louisianne removed the rubber gloves she had been wearing, rolled them up, and wearily tossed them into an old, distempered sink that stood awkwardly in one corner.

She went to Floy, kissed her, and put one arm around her as she looked up at Winterhagen. "Would you like to inspect?"

He took off his beret and lit a Gitane, using the match to light a kerosene lamp. The half-hour of electricity the Germans gave Parisians had been used up. Winterhagen lifted the lamp and held it to the sisters' hair, and Floy realized it had only just been dyed that odd red color.

"It'll do," Winterhagen said. He turned and stared pointedly at Louisianne's faded yellow-white hair.

"By the morning, Winterhagen, I shall be a not quite so ancient brunette."

"Very good. Now, ladies, will you please join Colonel Violet in the other room and put on the clothes he has made ready for you."

"What is he colonel of?" Ilone asked, putting one thin hand to her neck, suddenly aware of her undressed state.

"Les Fleurs du Mal," Winterhagen said. "An upright underground organization. Madame," he went on, pointing to Louisianne, "is known as the White Rose. She runs the show."

Bewildered, they left the room, and Winterhagen, taking the lamp, approached Floy, putting his hand to her thick, nearly black hair, holding a few strands to the light.

"It won't dye," Louisianne said, having put on the rubber gloves again. She applied a dark liquid to her own hair. Businesslike, as if she dyed her hair every day, she began rubbing the liquid in.

Her arms are too thin, Floy thought. She hasn't been eating enough. None of them had. They had all traded their food rations for milk for Curry.

"No," Winterhagen said. "It won't dye. It will have to be cut. I've bought a wig." He went to a rusted metal cabinet and removed a large parcel, which he undid. "Genuine Polish hair," he said, showing them a platinum-colored wig. He turned to Louisianne. "Do you know anything about cutting hair? I want it short, boylike. I want her to look as if she comes from a well-to-do country family."

"I've never cut hair in my life," Louisianne said, surveying her own hair in the cracked mirror above the sink. The dye on it was fermenting and bubbling. She placed a rubber cap over her hair and carefully removed the excess liquid from her forehead. Then she turned to look at Floy. "I can try, however. You do have scissors?"

"I have a better idea," Winterhagen said. "We'll get Sacha, Colonel Violet, to cut her hair. Pederasts are very good at such things, I am told."

"You really are the most reprehensible person," Floy said. "I've never met anyone who . . ."

"Whisper," he admonished her, as he went to get Sacha to cut her hair.

"Why are we putting up with him?" Floy asked her aunt.

"He's our only chance."

Chapter Twelve

The Weinberg sisters and Winterhagen slept on the floor in the outer room. Sacha had taken the leather chair.

Floy and Louisianne slept on the narrow bed in the bedroom. Floy felt naked with her new cropped hair. Annoyingly, Sacha had been quite expert about cutting it.

"Your poor old Sacha," he said, "can always find work in a *salon de beauté,* if necessary.

Louisianne held her in her arms. She had never welcomed physical contact except on rare and needy occasions. Floy thought that this may have been the rarest and neediest occasion of all.

"Curry is safe," Louisianne reassured her. "Alouette is going to rendezvous with us in a few days when we get into the *Zone Libre* and bring him to us. You mustn't worry about him."

"I'll try not to, Auntie." She felt like a very small girl, like that girl who had visited Louisianne years before, young and too innocent and sadly plain.

"As long as Chambertin doesn't know about him," Louisianne said, "he is quite safe. Now try to sleep."

But neither of them could. Floy said that Winterhagen had told her about the transmitter, about Les Fleurs du Mal. "Of course I knew you were doing something, but I suppose I didn't really want to know what it was."

"It started with Billy," Louisianne said. "He returned from Spain with a very good idea about what was going to happen in Europe. He said from the beginning that we had to do something. Early on he helped to get what the Germans, with that remarkable facility they have for the unfelicitous phrase, called 'political detainees' out of Germany and into France.

"When it became obvious that the Germans were going to move across Europe, that people would eventually have to leave France, he set up an underground system for getting them out. When he was directing films openly he traveled all over and you know how easily he made friends. But as a not very welcome alien living in France but not allowed to work, he needed someone to help.

"That was when he met Sacha, who was heaven-sent. Between us, Sacha and I traveled—you remember those odd weekend jaunts of mine—and established safe houses, contacted and hired *passeurs*.

"We got information from spies, of course, and also from escaping Jews, which we transmitted to London first and then to De Gaulle. Number 33 was a perfect place, with its apartments suddenly emptied after the armistice by fleeing Americans, to put up fleeing Reich enemies.

"Billy was a brilliant organizer, and Sacha and I both have good memories for names and places.

"Billy, in one of his usual whimsical moods, named our group Les Fleurs du Mal and gave all of us those ridiculous code names that Winterhagen has such fun with.

"We were all frightened when Chambertin became enamoured of you and you began to have those lunches with him. But Sacha thought you would keep him non-suspicious, as he put it, and I think you did."

"Billy . . ."

"There's a traitor. We don't know who or where or at what level in the organization—but someone betrayed him. Why they didn't betray me and Sacha and half a dozen others is one of the great unsolved mysteries, but there it is.

"The other mystery is how Billy managed to last under Gestapo interrogation without giving us all away. I don't like to think of what my poor Billy went through before that final indignity. You know, I haven't mourned for him yet. I'm waiting. For this occupation to be over, for the war to end, for the traitor to be discovered. Then I'll mourn."

"Has the same traitor given you away now?"

"I don't know. So many come through my little office. One of them might be a double agent. Or perhaps the Germans simply got smart. All the tenants registered for the apartments at number 33 either fled France long ago or exist only in the Protestant cemetery at St. Cloud.

"Luckily only Sacha and I know who all the members of Les Fleurs du Mal are. Well, perhaps Winterhagen does, too. During the last few years he has gotten hundreds out of France and he has had to work with many of our people."

"How did you know, today, that you had to leave?"

"DeFarge went to lunch. She never does, but today she told Sacha she had an errand. She never came back. We found her black oilcloth shopping bag, with her knitting and her papers, on the counter in the loge. Then one of our people in the local prefecture told us she had been picked up by the Gestapo. She's very brave but she's not brave enough to last under their questioning. We transmitted, immediately, to De Gaulle, who ordered us to leave. He wants us in London. We have the names, you understand. With those names, those contacts, he can establish an effective resistance on French soil. It is important Sacha or I get to London, to De Gaulle."

"And Winterhagen can get us out?"

"He's been working for us since the beginning. He's the best *passeur* in France. He has an uncanny knowledge of people and places. He creates brilliant disguises, new identities. He understands the German mentality.

"But he does it not for *patrie*, only for money. He

113

wasn't going to take us at all, but the Weinberg girls appeared at the right moment with the right number of diamonds."

Floy stared up at the ceiling with its peeling plaster and after a moment asked why she was being taken out. "I have no money. I am politically negligible. I'm not particularly good at this sort of business. Perhaps I should get Curry and go quietly with the other American women to the Vosges . . ."

"You don't suppose Chambertin would let you go quietly to Vittel now, do you? After he's found the transmitter in my office? He must believe you are a member of Les Fleurs du Mal, that you were 'working him' during those lunches. Can you imagine how he feels? So very thoroughly betrayed. I couldn't leave you to him, my dear. You must come with us."

"And Curry?"

"I'd stay myself before I'd leave him behind." She kissed Floy good night and closed her eyes, giving in to her exhaustion.

Floy, comforted by the nearness of that too-thin, elderly body, surprised herself by falling asleep almost as quickly.

It was still overcast and humid in the early morning, when Winterhagen woke her. A window had been opened, but there was no breeze. The stale smell of burned cooking oil seemed more pungent than it had the night before.

"I do not cut hair," Winterhagen said, taking her to the cracked mirror above the sink, speaking conversationally, as if this were his usual morning routine. He was dressed, shaved, polished. "But I am a genius at makeup."

He tweezed her eyebrows painfully, replacing them with Garbo-like arches. "The trouble is," he said, as he worked, "Chambertin has such a clear idea of what you look like." He stood close to her, stepping back every few

114

moments to observe his work. "And there are all those publicity snaps they'll pass around." He applied rouge to her cheekbones and bright orange-red lipstick to her lips.

"I am afraid you are going to have to do your own nails," he said, handing her a bottle of flame-red nail lacquer.

He took a flowered print dress out of the metal cabinet. "You are to be a victim of the cinema," he told her, giving her large paste earrings and a pair of dark, stiletto-thin high heels.

She put on the dress carefully, trying not to smudge the nail lacquer. "I would have thought you would cast me as a schoolteacher or a waitress." She got into the shoes and, teetering, not used to their height, put on the earrings. "Someone as far from the cinema as possible."

"As we speak, Chambertin is having schoolteachers all over Paris woken up to see if they have dark-green eyes." He placed the platinum-blond wig on her head, carefully adjusting it. In the mirror it seemed quite genuine.

"You give him too much credit," she said, thinking she hadn't given Winterhagen enough. She never would have recognized herself; her eyes were so heavily made up that it would be impossible to tell what color they were from any sort of distance.

"You don't give him enough. Now stand up and move about."

The heels made her take tiny, mincing steps. "Good," he said. "The walk is the hardest to disguise. But those shoes do it for you. You look infinitely available."

He gave her the red hat, the *faux* orchids replaced with a large paper rose. "Pretend you're sultry and alluring. You are to travel as my wife."

"You don't look like someone who could ever have a wife." He turned away from her for a moment, looking for his silver cigarette case, finding it, lighting a Gitane, clasping it between his teeth. There was something in his

115

face that suggested she had hurt him, but it was soon gone.

He had slicked back his hair so that it looked like a sheet of black macadam. He wore a broad-shouldered jacket, patent-leather shoes, a tie that begged for attention.

"We are dancers, much favored by the Germans because, according to our papers, I have a German father. The name, Winterhagen, often comes in handy." He held out their passports, their identity cards, and their *Ausweise* —the official exit visas issued by the Germans. "You are to be my French wife. My silent French wife."

"My accent is impeccable."

"On screen and only after a fashion. In real life you are too literal, too accentless. And you have a distinctive American tone, as if you've drunk too much whiskey. You will be my silent French wife."

She followed him into the front room. Sacha's chestnut-brown hair had been grayed at the temples, the rest darkened, the whole neatly combed. He wore a dark, expensive suit, a homburg. There were gold-rimmed glasses on his nose, a black band of mourning on his arm.

"Your poor old Sacha is an aristocrat," he said, smiling that sweet smile. "Louisianne is my older sister. I have lost a son in the Norwegian campaign. We are *très, très triste.*" He laughed. "Winterhagen is good, isn't he? You look exactly the sort of trollop the Germans stand in line for. Winterhagen should be the director, not your poor old Sacha."

Louisianne emerged from the WC, carrying an ebony cane, dressed in gray, pince-nez hiding her remarkable eyes. Her hair was the same color as Sacha's—they could find only one brown dye.

The Weinbergs were dressed as lay sisters, with long white veils covering their new red hair, gray-and-white habits giving them a boxy, asexual look.

"I should like to know," Ilone said, towering above her sister, "why we had to color our hair when we are to wear veils."

"You'll understand," Winterhagen told her, "when and if you reach stage two of our little trip." He looked at each one of them, and there was silence in the room. He handed out false sets of papers, ration books, a German *Ausweis* for each of them.

"We are all," he said, "to be on the eight o'clock train leaving for Lyon from the Gare de Lyon."

"Then we rendezvous in Lyon," Sacha said comically, putting the homburg on his head.

"No. They expect us there. We rendezvous in Vichy. Ilone and Chantil are to leave the train at Villefranche-sur-Saône. They are visiting other members of their order. Look for a priest driving a Delage."

"I haven't the faintest idea what a Delage looks like."

"I know," Chantil said. "They're black and extremely racy. John van der Veldt had one and he always . . ."

"This Delage is a sedan," Winterhagen said. "The priest will wave to you. Get in, and he'll drive you into Free France over the demarcation line, avoiding the somewhat rigorous border inspection.

"After you cross, change into black peasant dresses the priest will supply you with and tie babushkas on your head. You will get back on the same train you left, only this time you will take seats separately in third-class coaches. At Lyon you do not leave the station. You switch to the train for Vichy."

"Vichy," Sacha said. "But Vichy is . . ."

"The last place Chambertin and company will be looking for us. There will be a green bus parked across from the station in front of the Hotel du Pays. It will be marked 'Hotel des Sportifs.' It is an old bus powered by a new gasogene engine. Get aboard quickly when you see it, ladies."

"And if there is no green bus with 'Hotel des Sportifs' on it?" Ilone wanted to know.

"Then I am dead or in prison and your goose is cooked." He turned to Sacha and Louisianne. "After the train crosses over into the *Zone Libre* and you pass through inspection—I assume you will pass through—a car will be waiting for you. A Mercedes. It will take you to a barge, where you will find a fisherman and his mother. You will sail down the Yonne.

"Waiting for you near Joigny will be a familiar farm-girl and a boy. You will become a bourgeois couple, Pétainists and grandparents, traveling to Vichy, where you will be taking the waters and giving the Marshal moral support. Your daughter died in childbirth and your son-in-law is stationed in Algeria, which is why you have the child."

"My child?" Floy asked, to be certain.

"Your child."

They drank acorn coffee and ate gray, sour bread, standing up.

"I can't eat," Ilone announced. "I cannot touch a thing. Grandfather was a rabbi." She touched the silver cross Winterhagen had hung from her thin neck. "I can't eat." Chantil ate Ilone's bread but forced her to drink the bitter ersatz coffee.

The sisters were the first to leave, escorted down the steps by Winterhagen, directed to the Odéon metro station, where they were to take the early-morning train to the Gare de Lyon. Each carried an imitation leather grip, their papers at the top, their hearts—as Chantil said—in their mouth.

"What if they stop us?" Ilone asked at the door.

"Oh, they're certain to stop you. There's been a crackdown on *passeurs* and their clients lately. Simply show them your papers and keep your eyes on your shoes. They will be polite unless they arrest you."

"What will happen to them if they're caught?" Floy asked, when Winterhagen returned.

"They'll be shipped to a concentration camp in eastern Germany, where Ilone will die in a month and Chantil in half a year. But I don't think they will be caught. They've managed to get out of Holland and they found Louisianne and a way out of Paris. They're resourceful. Of course, a lot depends on luck."

"Let us hope your poor old Sacha has luck," Sacha said, kissing Floy, holding her for a moment.

"I won't say good-bye," Louisianne said. "We shall meet in Vichy of all places in a few days. Curry will be with us." She looked at Winterhagen with her clear gray eyes. "Take care of her," she said, managing to make the words sound like both a warning and a special plea. She kissed Floy and was gone.

A car, an old Horche with German plates, had been arranged to take them to the station. "He is a valuable property, after all," Winterhagen said as Floy watched through a gap in the blued window. "I thought a German car would be best."

"And how do we get to the station?" Floy asked, alone with Winterhagen in that dark, low-ceilinged room.

"My wife and I," Winterhagen said, lighting a Gitane, clasping it between his teeth, and taking her arm, "walk everywhere." They walked across the Chinese restaurant. The thin Chinese waitress sat drinking tea, ignoring them. "It is good for our leg muscles—we are dancers, after all —and it is cheaper."

He dropped an envelope on the table next to the girl's cup and led Floy out onto the sidewalk.

The skies had cleared. It was a sunny September morning, the glorious summer holding into the fall. The protective grilles were just being removed from the cafés; people in the apartments above them were opening their blue windows, preparing for the day. It could have been any autumn morning in Paris. Only the noises had changed; the sounds of traffic were gone, replaced by a precarious silence.

"I wonder if I'll ever see Paris again?" Floy said, adjusting the red straw hat, the paper rose bouncing. She wondered if the war and the occupation would ever end. If they were going to live out their lives never knowing peace.

Winterhagen moved too quickly to give her time to reflect. He carried a cheap brown-and-white houndstooth suitcase they were to share. He moved, with his hand on her elbow, guiding her, as if he were impatient to be at their destination, as if he were impatient with his wife's vanity, those high-heeled shoes holding them both back.

"I'm frightened," she said, making that confession with some effort; but he ignored her fear.

"You must play this role with great attention to detail. You are a cheap woman with a certain allure and you know it. In your films you were always too expensive, too *snob*, which was your appeal, I suppose. Now you are the opposite. A dancer's wife. Foolish, venial, a privileged hanger-on of this new German France, thanking your lucky stars you were smart enough to marry a man with a German father."

"I'm not that good an actress."

"I commiserate. You have been asked to play a game, an absurd charade. The worst that can happen is that you will be tortured to death. But I am not concerned with one American woman's faulty life. I am concerned, mademoiselle, with my own safety . . . *my* life."

He picked up the pace, forcing her to keep up. "If I am hard on you, if you find yourself in embarrassing or difficult or even impossible situations, you must not say you have not been warned. It is, however, not too late. You can still remove your platinum hair, throw away the red hat, and return to number 33. Chambertin, they say,

120

is obsessed enough to allow that—perhaps. It would be worth the gamble."

"If it weren't for my child, I would go back."

He looked at her for a moment, and she wondered what he thought of her. "It would be safer for you if you went back. I am not a café waiter escorting you into *Zone Libre*. I am more dangerous than that. The Gestapo wants me because I break their laws. *Les services*, Les Fleurs du Mal, will want me if your precious Colonel Violet is taken. If either the Gestapo or *les services* finds me, they won't be kind to you. Even if he wanted to, Chambertin couldn't be kind to you."

They crossed the Seine on the Pont d'Austerlitz. The river looked sad and dirty; several men in tattered clothes huddled under the bridge's gray ramparts, sharing a drink from a metal cup.

"Your coming with me has one bright side," he said, and laughed. "No other *passeur* could get you out of the railroad station, much less into Spain. Chambertin is looking for you and he usually finds those he looks for. He is like a lean, blond, elegant cat, with those blue glasses. And you are his particular mouse. The longer it takes to find you, the more he will enjoy playing with you.

"But I know the escape routes and the options we have. I know the way he and his pals think. Best of all for you, I am determined to save my own skin."

"And I am determined to save myself. And my baby. Do you hear me? I have a son. His name is Curry Devon. I love him more than I love anything in this world. He needs me. And so I will come along with you, though it's clear you don't want me."

She had been talking too loud and walking too fast. She was breathless as they came up onto the first level of the Gare de Lyon. She saw from the clock in its mock Gothic tower that they had five minutes to board their train. Winterhagen had timed it well.

He handed her the brown-and-white suitcase while he got out their tickets. She secured the red straw hat over her new, furious blond hair with her free hand, realizing he had made her too angry to be scared.

She felt nearly brave as they entered the Gare de Lyon, Floy carrying the suitcase, Winterhagen holding their tickets.

Chapter Thirteen

Floy didn't feel nearly so brave as she followed Winterhagen through the crowded terminal. Gestapo agents stood at the ticket booths in the entry corridor, listening to each potential traveler request tickets, interrupting them to check their papers and their *Ausweise*, arresting them for any infraction.

She realized how important it was that Winterhagen already had their tickets. He took her arm and the suitcase and led her into the central terminal. The café, at the foot of a pair of winding brass stairs, was filled with restless travelers drinking ersatz coffee.

Winterhagen stopped at the newspaper kiosk and bought a fashion magazine. He handed it to Floy ungraciously, as if she had demanded it. He took her arm again, looking up at the clock above the café. They had three minutes.

He walked her quickly to the gate. They were stopped, as she knew they would be, a few feet away. Floy, despite her resolve, cried out.

"Madame is nervous," the plain-clothes Gestapo man said in heavily accented French. One always could spot a Gestapo man, Floy thought, filling her mind with factual data, blotting out the darkness and fear and her imagination. They wear thick brown suits, she told herself, even on warm days. And brown shoes and brown ties. They have shaven necks, cropped hair. They are always scrupulously polite.

"We are late," Winterhagen was saying, in such perfect low Berliner German that the Gestapo man smiled. "Papa made certain that I learned the mother tongue," Winterhagen explained. The Gestapo man congratulated him, handed him their papers and their *Ausweise*, and gave them a quick, dismissive bow.

"Auf Wiedersehen," Winterhagen said, and Floy glanced at the Gestapo man, who was staring at another couple as they walked toward the gate. She knew what the novels her mother read meant when they said the heroine's heart stopped. Her heart quite literally stopped for a moment. For behind the Gestapo man, reading a copy of the anti-Semitic, obscene *Au Pilori*, was Rivet, in his soiled white suit. He was working a toothpick around his small yellow teeth. He didn't appear to recognize her.

"What happened?" Winterhagen asked as he hurried her through the gate, showing his tickets and the *Ausweise* to more guards, more Gestapo, sensing from the way her body had stiffened that there was a new danger, either real or imagined but one to be dealt with.

Inside the gate, at the foot of a first-class coach, he stopped to fool with the catch on the suitcase, and she told him about Rivet. He pretended to have trouble with the strap while he told her to look in her compact mirror, to adjust her makeup, to see in the mirror if Rivet was watching.

She did so, using the tip of her forefinger to erase a smudge of lipstick. "No. He's reading *Au Pilori* and occasionally glancing toward the café, as if he's expecting someone."

"You," Winterhagen said, standing up, picking up the suitcase with one hand, taking her elbow with the other. "It's you he's expecting."

The train began to make moving noises. Someone blew a whistle. He helped her up into the first-class carriage, dismissing an aged conductor with an airy "I know my way." The man Winterhagen was playing would never spare a franc for a tip.

"Do you think he saw me?" Floy asked.

"We'll have to wait and see," he answered as he slid open a compartment door and stowed the suitcase on the rack above the green plush seats.

She sat down with relief. "How did you manage first class?" she asked, wondering if Rivet had alerted the Gestapo, if at any moment the compartment door was going to slide open again.

"We are patriots, after all," he told her, brushing the seat before he sat down, as if his trousers weren't far more dusty than the upholstery. "And don't take off your hat," he said, as she began to do so. "You are far more chic with it on, *chérie*."

He gave her the magazine, and she looked at the cover. It showed a thin model in a mink coat and pastel-colored gloves. But Floy didn't see her. Her feet hurt from the stiletto heels and her stomach was sour and her mind was working on what felt like an infinite number of levels, variations of fear.

She looked down and saw that the print from the badly manufactured magazine had come off on her fingers. She closed her eyes and saw Rivet and that thin, sparse, yellow mustache and behind him she saw Chambertin with his blue smoked glasses; and then she opened her eyes and looked at Winterhagen, adjusting the creases in his trousers. He played his role consummately, patting his slick oiled hair as if it wasn't already cemented into place.

It was at that moment that she realized she trusted him. He was professional. She didn't like him but she knew she could rely on him, and that calmed her.

She put the magazine aside and stared out the window. An old woman held a small boy's hand as the train began to move, seeing off a passenger in another car. He was about Curry's age, with sausage legs and a bad boy's smile. A sudden need to be with Curry, to touch him, came over her with such force that she nearly missed Winterhagen saying under his breath, "We have company."

The door slid open, and Floy turned and saw an SS captain's death's-head insignia. For a moment she felt total terror, paralysis, an inability to react in any way except to be still, a fox confronted with hounds.

Winterhagen stood up, bowed, and brought out his Berliner German like a virtuoso displaying his best piece. There was every reason, his manner said, why the captain should be sharing their compartment. The first-class coaches on the Paris-Lyon-Marseille *rapide* had been reserved for Germans and Frenchmen associated with the occupation. The *Hauptscharführer*—looking like a sturdy *wurst* in his black tunic and jodhpurs—took Floy's hand, raising it to his lips as Winterhagen introduced her as his wife.

She managed to smile.

The captain was followed into the compartment by his aide, *Untersturmführer* Klaust. He was thin and pale, as if he had spent the summer in an office. The mirror-like shine on his black knee-high boots was hypnotizing, but Floy managed to give him her hand to be kissed, to be held a moment too long. She smiled again. This is easy, she told herself. I'm not giving them my hand to be chopped off, to have the fingernails ripped out. They are only kissing it.

She returned to her magazine, forcing herself to read about short skirts and rayon lingerie, as Winterhagen sat down, as the captain and his aide took seats across from her.

Floy read as if she were going to be tested, as if she were thoroughly absorbed. But still she could hear Winterhagen and the captain discuss, in German, Berlin nightlife and the women they had known in that city.

"Did you know that Jewess in the Alexanderplatz with thighs as big as a man's chest? . . ." the captain said, while *Untersturmführer* Klaust—made brave by the other men's stories of their conquests of Friedrichstrasse prostitutes—studied Floy's legs.

At least she didn't have to talk, to play out her role. She had always been most effective when her dialogue was limited. She stared out the window at the red-tile-roofed houses, the small, safe villages. It seemed as if they had always been there. Then she saw the lieutenant's reflection in the glass, giving her an amorous, calf-like stare, and she returned to her magazine.

"I thought this was supposed to be *rapide*," the captain admonished the old conductor in German-gymnasium French. He had put his head into the compartment to announce that the first-class dining car was open.

He stared uncomprehendingly at the captain and, closing the door, moved on.

"The railway workers are the worst," the captain said, returning to German. "Slowdowns. Always slowdowns." He stood up, looked at his watch, and asked if Herr and Frau Winterhagen would care to join him and his aide at second breakfast, a new meal installed on French trains.

Winterhagen excused himself and his wife. "We are slimming," he said.

The captain smiled benevolently. "Slimming" was a euphemism employed by Frenchmen when they couldn't afford a meal.

"No ration cards required," the captain assured them. "And no money. I like you, Herr Winterhagen, and Klaust is in love with your wife. It would be our treat."

"*Danke schön*, but no. We had a large meal with my cousins in Paris this morning."

"I would have given my eyetooth for a cup of real coffee and a genuine croissant," Floy said, when they had left.

"And a great deal more if anyone had recognized you. You understand German?"

"A bit."

"Why weren't you red with shame during that conversation about Berlin's nocturnal ladies?"

"I never turn red with shame. Only gray with anxiety." She felt better, calmer. They had left Paris. They were in the country. The sun had begun to look like it had in the summer, bright and yellow and comforting. "How much longer before we cross the border?"

"An hour or so."

She sighed and at the same time looked up from under the brim of the red hat. She saw him, then, in the corridor, and all the fear came rushing back.

She saw his pretty boy's face first as a reflection in the door's window as he navigated from one coach to the next. And then she saw Chambertin himself as he passed their compartment, headed for the dining car.

He glanced in at their compartment through his blue glasses. But evidently all he saw was a cheap woman in a tasteless hat, bending over to retrieve her equally inexpensive companion's cigarette case.

"What is it?" Winterhagen asked.

She told him that either Chambertin was on the train or she was hallucinating. "Certainly he would have driven," she said. "He never goes far without Rivet, without his Hispano-Suiza . . ."

"Some of the roads leading to the border have been ambushed by *les services*. All the brass headed for Vichy is taking the *rapide* via Lyon lately."

"Chambertin is headed for Vichy and we are headed for Vichy. Isn't that called putting one's neck in a noose?"

"He might be going to Lyon to wait for you there. Ninety percent of the escapees go through Lyon. He'll never suspect you are headed south via Vichy, even if that is where he's going. Still, we'd better get off before the border. Your disguise is good but not flawless. The border inspection can be thorough."

"Shouldn't we warn Louisianne and Sacha? He knows both of them . . ."

"They're not on the train."

"But you said . . ."

"I misled you. And the Weinbergs. In the event we were caught and questioned. Colonel Violet and his White Rose should have crossed the border half an hour ago in the back of a truck that delivers horse meat with a perfectly legal *Ausweis*. They will arrive in Joigny early this afternoon, if all goes well."

She looked at him, and even her fear of Chambertin was submerged for the moment. "There's something else, isn't there?"

"Yes," he agreed, lighting a Gitane, clamping it between his teeth. "There's a traitor. Someone gave Louisianne away; someone told them about the transmitter, about her activities. Too many of our men have been picked up lately. Too many safe houses have been raided."

"Who?"

"I don't know. Could be anyone in Les Fleurs du Mal. Or anyone near it. From DeFarge to the priest in Bayonne who hides Jews in the sacristy."

"Me?" she asked.

"Yes. It could easily be you."

The *Hauptscharführer* and his *Untersturmführer* re-entered the compartment at that moment, belching politely behind leather-gloved hands. They smelled of beer and schnapps and smoked meats.

Floy turned her eyes to the window, not able to look at the magazine's bleached pages. She watched the green farms and the thin cows and she saw a family in one of the tile-roofed houses sit down to what for them was a midday meal. She wished she were with them, that she and Louisianne and Curry lived in one of those tile-roofed houses and were sitting down to *pot au feu* and young red wine.

She wondered if Winterhagen seriously suspected her or if he was engaging in one of his techniques to keep her from thinking of Chambertin, to keep her from losing control.

"It has been a lovely summer, madame, has it not?" the lieutenant finally found himself able to say in formal, stilted French.

She began to answer when the conductor slid open the door to announce they were about to enter Villefranche-sur-Saône.

"Our stop," Winterhagen said, standing up, getting the suitcase from the overhead rack.

"I thought you were going on to Lyon," the captain said, perplexed. "You said you had an engagement at Chez Felix . . ."

"Yes. But we are visiting my wife's aunt in Villefranche-sur-Saône first. Tomorrow we go on to Lyon. *Auf Wiedersehen*," Winterhagen said, and the captain was forced to stand, to bow, to click his heels together, while Lieutenant Klaust, who would have liked to kiss Madame's hand again, followed suit.

"*Heil Hitler*," the captain said, extending his arm as far as he could, given the height of the compartment's ceiling.

"*Heil Hitler*," Winterhagen answered, allowing Floy to precede him into the corridor, following her, sliding the door behind him, smiling through the glass at his perplexed friend the captain.

They were forced to wait in the narrow corridor while the train inched into the station.

Behind them two people entered the carriage, coming from the dining car.

"Why do the French trains get consistently slower?" one of the men, a German speaking in French, asked.

Winterhagen turned and then asked Floy if she had remembered her magazine, putting his hand on her shoulder, signaling her not to look back.

"The Jews." The distinctive voice seemed to fill the corridor. "They're behind the slowdown."

"I do think, Chambertin, that French Jews are the worst Jews. You were far too good to them."

"What do you suppose Jean-Louis is going to feed us?" Winterhagen asked, not taking his hand from her shoulder. "Not rabbit again. I couldn't eat another rabbit stew. A good beefsteak would be too much to ask, I suppose."

"In reality," Chambertin went on in what Floy recognized as his educator's voice, "there are no French Jews. Never were. Jews are an international phenomenon."

She began to shiver uncontrollably. The white paper rose on her hat began to bob up and down. Winterhagen moved closer to her; his body pressed up against hers, but that didn't help.

"Is something wrong?" Chambertin asked. "Your companion appears to be ill." He spoke in French.

"A nervous disorder," Winterhagen answered in German. "My wife will be fine once we get her into the air."

"My friend is a doctor," Chambertin said, switching to German. But the train gave a jump and then a lurch and finally a last false start and then began to pull into the station.

The elderly conductor helped Winterhagen get Floy down the steps and into the station. It was a small, stone station, cool and dark.

Winterhagen, true to his role, reluctantly tipped the conductor while Floy sat on a wooden bench. She began to remove the hat, but Winterhagen stopped her. "Better leave it on, *chérie*." As if its bright red straw and insecure paper rose were somehow beneficial to her health.

* * *

Chambertin made his way back to his own compartment and listened only half-heartedly to his companion's views on the Jews. He watched through his blue smoked glasses as Floy, insecure on her high heels, was helped by Winterhagen and the conductor into the station.

His friend, a great admirer of Pétain, talked about a new, "pure French" racial theory.

Suddenly Chambertin stood up, excused himself, and moved quickly to the compartment where the two German SS officers were watching the conductor return from helping Floy into the station.

There is still time, Chambertin thought, as he identified himself to the officers. The train could be stopped. But he wasn't certain. He said he thought he recognized the young couple who had been sitting in the compartment. "Cinema people, aren't they?"

The conductor had boarded the train, and the engineer's whistle could be heard.

"No," the captain said. "Dancers."

"French?"

"He said he was half German. She appeared to be French. She didn't say very much. They were supposed to be going on to Lyon, but they suddenly got off the train to visit with her aunt. They seemed to be family-oriented. Wouldn't have second breakfast. First they said they were slimming, they they said they had eaten with his cousins. What Frenchman, begging your pardon, monsieur, ever refuses food, I should like to know?"

"Did he mention his name?"

"A German name. Winterhagen."

There was silence as the train began to move. Chambertin looked at the emergency cord.

"She had extraordinary eyes," Lieutenant Klaust said. "The color and depth of Burmese emeralds."

"Emeralds," the captain said reproachfully, "do not come from Burma." He looked up at Chambertin, whose hand was poised in midair, reaching for the cord which would stop the train. "She seemed either nervous or ill. A neurotic woman."

"I've never seen anything to approach those eyes," Lieutenant Klaust went on, despite his captain. "I couldn't stop myself from looking at her."

Chambertin, suddenly and decisively, let his hand drop to his side. He thanked the two officers, bowed, heiled, and left them to each other.

"Extraordinary eyes," the lieutenant said again.

Chambertin stood outside the compartment for a moment, his hand grasping the brass handle with such strength that it turned blue-white.

The captain looked at him through the glass, and not liking what he saw, turned away. Chambertin moved on. The captain lectured his lieutenant on manners becoming to an officer for an uncomfortable half-hour. At the end of the lecture he felt only a little better.

Had he been a more honest man and only a bit introspective he might have admitted that the sight of the Frenchman, Chambertin, grasping the door handle, his smoked glasses momentarily removed and his eyes more white than blue, had frightened him.

They couldn't have paid him a million marks to have looked at the images that man was seeing at that moment.

Chapter Fourteen

In the sunlight Winterhagen saw that perspiration had blotted the makeup he had applied to Floy's face that morning. She had put on new lipstick but too heavily. The red hat and the blond wig remained as they had throughout the trip, immovable. The white paper rose bobbed up and down.

"I look disreputable," she said.

"Finally," he said dryly, but he was relieved that she had regained her voice, that she seemed in control again.

He took the suitcase, tucked her arm in his, and led her to a café he knew on the Place Carnot. They sat at an indoor table with a cloth on it. The waiter was an old man who wore a Pétain pin in his lapel. After he had taken their orders Floy went, according to Winterhagen's instructions, to the ladies' room.

She packed the blond wig, the stiletto heels, and the cheap print dress into the brown-and-white suitcase. She told herself that if she ever saw another houndstooth suitcase, she would kick it. She avoided looking at herself in the mirror. She felt embarrassed. I haven't been all that brave, she told herself. And then she put on a dark cotton dress of no particular color and the wooden clogs Frenchwomen were forced to wear owing to the scarcity of leather.

German soldiers need leather, Floy thought, as she remembered Lieutenant Klaust's knee-high boots, his gloves.

But it was a relief to get rid of the wig, to run her

fingers through the short, boyish haircut Sacha had given her.

For a moment, in that narrow, not very clean ladies' room, she allowed herself to think of poor old Sacha, of Louisianne, of Curry, as they sailed down the Yonne on a barge. Curry would like the barge. He liked anything to do with transportation. She refused to allow herself the thought that Louisianne and Sacha hadn't met him, that something had happened. It was a good day for sailing, she told herself.

She closed the suitcase, put the red straw hat back on her head, per instructions, and wondered if her feet would survive the wooden shoes.

"How do you feel?" he asked. He had ordered a *fine à l'eau* for himself, a vermouth for her.

"My feet feel as if they're in an iron maiden, but other than that, I'm better."

He had changed his persona in the fifteen minutes she had been gone. Somewhere he had washed his hair. It was still damp but a shade lighter without the oil and carelessly combed. He had put on tortoiseshell glasses, gotten rid of his jacket, and removed his tie. A rope belt replaced the suspenders he had worn, and his trousers had lost their pleats.

He had become—she suspected with the Pétainist waiter's help—the consummate Parisian journalist, cynical and idealistic.

"We are of the Catholic left," he told her. "On holiday." He was relieved that her natural color had returned, that she could drink vermouth with a steady hand. "We are interested in ideas, in the mind, in the Truth that a liberal Catholicism purveys. We are also interested in cheap wine and American cigarettes, though we drink and smoke what comes our way." He took his silver case from his trouser pocket and lit a Gitane, clamping it in his teeth, talking around the blue smoke.

"You are very good. You should have been an actor."

"You are now," he told her, "Madame Camélia Pardieu, the dowdy wife of a left-leaning Catholic journalist." He reached over and plucked the white rose off her hat, putting it into his pocket. "Though he is not so left-leaning that he cannot make peace with the Fascists. We are both good at compromise." He sat back and finished his *fine*. "Are you still frightened?"

"Yes. But not *so* frightened."

They left the café, and he told her she could get rid of the hat. He put a rock in it and threw it into a stream they had to cross. He gave her a plum-red woolen beret to put on. It was such a relief to get rid of that hat

"Why couldn't I have packed it in the suitcase in the café?"

"A woman in a red hat was seen going in. She had to be seen coming out."

A farmer driving a gasogene-powered truck picked them up a mile from the café on Route 13.

Floy watched as Winterhagen chatted easily with the driver, joking with him about the *sales Boches*, about De Gaulle and Laval, agreeing with the farmer's homage to the little marshal, Pétain.

She felt relieved. He's my only hope, she thought, as he put his arm around her in the protective gesture that was expected of a man like him toward a woman like her.

But she realized now that he was far more complex and dangerous than he had appeared as the substitute tango dancer or the *passeur* dealing in the patch of sunshine at number 33. Then he seemed just one man. Now, in half a day, he had become several, exhibiting a chameleon-like ease with each new character he assumed.

She knew he was at his most selfish, his most disagreeable, at those times when she was most frightened. That his rudeness served to knock her out of her self-involvement, to help her overcome that paralyzing fear.

He had given her the key to equalizing her anxiety: anger. She would never have gotten out of the Gare de Lyon without it.

The farmer left them off at a secondary road an hour west of Villefranche-sur-Saône.

"What is Le Soleil?" Floy asked, as they turned off the paved road and trudged up a steep dirt path under a sign resting on white concrete pillars. It read, in black letters: *"Le Soleil. Privé."*

"Le Soleil is a nudist camp," Winterhagen said, moving ahead of her. "What the Americans call my ace in the hole."

Le Soleil was established as a nudist spa in 1922, devoted to air baths, to the "naturalist" life. Then it was frequented mainly by Americans.

But in the late twenties it turned serious, playing host to middle-aged bourgeois who believed in the health benefits of living unclothed one week each year.

It had been built and decorated by a firm believer in the International style of design. Black-and-white cottages faced the natural pool created by the clear, cool waters of the Saône.

In keeping with the International motif, the entrance to Le Soleil was through a black-and-white stone building, purposely austere, that served as the general office, dining room, and home for the owner/managers.

To Floy it seemed as far from *le soleil*, the sun, as a nudist camp could get. She stood in the center of the main building on a white-painted stone floor, surrounded by leather-upholstered chrome furniture, which needed rechroming. Tiny pits of rust disfigured the chairs and tables.

Winterhagen rang a metal hotel bell that stood on a desk, and immediately a nut-brown man popped out of an adjoining room, like a surrealistic jack-in-the-box. He had a shaved head, faded blue eyes, a wirelike body. He was short and nude and reminded Floy of a friendly lizard.

"Diderot!" Winterhagen said, and the two men embraced. It should have been an absurd moment: Winterhagen so fully dressed, so fully grown; the little man too thin, too nude. But it wasn't. Genuine affection made that moment real, surprising Floy. She wouldn't have guessed Winterhagen could have felt—much less expressed—warmth for another man.

"You are our last guests, Monsieur Pardieu," Diderot said, winking, pointing his head in the direction of the room from which he had come. Talking too loudly, he picked up their suitcase and led them through French doors toward the cottages that stood in a semicircle on the crest of a hill overlooking the pool and the Saône.

"Next week," Diderot said, when they were far enough from the main building not to be overheard, "the *Boches* take over. Between you and me, Max, I don't think they intend to operate a nature camp." He stopped and gestured to a point just inside the camp's gates where thousands of feet of rolled barbed wire lay. "Does that look like nature-camp material to you?"

"Who else is here?" Winterhagen wanted to know as they proceeded up the hill toward the cottages.

"Two Swedish couples who come every year and an old battle-ax and her husband from Nîmes, friends of Irme's. All O.K."

Winterhagen took a Gitane from his silver case, clamped it between his strong, white teeth, lit it, letting smoke escape. "And how is Irme?"

Diderot shook his head and looked at Floy. "My wife," Diderot said with such despondency that Floy didn't know whether to laugh or commiserate.

She came out of the office at that moment and gave a long, low whistle that made Diderot stand up straight, as if he were snapping to attention. She was nude except for a black snoodlike arrangement she wore to keep her dark hair in place. Rail-thin, tall, and implacably angry, she beckoned to Diderot. He shrugged, apologetically set the suitcase on the porch of the last cottage in the semicircle, and went to join his wife.

The inside of the cottage, like everything at Le Soleil, was scrupulously black and white. The spread on the bed was made of hand-knit black and white squares.

Exhausted, Floy sat on the bed, kicking off the wooden shoes. She closed her eyes and leaned her head against the black-and-white stucco wall. Max stood at the window, watching Irme and Diderot argue. From that distance and through the narrow window they seemed like a Punch and Judy for adults.

"It's Irme who arranged the sale of the camp to the Germans. Her father was the architect who designed and built Le Soleil and, falling in love with his own work, eventually bought it. It belongs to Irme, but Diderot— for the first time—has made an objection. To the sale. She argues that the Germans could have simply taken the camp without paying. Or the Germans could have given them worthless scrip for it. "But though he's frightened of her, he's angry. He hasn't slept with her since the papers were signed, and Irme can't stand that.

" 'At least the Germans get things done,' Irme keeps saying. Potato bugs, Diderot calls them. 'Yes,' Irme retorts. 'The French grow the potatoes and the Germans eat them.' I like to listen to them squabble. Irme blames me for what she calls Diderot politics."

"Where do you know them from?" Floy asked. He hadn't seemed like a man who would have friends, who would be interested in a couple's undisciplined domesticity.

"The old days. They had a magic act before Irme's father died and left her Le Soleil. Diderot specialized in

139

pulling rabbits out of hats." He stopped and turned away from the window. "We're in for it now. Irme is headed our way."

She knocked on the door, opening it without waiting for an answer. Floy thought she should have seemed absurd, standing in front of them in that snood and low-heeled shoes with turned down white socks and nothing else. But she didn't. She only looked hard and angry.

"You'd better get out of those clothes, Max," Irme said. "And you, too, madame." She uttered the word "madame" with terrible scorn. "We still have rules at Le Soleil, you know."

She looked once more at Floy with distrust and then something more—recognition?—and turned and left.

Diderot's head appeared in the window at the back of the cabin a moment later. "You must show yourselves at the pool, or the others will ask questions. Irme will be quiet as long as no one gets suspicious. As long as I'm not in danger. It's hard on Irme," he said. "She loves Le Soleil as much as her father did and she thinks selling it to the Germans is one way to preserve it. She is wrong but she doesn't understand." His round, dark, shaven head disappeared as Irme whistled from the main building.

Winterhagen began unbuttoning his shirt. He folded it neatly, putting it on a shelf in the black-and-white-painted pine cupboard. He removed his trousers, his socks, his shoes, and put them all away neatly.

"You don't wear undershorts either," Floy said.

"They get in my way," Max answered, just as Curry Greene had, giving her an odd sense of *déjà vu*, of having been there before.

He stood in front of her, staring at her. A thin line of black hair ran down his chest. He had long, hard, beautifully defined muscles, like a man who makes his living by physical labor. He reminded her of a Géricault painting she liked of a young man, nude, stoking a fire.

"You must take off your clothes and come with me to the pool."

"I know." She felt paralyzed again. And she felt awkward. He was as natural without his clothes as with them. He turned, and she looked at his muscled back and then looked down and then tried to get undressed. But her fingers seemed to have stopped working.

"Do you want me to help?"

"No. I'll do it myself, thank you." She felt idiotically polite, a fifteen-year-old virgin. "Perhaps if you wait outside?"

She heard the door close. Some woman of the world, she told herself, seeing him through the narrow window. He stood very still on the porch. It reminded her of cottages at the New Jersey shore, of her youth.

She struggled out of the cotton dress, watching him. His black eyes were half closed, his thick lashes making them obscure, difficult to read. He was studying the group sitting at the far side of the pool, as she studied him.

Before, she would have guessed he looked like a Roman without clothes, thick and intimidating. But in reality, he was classical, a Greek statue so beautifully made that she finally had to look away.

Undressed, she took one of Billy's prescribed deep breaths and, intensely aware of her nakedness, prepared to join Winterhagen on that reminiscent porch. She understood, as she tentatively pushed open the screen door and he turned to look at her, why she had assumed from the first that he was a cafe gigolo: A great many people would pay to hold that body in their arms. She didn't like herself any the better for that bit of understanding.

It was another difficult social situation in which Winterhagen seemed at ease. He didn't appear to notice that they were both nude, that she was considered a desirable woman. He spoke to her as one might speak to a bright but not quite mature child. She was a problem, and he had to deal with her.

"You are uncomfortable?" he asked, taking her hand and holding it. "The others are watching, so we must pretend to be happy, affectionate. You might touch my cheek."

She did so but she knew it was a gesture Billy would have left, as he liked to say—putting on an American accent—on the cutting-room floor. Wooden, without feeling.

But Winterhagen led her down the porch steps as if it had been entirely convincing. "When we get to the pool, we'll dive in and frolic for the benefit of Irme and the others. You do swim?"

"Quite well."

"Excellent." He put his arm around her shoulder, and she felt as if she were being burned. If he noticed, he didn't react. He led her across the dark-green grass dotted with yellow wild flowers down to the natural pool. She was too aware of his body but she tried to smile up at him, to act as if they were indeed "air bath lovers" on holiday.

"Swim a bit and get out when you're tired and wrap yourself in one of Diderot's towels. Lay on the chaise at the far side of the terrace, away from the others, and lose yourself in the contemplation of Nature. I'll explain you suffer from melancholia."

"You won't be that wide of the mark."

He laughed, showing those white teeth. He had put away the tortoiseshell glasses. He looked so happy and healthy that she almost believed him. "After a short time you can stand up, without your towel, and return to the cabin. Pretend you are fully clothed if you have to, but you must move naturally. When you get to the cabin, try and sleep. It is going to be a long and difficult night."

"Today was duck soup, was it?" She knew she was taking refuge in wisecracks, being flip to hide her discomfort. But she was walking across a couple of hundred yards of grass, nude, with a man who looked like Adonis and she had, she hold herself, to take refuge in something.

At the edge of the pool he bent over and, holding her close for a moment, kissed her on the cheek for the benefit of those watching.

Floy concentrated on the pool, small and natural and very clear, fed by the Saône. The Saône was another hundred yards away from the pool, protected by the omnipresent barbed wire. On the far side of the barbed wire was Free France.

"We are doing this not as a challenge or as some student joke," he said. "We are doing this to save our lives. So smile. Laugh. You are an actress."

She used another trick Billy had taught her in what seemed like another life. She thought of what the aunties —Rose and Ida—would think of her strolling down a lawn, nude, in front of half a dozen strangers. And she did laugh.

"Very good," Winterhagen, a schoolmaster well pleased, said. "And now we swim." He dived in first, creating a perfect natural arc with his body. Floy followed. It was a relief to submerge herself in that cool green water. She had been so warm all day; she had felt filthy from the trip, dirty and fatigued from her fears.

The water made her feel, if not reborn, at least renewed. In the water she was in control. She stayed in as long as she could, until her fingertips started to pucker.

"Prunes," Curry had said when he stayed in his bath too long. "My fingers are prunes."

She put the thought of Curry away quickly and got out of the pool, using a ladder that led to a flagstone terrace bathed in the late-afternoon sunshine. She wrapped a towel around her and lay on a wooden chaise, her eyes closed, her face to the sun.

Winterhagen stood at the far side of the pool, as at

ease as if he were in a favorite boulevard café, chatting with two middle-aged couples. The Swedes, blond and in perfect physical condition, were easy to distinguish from the French couple from Nîmes. They were thin and bony and green-complected.

Floy looked up when she heard them laugh, and they all looked back at her, smiling affably. We are all on holiday.

She closed her eyes, falling into a light sleep. She didn't awake for nearly an hour, when she became aware that Irme and the woman from Nîmes were standing near her, talking.

Irme, looking like the stick doctors use to check for sore throats, was staring in Floy's direction. Through half-closed eyes, Floy saw the other woman, hirsute, staring as well.

She thought she heard them say, *Les Filles du Jour*, and the fear that waited inside her like a mortal enemy with a knife struck at her again.

She wrapped the towel around her and, resisting the urge to run, stood up as slowly as she could. Remembering Winterhagen's instructions, she removed the towel and left it on the chaise.

Nodding at Irme and her friend, aware of M. Nîmes staring at her, avoiding the area where Winterhagen and the Swedes sat drinking Subrovka vodka from a silver flask, she went back to the cottage, intensely aware of her breasts, of the way her buttocks moved when she walked, and of M. Nîmes following her every step with his narrow eyes.

Safely inside the cottage, she lay down on the narrow bed, pulled the black-and-white summer spread over her, and thought of her baby.

"*Moi*, Tarzan," Curry had said, hitting his little chest, after Alouette had taken him to a children's matinee at the Graumont. "*Toi* Jane," he said, pointing to Floy.

"I can see he already has a deep-seated Oedipal com-

144

plex," Louisianne had said, putting her arms around Curry, holding him to her. Floy fell asleep again with that image in her mind—Louisianne and Curry. She comforted herself by saying she would soon be with them.

Winterhagen came in some time later, after dark. He put a tray in front of her as she struggled to remember where she was. On the tray was a bowl of thin bean soup, several slices of white bread—the first Floy had seen in two years—and a glass of dandelion wine.

"Diderot makes the wine," Winterhagen said, as she drank it and ate everything on the tray as quickly as she could, as if someone would take it away from her.

"His code name in Les Fleurs du Mal is Dandelion. He doesn't like it, but he's not the sort who objects to things like that." He took the tray and put it out on the porch. "I told the others you were too depressed to come to dinner," he said, coming back into the cottage. Floy was suddenly aware again that they were both unclothed. Winterhagen didn't seem to be. "I think the old bitch from Nîmes knows who you are."

"I heard her mention Les Filles du Jour," Floy said, not looking at him. The electric wall sconce, in the shape of a mermaid holding a clouded glass torch, went out, the camp's quota of electricity for the day having been used up. Winterhagen lit a candle.

"The power of the cinema," he said. "It's a pity. But she won't know yet that you're wanted by the Gestapo. She thinks you've stolen a dirty weekend with me, for now. But we're leaving a trail Chambertin will pick up sooner or later." In the candlelight his body seemed red with life and energy.

He began to take their clothes from the pine cupboard and pack them in the suitcase, which he lowered out the window at which Diderot's head had appeared earlier in the day.

She was too tired, too aware of him to ask why. He blew out the candle and came to the bed. "We must sleep," he said, sitting on the edge. "We have only a few hours."

"In the same bed?"

He turned to look at her. She could just make him out in the moonlight that came into the room through the narrow windows. "I almost never make love to my clients, *chérie*. Not unless I am paid to. The price your aunt paid only covers my getting you to Spain. Now move over. I drank too much with the Swedes. I must sleep."

"I'm not going to sleep in the same bed with you."

"There is the floor." He lay down, pulling the thin spread over him, closing his black eyes.

Floy, knowing she was being unreasonable, childish, went to the window and stared out. Clouds had moved in and obscured the moon. She could hear the river and the crickets and what she thought were nightingales, but she wasn't certain this was either the season or the place for nightingales.

She tried to think of Curry, but that didn't work. She knew all too well why she wouldn't sleep in the same bed with Winterhagen. She wasn't afraid of his desire but of hers.

She thought she had never felt so adrift, not even on that ship, when all she could think of was that she was pregnant, facing an abortion, and her lover was not only dead but had been married to poor fat cousin Gloria.

But Billy had been there at the end of that voyage to help, to be depended upon. Now she was dependent upon that man in the bed.

She began to cry, hating herself for her self-pity; still, she couldn't stop. She wondered if she shouldn't have taken Chambertin up on his offer. She would have been safe, well fed. She wondered how he would have re-acted if he knew about Curry. So many people didn't know about Curry. Her mother, the aunties. She had let them think she had had the abortion. Curry would be a surprise to them as well as to Chambertin.

She supposed Chambertin would have accepted Curry. And I would only have to stop myself from throwing up every time he touched me.

She wondered if she was hysterical and then she realized he was standing behind her.

"I won't make love to you," he whispered. "I will only hold you. Please come to bed." He turned her to him and put his arms around her. "It is too late and things are too difficult for us to keep up all the varied pretenses. You are not a sophisticated movie star and I am not—at this hour, at any rate—a hardened gigolo. We are just people, Floy, frightened and in need of the comfort we can give each other."

She moved her face up to his, giving up her pretenses. "I want you to make love to me."

He took her hand, kissed it, and led her to the bed. He lay down next to her. She could feel his muscles relax as his hands began to caress her. Her body, which she had thought of as a controllable, purely functional organism—immune, since Curry Greene, to sensuality—betrayed her.

As he kissed her, his tongue finding hers, he entered her, and she lost all that carefully nurtured, exquisitely hidden control. He was tender and passionate, making their lovemaking last as long as he could. She was conscious only of him.

"Did you really believe I was immune to you?" he asked, holding her with one arm, clamping a Gitane between his teeth, smoking. "I have wanted to make love to you from the first moment I saw you, when you came bursting into your aunt's office to find bandages for your son." He looked at her and smiled. "You're not crying again, are you?"

"Yes."

"May I inquire why?" He removed the Gitane and kissed her shoulder. "You have the loveliest shoulders."

"I hate myself for seducing you," she said, ignoring his kisses, turning away. "I hate myself for enjoying our lovemaking so much. I was perfectly content to lead a celibate life and now I won't be. I know that. I'll want to sleep with you again. And you're such a thoroughly bad hat, as my Auntie Ida would say. Too reminiscent of another bad hat I knew long ago."

"Someday, Floy, I will tell you the story of my life, and you will not think I am such a 'bad hat,' perhaps. In the meantime, we must decide whether to sleep or to make love again." He put the cigarette out and moved on top of her, fitting his body to hers so that she could feel how aroused he was. "I am afraid, Floy, against all common sense, we are going to make love again."

As his spoiled cupid's lips found hers, as he began slowly, with infinite care, to enter her again, she wondered if it were the fear that had made her sensual again, that had broken through the barrier she had put up when Curry Greene had gone so irrevocably out of her life.

And then she stopped thinking and gave in to that solace she had denied herself for so long, that absolute comfort Max was able to give her. And she was able to give him, Floy thought, surprised.

She woke some hours later, when it was very dark, to find Diderot and Max standing at the foot of the bed, talking quietly. "We must move quickly," Max said and she realized that she was back in the real world again, that she had to keep going.

She asked for her clothes, but Max told her she would get them later, that they had to leave at that moment. Embarrassed, she said she had to use the WC, and both of them escorted her to the cabin set aside for that purpose at the far end of the cottages. The clouds had obscured the moon, and as she fumbled out of the WC, she nearly laughed. They were standing in a field dotted with dandelions in Occupied France, in the dark early-morning hours, about to escape into the Free Zone, all of them nude.

Silently Max took one of her hands and Diderot the other, and they led her down and around the pool, across the flagstoned terrace, to the barbed wire fence that separated the camp from the river bank.

It had become, under the trees, perfectly, acutely dark. Floy was focusing on the whites of Diderot's luminous eyes, when they disappeared. She began to panic and had started to ask what had happened to him, when Max guided her down into a tunnel under the barbed wire. Diderot had dug it at the beginning of the occupation for Max's clients. During the day it was camouflaged by the yellow-gray rocks that lay on both banks.

"Keep as close to the ground as possible," Max whispered. She could deal, she thought, with the dirt and the broken roots scratching her body. But it was the smell in that black and moldy and seemingly endless tunnel that made her gag and nearly loose control. There was a point when she would have gone back, or tried to. But Diderot's hand, reaching for hers, touched her at that moment and pulled her through, up onto the bank.

"Quickly," he whispered. "There are guards."

Max emerged from the tunnel a moment later and, stepping into the river, went under immediately. A few minutes later they heard a short, low whistle. He had reached the other shore.

As Floy stepped into the black water, there was a sudden flash of yellow light upstream, on the camp's side of the river. Diderot grabbed her hand and plunged them both into the river. They stood submerged up to their noses in the black cold water, facing away from the bank, as two border guards came around the bend.

The guards had heard the noise they had made getting into the Saône. They stood still, as did the dogs that accompanied them. The only sign of their presence was the continued sweep of their electric torches, bright yellow arcs lighting up the near bank of the river—that, and the heavy panting of their Dobermans.

Floy stood in the black water, waiting for the torch to be turned on her. She wondered if they would shoot first or attempt to arrest her. She was afraid to turn her head, to look at Diderot for instructions. She thought that when the yellow light caught her, she would make a try for the far bank.

The waiting seemed to go on forever. There was no way to tell whether they were standing behind her or had moved on, once they had turned off their torches. It was conceivable that turning off their torches had been a trick, that they were behind her, waiting for her to make a move.

She could feel the murky bottom of the river; the mud seemed to be sucking her down and in. She fought with the downstream water to remain still, and then something touched her foot and wrapped itself around her ankle. She remembered diving into a nest of water moccasins when she was a girl, and she started to shake with the effort not to shout. In her mind she saw those thick, milk-white snakes crawling up her leg.

And then suddenly there was the sound of men singing. The guards had moved on and had begun to sing in German a melancholy country song. Diderot reached over, gave her a push, and she swam faster than she ever had in what she hoped was the direction of the Free Zone.

She reached the far bank quickly, scratching her skin as she scrambled up the steep bank, absurdly being pushed from behind by Diderot. Max's hands found hers and he helped her up the last few yards of mud and wet grass.

"Sacha should have this entrance on film," she said, and began to laugh. Max put his fingers across her lips.

"*Courage,*" he said, and she knew how frightened she was, how close to hysteria.

A false dawn had come up, and she looked down at her body, wet and raw with scratches, dirty with mud. It felt as if it belonged to someone else. Someone younger and more naive. She felt especially nude, as if making love with Max, after all those years of not making love with anyone, had cracked the hard shell she had developed. She felt so unprotected, so totally unclothed.

"My dress," she whispered urgently, and Max took her to a piece of flat land where two new suitcases sat side by side as if in an avant-garde painting. There was a cheap painted metal one for Max and a small, anonymous leather overnighter for Floy.

Silently Diderot offered her a flask filled with gin.

"Dutch courage," he said as she drank from it and handed it back, coughing from its strength. He replaced it in its hiding place in an ancient tree stump. "I keep it on hand for all of Max's clients."

"Mademoiselle is the last client," Max said. And Floy got into the dark cotton dress, the wooden shoes, thinking of the Last Gloves, the Last Maid, the Last Silk Stockings, the Last Client.

Diderot kissed her on both cheeks. "Don't go back," she said. "Come with us."

"That is all you need, mademoiselle, a five-foot-one nudist accompanying you, with his virago wife on his trail." He kissed her again and then, standing on his toes, kissed Max, said, "*Courage,*" and turned back to the river.

A few moments later they heard a quick, low whistle, signifying Diderot was back in Le Soleil.

Chapter Fifteen

The sun had come up in earnest, promising another beautiful late-summer day. They walked silently but not unhappily along a dirt farm road. I am in the *Zone Libre*, she told herself. Free France. The farm buildings with their red-tiled roofs lay on either side of the road, seemingly peaceful, remote from Paris with its German flags and ersatz food, its air raids and one-page news-papers.

"What now?" Floy asked, when they had left the farm road and had come to a secondary highway. Max was in faded workman's *bleus*, a peaked cap on his head, his free hand in his pocket, the other holding on to his grip. He looked so young, a farmer's son. "Where do we go?" She tucked her hand in his arm affectionately.

"*We* aren't going anywhere, Floy. You're going to have to make your own way to Châteldon. It's a town a few miles outside Vichy." He told her the name of the hotel she was to stay in and handed her an envelope filled with money.

She tried to see his eyes under the cap, but he had turned away to look behind them. She tried to remain calm. "Alone? I don't think I can travel alone. I know nothing about this part of France . . ."

"You have no choice, *chérie*." Quite suddenly he was the remote *passeur* again. "It won't be difficult. You can pick up a bus a little way from here. Speak as little as possible. Your new papers are in the overnighter. You are Madame Constantine, of Italian descent, on your way to take the cure in Vichy. At the hotel in Châteldon there will be cosmopolitan clothing. Do not trust the hotel's owner. He is only in it for the money."

"Like you."

"As you say." He bowed formally and stepped away.

"Why can't you come with me?"

"There are very good reasons."

"We're in the Free Zone. The *Zone Libre*. Chambertin can't . . ."

"He can do just what he likes. You couldn't be naive enough to believe that the *Zone Libre* is genuinely free, could you? Pétain is bending over backward to appease the Germans, doing everything for them but shining their boots, and who knows what he does at night? Now we not only have Chambertin and the Gestapo looking for you, we have the Vichy police, the Vichy secret police, and the pro-Nazi armed mobile troop."

"And Louisianne? Sacha? My baby?"

"I am taking care of all of them. We will rendezvous, as planned, in Vichy."

"That sounds like a boulevard song." She was trying not to plead with him, not to give in to her desperation.

"Let us hope we shall be singing."

He gave her her instructions for Vichy, and she tried to listen carefully, to remember. "If all goes well," he told her, "you will be reunited with your aunt and child very soon, traveling south to Spain."

"When?"

"It may take some time. There is a big war going on and a great many little ones, and wars tend to impede civilian progress. Be patient. Remember to be an actress. Your performance counts this time."

"Did last night count?"

He looked at her for a moment from under his peaked workman's cap and said finally, "No. We both needed

153

comfort, just as we both needed food and sleep. Think of last night as a necessity. Better yet, don't think of it at all. Put last night out of your head and concentrate on saving your life." He picked up his metal suitcase and walked away from her, lighting a Gitane. "*Courage*," he said, without looking back, a little cloud of blue smoke trailing him.

She walked for half an hour until she reached the *épicerie* where the bus was to pick her up. She had put away the sadness, the fear, and the feeling of being betrayed and was feeling oddly liberated. After all, Max hadn't led her on. She had said it herself. She had seduced him. It was her fault again, but somehow she didn't feel bad about herself. She only felt bad about the cracked fantasy she had created about Max. He was, after all, what he had always seemed: a fellow no better or worse than others, concerned, as he had said, for himself.

She felt peculiarly unburdened. It was a sunny, country September day. The air smelled fresh, clean. She took great breaths. In a short time she would be holding Curry; she would be with Louisianne and Sacha—if Winterhagen did his job, and she felt that he would. He was workmanlike. He wanted his money, so he would perform.

She thought of the previous night and shivered. "That bastard," she said aloud in English, surprising herself. She never cursed. She was too much her Philadelphia aunties' niece.

Resolutely she put him out of her mind as she saw and then joined a half-dozen peasant women standing in front of the still-closed grocery store, waiting for the early-morning bus to Châteldon. They wore kerchiefs and giggled like girls; they carried ill-disguised chickens, eggs, cheese, and other black-market products in their baskets.

Floy hunted in the leather bag, found a handkerchief, and tied it around her head. She offered to take one of the two baskets an older woman was carrying, and the woman agreed with alacrity.

She sat next to her in the back of the bus, and no one questioned her. The women talked at one another at the top of their not inconsiderable voices. They smelled of kitchens and dairies and exuded warmth. Their foray into the black market, into crime, made this bus trip an adventure for them, and Floy felt less frightened, less by herself.

If the bus is stopped and searched, she thought, I'll seem like one more peasant girl going to the town to earn a few extra francs. Her scratched legs, her short hair, the dark, shapeless dress, all added to the illusion.

She felt fatalistic, like Billy's Indian philosophers. She took one of Billy's deep breaths. I will do whatever I have to do, she told herself, to get through. She wanted to live. For her baby. For herself.

Most of all—she was feeling honest on that bus filled with gasogene engine smells and such blatantly honest women—she wanted to avoid Chambertin, his long, cold, blue hands, those nearly white eyes.

The bus pulled up in the center of Châteldon across from the farmers' market. Floy got off with the woman she had come to think of as hers, gave her the basket, and was sorry to see her go. She suddenly felt quite alone again.

Following Winterhagen's directions, she went to the section of the town behind the farmers' market and found, with little trouble, Le Cheval Gai, the hotel she was to stop at.

It consisted of two floors over a butcher shop, which, like the hotel, was owned by M. Motagne. The hotel's sign, a painting of a rather sad horse bucking, stood just inside the low-ceilinged, green-papered lobby. An

155

ill-looking clerk directed Floy to the butcher shop, where she found M. Motagne.

He was a short, fat, middle-aged man with gray, greasy hair and a two-day beard. His butcher shop specialized in horse meat—there was little else available, at any rate—and he was wearing a bloodied apron when Floy found him.

"I do not register my lodgers on any *fiche*," he said as he led the way up inhospitable stairs. "I do not provide breakfast or hot water and I only change the sheets after every third lodger." He wanted Floy to know the rules up front, he said.

Lodgers who didn't register didn't require much in the way of services, he reasoned. He charged four hundred francs per night, which was the price of a suite at the Ritz. He charged an extra hundred francs for not requiring Floy to sign the register.

"If *les flics* find I let rooms without registering my guests, it would cost me a lot more than a hundred francs," M. Motagne said, putting one red hand on Floy's right breast and the other on her left buttock as if they were about to perform some obscene dance. Floy pushed him away but not too forcefully, because she had no other place to go.

M. Motagne remained unperturbed. "You are too skinny for me, anyway," he said, shutting the thin, unlockable door after him. He neglected to give Floy the rag of a towel he usually provided. It was, after all, only a Le Cheval Gai courtesy and since she was not being courteous, neither would he.

He returned to his butcher shop, leaving Floy alone in the narrow, low-ceilinged room. She looked at the bed, decided that that would wait, and unpacked the overnighter. In a small case was a vial of Molyneux Number 5. It was like a message from Louisianne, and when she smelled that distinctive aroma, her spirits picked up. She spread a few drops of the perfume on the bed.

And then she lay down and tried to sleep. But the combined aroma of Molyneux Number 5 and the other non-registering guests' scents and sweat made her nauseous and ill. She lay looking up at the low ceiling, which desperately needed replastering, and fell, finally, into a long, exhausted sleep.

She woke fourteen hours later in the middle of the night, nearly retching from the smell of that mattress and that room.

She opened the shutters and looked out into the street, breathing deeply. She would have liked to have taken a walk, to have seen the town, but that was obviously not possible. Even in normal times women did not walk up and down the streets of Châteldon alone in the early-morning hours.

The clock in the church struck five, that hour when Göring and the Gestapo liked to strike. Such a terrible hour to be woken, carted off, tortured, beheaded. She didn't want to, but she thought of Billy, of that newspaper photograph, all the more frightening for its lack of clarity. At five in the morning, in that hotel room in Châteldon, she remembered the awful O of Billy's mouth and the axe in the corner of that cell and she wondered how she was to get through the next hour, to get through till dawn, without shouting.

Promptly at six the butcher's wife came in after a peremptory rap on the door. She was as fat as her husband, and her silk dress, bougainvillea-purple in color, had burst at one of its seams.

She carried a tray with acorn coffee, dark bread and, miracle of miracles, a pear. It was very small and very dry and very sweet.

"You are very kind, Madame Motagne," Floy said while she tried to keep her hand from shaking as she lifted the coffee cup.

"Just between you, me, and the lamp post, you may

call me Madame Hibiscus. It is," she said proudly, "my code name."

Floy began to thank her again, but she had already left, to return a moment later with a navy-blue suit, a prewar Chanel, once expensive and still beautiful. It came with dark blue high heels, a purse, gloves, and a dark-blue, medium-brimmed hat. In a gray carton was a simple cream-colored silk blouse.

"I could not get pearls," Mme. Motagne apologized. "I am sorry."

She had a mole with three hairs growing out of it on her cheek and an incipient mustache. "I wish I could offer you more," she went on. "My husband does everything for the money. I do everything for France. That is where we differ."

Floy turned so that Mme. Hibiscus wouldn't see the tears in her eyes, but Madame put one hefty arm around her, gave her a bear hug, and then handed her a mirror. "So young. So beautiful. But you must use the makeup." She pointed to a tray of pencils and rouge she had set up on a much-scarred wooden desk. "You must not cry. It will soon be over."

Floy sat down and, remembering Winterhagen's injunction to attend to details, began to apply makeup, giving herself new eyebrows, thicker than Garbo's, and a smaller, fuller mouth. She fixed the brim of her hat so that it shaded her eyes and put on the steel-rimmed glasses she had found in the overnighter.

"Bravo," Mme. Hibiscus said from her seat on the bed, clapping her big hands, as if she were at a play. "You look ten years older. Not like yourself at all. When I saw you in *Les Filles du Jour* I cried my eyes out. Now I would not recognize you. You look rich and perhaps a little ill. Not at all sympathetic."

Floy turned and smiled at this new friend. She wondered who had given Madame the name Hibiscus and decided that it suited her. She was colorful and open and impossible not to care for.

Mme. Hibiscus led Floy down the back stairs into the cobblestoned courtyard facing M. Motagne's slaughterhouse.

Floy nearly gagged from the smell, but Madame took her arm and led her into it. Sides of horses hung from the meat hooks, red, raw, and horrible. "One gets used to the smell," Madame said. "One gets used to the sight. One gets used to nearly everything except the *sales Boches*. Look at me: I've been married to Motagne for nearly thirty years. Oh, one gets used to everything."

She walked Floy through the slaughterhouse, past a young boy in a white apron splattered with blood, to the delivery area, where an ancient Renault, with a converted and noisy gasogene engine, was waiting. The driver, a husky young woman in a black turtleneck, was smoking a hand-rolled cigarette.

"Your taxi," Mme. Hibiscus said. She held open the door and beamed at Floy as if Floy were her daughter and not some stranger she had known only for a morning. She kissed her on both cheeks and whispered, "My regards to the White Rose. Without her there would be no Fleurs du Mal. All of us whose heart is with De Gaulle salute her. Tell her I am carrying on."

She touched Floy's gloved hand with her own red, rough one, and the girl put the car into gear and moved off. The last word Floy heard from the butcher's wife—from Mme. Hibiscus—was *courage.*

Floy didn't feel courageous wearing the Chanel suit, sitting in the back of the ancient Renault as it crawled along the empty, neglected road to Vichy. She felt second-rate, an impostor. Les Fleurs du Mal should not have been wasting their resources getting her out of France.

What had she been doing while Billy and Louisianne and Sacha were recruiting agents in Rouen, setting up safe houses in the Pas de Calais, delivering radio transmitters to Normandy and the Somme? While they had been establishing a central command post in Paris, securing new identities for the Jews who had foolishly taken refuge in France? While they had kept those Jews and French patriots out of the concentration camps at Le Vernet, Rivesaltes, Gurs?

She had been priding herself on being non-political, on being a non-sexual working mother. She had been lunching with Chambertin at the Ritz, allowing his obsession to feed her neurosis. (She thought of Curry Greene, of Chambertin, of Winterhagen, and another of Auntie Ida's expressions came into her head: "You certainly know how to pick them, kid. You sure know how to pick them.") She had been becoming mildly famous as a clotheshorse in films Billy and Sacha turned out without commitment. Their commitment had been elsewhere, along with their minds and their energies. Her mind and her energy, like her body, had been in hibernation. For better or for worse, she was awake now.

She thought of Billy and that execution room in Cologne, those open, senseless eyes. He, of all people, should have had a better death, Floy thought, as the car crossed the narrow bridge spanning the Lac d'Allier and entered the capital of the new, shrunken France.

Vichy—faded, middle-class, the sort of spa no one Floy knew ever went to—was now more alive than Paris. Cars, trolleys, people, moved about with dispatch and a sure sense of mission, crisscrossing its parks, which were surrounded by absurdly grand hotels and open-air cafés with carefully nurtured palms.

"*Vichy*," a newly painted sign read, "*Reine des Villes d'Eaux.*" Queen of Spas. It looks like a set for a musical, Floy thought. Chevalier, grinning from ear to ear, strolling through the Ancien Parc and up the steps of the Grand Casino, a pretty girl on either side, ready to try their luck at baccarat. She liked Chevalier only when he tried to sing in English: "Oh, thees eez my luckee day."

The driver, that big hulking girl, slowed down as she passed the Hotel du Parc, where Pétain had his seat of government. His offices were on the third floor, supposedly above the petty intriguers, Laval and Darlan. They held court on the first and second floors of the elaborate building with its Mussolini balconies and soldiers in French uniforms guarding the entrance.

There was a traffic tie-up—a bicycle had overturned—and her driver was forced to wait. Floy looked at the Hotel du Parc. Standing at the foot of its steps, working a toothpick in and out of his tiny yellowed teeth, was the unmistakable question-mark figure of Rivet. He wore his soiled white suit. The thin, yellowish patch of mustache above his thin little lips needed attention. His colorless eyes watched, idly, each car that passed.

Floy turned her head away carefully, knowing he couldn't see her in the back of the Renault, that the hat and the steel-rimmed glasses provided enough disguise even had he caught a glimpse of her. Still, she felt herself stiffen with fear, with the old, too-familiar anxiety as the car moved on, passing a series of luxurious hotels that had been taken over by foreign embassies and by Pétain for his government.

The Splendide was just off the promenade with its carefully kept parks and miniature golf courses. Floy wondered if Rivet played miniature golf in his free time; and then she wondered if he had free time, if he didn't spend every moment of his day waiting for her.

The car pulled into the circular driveway of the Splendide. It had somehow escaped the fate of its requisitioned sisters. Ornate, built—like the others—at the turn of the century, it had a marble facade that featured a pair of cupids holding a huge gilt clock above the enormous arch of its entrance. A boy in cream-and-gold hotel livery came out, opened the car door, and took Floy's overnighter.

Floy gave the driver a hundred-franc note, and the girl turned and gave her a smile. "Merci, Madame Constantine," she said, before driving off.

Floy followed the porter up the red-carpeted marble steps into the grand foyer that ran the full width and length of the hotel. Floor-to-ceiling windows—much valenced and draperied—faced the park. Its tufted lounges were filled with Germans. Germans in black leather and Germans in highly imaginative uniforms and Germans in diplomats' morning coats and Germans in rough tweed suits with gold chains decorating their paunches.

The German ladies wore off-white hats and pale dresses, reminding Floy of those organdy ensembles she had worn a thousand years before in Philadelphia. These were somewhat more flowery, despite the fact that summer was over. The German ladies had been told Vichy was in the south and believed it because of those carefully cared for palms.

"Madame Constantine," a not-quite-young *sous-directeur* greeted her. He had oily hair and wore a cutaway and had an air of masquerade about him, as if he were the man in the Laurel and Hardy film who was going to get a cream pie in the face. He took her to a reproduction inlaid desk, where he looked at her papers and registered her.

He stood up after filling out her *fiche*, returned her papers, and said, "Your suite is ready now, madame. Please. This way." He should have been convincing but he wasn't.

The suite overlooked the Quai d'Allier. She could see small sailboats and tourist schooners from her windows. The rooms were modern, in contrast to the determined *belle époque* of the lobby, upholstered in standard French 1930s gray *luxe*, Normandy-inspired.

"I am Monsieur Foucard," the man in the cutaway said, as he switched on lights and opened the radio console's doors. He turned up the Rudolf Friml music being broadcast by Radio Vichy. "I am also known," he whispered, "as Monsieur Lilac."

"I'm so relieved," Floy said, but he put his finger to his lips and led the way to the *salle de bain*.

He stepped into the long and narrow tiled bathroom, turning on the waterspouts in the stall shower and the marble tub.

"Your party will meet you by Friday, madame," he said, under the noise of the water. "The boy is safe. You will be notified when the rendezvous is to take place. You are to stay in your room as much as possible. Meals will be sent up. No. Please do not interrupt. We have no time, and I must tell you certain things.

"You have an appointment with Dr. Frenet-Haupt." He handed her a thick white calling card bearing the doctor's name and address. "He will prescribe the appropriate treatment of waters."

"What if someone asks . . ."

"You are a German general's mistress. You have come to take the waters while he is at the front. At the last moment your maid took ill, but you came on alone. It is very simple." He turned off the water and left her standing in the elaborate bathroom in her Chanel suit and steel-rimmed glasses, mindful of one fact. "The boy," he had said, "is safe."

"Restraint," Lilac said as he left, and she was surprised he hadn't said "*Courage.*"

"Damn bloody restraint," Floy said, but to herself, mindful of eavesdroppers, mechanical or otherwise. She ordered a bottle of vermouth, was told there wasn't any, offered to pay double the hotel price, and it arrived on a tray in under fifteen minutes.

She undressed, carefully putting away the suit and the blouse, as Winterhagen had put away his clothes in Diderot's cottage.

She poured herself a tumbler of vermouth, drew the curtains, because the relentless resort cheeriness of Vichy depressed her, and lay on the bed. She wondered what she was going to do with herself for five days. She wondered who and what Dr. Frenet-Haupt was and what help he was going to be, if any. She felt trapped inside a spy thriller that had lost its suspense; all she wanted it to do was end.

She drank the vermouth and got a little drunk and a little weepy. Despite how much she disliked him, she felt grateful to Winterhagen from the bottom of her heart for remembering to include in his message, "The boy is safe."

"My boy," she said to herself, "is safe."

Dr. Frenet-Haupt kept an office at 12 Rue Cailliou in the shadow of the Thermal Spa, which looked to Floy like a Turk's idea of a medieval castle.

However, the doctor's office, a gray stucco building with a mansard roof, couldn't have been more suburban. The entrance was reached through a fenced-in garden. On the gate a discreet brass plate read: "Dr. Frenet-Haupt. *Réducation et Réadaptation Fonctionnelle Remise en Forme.*"

"You are enjoying Vichy, madame?" Dr. Frenet-Haupt inquired as his nurse led her into the consulting room the morning after Floy arrived. "Madame de Sévigné, as you no doubt know, once said, 'Vichy is a bore. But that is the cure.'" He laughed as if it were the first time he had heard the anecdote.

He was a man in his early sixties with a Vandyke beard, morning jacket, a carnation in his lapel. "Madame de Sévigné adored white roses. I myself prefer the carnation. Such a simple, deceptive flower, is it not?"

The nurse, a stout, starched woman in a white uniform, shut the connecting door as the doctor took his seat behind a rosewood desk and motioned Floy to a red leather chair.

"There is no need for an examination, madame. I am in possession of your own specialist's report. A good man. A very good man. Now, there is a fellow who prefers violets. One cannot account for taste, can one, madame?"

Dr. Frenet-Haupt enjoyed the game. He would have strung out sentences for hours, loaded with references to flowers, had Floy not stopped him. If Lilac had been overly cautious, Carnation was wildly indiscreet.

"I am in a great hurry, Doctor," Floy said, smiling but firm. There was a time when she would have sat patiently through whatever nonsense the doctor cared to indulge in. Now she had other priorities. Being liked was way down the list. "Please," she said. "What is my regimen?"

He became serious at once. She was to follow his prescription exactly. "No deviations, madame. Each morning you are to go to the spring hall on the Rue du Casino. The first day an attendant will give you a numbered brass cup. Show them your prescription. Each time you attend you will ask for your cup by number and you will be given the proper dosage of water. I am afraid, madame, you may have to queue up. Vichy waters are suddenly popular again. The Germans are great ones for taking cures."

He wrote a few words on a slip of prescription paper. He stood up, handing it to her. There were two slips. One was the prescription. The other read: "Your contact at the spa is an attendant named Gardenia. She will tell you where and when the rendezvous is. Lilac is not to be trusted."

He took the second slip from her, tore it into a great many pieces, put them into a heavy glass ashtray, and set them on fire.

He waited until the fire had died out before he took her to the door, which, she saw, had not been perfectly closed.

"It is a pity," Dr. Frenet-Haupt said, unable to resist, as they walked through the reception room past his nurse's desk, "that lilacs do not bloom in the fall. *Au revoir, madame.*"

Chapter Sixteen

Floy didn't want to return to the Splendide, not immediately. She walked instead through the France district, a residential area near the Celestin Spring. She passed a playground with a puppet theater even more elaborate than the one that had once stood in the Champs, and stopped to watch a group of boys playing football.

They wore short trousers and deadly earnest expressions, which reminded her of Curry when he was intent on proving he could do something by himself. She wondered that these boys could be so normal when the world had been turned upside down.

But only my world is inverted, she reminded herself. If you weren't wanted by the police, if you weren't Jewish, if you lived in the Free Zone, why then you only had to keep your eyes half closed and your nose clean, as Jimmy Cagney said in a movie Curry had seen. For weeks after, that was his favorite English expression. Now keeping one's nose clean meant keeping out of politics, giving rubber-stamp approval to Pétain and his pro-German, supposedly French government.

It was far too late for Floy to keep her nose clean. She nearly laughed. It was as if she was appearing in an old-fashioned French farce. Was *sous-directeur* Lilac not to be trusted? Or was it the doctor who talked too much who was the traitor? Or were both working against her? And if either one was, why was she not in jail instead of in that tastelessly luxurious suite on the Splendide's third floor?

It was all a child's game, not even as seriously played as the boys' football on the Avenue des Celestins. Only the consequences had import.

As she walked up the Splendide's marble stairs, with its red carpet held in place by triangular brass clips, a little man in a dirty white suit stepped into the writing room.

She forced herself to continue to walk across the marbled, mirrored, many-columned lobby to the elevator. When it came, she decided she needed a magazine from the kiosk located just past the door to the writing room.

She looked in glancingly as she went to the kiosk and bought her magazine. Rivet was no longer in the writing room. Only three German ladies of indeterminate age, busy at the *faux* desks, writing postcards.

"May I help madame?" She turned to find Lilac in his cutaway.

"I thought I might write some letters," she said, pausing again at the writing room entrance. "But I've changed my mind. I think I shall go up to my rooms now."

"Very good, madame."

She left him, taking the elevator to the third floor, locking the door after her, knowing that was ridiculous. If they wanted to get in, a locked door wouldn't stop them.

She lay on her bed and thought that she had learned a few possibly important facts. That there was a door at the far end of the writing room leading into the Splendide gardens. That Rivet, who came and went that way, was watching her. That Lilac was indeed not to be trusted.

It was obvious that they knew who she was and where

she was. That they were waiting for Louisianne and Sacha to contact her. And then they would all be taken, along with the Weinbergs, Winterhagen, and her son.

She undressed and thought that she had better rinse out her underwear if she was going to arrive at the spring hall in the morning clean in body, clothes, and mind. Or if she was arrested. She nearly laughed. She was still her aunties' niece. Concerned about clean underwear, what the authorities would think.

She thought about Winterhagen not wearing underwear and then she thought about Curry Greene not wearing underwear. Someday, she said to herself, I'll meet a man who does wear underwear—long shorts, white and silky—and I'll marry him, and we'll live happily ever after.

But she didn't believe that. Winterhagen was another Curry Greene, all over again. Though this time she was quite certain she hadn't become pregnant. It's a time for death, she thought, not birth.

Underwear—she wondered if she was developing a fetish—made her wonder what state Curry's was in. She decided Alouette could be depended upon to keep it clean and mended.

And suddenly, while she was washing her slip with the bar of brown soap the hotel supplied, she began to cry.

She cried for herself, she knew that. It was so painful, so lonely being so totally by herself. Without Louisianne or Curry. Without the solace of even casual conversation. She was too afraid to speak to anyone. And then there was the knowledge that was with her all the time, the awareness that Chambertin was nearby, waiting to spring his trap.

Winterhagen had called him a big cat, and she remembered his feline elegance, those beautifully manicured fingers, and she felt an overwhelming revulsion along with the fear. It was as if Chambertin had managed to touch her once again with his obsessive, grasping hands.

She dried her eyes and hung up the slip. She was going to have to believe that the doctor had somehow gotten word to Winterhagen, that when the time came, he would be prepared for Chambertin's trap, aware that he was waiting.

The following morning she went to *les buvettes des sources*—the spring hall—looking for the contact Dr. Frenet-Haupt said would identify herself as Gardenia.

It was a large, oval building with glass tile walls and ceilings. Very white, medicinal. Attendants in white coats moved quickly, and there was a hushed, awed look about the patients.

A series of floor-to-ceiling mesh screens, painted white, had been arranged as temporary walls to keep the queues orderly. One of the women in starched white coats took Floy's money and directed her along the mazelike corridors created by the mesh screens. Another white-coated attendant gave her a numbered brass cup.

Yet another filled the cup with not very pleasant-tasting water. She was dismissed, but she had to wait for a group of German ladies to swallow and discuss their treatment before she was able to make her way through the mesh-screened corridors and back out into the Ancien Parc.

Lilac, in his cutaway, smiled at her inquiringly, as if she might have received the awaited message at the spring hall. Floy shook her head no and went up to her rooms and waited until it was time to turn the radio on for the BBC broadcast.

Of course, the BBC was proscribed, but she listened to it with the volume turned down and the bathwater turned up, as a great many French people did. As always, she was uplifted when she heard the broadcast's

170

signature, the opening bars of Beethoven's Fifth. That little bit of familiar music seemed to say that there was still sanity and reason in the world not very far away.

For a woman who hadn't paid very much attention to the world, she was now passionately involved.

The announcer, in those perfect BBC tones, read out the messages, half of which were obviously in code. "The barber wants Michelle to stop in tomorrow. Linda sends her love to Leighton. Marta regrets to inform Todd that the baby is no longer safe . . ."

Her baby, at least was safe. "The boy is safe." And then it hit her all at once with such impact that she had to sit down.

Her baby wasn't safe.

Lilac was the one who had said, "The boy is safe." But Lilac was a traitor, not to be trusted, working for Chambertin. So Chambertin knew about Curry. Perhaps he always had.

She switched off the BBC and drank a glass of vermouth, which wouldn't, she knew, help. She paced the room as if she were in a cage. She wished she knew how to pray.

"The boy is safe," Lilac had said.

So Chambertin knew. He was aware of her weakest, most vulnerable spot. She hated to think what Chambertin was capable of doing to her baby, her son, her Curry. She thought of Billy and cried out and was aware that she was losing control. She took the bottle of vermouth to bed and finished it, forcing herself not to move, not to cry, to take deep Hindu breaths à la Billy.

She made herself follow a routine each day. She spent her mornings in her rooms, reading magazines, listening to Radio Vichy, Radio Paris, and that most innocuous Radio, Geneva. She ate the food sent up from the dining room. She tried to appear calm, assured. She tried not to let all the fears rise up and fill her mind with that panic

171

that made her want to run screaming into the street, crying for her baby.

Each day she told herself she had to wait.

And each afternoon at the spring hall she had to stifle that impulse to shout at the women in the starched white coats who calmly handed her her brass cup and urged on the German ladies who wanted to chat over their water and block the narrow mesh corridors. Which one was Gardenia? She looked into each of the attendant's faces, but there was no sign.

Lilac continued to smile at her inquisitively, and Rivet continued to appear, just for a moment, twisting the screw of her anxiety.

On Thursday she bought a gardenia in the Splendide's florist shop for more money than she would have thought possible and wore it to the spring hall. She stood as long as she could in front of each attendant, the inappropriate gardenia on the Chanel suit's lapel, hesitating at each station in the spa as if they were stations of the cross.

But the attendants treated her as another foreigner, keeping their eyelids lowered, giving her her change, her cup, her water, waiting for her to move on.

She couldn't return to the Splendide. Those well-appointed rooms only served to heighten her anxiety, to make her feel as if she had already been taken, imprisoned. The boredom was very nearly as punishing as the fear.

Instead she walked to Dr. Frenet-Haupt's office on the Rue Cailliou in the shadow of the surreal Thermal Spa.

"The doctor is not in," the nurse said. She was big and blond but moved like a small woman, taking tiny steps toward Floy, who stood in the center of the waiting room.

There was something Lilac-like about the nurse's expression, a kind of muddy, suppressed exultation. "I shouldn't be surprised," the nurse couldn't keep herself

from saying, "if we don't see him for a good long time."
She smiled, a vindictive smile, like a girl who wins a
game unfairly. "I wouldn't be surprised if we don't see
him until the carnations bloom again, Madame Constantine. If then."

"When he returns," Floy said, her dislike giving her
poise, "will you tell him I called?"

"If he returns."

Dr. Frenet-Haupt had been taken. He had talked too
much about flowers. He had been too relaxed about
half-closed doors. He hadn't been cautious about who
worked for him. He was in a Gestapo jail now, and Floy
hoped it wasn't in Lyon. She had heard the stories of
Klaus Barbie and his bullwhip.

Her first thought was not to return to the Splendide.
To run. But where? She had no idea where Louisianne
and Sacha might be, where Curry was. She had to return
to the hotel. She had to wait there. The others hadn't
been taken; if they had been, she would have been also.
As she waited, the Gestapo waited. She wondered how
long they would wait, and suddenly knew. Lilac had
told her she was to remain in her rooms until Friday.
She had until the following day.

She would go to the spring hall on Friday for the last
time. If there was no message, no sign of Gardenia, she
would attempt to escape. She had a plan in mind: to get
back to Châteldon, to Mme. Hibiscus. It was a plan
that didn't give her much hope, but it gave her a certain
amount of that commodity all the members of Les
Fleurs du Mal seemed so anxious to give her: courage.

When she first began appearing in films, she would
spend as much time with Curry as possible and only at
the last moment head for the studio, nervous and empty.
When Billy found out she came to the studio without
eating, he grabbed her by the arm and pulled her out
onto the street.

"Children who don't eat their breakfast always look like you do now: peaked and crabby." He took her to the Poste Café around the corner from the studio. "It is why the English are superior to the French: think of English breakfasts." He made her eat several liberally buttered croissants covered with strawberry jam. He forced her to drink two large cups of hot chocolate. "There are no kippers, but this will do. How do you feel now?"

"Like a Strasbourg goose at pâté-making time."

"Nervous?"

"I'm too stuffed to be nervous."

"Exactly." He hummed a few bars of "Tit Willow" as he led her back to the studio and Sacha, whom he had kept waiting while he force-fed Floy.

So on that overcast Friday morning in Vichy, dressing in the Chanel suit, deserting the overnighter and putting the money and her papers along with clean underclothing in her purse, she descended to the Splendide's lobby. Taking a breath, she stepped into the Splendide's grand salon, where breakfast was being served.

"What are you doing?" Lilac, concerned, asked as she passed him to enter the dining salon.

"I'm so tired of cold food in the morning," she said, but she knew that wasn't what he meant. She had left the steel-rimmed glasses behind and carried her hat. She had put on her own makeup and done her hair in as close a semblance to the old way as she could.

She wanted to look beautiful and glamorous, because she knew beauty and glamour were weapons. "I need a hot meal," she said, stepping into the marble-floored room, with its gray walls and sleek nautical decor.

"I am sorry, madame," the waiter told her. He had an unfortunate long nose and a concerned look in his tired eyes. "No croissants. We do have brioches." She ordered brioche and extra jam and a pot of acorn coffee and a

174

slice of ham. She wanted to be certain to fill up that empty space before she went for the last time to the spring hall for that message she wanted so badly.

She saw Rivet as the waiter brought the coffee. The waiter looked up at the same time and saw him too. Rivet was just tall enough to look through the porthole windows of the doors leading to the salon.

His face was framed in that oval window, smiling at her, and she had to put her cup down. It was the first time she had seen him smile. Usually he looked worried, as if the tooth he was working on was bothering him and he was afraid it would cost too much to have it fixed.

Behind and above him she saw Lilac, serious. He was, she realized, afraid of her. If she were to get word to Les Fleurs du Mal, he wouldn't have much to look forward to.

She turned away, concentrating on the brioche, on the ham, avoiding the trio of Germans in Vichy on business at the next table, who were eying her, giving her a signal that they would enjoy a little company.

One of them went so far as to whistle, and she looked up but she didn't see the whistler's florid, round face. She was looking past him at Chambertin.

It was almost a relief. She had felt his presence since she had come to Vichy, and it was better for her to see him in person. He was being shown to a table on a platform, obviously where the premier tables were kept. He sat with two men, one dimly familiar from photographs in *Le Matin*, an official in the Pétain government.

Chambertin took a moment to get settled and then looked up directly into her eyes, as if he had known she would be there, as if he had planned the meeting.

He removed his blue-lensed glasses for a moment and stared at her with those nearly white eyes, frightening her. She wasn't flattered that he was still obviously obsessed with her. But it wasn't with her. It was with

175

some fantasy he had created. The intensity of that look nearly paralyzed Floy. But then he replaced his glasses and turned to his companions as if she weren't there.

She drank a second cup of acorn coffee and turned casually away from him. Rivet was still at the porthole window, a purser uncertain of the weather, hoping for a bad crossing. She wondered if she could get past him into the writing room and out the garden door. It seemed unlikely.

Oddly, she was suddenly clear-headed. Two Gestapo men in brown suits stood on either side of the dining salon's French doors leading to the Rue Rambert, effectively cutting off that exit.

She thought of Billy and the axe and the prison in Cologne. She had been in Cologne once. It was a gray, businesslike place. They were on location, and the assistant director had called it, matter-of-factly, the Catholic north.

"Is Madame finished?" The long-nosed waiter with the plaintive eyes bent over her. "More coffee, perhaps?"

"Yes. More coffee. Please."

As he poured, he spilled some on the tablecloth. He sponged it up with a napkin. "Buttercups are lovely this time of year." He placed a serviette under the cup. "Through the kitchen. Turn right. The door is open. It leads to Avenue Victoria."

He bowed. "I am so sorry, madame." He moved off through the kitchen doors, floor-to-ceiling swinging panels a few feet from Floy's table.

She took one of Billy's Hindu deep breaths and turned over the café table as she stood up. The steaming pot of coffee broke on the marble floor, splattering the German businessmen, leaving a growing stain on the red carpet-runner.

She left as two waiters and the *maître d'hôtel* tried to save the carpet, to right the table, while the German businessmen, sputtering, burned, got in everyone's way.

She ran through the kitchen door, turned right, and passed Buttercup as he set up a tray in the center of the corridor. On it was a tower of Hotel Splendide china.

"*Courage*," he said as she ran.

She sped through the open rear door and moved quickly along a service alley, not looking back. She heard Rivet swear as he crashed into Buttercup's china tower, but knew that wouldn't stop them for long.

At the end of the service alley she had a choice of going to the right onto the Avenue Victoria, a busy shopping street, or going to the left, back into the hotel via the garden off the writing room.

She went through the garden into the writing room, reasoning that would be unexpected. The three German ladies, again writing postcards, looked up. She smiled at them and nodded. They smiled and nodded back and returned to their postcards.

She went out into the lobby carefully, but it seemed deserted, at least by Rivet and Lilac.

Calmly she left the Splendide by its red-carpeted marble steps and crossed into the Ancien Parc, making her way to the spring hall, taking deep breaths all the way, refusing to think.

It was more crowded than usual; new German ladies with husbands stationed in France had arrived for a weekend of health.

Floy received her numbered brass cup from the attendant, waited a moment, and then joined the queue of German ladies inching through the wire-mesh corridors.

As she got closer to the attendant dispensing water she looked back. Chambertin had joined the queue.

The women nearest him tittered. German men did not line up to drink health waters. At least not in Vichy, France. He smiled and bowed at the ladies and attempted to get around them, to catch up with Floy.

"*Nein*," a buxom *frau* said to him, flirtatiously waving

177

her sausage of a finger in his face. "We all wait our turn. Like in Germany. Now everyone is orderly here."

He looked at her as if he would knock her down, but even if he had, there were twenty others he would have had to get by, all as stalwart as the woman in front of him.

He would have to wait for an opportunity to get around them.

Standing sandwiched in between those hefty German women, he looked like one of their sons, dragged along unwillingly on an excursion he would rather have missed.

As the line doubled and snaked around the spring hall, Floy found herself next to Chambertin, separated by the thin, impenetrable mesh curtain-wall.

He stared at her. The blue lenses in his glasses reflected the mesh curtains and Floy's own oddly composed face.

"You seem more available in your new outlaw career," he said, finding his voice. "Freer." She saw the blue Schmeisser pressed up against his suit jacket. "The old Floy would not have walked out on a restaurant bill. Not if her life depended upon it." He moved his face closer to hers, and she could smell that distinctive perfume from his black soap cutting through the spring hall's disinfectant.

"That is the crime we are going to arrest you for. Not paying your breakfast bill. We'll begin with that."

The line moved ahead. He pushed a woman aside so that he could remain next to Floy. The woman called for the police in an outraged voice.

"We arrived at Le Soleil an hour too late." She could see the nearly white pupils contracting behind the smoked glasses. "It must have been amusing swimming in the nude with your lover."

The line moved again, and he pushed more women out of his way. A general call for authorities rose up. Queue-jumping wasn't tolerated in Germany.

Chambertin ignored them, too intent on keeping up with Floy. He pressed up against the mesh, trying to touch her, to hold her back. "What is he called now? Still Winterhagen? We thought he'd try to save you, but it seems he's given you up. It's too late, at any rate. Now we have you. And of course we have the boy."

She put her hand over her mouth so as not to scream.

"He's bright. How old is he? Four? Five? He is not so very forthcoming yet."

The women in front of Floy had gotten their water. Two French policemen were crossing the lobby, accompanied by three of the more outraged women Chambertin had pushed aside.

Floy automatically handed her cup to the attendant, pushed by the woman behind her. "Gardenia," the attendant said. "They're waiting across the park for you in a green bus. Hurry."

Floy dropped the cup and ran as Chambertin broke through the queue, trying to reach her. Two hefty ladies blocked him at the last moment, delighted to keep him trapped. "We have him here, *Herr Direktor*," they said, exultant, as the police and a man in a dark suit came through, "this damn queue-jumper."

Floy emerged in the Ancien Parc and ran toward the Casino. On the far side of the street she saw the green bus, its motor running, its windows painted blue.

She continued to run, not looking back, even when she heard Chambertin shout, when someone blew a whistle, when the sounds of men in heavy shoes running along the pavement became insistently loud. And there was another, more subtle noise, one she didn't or wouldn't recognize.

She just managed to get aboard and the door shut behind her when she realized that unfamiliar noise was the sound of bullets. They had been shooting at her as she ran across the park.

The bus pulled away as Louisianne pulled her into a seat and put her arms around her. A car followed them and stopped as another car hit it broadside. There was an explosion, and the resulting fire blocked the Rue du Casino, allowing the bus to turn left on the Boulevard de Russe. It crossed the Lac d'Allier over the Pont de Bellerive undeterred. It then headed north on Route 9A, reaching Clermont long before cars could be mobilized to follow.

The Weinberg sisters, Ilone and Chantil, sat on the back bench of the bus in their peasant dresses, Ilone's eyes firmly shut.

"You can open them," Chantil said, unscrewing a flask, pouring brandy into the cap, which doubled as a cup. "They stopped shooting a quarter of an hour ago."

She handed the brandy to Sacha, who passed it up to Louisianne, who held it to Floy's mouth, forcing her to take some.

Floy swallowed a few drops and coughed. "Curry," she managed to say. "They've got Curry."

"They most certainly do not," Louisianne said in her no-nonsense voice, her gray eyes alive with anger. "When we learned that the Gestapo were visiting all the farm families in Joigny, we had Alouette meet us with Curry in Beaune. Winterhagen managed to take them to a place only he and I know, and they're safe now for the time being. He'll have to move them again soon."

"You swear he's all right? You're not telling me that simply to . . ."

"Would I?" Louisianne asked.

"No," Floy answered after a moment. "You wouldn't lie. Not your style, Auntie." Floy closed her eyes, asleep in her aunt's arms.

"Is she all right?" Sacha asked.

"Yes. Only exhausted with fear and worry."

Louisianne looked toward the front of the bus as it

careened down a dusty country road. In the driver's rearview mirror she saw Winterhagen's black eyes staring at Floy.

And then he turned his concentration back to the road leading south.

Chapter Seventeen

"I thought we were in a green bus," Floy said several hours later, opening her eyes, sitting up, refusing the flask Sacha offered her. Her mouth felt stale and dry.

"We changed to a gray one in Clermont-Ferrand. Winterhagen's theory again. They'll never think, he says, to search for a gray bus. According to him, the Gestapo are now combing central France for trucks, ox-drawn peasant carts, and groups of refugees on foot." Louisianne smiled. "He says he knows how they think. Let us hope and pray that he does."

"You like Winterhagen, don't you?" Floy said, surprised.

"Yes," Louisianne answered. "A couple of decades ago I would have tried to make a *lapin* out of him. He's so very much a man."

Floy looked for him in the driver's seat. Instead, Chantil Weinberg was in the seat, her plump hands authoritatively on the wheel, her chubby, earnest, and pretty face screwed up in concentration on the dark road. They were driving without lights.

"Chantil," Louisianne explained, "drove ambulances in Holland during the blitzkrieg. She does far better than Sacha, who tends to go too slow. My driving was always more a fanciful desire than a wish fulfilled. Winterhagen had to sleep."

Max was spread out full length on the back bench, his hands folded under his head, his cupid's lips slightly pursed, his dime-store lashes thick and black against his cheek. He looked like the worst boy in class caught napping again.

Sacha stood at the front of the bus, a map in his hand illuminated by a small flashlight held by Ilone. She was breathing heavily, her mouth slightly open. She wasn't used to any of this. She wanted to be back in her father's house in Amsterdam, ordering the servants about.

"I never thought I'd see you again," Floy said, and her aunt put her arms around her and Floy allowed her head to rest against Louisianne's bony shoulder. "I kept dreaming I was searching for Curry. I would be running from place to place, but he was always a jump in front of me, as if we were playing some mad child's game. He is all right, isn't he, Auntie?"

"He's fine. Well hidden and cared for." Louisianne paused and looked into her niece's eyes with her own uncompromising gray ones. "You mustn't feel so guilty, Floy."

"I don't," she said too quickly.

"Yes, you do. You feel guilty because you could have left France with Curry when there was still time. You feel guilty about your cousin Gloria and Curry's father, and you feel guilty about having an illegitimate baby.

"You've been carrying around a sack of ashes for years. You're Rose and Ida's niece as much as you are mine. I believe you allowed those lunches with Chambertin to take place as a kind of atonement. Now you feel guilty about him. About leading him on.

"Well, you've paid. Now you can put it all behind you. I forbid you to feel guilty anymore, Floy. I want you to live your life now. You've got so much to live for."

She held Louisianne's hand against her cheek. "You're right, of course," Floy said a few moments later. "But the one guilt I can't expiate is not getting Curry away. When Chambertin said he had him, I became certifiably insane. All I could do at that moment was run. When do you think I'll see him, Auntie?"

"For better or for worse, we are currently married to Winterhagen. We have to wait until he says we can go to him. I am as anxious as you.

"But Winterhagen is in charge. It was he who went and took Alouette and Curry to where they are now. The rest of us sweated and complained in a little room above the butcher shop in Châteldon, waiting. I can't tell you how depressing it was. Chantil kept organizing charade games."

"Hibiscus?"

"Without her I would have died in that room. She brought us the news and finally, when I thought I couldn't stand it another moment, she smuggled in a radio. When Winterhagen returned, he would only say you were *brûlé*. We had to wait, he said, to see if you would cool off."

"He wanted to leave me, didn't he?"

"He said he would get us to the south and return for you, but we all knew that it would be too late. He said he was being paid to get Sacha to London and the Weinbergs to Lisbon, and everyone else was excess baggage.

"We took a vote. Madame Hibiscus insisted on casting a ballot as well. It was nearly unanimous that we wait for you." Louisianne glanced at Ilone, and Floy knew that Ilone would have gone, that she would have done anything to be safe. Floy could hardly blame her.

"How did Winterhagen vote?"

"He abstained." Louisianne looked at her niece. "Still, he did go to rescue Curry and he didn't have to hold that balloting."

"With you on the scene? I think he did have to hold that balloting."

"I don't know how he managed to set up that commotion in Vichy. That's the sort of skill that makes him so valuable to us. He's a natural resistance fighter. *Les services* is going to miss him when he's gone. He knows

184

people everywhere. Unfortunately someone gave your doctor, Frenet-Haupt, away. They picked him up soon after you saw him."

"Probably his nurse."

"Winterhagen says it's someone high up in the organization. 'One of your damned bloody flowers,' he said to me when we learned about Frenet-Haupt."

"You know, of course, that Lilac is a traitor."

"Yes. But there's a more important traitor. There's a rat among the mice. Lilac will be taken care of, at any rate. If he hasn't already."

They rode through the dark for some miles before Floy said, "Do you think your traitor told Chambertin about Curry?"

"No," Louisianne said. "He wouldn't have to. Chambertin knew everything all along. From the beginning, you were followed night and day, your past looked into, the apartment house put under surveillance.

"I've been thinking, and it seems to me Chambertin has known about Les Fleurs du Mal for some time. He knew everything that went on in our household. I think it was Chambertin who arranged for Billy's arrest. He was afraid of Billy. Afraid—I see now, with the great clarity of hindsight—that Billy would identify the informant in time. In those last weeks before his arrest, Billy was behaving oddly, as if he were suffering from some great disappointment. I believe he knew who the traitor was but didn't want to admit it."

"But why did Chambertin wait to arrest everyone?"

"There was you, to start with; though he knew so much, he must have known you had nothing to do with Les Fleurs du Mal. No. I see now that along with the genuine refugees and informants, we were receiving and passing on double agents, misleading information. It's a bitter pill to swallow to think that we were in the end working for the Germans, for Chambertin. We were —certainly after Billy was taken—very useful to them.

He probably should have arrested us earlier, but there's his tragic flaw: He likes to toy with his mice before he eats them."

As conversationally as she could, taking her aunt's hand, Floy said, "Do you think we'll ever be safe again, Auntie?"

"Tonight we shall be at least more secure. We're going to a safe village. Winterhagen wants us to stay there for a few days, cooling off again, while he attends to other Fleurs du Mal business. I've agreed. It's better for us to go to ground and let them think we've disappeared."

Floy looked up at Louisianne's perfect profile. She had never felt more in need of her aunt's measured sanity, of that voice of calm authority. "You must be very important to *les services*."

Louisianne laughed. "I've been a fool, had by Chambertin. The White Rose! I was necessary in the beginning. I am good at organization, at details, at seeing both sides of problems. But Billy was the key. He had that rock-hard determination and that golden idealism.

"They all admired him, despite what one rural teacher kindly called 'the little lord's eccentricities.' You should have seen him drive into a tough French farm village in that yellow car of his and wrap those French cowboys around his little finger in half an hour.

"Sacha has inherited Billy's mantle, and that's all to the good. He never forgets anything. He remembers everyone's name, how many children they have, where they went to school. But he is not a politician or a soldier, so they trust him."

"Do you trust him?"

"Sacha is the only one—besides myself and possibly Winterhagen—who knows everyone in all the movements, and there are more movements in France than there is tea in China. There's the Left and the Middle and the Right. There are the Catholics and the Communists and the anti-Vichy and the anti-De Gaulle and the pro-Vichy and the pro-De Gaulle. Then there are dozens of splinter groups, all with their own idea of how France should be governed if Germany ever gets out . . . if Germany is ever defeated.

"That is the one idea that unites all of them: that Germany shall be defeated. What De Gaulle desperately needs now is to win them all over to his side, to unify them under his command so that when the time does come for an invasion, he has an effective home army.

"Most people believe Sacha is the man to unify all the *services*. The British think so, and so does De Gaulle. The Americans are backing their own man, but they always do. Sacha is going to London to be briefed by the General himself, and then presumably he will return to France with a new persona, ready to begin."

"I should think De Gaulle would automatically dismiss Sacha, given the fact poor old Sacha prefers men in bed to women."

"As long as Sacha doesn't put on a gown and high heels and commit fellatio on a barge floating down the Seine with a member of the German High Command, he is politically expedient. The General needs poor old Sacha now."

"And you?"

"He draws the line at American women of a certain age. I'll go to London with Sacha but I imagine they'll put me in a little room in South Kensington and try to forget me. I'll wind up, I greatly fear, in Philadelphia with dear Rose and Ida. It's my fate to be the eccentric sister who lived abroad too long, insults visitors, and cries after one glass of champagne. How I loathe and despise Philadelphia. The thought of all those red-brick houses on those narrow streets filled with people with narrow minds is almost more frightening to me than a German prison camp."

"Sacha won't let them send you back."

"I'm not certain he'll have much to say about it."

Winterhagen woke up at that moment and, instantly alert, moved up the bus toward the driver's seat. He nodded at Floy, perfectly serious, as if he had seen her only a little while before.

"You are well?" he asked and, not waiting for an answer, forced Chantil to change places with him. Chantil, aggrieved at having to give up the wheel, went and sat next to her sister. Sacha, with that characteristic civility, offered to read the map, but Winterhagen said he knew the roads, that Sacha should try to get some sleep.

Sacha came down the aisle, gave Floy that surprisingly sweet smile of his, and took a seat. It was clear he felt, like Chantil, rebuffed by Winterhagen.

"I think Winterhagen is the only person I've ever known Sacha to dislike."

"Sacha has good reason," Louisianne said. "Winterhagen is the best *passeur* we have ever had. And the greediest. We have had to give him huge, important sums to get certain men out of France and even out of Germany. The money came from De Gaulle, who got it from Churchill in embarrassing little stipends.

"And always Winterhagen's price rose. We paid because he delivered so consistently. Now he announces he is retiring. Now, when we need him most of all, he is leaving. One of his conditions for getting Sacha out was a British passport, to be handed over to him in Spain. Worse, we don't know half his sources. He refuses to divulge them. He says he won't put other men's heads in Fleurs du Mal nooses, that we're not to be trusted.

"I've argued and even pleaded—not my strong suit—but he says we're too dangerous now. He says he's too dangerous now. They're beginning to know who he is, and he doesn't want to die a rich man in a German torture chamber.

188

"There's something else, something he won't say. But what is clear is that he's going to take his money and set himself up in Portugal or preferably America, if the Americans will let him in.

"He appears to care nothing for his country, for the freedom of his people, for justice. He's a man without a country at a time when men are dying for their country everywhere.

"He is a brave man, but I'm not certain he is a good man. What I do know, Floy, is that he's not a man to fall in love with."

"Love? I can't think of a man—with one obvious exception—I dislike more."

"It's not a time to fall in love with anyone," Louisianne said, as if she hadn't heard, while the bus drove into the safe village.

They were to be divided up among a series of safe villages, Winterhagen said. They were in the Lozère district, not far from Grand Combe. They had traveled throughout the night on a series of roads most of which were not on any map. They were all apprehensive and at the same time relieved. They were in a safe village.

When Winterhagen announced the dividing up, Louisianne objected. "I thought we were all to be in the same village."

"The plan has been changed," Winterhagen said with finality. "It is safer this way."

"Safer for whom?"

"All of us."

It was early morning in that first safe village. Once modestly affluent, it was now the center of a farming community that had long passed its peak of productivity. The village was made up of three or four blocks of dusty, nineteenth-century buildings with a café, a post office, a general store.

In that late-September morning light—hazy and warm—it seemed to Floy as if they had arrived in another, more secure time.

She was attempting not to worry about Curry, to reassure herself that Alouette was taking proper care of him, that he wasn't missing her too much, that Chambertin was concentrating on finding her and not Curry.

The gray bus pulled up in front of the largest house in the village, a red-brick box owned by the mayor, who also owned the area's principal farm.

"Madame," Winterhagen said, turning, looking at Louisianne, "will be lodged here."

"Couldn't Louisianne and I stay together?" Floy asked, grabbing hold of Louisianne's hand. She had a sudden presentiment, an irrational feeling about that red-brick house.

Louisianne embraced her and kissed her on her forehead as she had done when Floy was a child visiting Paris for the first time and in love with all the Parisian men who wore tight suits and ran everywhere. She felt like a child. Winterhagen lit a Gitane and clamped it between his teeth, impatient. Floy held on to Louisianne, not wanting her to go.

"He knows what he's doing," Louisianne said. "If there's a *rafle*, a raid, then they might just get one of us and not the lot." She put something in Floy's hand, found her traveling bag, and stepped out of the bus and into the open door of the mayor's brick house.

Winterhagen had left the bus to help Louisianne, but she refused his hand. An old man, the sort of scruffy pensioner who haunts France's villages, wearing a paper poppy commemorating his participation in the last war, stopped Winterhagen and said a few words to him.

Winterhagen put his hand in his pocket and came up with a few coins. The old man moved on as Winterhagen reboarded the bus.

"Sentimental of you," Sacha said as Winterhagen got behind the wheel, took a last, uncertain look at the red-brick house as the door closed after Louisianne, and drove on.

"I'm a bleeding heart," Winterhagen said. Floy too looked at the door closing after Louisianne and then she opened her hand, knowing what she would find there.

It was the emerald Louisianne had given her when she was a girl, her first jewel. Louisianne had remembered to take it from the apartment on the Rue Balny d'Avricourt before she had left.

Chantil, who had taken the seat across from her, looked at the emerald. "Very beautiful," she said. "Fine quality." She helped Floy put the chain around her neck, fumbling with the clasp with her fat fingers. "It is like your aunt, whom I have come to admire. Full of color and light. Very deep. You are lucky," Chantil said, and Floy knew she meant she was lucky to have Louisianne as well as the emerald.

The bus stopped at the far end of the main road behind what appeared to be an abandoned barn. Sacha was to hide there. A local member of Les Fleurs du Mal would supply him with food.

"Reeks of authenticity," Sacha said, gazing at his new home. "Your poor old Sacha likes the location. So genuine." He kissed Floy and smiled that surprising sweet smile at the Weinbergs. "I'm not, however, at all certain about the casting. *Au revoir.*"

The Weinbergs were divided among the café owner and the postmistress.

"But I thought this was a safe village," Chantil said as she went off unwillingly with the postmistress. "If it's safe, why split us up?" She didn't like the look of the postmistress, an elderly virgin, and vice versa.

"Safe villages get raided," Winterhagen said, driving away. He stopped in front of an ancient wooden and shingled house with a mansard roof and heavily curtained windows.

"It's all contradictory," Floy said, liking the look of the house as much as Chantil liked the look of the postmistress. "You said we were to be parceled out among a series of villages. Now we're all in the same village in different houses." She looked at him, but he only said, "You must be patient."

"What did that pensioner say to you, the one you gave the coins to?"

"Nothing you should know."

"Where is my son?"

"He is safe."

"When can I see him?"

She was standing next to him in the narrow bus entry but all she felt was fear and a cold sort of anger. She didn't want to go into that dark house. "I want to see him." Her voice broke. "I want my baby. I must be certain he's safe. How do I know he's even alive?"

"The boy is safe."

They were the same words Lilac had used, and she shuddered. She looked into his black eyes. "You have no compassion. Either you never had it or it has been burned out of you. You could never know what it means to have a child, to be uncertain of his safety. I am sorry for you."

She turned and left the bus, walking up the broken concrete steps that led to that depressing house. She refused to think of Curry or Louisianne or that man driving the bus. She couldn't imagine how she had let him make love to her. I might as well have gone to bed with Chambertin, she thought. They are both monsters, only different breeds.

I am absurd. A rumpled American woman in an unpressed Chanel suit, coming off a bus with no suitcase, only fresh lingerie in her purse and irrational guilt in her soul.

She opened the front door and looked down a long, dark, fussy foyer. She sat down on a bench and closed her eyes.

"The boy is safe," Winterhagen—and Lilac—had said.

Chapter Eighteen

An old man wearing a frayed alpaca sweater came down uncarpeted stairs and sat at the end of the rough wooden bench as if he were joining Floy in a doctor's waiting room. He held a repaired malacca cane and wore trousers that had been machine-made in the last century. His mouth worked continually, and his eyes stared, unfocused, at a painting on glass hung on the wainscotted wall three feet in front of him. The painting, from the twenties and Japanese, showed a blue swan diving into a white lake.

Floy stared at it and then at him. "I am Monsieur Dot," he said, refusing to look at her. "It is no good asking me questions. My daughter, Madame Jbert, is in charge. I know nothing. Absolutely nothing."

He smelled of mothballs and old sweat; his red-ringed eyes were rheumy. "You are to wait in the parlor," he said some minutes later, and laughed a little to himself. Floy realized that he was attempting to draw out the encounter, that he was excited. Her arrival, for him, was an event.

The dark entry hall with the diving swan combined with M. Dot's personal aroma was too much for her. She stood up and went in search of the parlor. Pushing aside heavy sliding doors, she stepped into the parlor, which was filled with massive nineteenth-century furniture centered on a yellowed marble fireplace. It was hot, stuffy. She sat on a horsehair-upholstered sofa. A little cloud of dust rose around her.

She started to cough and thought about attempting to open the windows. They looked as if they hadn't been open in decades. She didn't have the enterprise to work her way through the rust-colored and dusty drapes with their faded ball-fringe and the gray lace curtains under them and the thick, yellowed shades under the curtains.

"I'm safe here," Floy thought. "As long as the Gestapo try to get in through the windows and not the door."

She wanted to cry but she found she didn't have any tears left. Instead she examined the room, noting the daguerreotypes on the papered walls and the fleur-de-lis design of the dark-red carpet.

She refused to give in to her longing for Curry, her need for Louisianne, to that sense of being betrayed by another man. Curry Greene and Max Winterhagen. Neither of them understood, she thought. Neither of them had felt anything for her but a momentary need to possess.

She refused to give in to all that accumulated self-pity. She tried to interest herself in the faded sepia photographs of women in sateen dresses holding parasols, of men in top hats and whiskers.

It was no good, and just as she was about to go to the entry hall and despite his plea of ignorance ask M. Dot questions, his daughter, Mme. Jbert, appeared.

"If there's something to eat," Floy said, after they had tentatively introduced themselves. "I haven't had anything since yesterday and I would be quite willing to pay . . ."

"This isn't a hotel," Madame Jbert said, removing her black hat, looking at Floy as if she had decided Floy was getting no more than she deserved. "I have to get you out of sight. Follow me."

Mme. Jbert was a mean, lean woman somewhat over thirty and under fifty. She had a high forehead, fair brown hair, and a small pointed chin. She might have been, if not pretty, at least attractive. But there was an abruptness about her that defied sympathy.

She went quickly up the narrow wooden stairs that led to the second floor and, standing on her toes, brought a set of folding steps down from the ceiling.

"Not a word while you're up here," Mme. Jbert said. "The last one talked to himself and he had to leave. You'll never know who is in this house, and the sounds from the attic are magnified."

Floy went up the ladder-steps into a low-ceilinged attic. It was nearly empty, filled with dust, and impossible to stand up straight in, except at the very center, where the roof peaked.

"I will bring you something to eat as soon as I see to my father," Mme. Jbert said. And Floy realized Mme. Jbert was tired and frightened too. But before she could express sympathy, Mme. Jbert had descended the steps and put them back in their place, folded against the ceiling.

There was no window in the attic, only a small vent, which let in a certain amount of air and light but not enough of either. She wondered how long she would have to remain in this new prison and thought of the Splendide's rooms with near-nostalgia. There were two items of furniture in the attic, the necessities: an old flowered and cracked chamber pot and an ancient straw mattress held together by a gray, worn cotton sheet.

Floy thought of the Splendide's radio, of the magazines, and realized she had nothing to read, nothing to listen to. Her hours would be spent in waiting.

The mattress exuded a familiar, piercing odor, reminding her of the one in Mme. Hibiscus's husband's room over the butcher shop in Châteldon. It was an insistent odor, made up of the smells of the man who talked to himself and the other émigrés escaping south by means of Winterhagen's expensive escort service.

She had used up the last of the Molyneux Number 5 in Vichy, but it would only have compounded the smell. She lay down on the mattress anyway, preferring it to the unfinished wooden floor. She wondered if Curry was in such an attic room somewhere with Alouette. He wouldn't, Floy knew, last very long in such a place. He was too noisy, too inquisitive. She hoped and prayed her boy wasn't in an attic room like this one and tortured herself with the possibility that he was. Winterhagen would only consider Curry's safety, not his comfort.

Suddenly the trapdoor opened, a tray was pushed up, and the door was shut after it. On it was a plate of boiled potatoes, dark bread, a cup of thin soup. There was also a glass of red wine and a small, lit candle in a ceramic holder.

The candle somehow made it all seem better. The room appeared larger, the meal finer. She ate carefully, the potatoes first. They were mealy but white inside and smoking. She couldn't remember potatoes ever tasting so good.

The soup tasted thinly of celery, and she ate the rough wheat bread much too quickly. She saved the wine for last, hoping it would help her sleep. But she hadn't realized how thoroughly exhausted she was. Bone-tired, as Auntie Rose would say. Despite the acrid bed, the windowless attic room, she had no trouble sleeping.

In the morning, when gray shafts of light began to make their way through the vent, Mme. Jbert's flawlessly coiffed head appeared through the trapdoor like a ventriloquist's dummy, disembodied, surreal. "A message has come for you. You are to stay put for three days. Then someone will contact you."

Three days! She couldn't stay in that attic room for

three whole days. And three nights. "Do you have a book I might read?" she asked, desperate, before Mme. Jbert's head disappeared and the door was shut.

"A book?" Madame asked doubtfully, as if it were some foreign, unheard-of object. "What sort of book?"

"Any book. The Bible." They were certain to have a Bible. The Bible would get her through.

"No," Mme. Jbert said decisively. "We are freethinkers here." She shut the trapdoor.

I suppose, Floy said to herself, this is going to be beneficial to my character. No radio, no books to cloud my mind from the basic and essential agony.

When the evening meal—the only meal—was brought up, she had meant to ask for pencil and paper, any distraction. But the sight of the food was too much for her. She cried like a child, big tears rolling down her cheeks, when, the meal finished, she realized she had forgotten.

She tried pacing, à la Billy, but the roof was too low, except in that one isolated spot, and she continually bumped her head against the blackened rafters.

She thought she would save the glass of wine for the morning, the days being more difficult than the nights. But the moment the thought was formed, she drank it in one swallow, as if it might be taken away.

Despairing, she tried to sleep, but now sleep too eluded her. At night, in the totality of that darkness, all the images she wanted to avoid came rushing back. Billy's head on its side, his mouth a round O, and a black pool of blood where his body should have been. Chambertin's long, narrow, nearly blue fingers touching her, wanting her. Curry, alone and frightened in some other airless attic room, calling for her.

She put her hands to her bosom and found the emerald. She understood suddenly why people wore crosses and medals and talismans. She held on to that emerald, and it was as if some of Louisianne's serenity and self-assurance had rubbed off to get her through the night.

When the sound of the folding steps being let down woke her from her light sleep, she was certain it was morning and Mme. Jbert had come to collect her tray.

But there was no daylight coming through the vent, and Mme. Jbert's head, made especially eerie by candlelight, instantly set off some interior alarm.

"Quickly," Mme. Jbert said, breathless with urgency and fear. "Hand me the tray. Put everything on it." She studied the tray. "The chamber pot. Quickly.

"Come with me," Mme. Jbert said, disappearing with the tray and the chamber pot. "As fast as you can."

Her muscles stiff from inaction, Floy climbed down the steps to the second floor. She could hear a distinctive, reminiscent rumble. The sound reminded her of the early days of the war, when the French Army went through Paris to the north. And suddenly she could identify that ominous noise.

"It's a *rafle*," Mme. Jbert said as the transport noise grew louder. Mme. Jbert set the tray and chamber pot on a table in the hall and took Floy's hand, leading her into a dark bedroom. Mme. Jbert handed her an old-fashioned nightcap, the sort French political cartoonists used to picture Chambertin wearing, sleeping with Hitler at Berchtesgaden.

"Get into bed. Quickly," Mme. Jbert whispered urgently. Floy got into the horrible-smelling bed with Mme. Jbert's father, M. Dot. She lay as far from him as possible, pulling the flannelette blanket up to her chin, realizing she was still wearing the Chanel suit and the Rue Rivoli blouse.

Her shoes. And the purse. She had forgotten them. They were still in the attic. She had started to get out of the bed when she heard Mme. Jbert overhead in the attic, hiding whatever would give them away.

The convoy's noise finally stopped. There was a long moment of complete silence. Then Floy heard Mme. Jbert close the trapdoor, put the ladder back in its place, and take the tray and chamber pot down to the kitchen.

Then, after another few moments of silence, there was an insistent knocking on the front door.

Floy felt as if she had become frozen, paralyzed in that foul bed. M. Dot laughed once and then began a series of bronchial coughs and spasms, which eventually segued into a steady, somnolent snore.

Under M. Dot's noises, Floy could hear soldiers, in bad French, demand entry. Then she heard Mme. Jbert open the door and ask what they wanted. But there was no answer. They pushed her out of the way, running up the bare steps in their jackboots.

They made the same noise they had the day they had come for Billy. Floy grasped her emerald and willed herself not to cry, to think of other things. She forced herself to think of Curry coming home from the Bois one summer day, having learned his first bad word, repeating it over and over. Alouette had threatened to wash his mouth out with soap, but Billy had made the mistake of laughing, and for days Curry would bring out that word at every inappropriate moment.

The door was flung open, and Floy lost that image of Curry with his little hand in Billy's, walking down the Champs, shouting that naughty word.

A German in a Vichy French soldier's uniform—German soldiers, according to the armistice, were not allowed in the *Zone Libre*—came into the room. He turned a huge flashlight on the bed.

The old man sat up for a moment, rubbing his red-rimmed eyes. "What is it, Marta? Who's here, Marta?"

Floy clutched the thin blanket, her face turned away from the flashlight, her eyes tightly closed. The nightcap, too large, had slipped down, covering her forehead, threatening to cover her eyes. She didn't dare move it.

She didn't breathe. She could only wait for the soldier's hands to pull the flannelette blanket away and expose the Chanel suit.

As he moved toward the bed, a long and brown rat, disturbed by the sound of the jackboots, by the tumult, jumped out of the shadows and ran across the bed.

The rat, the smell of the old man, and the closeness of the room were too much for the fastidious German soldier. "Just an old couple," he told his sergeant, backing out of the room, knowing he should have searched the bed for arms but too disgusted to do so.

"No weapons," he said. "Harmless," he went on. The sergeant looked at him suspiciously. He began to check his list, which would tell him who was supposed to live in this house and who wasn't, when the soldier stumbled on the rough wood floor, tripped, his torch falling and breaking.

"You are helpless, Hansfeldt. Genuinely helpless." The sergeant helped the boy to his feet and down the steps.

After what seemed like hours later, Mme. Jbert came for Floy and led her up to the attic. Floy stumbled too over Mme. Jbert's rough wood floors but she thanked God for them. She found the evil-smelling mattress and lay there, listening to the convoy move out of the village. Occasional flashes of headlight found their way through the attic vent, striping the ceiling like bars in a cell.

She wondered if she was going to cry and surprised herself by feeling, if not jaunty, at least not depressed. The Germans in their French uniforms had been outwitted by Mme. Jbert and M. Dot and the other citizens of that nameless safe village. She and Louisianne, Sacha and the Weinbergs were still secure. Mme. Jbert had said so.

"I must be getting tough," Floy thought. But there was a knock on the trapdoor, and once more everything stopped, and paralysis—that sickness of fear—took over.

But Mme. Jbert's neat head appeared, back-lit by light

from below. "I thought you might need this," she said, handing Floy a glass of the red wine.

Floy took it gratefully. "To you, Madame Jbert. To Free France."

Mme. Jbert's head disappeared, Floy drained her glass in the dark. Before she fell asleep she thought that at the least the night had not been boring.

Chapter Nineteen

In the morning Mme. Jbert—neat, sallow, unperturbed —put her head through the trapdoor, handing Floy a cup of bitter acorn coffee. She waited while Floy drank it, like a nurse at a sick patient's bed. Taking the cup, she said, "You may be here for some time. The Germans and the Vichy Gestapo are conducting a massive hunt for illegal aliens. It could be weeks."

Mme. Jbert disappeared, firmly shutting the trapdoor, replacing the collapsible steps quietly, decisively. And all the excitement generated by escaping the Germans the night before—all the hope—evaporated and Floy felt more trapped than she could stand. Before Mme. Jbert's warning, she could have stayed in that attic for days. Now she knew she wouldn't last the hour.

It must be safe, she told herself. They wouldn't return so soon. They have the neighboring villages to harass. They only come in the middle of the night. They have to sleep sometime.

She thought that if she could only see Louisianne, spend a few minutes with her, she would return to the attic and be all right. Louisianne would know more than Mme. Jbert. Louisianne, she thought, touching the emerald, would give her courage. Louisianne would reassure her about Curry. About herself.

She couldn't find her shoes or her purse. They had been taken by Mme. Jbert the night before and put away. She had a fairly accurate idea of what Mme. Chanel's blue suit looked like after three nights in that attic. It occurred to her that she hadn't seen herself in a mirror in quite some time. The aunties would approve. Rose and Ida always thought she spent too much time in front of a mirror. "Especially for a plain girl," Rose had said.

She brushed herself off as well as she could and forced herself to take her time. She would find Louisianne. Louisianne didn't think she was a plain girl. They would hide together. She was capable of nearly anything if Louisianne was near.

"I cannot stay here," she said aloud and in English, knowing what that last escapee must have gone through before he began speaking his thoughts out loud. "I can't stay here another moment."

The thought of fresh air made her fingers shake, and it took her several moments to work the trapdoor, to unfold the stairs. Her stiff muscles ached as she stepped onto the stairs that led down to the second floor.

The door opposite flew open, and Floy nearly shouted. It was only M. Dot in his tattered alpaca sweater and shiny trousers, staring at her as if he couldn't quite place her.

"I'm going out for bit," she said, her voice sounding unnaturally social, lah-de-dah. M. Dot looked at her with his rheumy eyes, and she thought he was going to attempt to stop her. But he only shook his head and went back into his bedroom.

In her bare feet she went down to the ground floor, relieved that there were no other sounds in the house, that Mme. Jbert was elsewhere. She put on a black shawl that was lying on the bench. In her need to get out of that house, she was willing to go barefoot, but she found a pair of wooden shoes under the stairs that fitted tolerably well.

There was a mirror in the entry hall, a concave one that made her look like a sideshow attraction. She stared into it, trying to separate the illusion from the reality.

She thought Auntie Rose was right after all. She was a plain girl. Pale and not very clean. But that was all to the good. She remembered Winterhagen's injunction to pay attention to details.

In her dark skirt and black shawl, her face devoid of makeup, she seemed sickly, a peasant's daughter, possibly deranged. By grief, she thought, taking one of Billy's deep Hindu breaths, stepping into the role, as both he and Winterhagen would have advised.

She opened the door and walked out. It was a gray, autumnal day, and the air smelled of dust, but it was fresh and reviving. It may have been grim and cool outdoors, but she was out of that room, away from that pervasive odor. She had to close her eyes against even that dim light, and it took a few seconds for her eyes to adjust.

She walked along the village's main street, staying close to the unpainted houses on her left. To her right, across the unpaved road, a second-rate sort of forest began. It had thin, undernourished trees, a dense yellow-green undergrowth. It wasn't anything like a story-book forest, though it managed to be both menacing and depressing. Like the village and Mme. Jbert's attic.

I haven't felt safe in this safe village, she thought, since we arrived.

There weren't many people on the street. A few old men and women. As in the rest of France, the young men were either in the Vichy Army or in German prison camps. Or hiding in the woods lest they be recruited—shanghaied—to work in German factories.

No one looked at Floy or questioned her being there. The people on the street, frightened by the previous night's *rafle*, were all intent on their own business.

When Floy reached the mayor's ugly brick house she knocked softly at first and then more loudly on the paneled wooden door. It seemed as if no one was there.

When she was about to give up, the door was opened by a fat man with a thin man's smile, tenuous and unbelievable. He continued to smile at her inquiringly.

"Madame White Rose," Floy said, and the man's smile grew larger, more suspicious.

"She was picked up early this morning. By friends."

"Did she leave any message?"

"No," he said and, still smiling, closed the door with finality, softly.

"Sacha," Floy thought. "I must find Sacha." She began to walk quickly back along the main street, her head down, that feeling of being trapped coming over her again.

Sirens sounded, tearing through the dusty country air, freezing everyone on the street in one position for a moment, as if they were all stopped in time.

Floy turned and saw three black Renaults speeding down a mountain in the distance, toward the village, their sirens going full blast. The Gestapo were coming back, and it was the middle of the day, not the night, and Floy felt certain they had returned for a purpose. This wasn't to be a casual *rafle*. They had come back for someone.

"Run," the little pensioner Winterhagen had given money to when they arrived said to her. "Run."

He, along with the others, vanished so quickly that it was as if they had melted. Floy took his advice and ran. She ran as fast as she could in the wooden shoes to Mme. Jbert's house. The door was locked.

The siren noise grew louder and suddenly stopped, and Floy beat on Mme. Jbert's door with both her fists.

"Go away," Mme. Jbert whispered from inside. "Leave us. Quickly. It is too late. Go." Floy stopped beating on the door. "You will get us all killed," Mme. Jbert, losing control, screamed through the door.

Taking off the wooden shoes, Floy ran instinctively across the road and into that poor forest. As she ran, she waited. For the siren to start up again. For someone to say *"Achtung!"* For a bullet from a blue Schmeisser to stop her.

But she managed to reach the forest without being stopped or apparently seen. She stood behind one of the larger trees, a huge and dark oak. She wrapped the shawl around her head so that only her eyes were uncovered. She looked around the tree and saw that the black Renaults had stopped in front of the mayor's red-brick house. The drivers—Germans in civilian suits—stood smoking cigarettes, relaxed, leaning up against the fenders of their cars.

Floy looked down and saw her pale legs and rubbed dirt on them and on the wooden shoes.

"I am a master of camouflage," an actor had had to say to her in a recent Sacha film. He was a handsome man, half Hungarian, half French, who hadn't been able to say the words without laughing. Everything had made him laugh. He had escaped to America not long after, because he hadn't wanted to go and entertain the German troops with Pierre Fresnay, Arletty, and Tino Rossi.

One of the soldiers in front of the mayor's red-brick house laughed, not unlike the Hungarian-French actor, and the others laughed too. Soldiers smoking, joking, standing around without much to do. Soldiers on a routine mission anywhere.

Floy stood behind that big, dark oak tree for nearly an hour without moving, her eyes on the Renaults in front of the mayor's house.

Finally the door opened, and Rivet came out. He wore a new white fedora. He kept his hands in his filthy jacket pockets, his lips pursed, a toothpick in his mouth.

He might have been a solid homeowner, stepping out for his morning walk after a late breakfast, working that toothpick in and out of his tiny ferret teeth. Except for that suit, that pointed nose, that tiny yellow toothbrush mustache. No. Even in that unsafe safe village, he looked as if he were on the Boul' Mich', a second-rate procurer.

She waited, expecting to see Chambertin, steeling herself for those blue-lensed glasses and nearly shouting out when she saw Louisianne come from that red-brick house.

Both her hands were wrapped in white cloths, which looked as if they might have been kitchen towels. Louisianne held her hands out in front of her some inches from her body, as if they were museum-quality pieces of especially fragile porcelain.

As Floy watched, the white towels miraculously became pink. And then the pink was streaked with dark red, and finally the towels became solid red as blood soaked through from Louisianne's hands to the towel's outer layers.

Intuitively, without having to reason it out, Floy knew what they had done to Louisianne. She had heard about it but she hadn't believed it. It was called the door torture. Floy had thought it was only one more hideous fantasy attributed to the German occupiers by their French captives.

They had taken Louisianne's long, fragile fingers and placed them in the open space between the hinges of one of the heavy paneled doors in the mayor's house. Then they had slammed the door shut, breaking Louisianne's fingers, crushing them. Open and shut. Open and shut. Until the blood gushed out of her fingers like water from a fountain, and still Louisianne wouldn't tell them where the others were. Or where she thought they were. Because the truth was she didn't know.

But those men in the mayor's dining room weren't interested in the truth. They were only interested in finding the others.

So they had taken her other hand and placed it in the open space between the hinges of the dining room door . . .

Louisianne, her hands wrapped in the blood-soaked towels, tripped as she walked down the mayor's steps. One of the soldiers reached out to help her, but she regained her balance and moved away from his outstretched arm, as if accepting his help would befoul her forever.

She was as pale as the linen-white walls of that little office off the salon at 33 Rue Balny d'Avricourt, where she had kept her transmitter, her lifeline to London and De Gaulle. Now they knew all about that and they would want to know more, and the door torture was so obviously just a make-do-step, an on-the-scene convenience. More sophisticated inducements to confession awaited her. She was aware of that.

Still, Louisianne held her patrician head high, and as she approached the car, she looked around for a moment, taking a last deep breath of air. A soldier held the door open for her, and she got in with difficulty, being careful of her hands, staring straight ahead, as if the village and the soldiers and the torturers had ceased to exist for her.

Tears streaming down her face, her hand grasping the emerald under the black shawl, Floy wanted to run to Louisianne, to hold her, to console her, to kiss those broken hands. Louisianne wasn't a vain woman, but she was proud of her hands.

But Floy's brain was working as fast and as hard as her emotions. She knew Louisianne wouldn't have wanted that consolation, that she would have thought it a weak, suicidal, and pointless gesture.

Instead Floy stood behind the black oak, her tears soaking through Mme. Jbert's black wool shawl, as the mayor, that fat man with the thin perpetual smile, stood on the steps and waved as the Renaults moved on.

Through the rear window of the last car Floy caught a glimpse of blue smoked glasses and a boyish, blond head and then a last sight of Louisianne, sitting very straight, her hands held slightly in front of her. Her face was rigid, noble, proud. It was as if she were not in that car with Rivet in the front seat and Chambertin sitting next to her on one side and a bored German soldier on the other. It was as if Louisianne were alone.

"Courage," Floy whispered. *"Courage."* She was well aware that she wasn't saying it for Louisianne but for herself.

Chapter Twenty

She stood in the forest until well after dark. There were no lights in the village houses. Not even candle-light. It was as if they had all gone into mourning. Or run away. Mme. Jbert's house seemed especially dark.

A truck without headlights drove slowly into the village from the south some time near ten o'clock. It stopped at the café and the post office, picking up passengers. When the truck reached the barn, Floy forced herself to leave the oak and race across the road, reaching the truck as Sacha was getting aboard.

He helped to pull her up into the back, where Chantil and Ilone had arranged themselves between crates of fruit, cabbage, and lettuce. They were eating apples and small squares of white soapy cheese. They stopped, guiltily, when they saw her. The doors were shut, Sacha turned on a small electric flashlight and the truck began to move.

"You must be hungry," Chantil said, offering Floy her bit of cheese. "The postmistress gave it to me before I left. She reminded me of my *kinderteacher*: mean but not so bad after all."

Floy said she wasn't hungry. She sat on a crate of apples, Sacha next to her, his arm around her. The curtain separating the driver's cab from the van was pushed aside after a few miles. Winterhagen was at the wheel.

"She's alive," he said, meeting Floy's eyes in the driver's mirror. "She's in a prison outside Vichy."

"They won't torture her anymore, will they?" Floy

asked, knowing as she said it how absurd it was. "It's encouraging, isn't it? Her being in Vichy. After all, she is American-born, and Vichy still has relations with the Americans, don't they? There is a chance, isn't there, that she'll be all right, that they'll arrange some sort of trade?"

Sacha hugged her to him, but she only wanted to hear what Winterhagen had to say. She couldn't see him clearly, which was all right. She didn't want to see him clearly. She didn't like him but she knew he wouldn't lie to her. Not about this.

"They're transferring her to Santé prison. Then to Fresnes and then Saarbrücken. It's what they always do when a prisoner's been designated NN."

"What does NN mean?" Floy asked, not at all certain she wanted to know.

"*Nacht und Nebel.* Night and Fog. Hitler is supposedly responsible for the phrase. It's used for prisoners who are considered so dangerous that they are cut off from all contact with the outer world."

"Was Billy NN?" Sacha nodded, saying that he was.

"My God." Floy thought of that axe in the corner of the *Le Matin* photograph. "They wouldn't . . ." She couldn't say it. She saw Billy's head and that black pool of blood and she had to bite her lips to keep from screaming.

"She has a chance," Winterhagen said. "We have a man, a guard, inside the Vichy prison. He's going to try to get a capsule to her. Pray that he does get it to her."

"How much time does he have before she's transferred?" Sacha asked, because Floy couldn't. She had sunk down onto the floor of the truck next to Chantil, who put her warm, motherly arms around her.

"She's being transferred tomorrow."

They arrived at the warehouse, a huge barn of a building just outside Aix on the Marseille road, in the early morning. It was owned by a member of Les Fleurs du Mal, Pierre Le Levandou, who was named after his native village. He had very white hair, a huge mane of it, and was six feet four, with broad shoulders and an enormous paunch developed over fifty years of over-eating. He made both Winterhagen and Sacha seem puny in comparison and did everything on a large scale. His whisper was another man's shout.

He had had two sons, both killed in the war. He had offered his services, early on, to Billy. His business put him in a peculiarly ideal position. Buying the produce of vineyards—many of which straddled both the occupied and unoccupied zones—and delivering wine allowed him to travel freely. He was one of the first merchants to get an *Ausweis* from the Germans, who were among his best customers.

In the beginning he transported British soldiers stranded after Dunkirk from the occupied zone to the *Zone Libre*. He would put them in his trucks and let them off at one side of the vineyards and they would walk across to the other side in the *Zone Libre*. He would pick them up again and take them either to Brittany, where boats were waiting to take them to England, or to Perpignan, where they were smuggled over the Pyrenees into Spain.

His trucks were equipped with genuine engines, and his gasoline ration was the same as that for emergency vehicles. Billy had often said it was a good thing Germans knew nothing about wine, because Le Levandou's was among the worst.

They sat in the truck in Le Levandou's warehouse, waiting for an all clear.

"They won't expect us to have headed southeast," Winterhagen said in answer to a question of Sacha's. "We have had to change our plans again."

They had had to change their plans, Floy knew, be-

213

cause Louisianne had been taken and the door torture was child's play compared to what they would eventually do to her. Louisianne would certainly eventually give away whatever she could to make them stop. There were no heroes, Winterhagen had said. No one could hold out against the Gestapo's torture machine. There were only traitors, saints, and dead men. No heroes.

So they had had to change their plans. Chantil took Floy's hand and held it while they waited for Le Levandou, and Floy thought it was remarkable what solace a stranger's touch could give.

At noon, while Le Levandou's workers were taking lunch in a building set aside for that purpose, he led them out of the grocer's truck and down into a cellar below the warehouse. It had a modern bathroom, food, and water supplies and was one of the primary stations for those escaping from the north. Le Levandou and his sons had planned to use it as a bomb shelter when the war that never came extended to the south.

Chantil and Ilone crowded into the bathroom. "Soap," Chantil said, as if she had discovered gold. "Real soap." There were tears in her eyes, and even Ilone managed to smile at her delight.

Floy sat on a cot and looked up at Le Levandou. "Is there news?" she asked.

"Yes," he said, after looking at Winterhagen. "She has been moved to Santé prison in Paris. They're being quick about it. Afraid of American pressure on Pétain, I suppose."

"Did she get the pill?"

"No. They searched all the guards in the Vichy prison early this morning. Our man managed to take the pill himself when he realized they knew who he was. Someone must have put the finger on him. A traitor."

There was a long silence, and then Floy asked, "What will happen to her next?"

"There may be a trial." He rubbed his huge hands

214

together, a despairing gesture. "There may not be a trial. She's NN. We don't know."

"Is she being tortured?"

'She's being questioned."

"So she's being tortured."

Floy lay down on the cot. She could hear the sounds of Ilone and Chantil in the tub, washing, complaining, and—incredibly—laughing.

She kept thinking of the tortures the Gestapo were reputed to use. There was the one in which the victim's head was held down in a lavabo filled with water, the torturer pulling him up just before he drowned, then repeating the process over and over again.

They were said to fasten electrodes to nipples and testicles and turn on the current in bursts.

Hot needles were shoved under toenails, fingernails slowly pried off with hot pincers.

In the beginning, Floy hadn't believed that men could do such things; she had set the tortures down to French imagination. Now she believed them. Still, they sounded like a boy's idea of torture, taken from penny magazines.

"She'll be all right," Sacha said. "Your poor old Sacha guarantees it."

Floy stood up and moved away from him. "She won't be all right, Sacha. She'll hold out as long as she can against those butchers, and then, when the last cigarette is ground into her skin, when the last electrical bolt is shot through what's left of her body, she will tell them what she knows. Because everyone does, finally, unless they're lucky enough to die first.

"In the end they'll take her to Cologne for that final indignity. They'll kill her as they did Billy, with their filthy, barbaric axe. And they'll photograph it and print it in the evening *Le Matin* for the edification and education of their French subjects."

She stared at Sacha with her furious green eyes as if

it were he who was responsible, as if Sacha were going to wield the axe.

"You'd better cry," he said. "Cry with your poor old Sacha. It won't do either of us any good holding it in." He held open his arms, but she didn't go to him.

"I can't cry, Sacha. Not now."

Le Levandou came down a ramp, wheeling a huge cask of wine on a dolly. He opened the cask with a steel lever and began to remove clothes from it like a street peddler purveying dubious wares.

"Ladies," Winterhagen said, as the Weinbergs emerged, pink and scrubbed, from the bathroom. "Please put on these clothes as quickly as possible. We are going into hiding again."

"Not into another little room," Ilone said, going pale.

"No," Winterhagen said. "You will be more comfortable physically in the next location."

"I suppose we're *brûlé*," Chantil said, examining the green and diaphanous tea gown she had been given.

"Sizzling." Le Levandou smiled at her. He liked his women plump.

Winterhagen told Sacha to take off all his clothes, while Le Levandou handed Floy a cream-colored dress that smelled of pressed violets.

"It was my wife's," Le Levandou said. "You will be careful, won't you?"

"Very careful." She asked if there was time for a bath before the ceremony. It was a bridal gown, complete with shoes and veil and long gloves. Winterhagen said she might have a bath.

She soaked in it until he called her. Revived—who had ever supposed a bath would be such a luxury?—she put on the gown and the veil. There was a narrow mirror on the back of the bathroom door. She saw herself in it and thought she looked like a mannequin in a shop on the Rue Rodin—an unreal, uncertain bride.

216

When she went into the outer room, they all stopped for a moment and looked at her.

"Is anything wrong?" she asked Winterhagen, but he turned and continued bandaging a naked Sacha.

"You are so beautiful," Le Levandou answered for them all. "In this new German world we do not see such beauty very often. You are to be congratulated, mademoiselle."

Ilone and Chantil returned to their wardrobe. They were wearing provocative tea gowns. Under the see-through lace they wore skin-colored slips. The effect was as if they were nude under the gowns. They had on Place Pigalle streetwalker heels and paste diamond earrings, and their dyed red hair had been piled high on their heads, their lips painted scarlet. They looked expensive and professional, a working man's dream of a high-class whore.

Sacha lay on a stretcher, bandages reaching from his head to his toes. "Your poor old Sacha has had one terrible accident," he said, giving his surprising sweet smile to Floy.

"He'll recover," Le Levandou said dryly, and then the door flew open and an SS *Oberführer* stood in the doorway and Ilone screamed.

It was Winterhagen wearing the black tunic and jodhpurs, the highly polished boots and death's-head insignia of an SS officer.

"I am to be the groom," he said, clicking his heels, bowing German-style.

"You nearly killed my sister," Chantil said.

"I apologize. I didn't realize I was so effective."

"Too effective by half," Chantil said, refusing to be mollified, waving a handkerchief in front of Ilone's somewhat worn nose.

Taking off his cap, Winterhagen helped Le Levandou slide the immobilized Sacha into an empty wine cask.

The Weinbergs, complaining, were loaded into similar casks and put on the dolly. Lids were nailed shut over them.

"They'll suffocate," Floy protested.

"No, they won't," Winterhagen told her. "There are air holes throughout." Le Levandou was to take out a delivery truck that afternoon. Sacha was to be unloaded at the Our Lady of Mercy Hospital in Toulon along with the medicinal wine the hospital officials had contracted for. One of the nuns had organized her own resistance group within the hospital. Sacha would be taken to the critical wing, where he was to be given a room and an identity as a burn victim.

"The Germans loathe hospitals and are afraid of nuns. Colonel Violet—your poor old Sacha—will be safe until we think it's time to move him."

The Weinbergs were being trucked to Marseille and unloaded with the weekly supply of wine at Chez La Tourette, a bordello popular with German officers.

"Madame La Tourette's mother," Le Levandou explained, "is in a concentration camp in Poland, but the Germans haven't tumbled to that yet. Occasionally a German officer is missing after spending a night at Madame's, but there has never been any suspicion. Madame keeps such a nice, *gemütlich* house."

"What if one of the German officers has a yen for one of the Weinberg sisters?" Floy asked.

"Both of them," Le Levandou answered, "suffer from what Madame calls the Italian disease. In a week or two they will be available for duty again. In a week or two they—and you—should be in Spain."

"And my marriage?"

"It has already taken place," Le Levandou said, helping her into a cask. "You and the young officer are going on your honeymoon to Monte Carlo—in Monaco, that unaligned little principality where a Parisian *carte d'identité* is all the papers you need.

"Your friend Madame Maude Hamilton has thought-fully provided you and Winterhagen with a honeymoon house."

"When will I see my son?" she asked, looking past Le Levandou at Winterhagen. "I must see him."

"You will," Le Levandou said as Winterhagen turned away and got into another cask. "In good time. *Courage.*" He began to nail the top closed.

Chapter Twenty-one

Maude Hamilton had, after some thought, decided to be perfectly safe and uninvolved. Or as perfectly safe and uninvolved as she could be under the circumstances.

The woman Maude had hired to "do" for her after her effortless escape from Occupied France had seemed as innocuous as the Monte Carlo skies. She had turned out to be the contact.

"You could have knocked me over with a feather," Maude said when she told the story. "This perfectly stunning little old *bonne* was a spy for Les Fleurs du Mal. It took her nearly an hour to convince me that she hadn't gone clean off her rocker. I'm afraid I kept saying. 'Sure, you're with *les services*, and I'm Mata Hari. Now how about lunch, ducky?'"

But after that hour, when Maude was finally convinced, agreeable, tiny Mme. Bertrand felt it her duty to describe what the consequences of involvement might be, scaring Maude half to death.

"You certainly don't pull your punches, do you, dear?" Maude said, and poured herself half a glass of black-market gin.

"I should not want you to blame me, madame, if something terrible happens."

Putting the boy and his cowlike nurse—Alouette, I ask you!—in the upstairs apartment had been one thing, it seemed. She couldn't have known, she could always say, that they were refugees from the Milice and other

220

Vichy police. Boys and their nurses were still innocent enough.

But she could hardly plead ignorance when Floy and her *passeur* came to pick up the boy and stay for a few days and possibly a week, pretending to be a newly married couple on honeymoon with the bride's son from an earlier marriage.

Then she could be charged with aiding and abetting a known enemy of Vichy France—not to mention Nazi Germany—and she could be extradited from Monaco and sent north to prison and torture and certain death. I'm not ready to die yet, dear, she said to herself.

In the end she decided—well, she felt she had no choice—to let Floy stay upstairs in that tiny apartment with the nurse and the boy and the *passeur* and, for all she knew, a private priest and a personal dwarf.

Maude was going on holiday with her "friend." He was a major in the Bersaglieri, the exclusive arm of Italy's army. He had been urging her for some time to go to Italy with him for a holiday. And though merely looking at pasta put on pounds and she loathed opera and other people's unpredictable theatrics, Maude had said she would like to go.

The most peculiar people, Maude thought, are working against the Germans and their chums the Vichy French. Poor little frail Mme. Bertrand! The strangest people were being brave. She decided that she would have to be one of them in this one not especially daring incident. If only for Floy and that boy with the dimples and his mother's emerald-green eyes and that sly, endearing way of looking at one, as if he were always cooking up trouble. Maude had quite fallen in love, she knew, with Floy's Curry.

It's a sign of the times, she had thought, as she supervised Mme. Bertrand's somewhat erratic packing, that I'm doing this. I'm a great big selfish woman who has never given a thought to another living soul and suddenly I'm making myself uncomfortable and perhaps putting myself in danger for a movie actress and her illegitimate son. She couldn't begin to imagine what her husband, poor Peter, languishing in a German prison camp, would say.

She put her hand to her pink-blond hair, set in not very convincing waves, and laughed, putting the idea of personal danger out of her mind.

But if the Gestapo, or whatever the local Monegasque branch of spies and informers was called in this (ha ha) nonaligned principality, were to find out she had given her flat to Floy, there would be consequences.

And Maude was under no illusion that that handsome and much too young macaroni major could save her. The Monegasque schoolboys paraded up and down in front of the Bersagliere sentries guarding his office chanting:

Giovinezza, giovinezza
Primavera di bellezza.

Springtime of beauty, indeed. He was the sort of man, Maude knew, who would end up dyeing his hair an improbable black and wearing corsets.

She wanted to leave Floy at least a note but she was afraid. That was all they needed, written evidence. So she contented herself with buying Curry a wildly extravagant sailor suit and filling the apartment kitchen with every luxury available that week on Monte Carlo's thriving black market.

She kissed Curry, holding him tight, tipped his nurse with tinned American ham, and allowed Antonio to sweep her away in his muscular arms and open car.

A photographic portrait of him stood in the place of honor in the little flat, his Roman head sporting an intricate example of Italian military headgear, complete with feathers. Curry turned it face-down, and Alouette giggled. All that smoldering self-esteem depressed both of them.

They waited anxiously for the surprise little Mme. Bertrand had promised them. She had an ugly little white dog with black spots named Piéro. Maude had banned him from the house, but the moment she was gone, Mme. Bertrand had brought him in.

Curry was delighted. He was a solidly built little boy who had become thin during the past weeks. He looked especially pathetic in the de luxe sailor suit—its design loosely based on the uniforms of the French navy— which was a size too large. They had had to roll the sleeves up.

He was so very alert, so bright that little Mme. Bertrand had kept the surprise vague, in the event something went wrong. She watched Curry play with Piéro on Maude's China export rug and thought that anything could happen. The truck might be stopped. The limousine carrying the young SS officer and his bride might be held up by the authorities, their papers inspected, her face recognized. They might have been betrayed. Too many members of Les Fleurs du Mal were being betrayed lately, little Mme. Bertrand thought. Her code name was Tulip.

"Is the surprise my mother?" Curry asked, catching her unawares.

"No," little Mme. Bertrand said, clasping her hands together in an uncertain, nervous gesture. "You are not to know."

He sat on the floor with the white dog in his hands, looking like an illustration from a turn-of-the-century children's book. It was much too late at night for him to be up, but Alouette had long ago lost control over him—from the moment they had left Paris, headed for Joigny, to which she longed to return with all her simple heart and soul.

Alouette was thinking about the charms of Joigny and its beautiful river Yonne when she heard a key in the lock. She assumed it was Maude, returning for some forgotten but necessary item of clothing, and continued to daydream about that recent trip she and Curry had taken down the Yonne on a barge commanded by a Resistance couple.

The door opened, and her daydream was dispelled. An SS officer stepped into the room.

She would have screamed, but he removed his cap in time and she recognized M. Winterhagen.

"*Bon Dieu*," little Mme. Bertrand said, "you scared us."

Alouette, sleepy, stood up and curtsied. M. Winterhagen had taken them off the barge at the point where the Yonne meets the Loire at Decize and driven them all through the night to Monaco. Alouette had fallen asleep, but Curry had remained up, standing next to M. Winterhagen in the bus, asking questions.

In the morning, when he had left them at that narrow, tall house in the hills above Monte Carlo, Alouette had apologized for Curry's questions. Curry was asleep in Maude Hamilton's arms in the upstairs main bedroom, both of them cuddled in the center of the most fantastic bed Alouette had ever seen.

"I needed him," Max had said. "To keep me awake." Max had smiled then, revealing strong white teeth, and Alouette had put herself to sleep with the memory of that smile all through this long, tedious wait.

Curry, holding Mme. Bertrand's little dog, looked up and then away. "That's the enemy's uniform," he said rudely.

"It's a disguise," Winterhagen said, and then Curry put the dog down and was in his arms.

"I've been so worried," Curry said, using one of Maude Hamilton's stock phrases, his little brow wrinkling up like hers. Winterhagen held him for a moment, kissed him, and then set him down. He turned and opened the door. Floy stood there in Le Levandou's wife's thirty-year-old wedding gown, her eyes red.

"I didn't want you to see me crying," she said, coming into the flat, taking Curry in her arms, holding him to her, burying her face in his neck, breathing in his little-boy smell as if she could never get enough.

"Women are allowed to cry," Curry said, with Alouette's wisdom.

"So are little boys," Mme. Bertrand said.

And then his own tears spilled over as he held on to his mother as tightly as he could, clinging to her as he hadn't done since he was an infant. "I thought you were never going to come," he said, sobbing. Floy kissed his wet cheek, squeezing her eyes shut, trying to hold in her tears. "I thought you had left me for good."

"I'd never leave you," Floy managed to say, and then Alouette, with an uncharacteristic display of tact—a fine sense of what was right—took Floy by the arm. She led her, still carrying Curry, into the big bedroom with the lavish bed, so that mother and son could be alone.

In the morning Floy found Winterhagen sitting on the narrow terrace overlooking Monte Carlo, drinking genuine tea, eating an omelet made from fresh eggs. It was a bright Indian summer day with a light, cool breeze coming from the Mediterranean, which was an unreal blue in the near distance.

Winterhagen finished the omelet, explaining, "Madame Bertrand has been kind. Would you like something?" He wore a light tan suit, an open-necked shirt, a scarf. He looked as if he had always lived in this house on the Riviera, as if he ate fresh eggs and drank genuine tea every morning.

"Tea," Floy said, sitting opposite him. Winterhagen called out to Mme. Bertrand to make fresh tea, to bring another omelet in the event that Floy changed her mind.

Floy wore one of Maude's inappropriately luxurious dressing gowns. She herself felt inappropriate, tired, relieved, anxious. "Curry's still asleep. He said you were extraordinary during that night ride." She didn't like giving him her son's compliments but she felt she had to be fair. "You're his new hero."

"Who was his old one?"

"He had several. Billy. Sacha. The man DeFarge used to get in to scrape the cobblestones."

Mme. Bertrand brought the tea and eggs, placing them in front of Floy, beaming at Winterhagen and his empty plate as if he were the spoiled son of the house.

Floy pushed the eggs aside as Mme. Bertrand retreated. In that brilliant sunshine, under the too-blue sky, with the toy town of Monte Carlo below them at the edge of the Mediterranean, all the details of the Gestapo torture machine forced their way once again into her consciousness: that terrible, indelible photograph of Billy's death, Louisianne's bandaged hands turning pink and then red as she held them out in front of her.

"I do understand," she said, sipping her tea, trying to focus on the present, "why we are here and the others are in hiding. You're afraid Louisianne will talk before they pack her off to Cologne, aren't you? You're afraid she knows too much about your plan . . . that she'll give you and us away. You're afraid she'll break, aren't you? Do you know what, Winterhagen? I'm afraid she won't."

Don't be heroic for us, Auntie, Floy said to herself, turning away from Winterhagen. Tell them what they want to know. Winterhagen is smart and he wants to save himself more than anything else. He'll find another way to get us out. Tell them, Auntie. Please.

But even as she offered up that prayer, she knew Louisianne wouldn't have listened if she could. Louisianne would hold out until the last bone had been broken, the last organ damaged, the last possible indignity delivered.

"And we're going to wait here drinking tea and eating omelets until she either tells them or dies. Isn't that true?" He kept his eyes on the sea, the baroque town.

"Isn't it?" she asked again, her voice sounding loud and unpleasant.

"Yes." He turned to look at her. "But it shouldn't keep you from eating your omelet."

She pushed the plate to the edge of the table until it fell, breaking on the Spanish tile floor.

Winterhagen lit a Gitane, clamped it between his teeth, and let the gray-blue smoke escape into the air. Mme. Bertrand came out, and Winterhagen helped pick up the pieces of Maude's second-best luncheon ware.

Floy stood up and went inside. She was behaving badly, unPhiladelphia-like. She didn't care. For no reason at all she saw Chamberlin, his nearly white eyes insane with his need for her, his long white hands reaching out to touch her.

She hated herself for allowing those lunches at the Ritz. For taking part in that night at Le Soleil.

It seemed incredible, but soon they had all settled down into a routine.

"Routine," Auntie Ida had once said in her Ten Commandments voice, "is the great tranquilizer."

Floy decided that Auntie Ida was right.

A tranquillity new to her, bittersweet, settled upon her. In the mornings Winterhagen disappeared. Les Fleurs du Mal business, he said. Floy, dressed in a babushka and a housedress little Mme. Bertrand—Tulip —had managed to get for her, took the role of Curry's nurse. She and Curry would walk away from Monte Carlo into the hills and mountains.

Curry was curious about everything. He asked questions about carts carrying manure. Old churches, bridges, mills. The Spanish lilac that grew over the mountainside and made it fragrant. The well-kept gardens of the villas dotting the mountains and the pigeons flying over the Mediterranean.

Some of the peasants were yellow and thin, having

227

little to eat but chick-peas and rutabagas. But most were healthy, buying rice from the Italian soldiers who smuggled it in from across the border, purchasing meat of a doubtful quality but still meat.

The shops in the tiny villages, unlike those in France, had products to sell. The windows were filled with ersatz honey, called colonial honey. Candies made from crushed and rotting dates. Coffee made from burned barley. Rutabagas and Jerusalem artichokes. Cans of condensed milk, for which one needed a coupon. But in France even these poor foods were difficult to come by. Monaco was affluent in comparison.

She and Curry had a favorite spot, a peak overlooking Monte Carlo. The absurdly grandiose Hotel de Paris and the Casino with its gardens looked like elaborate toys in a rich child's miniature village.

"You're sad, Mama?" Curry asked as he ate the canned chicken and asparagus Maude had left for them. There were rolls, too, supplied by little Mme. Bertrand, who bought bread tickets peddled illegally by hotel porters. The rolls were white and soft, and Floy treated them with respect. She regretted the spilled omelet. She ate everything carefully, thoroughly.

"I'm worried about Auntie Louisianne," Floy said. "But I am not sad. I am resigned." It took her some little time, picnicking on that peak overlooking Monte Carlo, to explain "resigned" to Curry's satisfaction. He had an insidious way of forcing her to dissect words until there was nothing left.

Floy attempted, on those long, comforting walks, during those well-supplied picnics, to speak English, but eventually they would lapse into French, her fault as much as his.

"I speak good English, sister," he said, having been taken to Hollywood gangster films from his earliest days.

"You speak lousy English, brother," Floy told him.

228

"It's going to be difficult for you in America, unless we practice."

"I shall teach them flawless Parisian French," Curry retorted, which sounded so like Louisianne that Floy had to turn away.

They would return to Maude's house in the late afternoon, have an early supper, and retire to that enormous bed in the master bedroom. Floy sat up reading, electricity and books still new indulgences. Alouette slept in her own narrow room, while Winterhagen slept on the sofa in the salon.

Floy would find him there each morning, wrapped in a thin blanket, a Gitane clamped between his white, perfect teeth. He would shake his head no to that unspoken question always between them. Louisianne was still alive, still Night and Fog, still being questioned.

On the fourth day of their stay, he asked her over breakfast if it were possible for Curry to spend the morning with Alouette. 'I have an errand at the Hotel de Paris. It would be better for the errand's success if you were to accompany me. We are, after all, a honeymooning couple and by this time we should make an appearance together."

She put on a dark dress Maude had left for her that made her look older.

"You've done something effective with your makeup," he told her, when she came out of the bedroom. "Sophisticated and distancing. More *femme du monde* than bridal, and quite correct. A woman on her second marriage. You've become proficient at disguise."

She looked at him, and not with affection. "A fitting end to a glorious career in the French cinema," she said. "A master of disguise."

If she looked like a woman of the world embarking on a second marriage, he looked like the quintessential

229

Côte d'Azur male, marrying for the only possible reason: money.

Winterhagen took her arm when she had put on the large, round-brimmed hat she had found in Maude's guest closet. She hadn't thought of their night at Le Soleil since they had arrived in Monte Carlo. She hadn't thought of him sexually or, she supposed, in any other way except with dislike.

She blamed him for Louisianne's capture, unfairly. Still, she couldn't think of him without thinking of Louisianne, without counting the days Louisianne had been undergoing the Gestapo version of questioning.

"Do they pay you extra for errand service?" she asked, preceding him into the old Daimler taxi that waited for them, moving her arm away from his hand, sitting on the far side of the car.

"Certainly. Otherwise I would not do it." He leaned across the seat and adjusted her hat. "You don't want to look like Dietrich on a spy mission," he said, turning the brim up. "And you do want to smile a bit. You've got what you wanted, after all: a handsome husband, a Monte Carlo honeymoon." He looked at the driver looking at them in his rearview mirror and then he kissed her on the lips. She waited until he was through and then reapplied lipstick.

A band in bright white uniforms was playing Offenbach in the space behind the opera house where the white wrought-iron tables and chairs of the Café de Paris were scattered.

Handsome, elderly couples, a little bewildered by what was going on in the outside world, sat listening attentively. They didn't understand Pétain or Hitler or Roosevelt. Offenbach they understood. They always had.

The women wore white gloves, and the men's linen jackets were correctly pressed.

Winterhagen walked Floy through the gilded, crystaled opulence of the Hotel de Paris's lobby with one hand on her elbow, the other in his jacket pocket. He had assumed a new kind of authority, a change of posture and of facial expression. The *sous-directeurs* and the porters, the lobby waiters and the concierge all bowed to him in deference. Monaco was a small town. Everyone knew Max was the young SS officer on honeymoon.

The Italian Gestapo agent, Sortino, sitting on the green plush sofa under a heroic painting of Diana and the hunt, turned a page of *Die Stürmer*. He didn't read German, but the illustrations were graphic enough to hold his interest. It was an anti-Semitic weekly his mother, who worked in the German embassy in Rome, sent him. She thought it might help his career. All the big shots, she wrote, read *Die Stürmer*.

Sortino was a thin, balding man with a nose that was too wide and had earned him much unwanted attention as a child and later at school.

Sortino knew very well who the young couple walking across the lobby were and he looked away. Some Gestapo men outranked SS *Oberführers*, but Sortino was not among them.

He had had a long talk with his chief informant, little Mme. Bertrand, the evening before. She had come to his room late at night to report. Little Mme. Bertrand had said the couple had not come out of their bedroom since they had arrived, and it was a shame, considering her son from the first marriage was in the same flat.

Little Mme. Bertrand, who exhausted Sortino with her reports and the details she put into them, had clicked her tongue annoyingly.

Sortino studied Floy's thighs under the dark dress as she walked across the lobby. He decided he would pay a visit that night to a woman he knew. She didn't charge very much. Of course she didn't look very much like the SS officer's bride either.

Floy and Winterhagen walked through the muraled corridor that led to the terrace restaurant overlooking the gardens and the Mediterranean. "The most beautiful summer in a decade" had continued into the fall. The sun was shining, the sea was especially turquoise. A flawless Monte Carlo day.

The *maître d'hôtel* showed them to a table on the first terrace. Winterhagen pressed money into his hand. He bowed. There was no war, that bow seemed to say to Floy, no concentration camps, no torture. Not on the first terrace of the Hotel de Paris there wasn't.

Strains of Offenbach were carried to them around the hotel. Winterhagen took Floy's hand, turned it over, and kissed her wrist as if he couldn't bear to leave her for a moment, and then went to deliver an envelope.

The envelope was earning him ten thousand francs and would have cost him his life if the Italian Gestapo man, Sortino, took it into his head to come out of doors ... to wonder if it were merely coincidence that caused the SS officer and the old Russian count to go to the hotel's one unattended gentlemen's smoking room at that moment.

But Sortino was interested in the depiction of certain experiments German doctors were making on Jewesses, as pictured in the distinctive *Die Stürmer* style, and Winterhagen returned to his table, smiling at his bride.

"What do you suppose was in the envelope?" Floy asked. Nearly everyone at the dozen or so occupied tables had shown some interest in them. She asked that question not expecting an answer but because she had to appear interested in her new husband.

"Orders," Winterhagen answered unexpectedly. "New orders." He drank his *fine* and lit a Gitane. But here he held it between two fingers, absently flicking the blue-gray ashes into an ashtray. It wouldn't have done for the SS *Oberführer* to clamp a cigarette between his teeth.

"Les Fleurs du Mal," he went on, smiling as if he were complimenting her, "will need to take new names, new identities, new addresses. They will have to reform into new groups, establish new contacts, hide, dissimulate, start over."

"Because Louisianne was taken."

"Yes. And because someone gave her away."

"Who?" He didn't answer, and she said, "Why didn't they search the other houses again? Why didn't they find me, the Weinbergs, Sacha?"

"The mayor took his orders from Madame Jbert. He didn't know there were others in the village. He only knew of one member of Les Fleurs du Mal, the one he was sheltering, the White Rose. I assume he told the Gestapo about her the morning after that first *rafle*. There had been too many people around that night, too many witnesses."

"What will happen to him?"

"Nothing too pleasant. They may use him for a while to feed false information to the Gestapo, but eventually he'll find himself with a missing vital part. What I'd like to know is who gave him his orders? He's sheltered people before and not given them away. Who told him to turn in the White Rose is a mystery I'd like solved."

"I thought you didn't care about Les Fleurs du Mal, about the Resistance."

"I don't like being used." He drank his *fine*, taking her hand, looking around as if he didn't know their table was the center of interest, holding her to him, kissing her neck.

Floy held on to him for a moment, her eyes closed as if in passion. She wondered where that sexuality he had aroused in her at Le Soleil had gone to. That night seemed to her like a romance she had read, a film she had seen. Not real. Not about her and him.

They left the terrace and went into the wide, muraled

233

corridor that led to the main lobby. A woman came out of a small sitting room. It was apparent she had been waiting for them.

She touched Winterhagen's arm, and Floy recognized her. She still wore the chic little prewar hat with the veil and the expensive Mainbocher suit.

Behind her, holding on to her hand, was her son, only a year or two older than Curry but far more serious. Just as when Floy had seen her in the patch of sunshine in the courtyard of 33 Rue Balny d'Avricourt, there were tears in her eyes. But they were no longer tears of terror and fear.

"Monsieur," she said, "I saw you come in and I waited until we would not be overheard. I so want to apologize. Without you . . ."

"There is nothing to apologize for," Winterhagen said, retreating a step.

"Brazun told me it was you who persuaded him to take us with him."

"Madame, I am sorry to disappoint you . . ."

"We leave tomorrow, monsieur, my son and I. We are joining my family in North Africa. I do not like to think where we would be if it were not for you. The most unexpected people have been generous. Friends I trusted for years turned their backs on us. Odd, no, what people will and won't do in times like these?" She kissed Winterhagen on the cheek and then, holding her son's hand, retreated into the small sitting room.

"Would you kiss me, please, rather enthusiastically on the mouth?" he asked, putting a restraining arm on Floy's, keeping her from moving on into the lobby. "There must be a solid reason why it's taken us five minutes to cross forty feet."

She kissed him, telling herself she still didn't feel anything . . . that those corrupt cupid's lips pressed against hers might as well have been made of wax. It was all, she told herself, part of the job.

In the lobby Winterhagen assumed a sheepish, caught-out look, as he saw himself in a mirror, his lips and cheek smeared with Floy's lipstick.

He used his handkerchief and then took Floy's arm again, as if he couldn't bear to let her go.

The Gestapo's man in the Hotel de Paris, Sortino, sighed as they left, folded his German magazine, put it into the pocket of his worn jacket, and decided to see what, if anything, was happening on the terrace.

Monte Carlo, which had seemed such a promising post to both him and his mother, was proving to be a terrible disappointment.

In the car going up the mountain, Floy looked at him, amused. "So you're not such a tough guy after all."

"I'm pretty tough," he said, looking away from her, indicating the driver.

Before they entered Maude's house, as the car went back to Monte Carlo, she said, "You helped her, didn't you?"

"Who?"

"The woman in the two-hundred-franc hat."

"I never saw her before."

Chapter Twenty-two

Alouette had the grippe. She wrapped herself in blankets, turned on an electric heater she had found in one of the closets, and dosed herself with everything she could find in Maude's overstocked medicine cabinet. "One day. In one day I will be well," she promised.

"If you don't die of self-inflicted poison," Floy said, looking at the empty bottle of Milk of Magnesia on the night table, surrounded by other, less familiar potions. "If you need anything . . ."

Floy herself didn't feel as well as she might. She never did on the first day of her period. Little Mme. Bertrand bustled around the small apartment, dusting. The dog, Piéro, followed her everywhere and occasionally she reached into the pocket of her apron and gave him a piece of brown rock-candy, an expensive black-market indulgence.

The apartment suddenly seemed extremely small. Curry wanted to be entertained.

"Would it be possible," he asked Max, who was going out, "for us to take a walk together?" He asked this with deference, as if he already knew the answer was no.

"Quite possible," Winterhagen said, to Curry's relief and delight. "We will establish for all interested parties the legitimacy of our new relationship. A wife's new husband should get to know his stepson. We'll go to the beach. It is warm enough for swimming. There is a bicycle in the garage with tires in fair condition."

"I haven't a swimsuit," Curry said, disappointed.

"You can wear your underwear."

"And what will you wear?" Floy asked, amused. She lay on the sofa, drinking a cup of tea.

"I shall prevail upon Madame Hamilton's kindness yet again and borrow one of her husband's swimming costumes."

Floy left the sofa and stepped out onto the terrace to watch them ride down to the beach.

It was covered with white pebbles and quiescent pigeons. Fragrant oleanders still bloomed on the quay above. The water looked warm and inviting and absurdly blue. I'm nearly jealous, Floy admitted to herself as she watched. Curry so obviously needed Winterhagen's approval, his reassurance. It was understandable. He had lost Louisianne and he had lost Floy for a time. It would take a while to rebuild that security he had had. He was going to have scars. She knew that. Floy only hoped they wouldn't be too deep.

She went back to the sofa. Winterhagen had forgotten his silver cigarette case. She picked it up from the table where he had left it. It was small, flat, and beautifully etched in the Russian niello manner. She opened it, surprised to find two panels. In one were his Gitanes. In the other was a snapshot of a young woman with a great deal of black hair and round black eyes, a face filled with sympathy. She held a boy about Curry's age. He had Max's pensive expression and perfect features.

'His son and wife," little Mme. Bertrand said, pouring more tea for her, looking over her shoulder. "Before they were taken off to Oranienburg."

Floy looked up at her shrewd little face.

"Surprised? I may be the only person who knows everything about him. I've known him since he was born not too far from here in Menton, now held by the Italians. Oh, those terrible macaronis." She began to dust again.

"Tell me about him," Floy said, and Mme. Bertrand

brought another cup, poured herself tea, and sat down next to Floy, ready for a good, long gossip.

His father, she said, was a poor and last member of a family with a minor title. "Three lines in the *Almanach de Gotha*." He had used what money there was to become a lawyer, a great comedown in social status. He compounded his social disgrace (little Mme. Bertrand said, helping herself to a Gitane, lighting it) by marrying an actress.

"Fire and water. Lola lived to travel. Not to foreign places. Lola thinks there's only one country on earth and that's *la belle France*."

Lola adored touring, Madame went on, smoking her cigarette with her little finger well out. She hated Paris. She liked country music-halls jam-packed with families in their Sunday best, reeking of garlic and the Sunday stew, exuding good humor and beery breath.

"She spent her life pleasing them, traveling from one end of France to the other. Max's father stayed home in Menton, where he belonged, practicing law. His clients were what the British called 'our old pussies,' English ladies on a pension who wintered in Menton because the winter was mild and the living inexpensive.

"They had, unpredictably, a perfect marriage. Whenever she happened to be playing the Mediterranean, Lola would take a month's holiday, usually in September, and spend it with him. At the end of the month she'd kiss him good-bye and go on the road again."

"Was she good?"

"Marvelous. I never missed a performance."

Madame Bertrand flicked the ash off her cigarette and sipped her tea. "Lola never wanted a child but she made the best of Max. She took him with her. From the beginning he traveled with her troupe, doing a week in Le Havre, a two-nighter in Dieppe, ten days in St. Malo before heading for the interior: Rennes, Tours, Bourges. The big time: Lyon.

"He was sent to school in each village, always the object of much curiosity. An actress's son. Born, they said, to be bad. He got into a certain number of scrapes, naturally. But he also got his education then, learning about France's villages and hamlets, about the back roads and dirt roads and locally known cow paths that became so important to him when he started working as a *passeur*.

"He's a brilliant *passeur*," little Mme. Bertrand said, her hen's bosom inflating with pride. "Brilliant. He built a foundation, a network of friends during those years, and it's been those friends who have provided safe houses for his clients."

"Did he ever act with his mother?"

Mme. Bertrand permitted herself a smile. "From the time he was twelve he played the male ingenue. Lola kept him innocent, hiring elderly ingenues, ladies with bad breath or congenital difficulties not greatly noticed by the audience.

"He was a very pure boy, though to look at him, one would have never thought so. Lola taught him to tango, and I remember seeing one of her productions when Max performed. He wore gaucho trousers and a Valentino hat, and every woman in that audience held her breath during the entire time he was on that stage. The most respected woman in that audience would have gladly risked eternal condemnation for him, but it wasn't to be."

"He fell in love," Floy said, looking at the snapshot in the cigarette case.

"He was just eighteen. Lola had been offered a month's engagement in Strasbourg. She always hated it—so German, she said—but she took it. She was nearly forty then, claiming thirty—Max was a miracle birth—and getting tired.

"He met her there. She couldn't have been more inappropriate. An educated German Jewish girl with a rich father." Little Mme. Bertrand sighed, stood up, brushed the spilled ashes from her lap, fed Piéro a piece of rock candy, and gathered up the tea things.

"What happened to them?" Floy asked, looking at the snapshot of the girl with the poignant eyes who was holding that replica of Max.

"They married against everybody's wishes. They danced together. Tangos. They were successful for a time, working in the Chevaliers' company, appearing in two or three films. They had a son. They were very, very happy."

"And then?"

Mme. Bertrand bustled into the kitchen, Piéro behind her. "You should rest. I've said far too much. He'd kill me if he knew I've been talking about him." She stopped for a moment and looked at Floy without seeing her, her eyes glistening. "He's such a good boy." And then she began to clean the kitchen floor.

Later Floy sat on the terrace and watched as Max rode the ancient bicycle up the mountain. Curry, his head propped against Winterhagen's chest, had fallen asleep. They looked tan and healthy and tired. Once, Winterhagen bent down and kissed Curry's forehead. It seemed a natural gesture.

In the evening, after Curry had been put to bed and Alouette had announced that she was cured and Mme. Bertrand and Piéro had gone to make their report to the Gestapo man, Sortino, Floy found herself alone with Winterhagen.

"Imagine little Madame Bertrand being a double agent," Floy said, sitting on the arm of the sofa. "Difficult enough to imagine her being a single agent. She's remarkable."

There was a silence. "I saw the photo in your case,"

240

Floy said, breaking it awkwardly. "I didn't know you were married."

"I'm a widower." He sat down on the sofa near her, opened his case, and looked at the snapshot.

"Will you tell me about her? And the boy?"

He looked up at her and then back at the photo. "She wasn't beautiful. Not at all like you. Her features were too large and animated. She had enormous, poignant eyes. She spoke perfect, nearly Parisian French, though she was born in Germany. She had traveled all over the world, while I had traveled around the backwaters of France.

"At our first rendezvous I was terribly nervous. I had dazzled the fellows in Toulon and Chatellerault. She spoke about Cairo, New York, and London. To stop her, I kissed her. We were both virgins. She was as surprised as I was.

"Eva's father was violently against the match. Judge Kauffmann was an important jurist in Berlin who supposedly had the ear of Von Papen. When we married, he sent a note with a thousand francs, saying he didn't want to see her anymore.

"When we had a son, Nick, Eva wrote to him, but he didn't respond. Still, we were happy. We had moved from an apartment in the Rue du Four to the Rue Daguerre in Montparnasse," Max said, closing his eyes.

Floy felt a slight, sharp pang of jealousy. She found herself wishing she and Max and Curry had been happy, once, in an apartment in Montparnasse.

In 1936, he went on, after the Berlin Olympics, the Nazis began their major, unbridled assault upon the Jews. Eva was told by the Jewish emigrés streaming into Paris that her father was dying, that he had been stripped of his judicial post, that he was a prisoner in his house in the Bülowstrasse. Von Papen's ear had proved as false as the rest of him.

"You understand," Max said, "that in all this time we hadn't heard from him. And then, suddenly, one of those emigrés who constantly filled our apartment arrived with a scrap of paper."

It was a will. Judge Kauffmann had left everything he owned—which was to be confiscated by the Nazis—to his daughter. There was a postscript in which the old man begged his daughter for her forgiveness. He had written that he loved her, that he yearned for her presence, yearned to see her one more time. He had written that he gave his blessing to her marriage.

Eva packed at once and bought tickets for Berlin. Nick and his nursemaid were to accompany her.

"I want my father to see his grandson," Eva said. "I want him to know that there is new life for our family. I want him to hold his namesake in his arms."

Max had said that the judge would be horrified, that Jews never named their children after living relatives. Eva replied that her father wasn't that sort of Jew. She continued to pack.

It was November and it was cold and the refugees told her she was *meshuga*, crazy. It all happened too quickly for Max to say anything.

"I am a French citizen," Eva told the refugees. "My son is a French citizen. French citizens go back and forth all the time. My husband has impeccable Aryan credentials. I need to see my father once more before he dies. I need to forgive him."

"You'll never get him out," a little emigré named Ludden warned her. He always wore a skullcap under his hat. "Never." But Eva said she wasn't going to try to get him out. He wouldn't leave. She knew that.

"I only want to hold him once more. I want him to kiss Nicky, to know the pleasure of a grandson."

On no account would she let Max accompany them. "You are our lifeline," Eva told him. "You'll pull us back if we get stuck."

Max had accompanied them to the Gare du Nord. He had held her and his four-year-old Nicky as long as he could. Ludden, his skullcap showing under his black felt hat, waited with him while the train slowly pulled out, headed east.

Eva had taken a first-class ticket out of habit. She had let down the window in her carriage and stuck her plain, vibrant face out of it and waved. Nicky, held by his nursemaid, blew kisses at him.

"I wasn't much of a lifeline," Max said, stubbing out another Gitane in Maude's Lalique ashtray. "I never heard from Eva again. The nurse returned a week later, hysterical." She told him that Eva had been arrested the moment she arrived in Berlin. With Nicky.

Max tried to get to Germany, but he was stopped at the border.

A month later Ludden brought an emigré to the apartment on the Rue Daguerre. He had been on the train that had taken Judge Kauffmann, his daughter, and grandson to the concentration camp at Oranienburg.

"It wasn't a passenger train, you understand," Ludden's friend said. "It was a train for cattle. And the judge and his daughter and grandson weren't even in the same cattle car."

At the camp they were miraculously reunited. The old people and the young women with children were sent off, immediately, together.

One of the matrons, at the last possible moment, took Nick from his mother. Eva screamed and tried to get to Nick but she was beaten and kicked back.

Max stopped for a long moment and he lit another Gitane before he spoke again. "The trouble was Eva was six months pregnant. They might have let her go if she hadn't been pregnant but they had a new policy of getting rid of pregnant women. Too much trouble, I guess. And according to the Racial Laws, there weren't to be any more Jewish babies."

Eva was forced to keep marching. She found her father, who helped her. Ludden's friend said she was bleeding pretty badly, well worked over by the Nazis when she tried to get to Nick.

All of them—the young pregnant women, the women with young children, and the old people—were being sent into a huge brick building. A new Nazi experiment. They were told they were going to have showers, receive new clothes.

"Such a big building," Ludden's friend said in his Yiddish-accented German. "Big smokestacks. A terrible smell. Everyone in camp, even the Nazis, kept as far from it as possible."

He had escaped only a few weeks before.

"My wife?" Max had asked, not interested in Ludden's friend's escape, wanting to hear the final words.

"She was killed with her father in the big brick gas oven," Ludden's friend obliged.

"And my son?"

The gray little man, this escaped prison-camp inmate, looked up at Max and tried for a smile. Most of his teeth were either missing or brown stumps, and the smile wasn't nearly successful. "He's in the children's camp. He is safe for the time being. The matron protects him."

"Can I get him out? Any way?"

"There is nothing for you to do now. But I want you to help."

Nicky would be safe, the little man said, protected, while Max helped get certain people out of Germany and through France to Spain. Eventually the little man's organization—"a very poor organization"—would get Nick out of the camp.

"I want you to meet a man," Ludden's friend said.

The man was Lord Billy. Max became a *passeur* for him, for Les Fleurs du Mal. He spent the next few years escorting important German, Viennese, and Polish escapees across France into Spain, where British agents took over. He spent the next few years waiting for scraps, for little pieces of information about his son. He spent them mourning his lost wife, his Eva.

The war eventually arrived. That ridiculous, absurd one-month war. His father, who loathed and despised the Italians as only southern Frenchmen can, closed his house and took Lola with him to Switzerland a few days before the Italians took Menton.

"I fought in the Norwegian campaign," Max told her. "I thought we might win. Later, when I saw French officers at Fréjus toasting the Germans with champagne, I knew the war had been a farce, a mediocre politicians' effort to save what little face they had left."

He returned to Paris, to Billy and Louisianne. Ludden and his friend had long since disappeared. He began taking fugitives through France to Spain again.

"I was charging a great deal, saving money for my son. I knew when the time came it would cost a fortune in bribes to get him out."

He was silent for a long moment. The prewar Gitane, stale and dry, had gone out. His forehead was damp with sweat, and his eyes were wet with tears.

"And now," Floy asked, "you are going to quit?"

"They lied to me. Eva and Nick walked into that building in Oranienburg together. No one took him away from her. They didn't want four-year-old Jewish boys any more than they wanted unborn Jewish babies. Or their mothers. Nick and Eva thought they were going to have showers, to get clean. They took off all their clothes and folded them in neat little stacks, and then they went in and turned their faces up to the spouts from which they expected water and received poisoned gas.

"There was no maternal matron. Ludden and his friend used me. They were desperate. I'm not certain I blame them, though it wouldn't be wise to put me in a room alone with them. I've lived all these years with my vision of Nick and now I find it was a ghost that kept me going. My son's ghost. Ironically, they could have had me if they had told me the truth, but I don't suppose Ludden's friend could take that gamble."

Louisianne and Billy hadn't known, he told her. They had simply inherited him.

"How did you find out the truth?"

"Another Jewish refugee. He had been at Oranienburg and remembered Judge Kauffmann and his daughter and grandson. The refugee was in the detail ordered to gather up clothes left by the gassed Jews for the German Winter Aid program.

"He was surprised by Eva's fur coat. Most fur coats didn't reach the camps. He had seen them walk into the gas chamber, all three of them. He didn't know who I was. He had no reason to lie. Now there's no reason for me to help."

"You're going to retire?"

"It's time. The Germans are going to march into Vichy at any moment, and I don't want to be waiting for them. They scare me. And my compatriots in *les services* scare me—amateurs, at odds with one another, ready to use anything, anyone, for their separate causes. No. I am ready to leave now." He looked down once more at the photograph of his wife and child.

"You miss her very much?"

"I never supposed, after Eva, that I could love again." He snapped the case shut. "But the truth is that I knew that first day, when you crashed into Louisianne's office, concerned only for your son, that I could care for you.

"I knew that it wouldn't do either of us much good, but I lost control at Le Soleil. If Curry weren't asleep in your bed, I would attempt to make love to you again.

"In the beginning, I thought you were another upper-class American, an actress who didn't care for her craft, a female who lived for no particular reason.

"I take it all back. You live for your son, as I lived for mine. You are brave and intelligent and you do fight

for him, for what you believe. If you were what I orig-
inally thought you were, you would be with Chambertin
and the other monsters. No. You have given me courage,
Floy. I did not want to say this. I had not planned to.
But I love you, Floy."

He took her in his arms and held her close, and she
believed him. He kissed her with his spoiled cupid's
lips and she could feel his hard, strong body against hers
and then Curry called out from the bedroom. He was
having a nightmare.

She held on to Max for one more moment and then
she went to her son.

In the morning she woke up feeling suddenly, completely alive. She made a vow to herself. For the rest of
their time in Monaco she was not going to think of the
war, of Les Fleurs du Mal; and yes, she was not going
to think of Louisianne, if she could help herself.

She was going to put all the terror, all the anxiety
out of her mind—Rivet's soiled suit, Chambertin's nearly
white eyes, that axe propped up against that wall in that
prison in Cologne.

She was going to pretend to be free, to be in love, for
the next few days. It might be, she thought, our last few
days. At any moment the door could fly open, and instead of Max dressed up like an SS officer, the real Mc-
Coy might appear.

(Certainly Louisianne knew of Maude's house, of her
offer. Certainly her interrogators could get that piece of
information out of her if they tried, and Floy knew how
they were trying.)

But Floy wouldn't think of that. She had her son, alive
and healthy. She understood Max now. At least she understood him better. They would have the kind of non-
bed affair she had been denied when Curry Greene had
taken her to that apartment at the Wallingford.

She and Max, she thought, were going to be old-fashioned lovers. Curry was their unlikely duenna. They would all be able to get to know one another better without sex getting in the way.

"Such a good boy," little Mme. Bertrand had said of Max.

Such a good man, Floy amended, thinking of his dead wife and son, of his long, lonely despair.

Chapter Twenty-three

They had five more days in that haven from the outside world. During the days they went on picnics. Curry and Alouette carried the hamper. Little Mme. Bertrand allowed herself to be persuaded to come along on two occasions.

Curry listened carefully to everything Max said. He imitated his walk, his accent, the way he shrugged his shoulders. When he clamped one of Max's Gitanes between his teeth, Max gently took it away, explaining that smoking was not for boys who had to grow up but for men who had no place to grow but out.

At night Floy and Max held hands and sat on the terrace overlooking Monte Carlo.

"I feel a little ridiculous," Floy said, looking at the cinematic moon, "as if we're waiting for the orchestra to begin before we break into song."

He kissed her hand. "You are being courted," he told her. Before she went to the bedroom she shared with Curry, Max would kiss her good night with such sweet passion that she would prolong that kiss as long as she could.

He practiced his English, preparing, he said, for America. "I shall be an actor again." He was perfecting his accent, he told her, for Hollywood and Cecil B. de Mille. "Nick and I will learn American together," he said, when he invariably slipped back into French. Then he turned those heavily lashed black eyes away from her and corrected himself. "Curry and I."

During those five days she realized she not only loved him—desired him: she liked him. She saw in him the boy filled with sweet-natured naivete that little Mme. Bertrand still cherished.

They ate the food from Maude's black-market larder, and when it ran out—Alouette's appetite never diminished, not for a moment—little Mme. Bertrand supplied more. Max tried to pay her, but she held up a tiny hand.

"Oh, no, Max," she said in her singsong southern accent. "Madame Hamilton told me, 'This party is on me.' It is Madame's present."

Floy discovered Max could cook. "I can't boil water," she confessed. He looked at her sideways, to indicate no one had ever dreamed she could.

He was teaching Curry to make *oeuf à cheval*, egg on horseback. "When you are a road kid," Max told him, "you learn to make a few dishes."

"Am I a road kid?"

Max stopped beating the precious egg and looked down at Curry looking earnestly up at him. He so much wanted to be a road kid. Max bent down and held him for a moment. "Now you are," he said, and went back to his preparations.

Oeuf à cheval consisted of an egg on a slab of Gruyère cheese on a slice of *pain mie*, toasted in a hot oven until the white of the egg was firm, the yolk soft and fluid, and the cheese partly melted.

"Like so," Max said, flipping the *oeuf à cheval* onto Curry's plate.

"Men," Curry said to Floy as he ate, "are the very best cooks."

Floy and Max, who once had trouble making polite conversation, talked endlessly. About their pasts, their futures, Curry.

"He's the sort of kid," Max said, "you can rely on. He was very brave when he was separated from you. He would never ask for you directly. Only at night, before he went to bed, he would look up and say, 'Any word?' "

They avoided talk about the war, about concentration camps, Germans, the Weinbergs, Sacha. Floy deliberately spoke of Louisianne, carefully, mentioning her only in past incidents and anecdotes.

Louisianne was to be left outside Monaco, outside that magic world they were inhabiting with fresh eggs and milk and the diluted war news from Radio Monte Carlo.

But sometimes she would wake in the night from a light sleep, sweating, having dreamed of Billy in that windowless room in Cologne, of Chambertin in a white coat, waiting for her in a modernistic dentist's office. And of Louisianne, calling for her.

She would wake crying, and put her arms around Curry and hold him.

That piece of knowledge was always there, once learned, never really forgotten. It was always in the background, waiting to make itself felt like an incurable cancer. As long as Louisianne remained alive, a potential informer, they could remain in Monaco. When she was finally silenced, when she could no longer talk, they would have to move on. It seemed an extravagant price to have to pay for those few days. It seemed monstrously, grossly selfish, unfair. But there it was.

On that next to last night Floy dreamed only of Louisianne. In the dream she wore a toga and looked like a Parthenon statue, white and gray and stony. Majestic. She was to be killed. They—an amorphous they—had sentenced her to the Roman death for traitors. She was sewn into a sack along with a wild monkey, a poisonous snake, a fighting cock, and a savage dog. The sack was tossed into the sea. The animals went berserk. Only Louisianne remained calm as the sack disappeared.

"I've read too much popular history," Floy said in the morning, when she told Max about the dream. He took her hand and held it in his for a moment. She felt

251

spineless, soft, like the rag dolls she had had as a child. She needed Max's strength so very badly.

Late in the afternoon of that last day Max went to an assignation with the Russian count in the Hotel de Paris's only unattended men's room. The Russian count—Primrose—had a transmitter hidden in his hotel suite.

While Floy waited for Max to return with news, while she dreaded his return, Curry switched on the radio. He started with the circumlocutions of Radio Geneva, turned to the lies of Radio Vichy, and settled on the BBC and the opening bars of Beethoven's Fifth Symphony. They listened to the coded messages, the news of the war, as if they were listening to a radio play, fictional and not even faintly believable.

Max came in and looked at her carefully. "We're leaving tomorrow."

She didn't ask why or what the Russian, Primrose, had heard on his transmitter. She knew.

"Let's celebrate," Floy said. She was feverish suddenly. There was an odd, warm glow to her skin.

"All right," he agreed. "Let's celebrate."

They kissed Curry good night and told Alouette what would be expected of her in the morning and then they went out. Floy had found one of Maude's evening gowns, nearly the same green as her eyes. It exposed her back and her shoulders and was slinky in that special Schiaparelli thirties' manner, reeking of de luxe class ocean voyages.

Max found that he fitted into Peter Hamilton's dinner suit. Smelling of mothballs and Maude's Coty perfume, they rode the bikes down to the Casino. It was bathed in a yellow light and seemed more real than it did during the day. It was a building designed for the night.

They couldn't sit inside; they would attract too much attention. They walked through the gaming rooms, where monocled men in dinner jackets and women in evening gowns quietly played at losing money. He led her to the terrace, where he ordered champagne and *langouste*, and miraculously both were served after an enormous amount of money changed hands.

It had grown cool, like a genuine autumn night, and they were the only couple on the terrace. They sat at a table overlooking the Mediterranean. There was a full moon and stars, but the night still seemed too dark, as if it too had to cut down on the wattage.

The old Russian count peered out from the *petit salon* but didn't join them. The orchestra inside the salon played fox-trots one after another, and they danced. A reedy tenor sang in English, "Be Sure It's True When You Say I Love You, It's a Sin to Tell a Lie," and Max held her close.

"You've made me come alive again," he said, his lips against her hair. "You and Curry." He smiled. "This is no time to be in love."

"I'm too old to be in love," she said, kissing him, pressing her lips as hard as she could against those spoiled angel's lips.

And then the Russian, Primrose, came out and rather noisily lit a long white cigarette with a built-in filter, tapping time for a moment with one patent-leather-shod foot to the banal music.

Max took her arm, and they rode back to Maude Hamilton's guest flat in the hills above Monte Carlo. He held her close to him, and she knew his need for her was as great as hers for him.

"We're not too old to be in love," Floy said in the dark, warm Riviera night, as he held her. "We're too young to be living the lives we're enduring."

She kissed those spoiled cupid's lips once more and then went to Maude's absurd bed and lay awake next to Curry until the early morning. She washed and put on a dark traveling dress. She was now a bride at the end of a honeymoon with a second husband; almost happy.

Curry was told he would have to be quiet and calm and

253

listen carefully to Max, and he said, his eyes big with adventure and fear, that of course he would.

A diplomat's limousine had come to take them across the comic-opera border into unoccupied France. Before he closed the door, Max kissed little Mme. Bertrand on both her rosy cheeks.

"No good-byes," she said, turning away, her eyes filled with tears. She picked up the black-and-white dog and buried her face in its neck, looking like a schoolgirl. "You all be careful. You all must come back to me." And then in a low voice she said to Max, "Be a good boy."

The limousine stopped at a bus station a few miles over the border, and it was time for Alouette to say good-bye. She had been given her choice: to come with them or to return to her home in Joigny. She had chosen Joigny, but only Curry was surprised. He put his arms around her stout, red neck and Alouette cried, but it was clear she was longing for the farm, for her own family.

"Why now, Max?" Floy asked finally, as she knew she would. "Why have we left now?" The car drove silently, easily, through the Côte d'Azur hills toward Nice. Max had gotten out of his uniform and into a businessman's suit.

"The Russian, Primrose, received word that the Gestapo search for us has been called off. Or it appears to have been called off. They're too busy to be concerned with us. They are worried about an Allied invasion of North Africa and they're planning to occupy Vichy France shortly. It is time for us to move on."

"Why now, Max?" she asked again quietly.

He said softly, "*La Rose Blanche est morte.*" He looked at her with his black eyes and touched her cheek.

"How did she die?" She had to know. Though the Nazis had made reality worse than imagination, still, she had to know.

Max looked at Curry, who lay asleep, his head in

Floy's lap, his legs across Max's knees. "She broke a window in Santé prison," Max said softly. "She cut her veins with the glass. She bled to death. She was afraid she would tell them what they wanted to know during her next scheduled period of interrogation. They got nothing from her. Louisianne died a hero's death. She is a French patriot."

"That's so little solace, Max," Floy said, crying for her dead, brave auntie.

He took her hand, kissed it, and held it. "She died the way she lived, Floy: with nobility. She told them nothing. That can be said about very few long-term Gestapo guests."

She cried as the limousine began to drive down toward Nice. She cried with sorrow, with pain, and with relief. She would not have to remember Louisianne as she had to remember Billy, in that filthy black-and-white photograph taken in the prison in Cologne.

She could remember Louisianne as she last saw her, her head held high, so clearly determined never to give in.

Chapter Twenty-four

The limousine pulled into a garage in the back streets of Nice. Once a stable, it still smelled indefinably of horses and leather. Floy, Curry, and Max were taken by the proprietor into his office, while the limousine was put up on blocks, its bonnet open, a mechanic set to work on it, the chauffeur dismissed. The limousine was a legitimate Nazi official car, "borrowed" for the occasion. The real chauffeur was to pick it up in an hour's time.

The garage owner, a tall, worried-looking man with a shining bald head, had been inappropriately code-named Mimosa. He sat smoking German-issue cigarettes in his closet of an office while Floy and Curry stared at him and Max tried to see out the window, which had been covered with laundry blueing per the air-raid instructions.

"If Herr Lidermann's man had come and found his car not here, I would have been done for, I can tell you," Mimosa said. He looked at Curry looking at the German cigarette packs. "Black market," he explained. "The Germans use them like money. They're the worst cigarettes on the black market but they're the cheapest. What are you going to do?"

There was a clock on the wall, a prewar tire company promotion. It was ringed by a miniature tire and it moved with excruciating slowness.

"Why are we all watching the tire clock?" Curry

wanted to know. Max took a sheet of coarse paper from the garage owner's desk and taught Curry a battleship game which kept them both occupied until they heard a truck enter the garage.

Mimosa ground out his cigarette, put the butt in the pack, and—just in case someone was light-fingered—pocketed the pack. He looked startled as he went into the garage. Herr Lidermann's man had come for his master's limousine just as Le Levandou had come to pick up Floy, Max, and Curry.

"Yes, *mein Herr*," they could hear Mimosa appeasing Herr Lidermann's chauffeur. "Just one more hour. Not even that. Clogged. The terrible gasoline we must use because of this bloody war."

At the same time they could hear Le Levandou talking at the top of his considerable voice to the mechanic. "The damned *Boches*," he said, disregarding Herr Lidermann's man. "Now those bastards are stopping every transport throughout the south. Only the trains don't get stopped," Le Levandou said, complaining that his truck had been stopped and inspected four times in one morning. "The trains. They're one's only chance to get anywhere. The *sales Boches* are everywhere. I expect them to turn up here any moment."

"Monsieur," they heard Lidermann's chauffeur say in a thin, German-accented voice. "I am a German and I take great exception to what you say."

"You're a German?" Le Levandou boomed. "I don't believe it. You're too short. A German is supposed to be big and blond and . . ."

They didn't hear the rest of Le Levandou's ideal of German manhood, because Max had picked up Curry in one arm and grabbed a suitcase with his free hand. He motioned to Floy to take the paper they had been playing battleships on and cautiously opened a thin door leading to an alley. Floy folded the paper and put it in the pocket of her dress, following Max and Curry into the alley, silently shutting the door after her. Curry began to say something, but Max put his finger to his lips, and they moved along the alley, staying close to the buildings, coming out on a side street near the fish market.

"*Courage*," they could hear Le Levandou shout in his raspy voice. "We all need *courage* nowadays."

Max set Curry down, and the three of them began to walk quickly up the Avenue Thiers to the railroad station. Three black Renaults had pulled up in front of Mimosa's garage.

Floy wondered why there were always three. Two or even one would have been sufficient. She refused to think about Le Levandou or Mimosa. They would be let go. It was a routine *rafle*, she told herself, knowing that three black Renaults meant more than that.

They stopped in a doorway off the Avenue Malaussena. Max stood outside the tenement door while Floy went into the evil-smelling corridor and put a babushka on her head, wooden shoes on her feet, and an ancient sweater and a string bag over her arm, all of which Max had taken out of his suitcase. She didn't seem to be able to catch her breath. They had left the garage with only a moment to spare before the Gestapo came. They owed their lives to Le Levandou. She would have to be grateful later. She would have to concentrate now on not letting it become an empty gesture. Max gave her papers and money. She was going to have to go on alone. She would have to get her ticket by herself.

She came out of the corridor, bent down, and held Curry.

"Don't send me away again," he said, and she willed herself, commanded herself, not to cry, to breathe regularly.

"We are playing a game," she told him, trying for and nearly achieving a normal, even voice. "You are to be Max's boy for just a while. I will be watching you all of the time but you must pretend not to notice me. You must do what Max says. Call him Papa."

"Why?" Curry asked, suddenly a little, scared child; despite her resolve, her fear had communicated itself to him.

Max was better. "Because," he said, putting his hands on Curry's shoulders, "the people who are searching for us are looking for a mother and son. The Nazis. We're going to fool them."

Curry seemed satisfied. For a moment he had been about to cry but now he stood up straight, ready for battle. Max kissed her and held her for a moment, looking into her green eyes with his black ones. Then he took Curry's hand, and they went off up the Avenue Malaussena while Floy went directly into the train station, concentrating on Billy's advice. She took a long Hindu breath; she willed herself into this new role.

She stood in a queue for half an hour and purchased her third-class ticket while a Gestapo agent watched from behind the ticket seller's booth. He didn't ask to see her papers, but her hand shook, nonetheless, when she accepted the ticket. She bowed her head and moved away, catching sight of herself in a shop window in the station arcade. She thought she looked exactly what she was supposed to be: a scared country girl in wooden shoes, carrying a string bag, clutching an old wool sweater. Well, she was scared.

Max and Curry were sitting on bench seats in the second-class coach just ahead of the third-class carriage she was in. Max wore gold-rimmed glasses and had two pens clipped to his breast pocket. He looked shiny and eager to sell something, anything. Curry sat on his knee, apparently absorbed in the sights Max pointed out to him. Though they looked nothing alike, no one would have suspected them of being anything but father and son.

The journey, which should have taken two hours,

stretched out to nearly six. The French railway workers had drawn turtles in yellow chalk on the railroad cars, signifying a slowdown.

When cars were added at Toulon, a process that usually took a few minutes was dragged out to over an hour. The workers were objecting to transporting German troops across supposedly unoccupied France.

It began to rain in Toulon, and a fat woman with elaborate hair and a wet coat pushed in next to Floy. The damp and her neighbor's mildewed smell and cheap perfume made Floy nauseous, uneasy. She prayed that Le Levandou had somehow escaped, that he wasn't suffering for her. She longed to be up in the next car with Curry and Max. She felt a nearly overwhelming temptation to get up, to go to them.

She didn't, of course. An old man in a checked jacket a few seats behind her began to play a melancholy boulevard song on his accordion. The train finally began to move. But the last two cars remained in the station, improperly coupled, filled with German soldiers.

The accordionist stopped playing as three sets of police ran through the coaches. There were the Darlan police—France's own Gestapo, the Vichy police, and the Toulon police. If Chaplin were filming it, Floy thought, it might be funny: all those police in all those starched uniforms, running through the train.

She wasn't frightened. It was clear they weren't looking for her or for Max and Curry. They wanted the engineer, the man who had improperly coupled the cars bearing German soldiers.

The railway workers on the platform began to shout anti-German slogans, and the passengers began to cheer the railway workers, but by the time the train began to move, there was total silence inside and outside the train.

The engineer had been found, and for a moment it looked as if he would be shot right there in front of workers and passengers on the station platform. But the police and the German soldiers had eyed the sullen crowds and contented themselves with taking him off and allowing the train to move on. No one believed he would reach the prison alive.

"*Courage,*" someone in the crowd had shouted.

Floy never wanted to hear that word again. It always seemed to presage some catastrophe. Whenever someone said it—and someone was always saying it—she went all hollow and only wanted to close her eyes and black everything out.

As they approached Marseille, a conductor and a policeman came through, asking for papers. Behind the policeman was Rivet in his soiled, white suit, working his toothpick.

Floy stood up and started to go to Curry, to Max. But she realized in time that Rivet didn't know what they looked like. He knew only her face. She would be giving them away. She was still blocked from his view by the conductor and the policeman; he hadn't seen her yet.

She turned and walked slowly to the ladies' room. The door didn't open for a moment, and she thought someone was in there, but it had only stuck, having swelled up from the damp. She went inside without looking back and bolted the door.

Of course this was only a delaying tactic. They would open the door, check the ladies' room, and she would see Rivet's ferret face staring at her, waiting to take her to Chambertin.

There was a sharp rap on the door. "Tickets, please. Papers."

"One moment, monsieur," she said. "I am ill."

"We want your ticket and we want your papers now."

She hesitated. "I have a key to the door, madame," the voice said. "I am going to use it."

She released the bolt and opened the door, ready for Rivet's yellow teeth and little eyes.

"Sorry, mademoiselle," the policeman said, giving her

261

ticket to the conductor, looking at her papers perfunctorily. "We must check everyone."

She allowed herself to look to the left, to the third-class coach behind hers. She could see Rivet's thin back as he sauntered down the aisle, looking at faces.

She returned to her seat. Max looked back once, saw her, and, reassured, turned back to Curry. Her breathing, she realized, was erratic again. She wondered if she would black out, faint, but she had to be prepared for Rivet's return.

She stood up again. Her neighbor in the damp coat made a clucking sound of annoyance. Why couldn't the girl stay put? She couldn't see Rivet in the next coach. He must have gone on. She went back to the ladies' room and bolted herself in again. She waited there until the train pulled into Marseille. She waited for Rivet, but he never came.

In Marseille the rain had turned into a downpour of nearly storm proportions. It was a godsend for those wishing to leave the station unobserved. There was a great deal of confusion in front of the station, with two swastikaed limousines blocking the entry way, waiting for visiting Nazi officials, gasogene-powered trucks waiting to unload foodstuffs onto the train for its return to Occupied France, and a gigantic old Horche, maroon with gray trim. The Horche had pulled up in front of the official limousines, blocking their way.

A chauffeur stood holding the rear door open with one hand. In the other he held a maroon umbrella over the car door.

"Darling," an insistent voice called out from the back of the Horche as Floy appeared at the top of the steps under the station's marquee. She had left the babushka and the sweater in the station along with the wooden shoes. She had applied what Max called her Hollywood makeup and wore black pumps, the dark and useful traveling dress—chic again without the sweater, and the wooden shoes.

"Darling," that piercing voice cried out. "Over here."

A head belonging to a greatly transformed Chantil Weinberg stuck itself out of the rear door under the maroon umbrella. Her hair, now a rosier shade of red, was intricately curled. On top of it perched a magnificent purple hat strewn with once live, now stuffed pheasants. It was the sort of hat one wore to Ascot. Under it Chantil's plump face was thick with pancake makeup of an orange hue and a lipstick so dark that it was nearly black.

She motioned to the chauffeur to cut through the crowd, to provide cover for Floy. He managed to get to the marquee in the blinding rain, and Floy, under the umbrella, stepped out and ran for the car.

She reached it fairly dry, and was pulled into the back seat by Chantil. The chauffeur, sopping wet, ran around the enormous car to his seat.

"Curry and Max?" Floy asked, hugging Chantil, sitting back and laying her head against the plush upholstery, a little dizzy from lack of food, the long and frightening train journey, and Chantil's new and overpowering perfume.

"We're in the front seat," Max said, and Curry's head appeared over the divider. He had a moment to smile at Floy before he was pulled down again.

Sacha, who was playing the part of chauffeur, turned and looked at her as he tried to back the car out to the road. "They got in through the driver's door," he said, "while your poor old Sacha got soaked, escorting you to the car, claiming the attention of anyone who might have been interested."

"They all think Madame Bégonia has appeared to welcome a new girl to her house. Not an uncommon occurrence." Chantil crossed her silk-stocking-clad legs with great deliberation. She turned and with gloved hands drew a dark curtain over the rear window. "The real Madame, La Bégonia, has a terrible cold. Someone had to come, and we do not look unalike, though she is of course a good deal older."

Sacha had succeeded in getting the Horche onto the road and he drove the car slowly past sodden cyclists in the direction of Marseille's Vieux Port.

When he had reached the Canebière, its lovely old plane trees wilting in the rain, Curry and Max sat up in their seats next to Sacha.

"I want to sit with Mama," Curry said, sounding very much a small boy.

"It's all right now," Max said, and pushed Curry through the partition into the back of the car.

Curry allowed himself to be kissed by Chantil but then he folded up and went to sleep in his mother's arms as Sacha maneuvered the Horche into a narrow, cobble-stoned side street that ran under the balconies of Marseille's fish restaurants. He drove into the courtyard of a large, severely respectable, limestone-fronted house which had been built at the end of the nineteenth century.

They all waited while Sacha got out of the car and, getting wet again, opened the doors to the garage, which was built under the house and into the side of the mountain on which it stood.

"All of her girls are ravishing," Chantil whispered, so as not to wake Curry. "When her car is seen at the station everyone knows La Bégonia is picking up another new beauty for her house. There will be a lineup tonight. We shall have to say the new girl is ill with flu."

"Will they believe that?" Floy asked, amused by Chantil's authoritative delivery.

"Of course. La Bégonia has the approval of the German military machine unofficially occupying Marseille. She can do no wrong. She is fascinating, Floy. In some ways she is very much like Louisianne . . ." She stopped and put her arm around Floy. "We've heard. I'm sorry, Floy. I'm so very sorry."

Floy said she was sorry too, and then Sacha returned to the car and drove it into the garage and led them up a back stairway. They went up several flights to what Chantil—once again an authority on Madame Bégonia and her house—described with awe as La Bégonia's private apartments.

Max carried Curry into a bedroom that looked in the dim light as if it had come complete from the Ritz in Paris, right down to the paneled walls and gray drapes.

Max laid Curry on the bed, and in the candlelight Floy saw how tired Max was, how exhausting the trip had been for him. "You're not immune to fatigue either," she said, touching him.

"Only every now and then." He followed Chantil to the room set aside for him on the opposite side of the wide corridor. "In the morning," he said before he went. "I will see you in the morning."

Ilone, looking thin and worried in the tea gown Le Levandou had supplied her with, came in, kissed Floy on both cheeks, looked down at Curry, shook her head, and retired without saying one word.

Sacha had stayed behind, still dripping on the Aubusson carpet.

"You know, don't you?" Floy asked. "You've heard?"

"They told your poor old Sacha yesterday," he said, "when they transferred me from the hospital to the bordello." He gave her one of his surprising, sweet smiles. "It wasn't the worst way to die, Floy."

"No. She died without telling them what they wanted to know, so I suppose you're right, Sacha: It wasn't the worst way to die. She and Billy both died not so badly. It's odd; I never thought before that there were good ways and bad ways of dying, and now of course that's very clear. But I don't know how I'm going to live without her," Floy said, not caring very much, after all, how Louisianne had died. Only that she was dead.

Sacha held her for a moment, and then Max came in and said his sleep would have to wait, that there was someone both he and Sacha would have to talk to, and Sacha left with him.

Chantil asked if Floy were hungry, and Floy said yes, she supposed she was. Happy to play hostess, Chantil supervised a knife-thin waiter as he brought up two enormous bowls filled with rich bouillabaisse.

Curry, woken up by the aroma of the fish soup, sat on Floy's lap and finished his in record time. Immediately after, he was sleeping again.

Floy ate the bouillabaisse and drank a glass of white wine. She got out of her clothes, washed, and got into the bed, taking her boy in her arms, kissing him, thanking whatever god happened to be around that he was safe, that she was safe.

At first she thought she was too tired to sleep. The events of the day began to replay themselves in her mind like a news film out of control. But the wine and the anxiety worked together, and she slept, dreaming not of Rivet and his inquisitive nose moving through the third-class coach but of Chambertin and his grasping hands, his nearly white eyes behind the blue smoked glasses, reaching for her.

Chapter Twenty-five

She woke in the early morning and, looking around her, took a moment to realize where she was. She reached out for Curry, reassuring herself that he was there.

Then she laughed, thinking it was peculiar that she still could. What amused her was the room. The night before, in the dim light, it seemed as if it had been decorated by César Ritz.

She had missed the mirrored ceiling, the purple brocade tufts, the yellow satin sheets. Floy looked up at herself, with her sad eyes and skin made sallow by all that purple and yellow, and thought that it wasn't a room designed for early risers.

She kissed Curry and held him as he began to make wake-up noises. Then she looked up into the mirror again and realized that the rolled-up lump of blanket and pillow next to her was Max. He woke instantly, as he always did, perfectly alert. He smiled, kissed her, and got off the bed before Curry had completed his waking-up process, a protracted event.

Max put on his dark suit, but he took the pens from his pocket and no longer looked like a super-salesman. "I had to sleep with you two," he said. "My room was needed for business purposes. Last night was a busy night at Chez Bégonia. It always is after a *rafle*."

"Le Levandou?"

"And Mimosa. No more than we expected, but Le Levandou was always so careful. They must have followed him after he delivered Colonel Violet—your poor old Sacha—here from the hospital."

"Wouldn't that make Chez Bégonia a dangerous place to be?"

"Probably. We'd better move on quickly. Whoever is providing the Gestapo with information is somehow missing us. It's odd. Colonel Violet is the man the Gestapo wants."

"Do you know who the traitor is?"

"I think I do."

"I don't want to move on," Curry said suddenly, his eyes still closed.

"He's not sleeping," Max said, reaching down and tickling Curry under his ribs. Curry gave a shout, opening his eyes.

"Do we have to go on a train again?" Curry asked, jumping out of the bed, heading for the bathroom, an opulent affair Madame Bégonia had had installed.

"Perhaps just one more train."

Curry stopped at the bathroom door for a moment. "When do we get to go to America? I want to meet Monsieur George Raft." And then he said in heavily accented English, "He's one big tough guy, see?" And then, reverting to French, "He only travels in a big blue Cadillac."

"He's seen too many American films," Floy said. "So have I. The three of us—Louisianne, Curry, and myself—would go to the Graumont every Sunday afternoon. It was our way of keeping in touch."

He sat next to her and held her hand. "Are we going to get through?" she asked, looking up at him.

"Yes. We're no longer *brûlé*. The Germans are about to march into Vichy France. They're afraid that when the Allies invade North Africa, the south will rebel. Not likely with Pétain at the helm, but perhaps the Germans know more than I do. They're concentrating on rounding up local rallying figures, Resistance leaders.

"Like Le Levandou?"

He nodded and put her hand to his lips and kissed it. "You were so good on the train yesterday. My heart was in my mouth when I saw your friend Rivet. It was very bright, very intelligent of you to go to the ladies' room. It might not have worked but it was your best chance."

She shuddered, thinking of Rivet. "Chambertin?" she asked, forcing herself to say the name, to bring that fear into the open.

"He's keeping his hand in. Rivet's proof of that. Just in case you surface. But his main preoccupation now must be to get the Germans into Vichy France without a revolution.

"Two bombs exploded yesterday. One in Laval's recruiting office, moments before dozens of French workmen were about to be enrolled in the Fatherland's labor program. The French are getting more desperate, braver. The second bomb went off in Pétain's Legion headquarters. It killed half a dozen Pétainists. No. Chambertin has other things to worry about now."

Chantil announced over breakfast that she was going to stay. "La Bégonia needs me in her resistance work. She's not as strong as she used to be. I can be useful." Her chubby face was so earnest.

"If you stay," Ilone said, "then I stay. And we'll be caught, because I'm a terrible actress, as you know, and a fearful coward. We'll be shipped to a concentration camp in Poland and we'll be tortured to death while Papa and Mama wait for us in Lisbon. When they hear, they'll die."

Chantil, under that sort of pressure, capitulated, but it was obvious she thought she had found her niche. "I could have been of inestimable use," she said, echoing Bégonia, who thought she had found a capable, dedicated second-in-command.

They were to travel together this time. The rumors of German occupation of Vichy France were creating a new wave of refugees. Six wealthy families who had fled to Marseille from Paris were having their cars sent to Perpignan, on the east coast of France's Pyrénées-Orientales department, just below the mountains separating France from Spain. The families were attempting to reach Spain aboard two chartered yachts. They were to meet their cars in Barcelona.

The cars were lined up in La Bégonia's courtyard on that sunny morning. The October air was salty and fresh as they left Chez Bégonia through the garage. Ilone and Chantil were put into the trunk of the first car, a Packard limousine with enough space in the trunk, as Chantil noted, for two more Weinbergs.

Sacha declined Chantil's invitation to join her and her sister in the Packard's trunk. "Your poor old Sacha's afraid you'll try to reform me. You've taken your role at Chez Bégonia too seriously. I shall ride alone." He got into the trunk of a brown and white Delahaye.

Floy and Curry were to ride in the trunk of an ancient black Rolls-Royce.

"It may be painfully slow," Max warned them. "Curry, it is your job to care for your mama. You both must be very quiet." Max was going to drive the Rolls onto the train. When Floy protested, he said, "They still do not know what I look like, and we don't have enough drivers."

"Chambertin does. He saw you on the train from Paris. He . . ."

"Chambertin will not be inspecting chauffeurs on the train from Marseille to Perpignan."

"Rivet might. They may have gotten hold of a copy of our tango. They could have made a print . . ."

"And I will look nothing like the actor in that print."

It was true. He wore an old chauffeur's uniform, with baggy trousers and a cap a size too small. He walked with a limp. He looked old and irascible, a wealthy family's driver.

"It's a short trip to Perpignan, and there's no inspection until the border, by which time we will all have disembarked."

"Why can't we stay in the cars and go straight through to Spain?" Floy asked. She was too anxious, she knew.

"The border inspection is the most thorough in France. There won't be a piece of that car untouched by the time the border guards get through with it. No. We must cross the Pyrenees on foot. It is more difficult but less dangerous."

She didn't want him to shut the lid on the cavernous trunk. She wanted him to stay and talk, to reassure her. But he bent over and kissed them both, and the lid was shut, and there was a sudden and total darkness. Curry put his arms around her, frightened of that pervasive dark.

She whispered to him that he could see sunlight by looking in the several places around the lid where the insulation had worn away.

He turned to look, and Floy suddenly felt as if she would explode if she weren't let out of that confined space. She felt again the terrors of the claustrophobia that had assaulted her in Mme. Jbert's attic. She had to put her hand to her mouth so as not to scream.

"Take a deep Hindu breath, Mama," Curry said, repeating Billy's favorite panacea for fear and anxiety. "Breathe slowly. Deeply. It is going to be all right, I promise you, Mama. We are together. I am taking care of you."

"I know," she was able to whisper after a long, desperate moment. She took Billy's Hindu breath and let her body relax. "I'm all right now."

The cars were driven out of La Bégonia's courtyard, across Marseille to the train station. There were a few transferred to a loading platform and then onto the train. moments of delay while bribes were paid, and then the cars, labeled with Emergency Vehicle stickers, were

The train moved out with surprising speed, given the slowdown of the previous day.

There's always the danger, Floy thought, that some resistance movement may bomb the train, that we'll all be killed in a final irony by members of *les services*.

She put that thought away. She held Curry's hand and closed her eyes against those motes of sunlight finding their way into the trunk. This was not, she knew, the time to compile a list of catastrophes that could befall them.

Curry's small, sweaty hand was a comfort. Once, she had not been much at touching people. Now she wanted to touch people all the time. She thought of Chambertin's need to touch her. She remembered those lunches at the Ritz, when he helped her into her chair, when his hand grazed hers reaching for salt, for bread. She wondered if she would ever exorcise his ghost from her mind and then she heard Max's voice as he argued with the stationmaster. She thought that maybe she would, with Max's help.

Max was saying that he wanted to stay with his auto to make certain it arrived safely. He was inordinately proud of his old Rolls. But the stationmaster was adamant. "It is far too dangerous to allow you to stay here, monsieur, while the train is in motion. We have rules, still, monsieur. You will ride with the other passengers. And hurry. I have a schedule I must at least attempt to adhere to, monsieur."

As the train pulled out and gathered speed, she felt that irrational fear, that claustrophobia begin to take over again. But Curry began to sing the American songs Louisianne and Billy had taught him when he had barely learned to talk, much less sing.

"All your fears are foolish fancies, baby," he sang in

272

his delicious French accent, emphasizing it because he knew it made her laugh. "You know, *chérie*, that I am in love with you."

"Every cloud must have a silver lining," she sang back to him, playing their old game, tears in her eyes, the fear dispelled. By the time the train, for once not beset by slowdowns, arrived in Perpignan, she had taught Curry to sing "Chattanooga Choo-choo" and his new favorite, "I Don't Want to Set the World on Fire, I Just Want to Start a Flame in Your Heart."

The cars were driven off the special coach onto a ramp and then into a storage area to await transfer to the train headed for Port Bou in Spain.

Two vans, gasogene-powered, waited for them in the storage garage. They carried vegetables, which were to be sent to Germans living in Occupied France by the return train. Half would reach their destination, the other would go on the black market.

The vans pulled out of the station loading area and onto the Boulevard Conflent, following the Tet river east for a time, crossing it on the Pont Joffre, leaving Perpignan behind after a few miles.

The vans stopped and backed into a farmyard stable with open doors, and they all got out. A short, dark woman with gold earrings and a tooth to match stood in the center of the spotless stable—evidently horses had not been housed there for some time—with her hands on her stout hips.

"I am the Red Rose," she said with a great deal of pride, not smiling. "La Rose Rouge. You are in my stable, on my property. My husband does not approve of my activities and keeps away. You must do what I say and you must do it immediately or you will have to leave. I will not sacrifice him for you. I tell you that now, up front."

She smoothed out the fringe of hair she wore on her forehead and held out a strong, calloused hand to Curry.

"I am pleased to meet you, monsieur. You are hungry, I can tell from your face. Come. All of you." She led Curry to the largest of the stalls, where a table had been set up, a cassoulet in a huge orange pot placed in the center.

The pot was steaming, and the odor filled the narrow space.

"Madame," Max began, but Chantil interrupted him, her eyes, hypnotized, on the orange pot.

"Talk later, Max. Let's eat for God's sake."

The Red Rose smiled for the first time, amused. "Yes, eat, monsieur. There will be time to talk afterwards. And be easy. Your guide has arrived. He is up in the house, arguing with my husband. Politics."

She began to spoon cassoulet onto their plates, pointing to white bread and red wine, indicating they should help themselves. She stood leaning against a post, her hands working her apron, a bemused expression on her face, watching them eat, urging Curry on.

Floy hadn't felt so secure since she had left Paris.

Chapter Twenty-six

After that satisfying meal Curry fell asleep in Floy's arms. She carried him to the stall they were to share, putting him down on the mound of soft hay that was to serve as their bed. There were to be no sheets, no personal possessions of any kind. In the event of a *rafle* and a quick exit, the barn would have to look deserted.

"I was in prison one winter," Mme. Rose said. "My husband couldn't live through another episode like that."

The plates were cleared and left outside the side door, where Mme. Rose would pick them up later and carry them to the farmhouse. None of the girls who worked for her were to know who was in the barn. It would be dangerous, she said, for all parties. "The girls in Perpignan all have big mouths."

She stood at the head of the table, rubbing her calloused hands together, smoothing her bangs, attempting to find what she felt would be the "best" words. Then she gave up and spoke in her direct fashion.

"They raided Chez Bégonia this morning an hour or so after you left. La Bégonia has been taken in for 'questioning,' but she had a pill and we think she's dead. We hope she's dead.

"The nuns in the hospital where Colonel Violet was kept have been 'questioned' as well. Sister Iris died during her interrogation. The papal nuncio has made one of his feeble objections, but the hospital has been closed, the patients distributed among the other hospitals in the area. The rest of the nuns are to go on trial in six or seven months, we are told. Of course, by that time there will be considerably fewer to go on trial. Winter in German prisons isn't meant for religious types.

"There have been raids on *les services* throughout the south. Someone is talking. They've been preparing for this, it seems, so someone's been talking for a long time. And it's not a question of a girl with a big mouth. It's someone who knows a great deal. The guess is that the raids have occurred now because the Germans are going to march into Vichy France at any moment and they want as little resistance as possible."

"Does everyone know that the Germans are about to march in?" Sacha asked, amused.

"Everyone."

"Except," Sacha said, "your poor old Sacha and quite possibly the Germans."

"*Les cochons,*" Madame said, spitting on the sawdust floor, looking at Winterhagen, who was sitting still, one of the last of his Gitanes clamped between his teeth. "They've overrun Perpignan. They haven't come here for their annual holiday," Mme. Rose said sharply.

She blew out the three candles on the table, licked her thumb and forefinger, and carefully wetted the wicks. "You must all sleep now, except for you," she said, pointing to Winterhagen, "and you, Colonel Violet," she said, pointing with her long, accusatory finger at Sacha. "We must talk."

Ilone and Chantil went to their stall, like two horses forced to live together despite an incompatibility. They immediately began to argue. Floy lay down next to Curry in the adjoining stall, and because there were so many things she didn't want to think about, listened.

Chantil did not want to leave France. "I want to help," she said, pleading with Ilone for understanding. She had met people in Marseille, important people in *les services*, who thought she could be of use. "I speak German, Ilone."

"Like a Dutchman," Ilone answered in a harsh whisper. "Didn't you listen? They made a *rafle* on Chez Bégonia. La Bégonia is either dead or in a German prison being beaten senseless with a bullwhip. Those people you met, those very important people, are in prison or hiding in the country, without food or warmth. Food, Chantil, I feel I must remind you, is not unimportant to you."

"I want to go back, Ilone."

So Ilone delivered the *coup de grâce*. "You would kill Mama and Papa. If you want to kill Mama and Papa, by all means go back. You have my permission. When I'm sitting *shiva* for them all by myself in some hotel in Portugal, I'll remember you went back to be noble, to save strangers' lives. Yes. By all means. Go back, Chantil."

That went on for some time and afterward there was silence in stall number two and the only sounds were whispers coming from the far side of the barn, where Max, Sacha, and someone else were huddled.

Mme. Rose had waited until the women had gone to their straw beds before opening the side door and letting out a surprisingly shrill whistle, the sort French audiences give when unhappy with a performer.

A few moments later a big, dark youth, tall and gangly, slipped into the barn. He had a long, melancholy face and wore clothes a size or two too small, giving him the look of a child wearing hand-me-downs, a child growing too quickly.

"Cactus. Your guide." Mme. Rose folded her wrinkled hands with their gold rings in front of her bosom, amused by Sacha's expression.

"You? You are Cactus?" he asked disbelievingly. Cactus was responsible for taking hundreds of escapees over the Pyrenees into Spain. He was a Basque shepherd, but Sacha had expected an older man, someone of experience, not this gangling boy. "I've been wanting to meet you for quite some time," Sacha said, exercising his charm, giving his surprising sweet smile.

277

"Why?"

"To thank you."

"You are welcome, Colonel Violet, but I have been—as you have cause to know—well paid." Cactus was immune to charm. He looked at Max. "So. Now it is you who are leaving. I think it is just in time."

Max nodded his agreement. They had worked together often in the past and were evidently friends.

"Where are they?" Cactus asked, and Max led him to the stalls. Cactus took a flashlight from his pocket and shone it into both stalls, letting it play over the Weinbergs' tea gowns and high heels, move slowly over Floy's wooden shoes and Curry's sandals.

"They will never make it," he said, moving away, "never."

"If they were properly outfitted . . ."

"I might let them try," Cactus said in his odd, Catalan-accented French. He turned off the flashlight and looked at Max as if he was disappointed. "I did not expect, Max, a boy and three women, two of whom are not in what I might kindly put as their first youth."

"It is an emergency."

"It is always an emergency, Max." Cactus put his oversized hands in the pockets of his trousers and looked down at his enormous feet clad in climbing boots.

"How much?"

"Twenty-five thousand francs," Cactus said, looking up at Max, smiling.

"Done. Where can I get them outfitted?"

"You might try a fellow Billy used to work with," Sacha said. "He has a little shop in the middle of old Perpignan, just off the Place des Esplanades on the Rue Petite la Real. He is known as Orchid."

"Is he safe?" Max asked Cactus.

"I know the shop. I would wager that he is, though I have never dealt with him. You'd better go with a cover; pretend you are a simple tourist."

"Yes, a simple tourist buying warm clothes and hiking boots for a stroll over the Pyrenees."

"Shopkeepers in Perpignan believe anything of tourists."

"What happens when he asks for my clothes ration card?"

"Give him money," Cactus said. "Get them good boots. Warm coats. It is cold on the Pyrenees in October. But we must cross immediately, before the snows make the crossing impossible."

"What about the patrols?"

"The Germans and their dogs seem to have gone into hibernation for the winter. My last two crossings went without disturbance."

"I am not certain I like that."

"You are too cautious, Winterhagen," Sacha said.

"You think so?"

Max woke the Weinbergs and said that one of them would have to come with him and pretend to be his aunt. "I don't think it will be dangerous, but I offer no insurance, you understand?"

Chantil immediately stood up, but Ilone pulled her down and got up in her place. "You don't look like an aunt," Ilone said. "I do. Besides, it is my turn to be of use." Mme. Rose went to find Ilone wooden shoes and a coat to cover her tea gown.

"I should go," Floy said, coming out of her stall and Sacha laughed.

"Your poor old Sacha has never seen so many volunteers."

"I'm the actress," Floy persisted.

"You're also the best known," Max said. "They've never seen our faces. They might be waiting for yours."

"Take the boy," Cactus said. "Children are good for cover. He can be your son. You are a widower. She," he

279

said, pointing to Ilone, "takes care of the boy. It's his birthday, and you promised him an overnight hike."

"They won't believe that," Floy said.

"No. But if the Gestapo asks, the shopkeeper, Orchid, can say he believed that."

Max looked at Floy. "You'd better take Curry," she said, turning to wake him up. "We must have proper climbing gear."

In the early morning, when Floy woke up, she reached automatically for Curry. When he wasn't there she tried not to panic. Max had said it might take some time, that if Orchid could not be found, they would have to wait in a safe house that Max knew until the shop opened.

I am not going to worry, she said to herself. And there will be peace in our time. She stood up, pulling the blanket Mme. Rose had supplied around her shoulders. It was cold in the unheated barn, but she would have shivered anyway. She thought of Curry gamely going off with Max and Ilone. Before, she had wanted too much for him. Now she only wanted him to be safe and healthy.

As Sacha and Chantil came out of their respective stalls, bits of straw sticking to their clothing, the side door opened. Cactus came in, carrying several heavy brown coats and a canvas bag filled with thick-soled shoes.

"Where did you come up with these?" Sacha asked, examining them. "They look to your poor old Sacha like officers' coats."

"They are. I stole them from the depot in case Max comes up empty-handed. French officers won't be needing them much longer anyway."

"Why not?" a sleepy Chantil wanted to know. She also clutched one of Mme. Rose's blankets around her shoulders.

"When the *Boches* come into unoccupied France, they're going to disband Pétain's army and take all the French soldiers to Germany to work in the factories. They're all going to get double rations when they go, the *Boches* say."

"It's amazing," Sacha said, getting into one of the officers' coats, handing one to Floy, another to Chantil, "how much everyone but poor old Sacha knows of German plans."

Mme. Rose came in with a tray of steaming acorn coffee and large slices of recently baked rye bread.

"I think something's terribly wrong with me," Chantil said. "I'm beginning to like acorn coffee."

Mme. Rose watched as they ate, her arms folded across her large bosom, her one gold tooth glistening while she encouraged them to eat, while she apologized for the lack of butter, honey, jam.

When they had finished, she looked at Floy for a long moment and finally spoke. "You might as well know now. Winterhagen has been taken, along with the boy. It can do you no good to get excited. Mourn them later, when you are on the other side. In the meanwhile, Les Fleurs du Mal will see what we can do for them. You, Colonel Violet," she said, turning to Sacha, "must get to the other side. The entire movement depends on it."

"Who took them?" Floy asked, amazed at how calm she sounded. "Where are they?"

"My sister," Chantil said, looking very white and ill. "Where is my sister? She should never have gone. She was trying to prove how brave she was. She's not brave at all. Where is my sister, Madame Rose?"

Madame looked at Floy and then at Chantil. She sighed. "I will tell you what happened. I don't think it will help but I will tell you."

Max had reconnoitered Orchid's shop, but it had been,

of course, closed. He saw a light in the second-floor apartment and managed to rouse Orchid, who seemed to be what he was supposed to be.

Max, Ilone, and Curry had gone into the shop with him. Orchid said he didn't have enough boots on hand but he knew he could get them from a fellow who kept a shop on the Avenue Gilbert, on the far side of the Citadel.

"Orchid left them in the dark shop. Fifteen minutes later the Gestapo arrived. I don't think Orchid knew who Max was. He thought he was just one more nameless emigré. It seems he habitually gets money from both ends: the emigrés who buy his mountain-climbing boots and the Gestapo when he tips them off.

"He's been clever. He's never turned in anyone whom *les services* was interested in. He was afraid of reprisals. Now, of course, he has good reason to be."

"Where are they now?" Floy asked again.

"Winterhagen and the boy are at Gestapo headquarters. They've taken over the Hotel de la Tour. A big cheese, a French traitor, has them. He has a Hispano-Suiza and wears smoked glasses, even at night. My niece is a secretary for the Prefecture. The Prefect is in love with her. He tells her everything." Mme. Rose for a moment was lost in contemplation of that romance. "She gives him absolutely nothing."

"We must go as soon as it is dark," Cactus said. "Let us hope Max can hold out until then."

"Max won't talk," Chantil said.

"He will. Why do you think they took the boy to Gestapo headquarters. It's an old *Boche* trick. First they'll work on Max to soften him up. Then they'll begin to work on the boy. Max will talk."

"I'd like to borrow a shawl, madame," Floy said. Without a word Mme. Rose gave her the black shawl she was wearing. Floy draped it over her head and stepped into Chantil's discarded high-heeled shoes. She used Chantil's compact mirror to apply her film star makeup with a surprisingly steady hand.

"Listen to your poor old Sacha," Sacha said. "It won't do any good. You'll wind up in prison yourself. They won't hurt Curry. They couldn't."

"They could," Floy said, handing the lipstick and the compact carefully—she was being very careful—to Chantil. "He could."

She asked Madame to tell her how to get to the Hotel de la Tour, and Madame gave her directions and a warning. There weren't many strangers in Perpignan. Floy didn't want to be picked up en route.

"If I'm not back by dark, go on without me," Floy said to Sacha. "It is you who are important. I couldn't leave without Curry. Or Max."

She left, and they were all quiet for a long moment until Chantil said, "But if Curry and Max are with the Gestapo, where is Ilone? Where is my sister?"

Madame looked at Sacha and then at Cactus, who turned away, busying himself with the canvas bag filled with officers' boots.

"They shot her," Mme. Rose said finally. "The *sales Boches* shot her when she tried to keep them from taking the boy. He had begun to cry when they started screaming at him, waving their guns at him. Your sister picked him up in her arms and began to run. She got nearly a block before they caught up with her. They pulled the boy out of her arms and then they shot her. They wanted the boy, you see. Now sit down. I'm going to give you some brandy . . ."

"She never wanted to be a heroine," Chantil said, the tears rolling over her plump cheeks. "She hadn't even wanted to leave Holland. All she wanted was to be quiet."

She drank the brandy too quickly and began to cough. When she recovered, she went to lay down in the stall. She was back almost immediately. "What will they do with her body?" she asked Mme. Rose. "Ilone would have wanted a traditional Jewish burial, you understand?"

"I understand," Mme. Rose said, putting her arms around Chantil, holding her close. "I will try to find out where they bury her. After the war we can all rebury our dead."

Chapter Twenty-seven

Floy thought of Auntie Rose, who needed her morning walk. For digestive purposes. Floy had walked some four miles, across the Pont Joffre over the Tet river, and she too felt she had needed her walk.

For digestive purposes. There was no Billy or Sacha or Max to help now. She had to create her own role, devise her own dialogue, nuances. She was the star, the director, the producer. She took one of Billy's deep Hindu breaths, but for once it didn't help. This performance would succeed or fail—she refused to think of the odds—on her strength.

There weren't many people about, and fewer cars. She turned into the maze of medieval streets that all seemed to end at Perpignan's fourteenth-century Loge de Mer, lost her way several times, but finally found the Hotel de la Tour where Mme. Rose said it would be.

She wasn't at all tired. She didn't even think of her feet squeezed into Chantil's wide, short shoes. "I've energy to spare," she said, again echoing Auntie Rose, realizing that for the first time in a long while she was thinking in English.

The hotel was a large, square building of old red brick, dotted with cast-iron balconies. A banner advertising Pétain's substitute for Liberty, Equality, Fraternity hung from a third-floor pole: Work, Country, Family. A small and for once discreet German flag flew over the banner.

A familiar black Hispano-Suiza with Paris plates and

swastika hood-ornament stood in front of the hotel entrance, taking up most of the narrow, cobblestoned street. The car was highly polished, meticulously waxed. The hotel suffered in comparison with all that gloss.

Even the thought of Chambertin desperately trying to make love to her in the back of that car didn't stop her for a moment. She pushed the memory away angrily.

Appropriately, Rivet stood facing the street, propped up against the fender. He wore his soiled white suit and worked a toothpick around his small, yellow teeth, almost the same shade of tobacco-yellow as his narrow strip of mustache. His new fedora, now more gray than white, had been pushed to the back of his head as he earnestly manipulated the toothpick.

She nearly greeted him. It was as if she were unexpectedly coming upon an old friend not seen for too long a time. She almost felt affection, pity, for him. She felt as if she had known him for a lifetime.

As usual, he didn't see her. His narrow, yellow eyes were focused on a second-floor window in the opposite building, where a young girl was typing away at an ancient machine.

Discarding Mme. Rose's shawl, holding her head high, assuming a movie-star hauteur, she walked past the Gestapo guards standing like bronzed book ends on either side of the tiled entrance.

She could hear the click-click-click of Chantil's spiked heels as she moved across the tiled floor and she knew she was frightened. But she put that fear away—she had no choice—as she approached the concierge.

Behind him on the wall was another Nazi flag, the center of an arrangement of photographs featuring Hitler and Pétain. The hotel had been taken over, swallowed whole by the Nazis.

Floy took her time, looking around the lobby with distaste, ignoring the soldiers who guarded the elevator, the entrance to the dining room, the staircase. For the first time she noticed the belts all the German soldiers wore. They were broad, made of leather, and held together by round brass buckles on which was inscribed, "*Gott mit uns.*"

"I have an appointment with Monsieur Chambertin," Floy said to the concierge as if he wasn't there. He wore his hair in a greasy pompadour. "Which room is he in, please?"

The concierge wasn't certain what line to take. He equivocated. "I am afraid Monsieur Chambertin has asked not to be disturbed."

"You will be very sorry," Floy said in a perfectly audible, conversational voice, "if you do not disturb him. Immediately. In fact," she went on, lowering her voice only a little, "I can promise that you will."

She looked around the lobby again as if bored, refusing to let herself be frightened by those soldiers with their God-blessed belt-buckles and their cropped hair. She turned back to the concierge, whose forehead had gone red and his cheeks white.

"Very well, madame. I will put through a call to his suite. Who shall I say is calling?"

It would have been better, she knew, if she had been able to walk into his suite—Chambertin and his suites— unannounced. But the concierge had won a round. She was forced to say, "Mademoiselle Devon. Floy Devon."

He took a new, efficient-looking telephone from below his desk and held the receiver very close to his mouth. His hands shook. Chambertin would not be indulgent of service personnel's little errors.

He had a hoarse, whispered conversation and then after a pause a somewhat less whispered conversation. And then, smiling, using his flaccid hand to wipe the perspiration from his forehead, he said, "Mademoiselle may go up. I am sorry for the inconvenience, but you understand . . ."

She left him explaining and looked at the elevator

cage. It was gilded and small, manned by another Gestapo *manqué*, a French boy in hotel livery with a photograph pin of Hitler in his lapel.

She turned and walked up the majestic staircase—a leftover from the hotel's previous incarnation—climbing one flight of marble stairs. The elevator would have been too quick, too claustrophobic. She would have been distracted by the lapel pin. She needed all her concentration.

At the far end of the corridor stood a genuine German soldier. He was tall, husky, and there was a country boy's snarl on his face. As she walked toward him, Floy thought that stupidity must be a prime requisite for Gestapo guards. She felt she had to demean him in order not to be intimidated as he waited for her silently at the end of the red and white corridor.

She knew she couldn't afford to be intimidated. If it were only her life, her body, then she could have allowed herself that terrible luxury, fear. There was no question of being afraid now. She wouldn't let herself.

I am not playing a role, she told herself. I am a strong-willed, cynical woman, not even a little noble, coming to arrange a deal, an exchange, profitable to me.

She remembered Billy teaching her how to act in that studio on the Boulevard Richard Lenoir. And she thought of him, his head chopped off by a Nazi axe, carefully propped up by Nazi propaganda experts who were just doing their job.

She remembered Louisianne leaving the mayor's brick house in that supposedly safe village, her bandaged hands in front of her, not allowing them to help her down the steps.

It was a long corridor. It took all those memories, all her resolve, not to turn and run, not to stop, paralyzed, midway.

Not once did she allow herself to think of Curry or Max or the solace of their embraces. She knew she couldn't afford that comfort either. She had to get down to the business at hand.

I am brave now, she told herself. Far braver than that girl who left Philadelphia with a bun in the oven. Far braver than the neurotic woman who left Paris to escape a hotel-prison in the Vosges.

She felt, perhaps for the first time ever, that she finally knew who she was. Such a long and difficult maturing process, such a painful *rite de passage*.

She put her hand to her chest and found the emerald Louisianne had given her and saved for her, and then the dumb giant at the end of the corridor stood up, opened the door behind him, and directed her to another door, which led to one of the rooms that made up Chambertin's suite.

He had been waiting for her, but it seemed clear to Floy that he wasn't prepared. He stared at her with that not quite sane obsessive stare of his from behind his blue-lensed glasses. He still needed her.

He tried a smile, but it was too thin. He was still pretty but he appeared to be less boyish. He seemed, now, less whole—unformed, like a cake that hadn't been cooked long enough and had begun to come apart.

He held out his long, thin, blue-white hand, and Floy took it for just a moment, fighting back nausea, winning. He held her hand too long, and she could feel how cold, how lifeless it was. She realized in time that this was more difficult for him then it was for her.

He dropped her hand suddenly, as if it had burned him, and took a step back, taking off the blue smoked glasses. His nearly white irises looked transparent. They held that hard, neurotic look of desire she remembered too well. He would come away from those frustrating lunches at the Ritz wearing it, as if he was never to be satisfied, always hungry.

That unquenchable need for her wasn't flattering. It

wasn't Floy Devon he was obsessed with. It was a celluloid image, some terrible, unreal fantasy he had created and transferred onto her.

It was clear Chambertin wanted her as badly as before. Perhaps more so. He so very much believed he needed her. He was like an out-of-control adolescent finally in a room alone with his sex object.

It was what Floy had counted on.

Chapter Twenty-eight

"You don't look nearly as chic as you once did, Floy."
With an enormous, visible effort, he was controlling
himself. She could still feel the intensity of his desire,
nearly smell it. But Chambertin was ignoring it, attempting to put it away—like a housewife with an unexpected
guest, trying to shut the door on a closet filled beyond
capacity.

He had carefully closed the door behind her and was
resting his boy's hips on an old, large desk that took up
too much of the room, so much less *luxe* then he was
used to.

He had replaced the smoked glasses. But his voice
and his hands, grasping the edge of the desk, betrayed
his anxiety.

She felt, at that moment, nearly sorry for him. "I see
you've brought along all the necessities," she said, avoiding the door that led to the other room of the suite,
attempting a nonchalance she didn't feel.

There was Chambertin's Stavisky hat and the black
greatcoat he wore even in the warmest weather, spread
across a chair like an ornament. The blue Schmeisser,
beautiful and cold, lay behind him in the center of the
desk.

The room was permeated with the perfume of his
black soap, as if he had continually washed his hands in
the basin in the far corner. He lit a cigarette, an
Abdullah, and held it as if it were a delicate surgical
instrument.

"I try to travel with as little discomfort as possible," he said, avoiding looking at her, more in control.

There was silence. She tried to listen for sounds from the other room. Chambertin ground out the cigarette and looked at her through his blue smoked glasses, unable not to.

"You're more beautiful, Floy. Not nearly as smart, but life on the run seems to have appealed to you." It was as if he were taking stock of an expensive animal, one he hoped with all his heart to buy from a not-to-be-trusted trainer. "You're thinner but somehow more sensual. Now you could have an important screen career. Men would pay anything to see you."

She smiled and moved a step closer. Over the mantel hung a German flag. There's too much red in that flag, Floy thought. Too much blood surrounds that twisted *hakenkreuz*. She put her hand out and for the first time since she had known him voluntarily touched him. "I thought I might make you an offer, Chambertin."

He didn't say anything. He stood in front of his Nazi flag and looked down at her hand touching the fine cashmere of his jacket sleeve.

She moved her hand up to his shoulder and looked into his eyes. "I promise to stay with you for as long as you like, Chambertin. I'll do whatever you wish. I'll be whatever you want me to be. When you are finished, you can dispose of me as you like. *If* you let them go. I am asking you—I am begging you—to let them go."

He stared down at her as if now he would quite literally eat her. As if he were a starving animal and his prey—a meal that would save his life—was only inches away.

He kissed her, forcing her mouth open, holding her close so that she could feel how excited he was, how much his boy's body needed her.

With an enormous effort he pushed her away. He

laughed, but it wasn't his usual laugh. It was too high, too musical.

"Don't you realize," he said when he could, "that I have you now? That you've given yourself to me by coming here? That I can do with you whatever I want, and if you think you won't comply, I know otherwise. I know new tricks now, Floy.

"You're trying to make a deal, Floy, with currency that has lost its value." He saw her look at the Schmeisser and laughed again, this time with more conviction.

"You are not the sort of pet who kills people, Floy. You're the sort who goes meekly to the slaughter, sticking her own head in the noose, as you are doing now."

He lit another Abdullah, his hands still shaking as he held it. "Toward the end your aunt, Louisianne—such a curious name, such a curious woman—would sometimes black out and talk of rabbits. *Mes lapins.* But we were more interested in flowers.

"She told us all, finally. She gave you all away. Le Levandou. La Bégonia. The fact that you were headed for Perpignan. It wasn't easy and it took such a long time and a certain amount of skill. But in the end she told us everything. She took her own life then. Guilt, one assumes. Shame, perhaps. You wouldn't believe it, but some grow to like the questioning. To need the stimulation."

"I don't believe any of it."

"How do you think we learned of those sisters of mercy harboring Colonel Violet? Or about that safe garage in Nice? We could have picked you all up long ago, but it seemed easier, neater, to clean up after you, to wait for you here in Perpignan. It's been dull, I don't mind telling you. We've had to import our own distractions. Come and look. I've been handling this one myself."

He crossed the room and opened the door that led to

293

the other room, holding it open for her with mock courtesy. It was bare. The carpets, the furniture, the drapes, had been removed, the windows painted black. In the center of the room under a harsh spotlight, tied to a chair much too large for him, was Curry. He looked unharmed. His eyes were tightly closed. Floy couldn't tell if he was sleeping or merely blotting out the spotlight. He looked so vulnerable tied to that chair.

"Of course, we're waiting for more sophisticated equipment before we work on the boy." Chambertin stood in front of her, moving into the room ahead of her, keeping her from Curry.

Then she saw Max. He was also tied to a chair, nude, his head on his chest. Chambertin held Max's head by the hair, forcing him to open his eyes. He looked at Floy and then at Chambertin with his black eyes but he wouldn't say anything.

"A great hero, your Winterhagen," Chambertin said. "He won't be such a hero when he sees what we do to the boy." With the tip of his handmade shoe Chambertin touched the large toe on Max's right foot where the nail had been pried off. "Oh, we've only just begun. He has so much to tell us. In the morning, when our German friends return, we will start working seriously on the child. Have you ever seen a live animal skinned?" Chambertin asked, staring down at Max. "It is one of the less appealing sights . . ."

He turned around, missing Floy. She was standing in the doorway, holding the blue Schmeisser. He laughed a genuine Chambertin laugh. "Put it down, Floy. You don't suppose I'd be foolish enough to leave a loaded gun around, do you?"

He took a step toward her, reaching for the Schmeisser with his grasping hands, and Floy shot him, aiming for the gold swastika he wore in his jacket lapel, missing it, hitting his heart.

They were both surprised. He fell to the floor on both knees comically, one hand to his heart, like a suitor in an old play. "Floy . . ." he said, and then he fell over onto the floor, his hand still to his heart, his knees up in a fetal position.

Just like in the movies, Floy thought, wondering if now she was going to lose control, if she was going to scream or faint. She did neither.

"Do you need me, *mein Herr*?" the soldier tentatively asked from the corridor in German. He had heard the shot, smelled the cordite.

"*Nein,*" Max answered, calling out in Chambertin's voice and French-accented German. "I am teaching the prisoner new tricks."

"*Jawohl, mein Herr,*" the soldier said, and they could hear him take his seat in the corridor, amused, reassured.

"Put a towel under him," Max told her, not giving her time to fall apart. "We don't want blood seeping out under the door." He spoke to her in French, in a low, conversational voice—in Chambertin's voice. He knew the soldier's French was nonexistent.

She forced herself to move, to go into the other room, to take the towels from the basin, to put them against Chambertin's body.

One part of her mind focused on how much blood there was, at how round and dark the bullet hole in his chest had become. On how suddenly, irrevocably dead he was.

The other part of her mind was shut off like a water faucet. Eventually she would have to turn it on. Later. Later she would have to think, to feel. Now she had only to move.

The towel had Chambertin's monogram embroidered on it. It was oversized, thick, and smelled of his black soap. It sopped up most of the blood.

Floy stood up, avoiding Chambertin's face. She started

to go to Curry, but Max interrupted her. "Untie me first," he said, as if he were telling her he loved her, using Chambertin's staccato style of speaking.

She did as she was told. She was, she knew, afraid to untie Curry. Afraid that he was badly hurt, afraid that he was dead. If he was dead, she knew she would lose control: scream, shout, try to kill the automaton guarding the door.

"Murmur endearments," Max directed her. "You are teasing me. Remember, you are a delicious little piece, and I am going to have you sooner or later." He winced as she undid the ropes, which left deep marks around his biceps, his wrists, his calves. He stood up and swayed for a moment, reaching out, putting a hand on her shoulder for support.

Steadying himself, he said, "Untie Curry. Try not to let him speak. He's fine. He's tired and shocked but he's not been hurt." He let his hand rest on her shoulder for a moment and then moved away. "We must be quick."

She thanked God she didn't have to plan, she didn't have to think. Max was taking care of all that. She bent down and undid Curry's ropes. They weren't as tight as Max's. As she undid the rope around his ankles, his eyes opened, he looked at her, and he screamed. It was a terrible scream for a mother to hear. It came from the center of his being and it rocked both of them. She held him to her and soothed him.

"*Mein Herr?*" the guard, startled in spite of himself, called out.

"Fun with the boy," Max said in German, leaning into the room so that his voice would be in the right place. "*Nicht wahr?*"

"Come in here," Max told Floy and Curry in French.

She carried Curry into the other room, stepping carefully over Chambertin's body, not looking down, keeping Curry's face in her neck. He was shivering, and she knew it wasn't from cold.

"Mommy's here," she whispered to him. "It's all right now, darling. Mommy's here."

But he opened his eyes as she walked into the other room, before she was able to shut the door, and saw Chambertin's body banked by bloody, monogramed towels, and he screamed again. They could hear the guard chuckling to himself loud enough to make a good impression on Herr Chambertin.

"You're going to be all right," she said, holding him, cradling him as if he were a baby, kicking the door closed behind her.

"Of course he is," Max said in a no-nonsense voice. "You have to help us, Curry. We need you. Can you help us?"

"Yes, Max." He stopped shivering and got himself out of Floy's arms.

"You're all right?" she asked, not wanting to let go of him.

"Of course he's all right," Max said. "He's going to help us." Max was going through Chambertin's desk. He found his passport, his *Ausweis*, his orders signed by the *Kommandant* in Paris. "We need you, Curry."

"Are we going to get out of this, Max?" Curry asked in a small voice.

"Yes. Herr Chambertin is going to help us." He put all the papers in a leather portfolio he had found and suddenly sat down in the desk chair.

They both looked at him, surprised. "I am sorry to say that now you two will have to help me get dressed. I don't seem to be able to do it myself."

Floy turned to go back into the other room where she had seen Max's clothes, but he reached out and stopped her. "No, Floy. You and Curry are going to have to help me dress in Chambertin's clothes."

It took nearly half an hour.

"We have a little time," Max said, and she saw the

bruises on his body, dark-blue circles covering his chest, his arms, his legs. "The soldier thinks we are either making love or torturing the boy. We have plenty of time. It would look suspicious if we left too quickly."

He allowed Curry to help him with Chambertin's shirt but he let it blouse out so as not to have it touch his skin. He didn't say anything when Curry helped him into the trousers, but Floy could see that his eyes watered and his hands grasped the chair for a moment.

The worst were his feet. He put on two pairs of Chambertin's socks quickly, one on top of the other, to muffle the pain, to stop the blood. He looked straight ahead of him, but the tears of pain now spilled over.

"Max is crying, Mama," Curry said, looking as if he would, too.

"It's my turn," Max said. "Now please, Curry, help me into his boots." They were soft boots, a city man's idea of countrymen's footwear. They look about as rural, Floy thought, as the Rue de la Paix.

Slowly Max stood up and practiced walking. "Painful?" she asked.

"What do you think? But it will be all right."

He put on the Stavisky hat, and she draped the greatcoat over his shoulders. He hesitated for a moment.

"What is it?"

"I am afraid I will need his glasses," Max said, knowing how much she would hate going back into that other room. "I would go myself, but the less I walk . . ."

She forced herself to open the door. It was easier than she thought. Chambertin looked unreal, a wax figure curled up. She bent down. Already a different perfume— of blood and death—had supplanted that of the black soap. She removed the blue smoked glasses and pulled back. She hadn't expected his eyes to be open. They seemed now completely white, translucent. She reached over and closed them, because as hard as that was, it would be much more difficult living with the thought of them open, haunting her forever with that unsatiated lust.

They left the suite, Curry between them. Speaking Chambertin's pedantic German, wearing the Stavisky hat and the blue glasses, walking quite naturally, Max made a perfect Chambertin. Floy thought that even she would have been fooled.

In Chambertin's voice he told the soldier not to disturb the prisoner until morning. "When the new equipment arrives, when the specialists come, he will either change his mind or lose it." The soldier smiled appreciatively from ear to ear.

The boy, Max told him, was of no use. He was personally going to give him to the authorities to make certain he was shipped off to a work camp in the east. "The *gnädige Fräulein* and I are going to spend the night in less lugubrious circumstances, *nicht wahr?*"

The soldier put an appropriate smirk on his earnest, plain face.

"This could never happen in Germany," Max whispered in Floy's ear, as if he were making an improper remark, grabbing her arm, pulling her to him. "He's been in France too long." She laughed a little, lowering her eyes. He patted her rear appreciatively, for the soldier's benefit.

Curry, as instructed, kept a little away from them, as if he had already been discarded. The elevator operator kept his eyes on the machinery through what seemed an endless ride.

Max said in German that the operator needed a bath, and Floy said in French, "You mustn't say such things, Herr Chambertin."

She tried not to look at Curry standing in front of her, his little shoulders held back and his head held high because Max had said he had to be a good soldier.

299

She thought that if this were not the performance of Max's career, it certainly was of hers.

"March," Max ordered Curry, prodding him in the back, and Curry walked across the lobby in front of them quickly.

Max, using Chambertin's measured steps, followed, his arm draped around Floy's shoulder, the greatcoat around his. The matched sets of soldiers came to attention as they passed between them, their hands striking out, Heil Hitlers reverberating around the room.

Rivet, toothpick in place, raised a nearly nonexistent eyebrow at the sight of Floy and Curry. But he knew from past experience not to question his Chambertin. His eyes on Floy, he opened the rear door for the three of them.

Coughing, as if he had something caught in his throat, Max directed Rivet out the Avenue Grande Bretagne and over the Pont Joffre to the Avenue de Bompas.

As Rivet drove, Max carefully removed his right boot, closing his eyes for a moment. Then he handed Floy a very cold, obscene thing. She stared at it for a long moment. The blue steel Schmeisser.

"Stop the car," Max ordered when they reached the relative obscurity of the Avenue de Bompas. "She'll ride in front."

Rivet pulled the Hispano-Suiza to the side of the dark road, turning to complain. "Something's not right here," he started to say, but Floy had already gotten into the front seat with him and had put the Schmeisser next to his ribs.

Rivet looked at Floy with a droll expression, as if he were about to ask her how could she? She forced herself to reach into the soiled jacket of his suit, removing his revolver, handing it to Max. And then she reached down and removed the knife Rivet carried in a leather holster strapped to his thin, hairless ankle.

"Drive," Max said, resuming his own voice, directing

Rivet to the farmhouse. "Don't think you won't die if you decide to make trouble. We would like to kill you."

Rivet said he didn't want to die and he wasn't going to make trouble. He had a thin, oily voice. Floy realized she had never heard him speak before.

Without thinking, she reached over and broke the toothpick he held between his tiny yellow teeth. Only then did she feel he had been completely disarmed.

Max had Rivet park the Hispano-Suiza behind the barn; its elegant curves faded into the dark. Floy and Curry followed as Max marched Rivet into Mme. Rose's former stable.

A red-eyed Chantil, wearing a French army officer's overcoat and shoes, jumped up when they entered. She hugged Floy and Curry to her, tears coming into her eyes. "I am so glad," she said, choking on her tears and her words. "I am so very, very glad."

"The boy must eat," Mme. Rose declared, getting him out of Chantil's grasp. "Is he all right?" she asked Floy, looking at Curry carefully.

"I'm fine," he said, and Floy thought that he might be. "But I am hungry, Madame Rose." She took his hand in her calloused one and led him to the table, where a pot of beef stew sat. Sacha, who had been eating, patted Curry's head and stood up, embracing Floy.

"Your poor old Sacha knew you would be all right," he said. "I just knew it."

"How did you know?" Max asked, and then turned away, bringing Rivet into the dim light cast by the single candle.

Cactus, the Basque guide, uncurled himself from a dark corner. "We were just about to leave. Who is this one?"

"A traitor," Sacha said unexpectedly.

"You are the traitor, monsieur," Rivet answered, his tobacco-yellow eyes open wide with fear and something else. Anger, Floy thought. Sacha punched him in the mouth and then again, and they could hear an odd, hollow, cracking noise as Rivet's nose broke.

"Come," Sacha said to Cactus. "Let's take care of him right away. We can't leave him behind."

"Stop," Floy said, but Sacha grabbed Rivet by the neck of his filthy jacket and dragged him to the door. Cactus followed. Rivet started to shout something at Floy, but Sacha—Sacha?—hit him in the mouth again. They dragged him out, bleeding over that awful suit, and Floy felt irrationally, overwhelmingly sorry for that little Parisian gutter rat.

There was one more muffled shout as Sacha held Rivet and the Basque boy, Cactus, strangled him.

Floy looked at Max, but he turned away. She went to Curry, who had been shielded from the scene by Chantil's and Mme. Rose's broad backs. They were both encouraging him to eat.

Chapter Twenty-nine

Chantil, wrapped in her new French officer's overcoat, was helped into the huge Hispano-Suiza trunk. "I'm spending my war in the trunks of luxury cars," she said. She had kissed Mme. Rose, who had promised again to find out where they had buried Ilone. Mme. Rose very carefully did not tell her about the unmarked mass graves, the impossibility—because of the sheer numbers —of finding Ilone's last resting place. After the war (if there was an after the war: Madame was beginning to doubt that), there would be time for such confidences.

Cactus picked up Curry and placed him next to Chantil.

"You'll be all right?" Floy asked, not wanting to leave him.

"I shall teach Mademoiselle Chantil American songs."

"Not too loud."

"In a whisper," Curry said, and then the lid was put down and locked.

Mme. Rose had found a cap in her son's room that transformed Sacha into a chauffeur again. "Chantil is always in the trunk and your poor old Sacha is always at the wheel." He embraced Mme. Rose. "I will return the cap."

"He doesn't need it anymore," Madame said dryly. He had been killed by the Germans early on for helping escapees over the Pyrenees.

Max, directing everyone's movements, got himself, with difficulty, into the back of the limousine. Floy, wearing Madame's shawl, got in after him.

"*Après la guerre*," Madame said, "you will come back with the boy. Then I will demonstrate for you what a cook I am." She took Floy's hand and held it. "Look after that boy. Such a good boy."

She turned and went back to her stable to remove the evidence of their stay, to make certain that the earth over Rivet's grave was properly packed. "At least, after the war," Mme. Rose said, "we'll know where that one is buried."

Cactus remained with the car for a moment. "So you are not," he said, standing at the rear window, talking to Max, "walking over the Pyrenees after all."

"I couldn't walk over the Pont Royal," Max said, putting out his hand, shaking the guide's.

"You want your money back?"

"Credit it to the next group coming through."

"They'll stop you at the border."

"I have an excellent *Ausweis*."

"Better stay here, recover, and walk across."

"I'll get through. I have insurance."

Sacha started the car, and it moved off, leaving Cactus in the road, looking his age for once, young and a little sad. He hadn't really wanted Max to leave.

Sacha drove back through Perpignan and took the Avenue d'Argelès to Route 114, the coastal road. Floy held Max's hand. His black eyes were closed, his black doll's lashes lay against his pale skin. He's too still, Floy thought, and she put her head next to his to make certain he was breathing, as she used to do with Curry when he was a baby.

When she felt reassured, she turned to look at the coastal road. There were no other cars, no lights in the villages or in the farmhouses, the blackout being strictly enforced this close to the sea and the border.

There was a quarter-moon, and by its light she could sometimes catch glimpses of the Mediterranean. It was too blue, too calm in Monaco. Now it seemed black and infinite. She felt curiously alert and not at all despondent, just another fancy-free murderess escaping across the border into Spain.

At Argelès a sign in French, German, and Spanish alerted all drivers that the road was closed to civilian traffic. Max opened his eyes and told Sacha to take a right at a closed inn. There was a rough back road that led to Le Boulou, where they could pick up Route 9.

They drove through the Pyrenees, using the new tunnel the Germans had built so that supplies coming from Spain could reach Germany quickly.

At the far end of the tunnel Sacha spoke for the first time. "The border patrol is just ahead. Perhaps you should wake Max up."

"Max is awake," Max said, opening his eyes, staring past Sacha at a new concrete structure a mile ahead. Four guards stood under the glare of yellow lights, wearing crisp new uniforms, waiting for them.

"We won't get through," Floy thought, suddenly certain of it. In her mind's eye she saw them opening the trunk, getting Curry . . .

"You handle this, Colonel Violet," Max said. "You hand them the papers." He gave Sacha Chambertin's *Ausweis* and his passport, along with forged papers for Sacha and Floy. 'Let them get a good look at you, Colonel. There won't be any problem. You have a nice, honest face."

Max was too calm, more as if he was returning to a tedious business after an unsatisfactory vacation than as if he was escaping from the Gestapo.

The size and expense of the car, coupled with the Paris

license and the swastika hood-ornament, impressed the guards. They stood a little straighter as the car stopped. They saluted. The most senior detached himself and self-consciously marched to the car.

Floy tightened her grip on Max's hand as the guard, impressed but intent on doing his job, said, "Everyone out of the car, please."

Floy began to get out, but Max held her back. "Give him the papers." Sacha got out of the car and, Mme. Rose's son's hat in hand, gave the guard the passports, the *Ausweis*.

The guard examined them and then, startled, looked at Sacha and attempted to see into the dark back of the Hispano-Suiza. "One moment, please." He moved off quickly, forgetting to march, to confer with the other guards.

Max opened the rear window and put his head out. He wore the Stavisky hat, the blue smoked glasses. "I am in a great hurry," he said. "You are impeding the business of the Vichy State. I want all your names on a sheet of paper, immediately, along with your ranks and serial numbers."

The senior guard jumped to attention at the certain sound of authority in Max's voice. "I must place a call, Monsieur Chambertin. I have no orders . . ."

"Then do so."

Max closed the window while the guard disappeared into the border building. Two German soldiers, officers, came out to stare at the car and its occupants. They seemed less easily daunted. "Here already," Max said. "The rumors of German occupation of the south seem to have arrived after the fact, don't you think, Colonel?"

Before Sacha could answer, the French guard—his demeanor oddly altered, as if he was now less impressed —returned to the car.

Sacha rolled down his window. The guard looked at him and then into the back of the car and seemed about to smile. "You are free to move on," he said, after too long a pause, so Floy thought they weren't free at all. He handed the documents back to Sacha while two lower-ranking soldiers removed the barriers.

Sacha started the car, and Floy closed her eyes. She waited for the bullets, the sudden command to halt, the warning that they were all under arrest.

None of that ever came. The soldiers saluted, the Hispano-Suiza—Chambertin's Hispano-Suiza—drove unmolested across the border and on to Spain.

Sacha pulled to the side of the road and helped Chantil and Curry out of the trunk. Curry was asleep, and Sacha laid him carefully in Floy's arms.

"He sings beautifully," Chantil whispered, getting into the front seat with Sacha. "But his 'Chattanooga Choo-choo' needs work." She looked around her, her plump face creased and dirty from the trunk. "Are we in Spain?"

"Nearly," Max answered.

Sacha drove the last mile leading to the Spanish border. There was a great deal of ripped-up paper on that last stretch of road, looking at first like snow and then like the aftermath of a Fifth Avenue ticker-tape parade.

"French passports," Max explained. "The French rip up their papers before entering Spain. They all claim they're French Canadians so they won't be sent back. Most of them are sent back."

A tall, gray-white stone monument marked the border. On one side was carved the word "France"; on the other, "España."

The Hispano stalled just a few feet into Spain. Chantil suddenly began to cry, repeating her sister's name several times. Floy thought of Louisianne.

And then they were arrested by the Spanish police.

Spain, 1942

Chapter Thirty

The little band of Spanish militia, dark-skinned and very young, wore pressed uniforms. Pro-Fascist, they were bored with refugees with either no papers or suspicious ones.

Only the Hispano-Suiza and Floy's American passport, miraculously produced by Max, gave them pause for a moment, and it wasn't a very long moment.

The Hispano-Suiza was started, and one of the militiamen took the wheel, following his compatriot's prewar Fiat into a small, filthy town that didn't seem to have a name. The driver wasn't talking.

They were all herded into a police station lit by one light bulb. The glass in the windows had been broken during the Civil War and not replaced. Though it was the middle of the night, what seemed like the entire population had come out to look in the broken windows at the rich refugees, always a source of entertainment.

A motherly-looking man gave Curry a glass of milk that didn't smell as well as it might. He drank it anyway, sitting on a wooden bench, staring at the dark faces staring at him. He seemed to be enjoying himself.

Curry is my son, Floy explained carefully in rusty Spanish. *"Mi hijo."* The dignitary, the only fat man in the village, scratched at a boil under his chin, unimpressed. Still, she went on. Max was her husband. Sacha, her brother. Chantil, his wife. She was taking them all to America on her passport.

The dignitary ordered a beer, which made Floy want one more than anything else, but he wasn't offering. She stood up, but one of the soldiers stood in front of her, indicating she should sit down.

"What the hell are you two doing?" she shouted at Max and Sacha, "sitting on that bench, not saying a word, when any minute we might be sent back to . . ."

Max took her hand and pulled her down beside him, suggesting she should rest. The people at the windows looked on with unwavering interest.

The motherly man—who, it turned out, was a police-man whose uniform had been stolen—gave Curry an odd, elongated doughnut sort of cake. Curry offered to share it, but only Chantil, guilty-faced, took him up on it.

"I'm starving," she said, making a funny face when she bit into the hard dough. "Simply starving."

An hour or so later one of the original militiamen placed a yellowed piece of paper in front of the fat of-ficial, who had gone through half a dozen beers. The official's face turned red and then he left the police sta-tion without saying a word.

He returned an hour later, just when the crowd was getting bored and Floy had gone to sleep, to lead an escort of half a dozen soldiers. They flanked Floy, Max, Curry, Sacha, and Chantil as they were marched across the square to what Floy was certain to be a Spanish prison. Billy had talked about Spanish prisons.

It looked like a Spanish prison, but it turned out to be the town's hotel. It too had no glass in its windows.

They were escorted into a long, low room lit by kero-sene lamps. A new dignitary, stately, his arms crossed over his chest, was waiting for them.

He was of course not Spanish, but Floy was so tired and confused that it took her some time to realize it. He waited until the fat man in the blue suit had left with his militiamen before he looked at Max. "You took your

312

bloody time," he said in upper class Anglo-English French. "We had given up."

"The Gestapo isn't exactly handing out exit visas."

This new dignitary, thin and wearing a beautifully cut pale linen suit, shrugged his elegant shoulders and stood up, handing Max a dark leather envelope. "Your passport and the money. As requested. You'd better count it. When you have, will you sign this, please? Payment received. Merchandise recovered."

Max didn't open the leather envelope. He signed the sheet of paper and turned away. The Englishman looked at his thin gold watch, glanced at the paper Max had signed, and handed it back to him. "And here," he said, pointing to another line wearily.

He stood up. "Mademoiselle Weinberg," he said in French to Chantil. She was having trouble keeping her eyes open. The smell of the kerosene, the low-ceilinged room made her sleepy. "You are to be transported to Lisbon, where your parents are waiting for you." She opened her eyes, now alert. "Immediately. There is a van outside which will take you to a train. You may make it, but only if you hurry."

Chantil kissed Curry, shook hands with Sacha and Max, and then embraced Floy, enfolding her in her plump arms. She told Floy the name of the hotel in New York where her parents would more than likely be staying—"They always stay there and it's always dull"—and said if there was anything she could do . . .

"Mademoiselle Weinberg," the Englishman said, rubbing the bridge of his nose between his forefinger and thumb, "you must hurry unless you want to spend the night in the railroad station, not a pleasant prospect, I assure you."

"Don't go out of my life, Floy," Chantil said and was gone.

The Englishman was not quite able to hide his distaste for the emotion, for the place, for the not quite above-board transactions that he was engaged in. "Colonel Violet," he said, "there is a car outside which will take you to an airport where a Lysander is waiting to fly you to London and General de Gaulle." He held out his hand. "Good luck."

Sacha stood up, his chestnut-brown hair as untidy as always, his rumpled, handsome face slightly rueful. He gave Floy that surprisingly sweet smile. "You will not forget your poor old Sacha?" She went into his arms and hugged him. It occurred to her, inconsequentially, that she had never seen Sacha cry. "Whatever happens, you must always remember that I cared for you and Louisianne and for Billy—my sweet, ill-fated Billy—more than I have cared for any other people in my life. Unfortunately, sometimes ideas are more important than people."

She held on to him for a moment, not listening. It seemed to her that her last tie to Louisianne was coming undone. "After the war," she began, but couldn't continue.

"After the war," Sacha said, kissing her, "you will come back to Paris and make ridiculous films with your poor old Sacha once more."

He gave her his sweet, absurd smile and was gone.

Curry put his head against Floy's shoulder, and she put her arm around him. The Englishman looked at the three of them without kindness. "We've paid you," he said to Max. "You've delivered the goods. Somewhat late, but still you have delivered them.

"There is a car waiting to take you and presumably Miss Devon and her son to Barcelona, where letters of credit and other communications from her relatives in America await her. All per your radioed instructions. Is there anything else to say?" He held up the paper Max had signed. "I've only stayed because you asked me to. I should have gone with Colonel Violet."

On the paper Max had signed was a note he had

written, asking the Englishman to stay on, indicating there was more to say.

Max closed his eyes and opened them. "Has Colonel Violet's background ever been checked into?"

"Of course. I mean I assume he has been well-vetted by your people and quite probably by mine . . ."

"He's a double agent. His first allegiance is to Adolf Hitler. They've been using him to control us."

"But . . ."

"Poor old Sacha, the man you are all counting on to unify the Resistance in France, is its worst enemy. He learned to speak French when he was six years old. He has a German father and no mother. All the members of Les Fleurs du Mal who have been arrested in the past few weeks—and a good many during the past few years —have been betrayed by him. Including the White Rose and his lover, Lord Billy."

The Englishman looked at Max and then made the only gesture that would betray his feelings during the hour in that room. He touched his smooth blond hair.

"You are quite certain?"

When Max nodded, he said he would of course have to check on the allegations. He asked where Max would be staying and said if he didn't have a place—bloody difficult getting a decent room in Barcelona nowadays— he would call the Ritz and have them free a couple of rooms. "We will want to talk to you again in the morning."

"I hope so."

The Englishman held out his very clean, white hand and Max, after a moment, took it.

Max picked Curry up, and Floy followed them into an old black Ford driven by a man in the uniform of a *Guardia Civil*. The villagers who had remained in the square were rewarded by the sight of Sanchez's car driving off toward Barcelona, the beautiful American, her gigolo, and son in the back seat.

315

Chapter Thirty-one

The two rooms at the Ritz were a suite with one rather grand, nineteenth-century bedroom and a paneled dressing room that featured a gilt child's bed that had once, according to the porter, belonged to a child princess with an unpronounceable name.

Max, carrying a sleeping Curry in his arms, looked at Floy, who looked back at him and said, "Certainly you can't sleep in the principessa's bed. Curry will." She paused. "You'll have to sleep with me."

There had been time for questions during that long drive to Barcelona through the impoverished villages. But there were too many questions, and they had remained unasked.

Used to blacked-out cities, Floy was surprised by the lights of Barcelona. Barcelona was a late-night place, and there were still people, cars, entire families, walking up and down the Diagonal, the Paseo de Gracia.

The Spanish practice of blaring news over speakers in the streets, even in the early-morning hours, made her feel that despite the lights and the traffic, the war was following them.

Still, it was as if they had not only crossed over into a different country but crossed space to a distant planet. People were out at night without fear of arrest, of breaking the curfew. They were shopping and talking and sitting in well-lit cafés. Spain had already had her war, and it had left her poor and unhappy. But it was over.

Her dead could be properly buried. Her living could go about their business.

While Max bathed, Floy—just out of the claw-footed and oversized tub, that ultimate luxury—lay in the canipied Ritz bed with her eyes closed. She refused to think. She refused to allow Sacha's betrayal—poor old Sacha—to surface. She refused to think of Louisianne's death, of Chambertin and the bullet she had put in his heart, to destroy the moment.

I'm at the Ritz. I've had a bath with perfumed soap. Curry is safe behind those locked doors, and in a moment Max will come to me. We're free.

She opened her eyes to reassure herself that she was in that bed, in that illuminated city. And she nearly screamed. Max had left Chambertin's blue smoked glasses on the rosewood bureau. They stared at her accusingly. They seemed malevolently alive, as if Chambertin were still wearing them.

She fought off that familiar paralysis fear always brought and got out of the bed. She forced herself to touch those blue-lensed glasses and, holding them by the wire frame, she threw them out of the French windows.

After a moment she heard the lenses break as they hit the Ritz's cobblestoned courtyard. Someone—a waiter, she thought, from the all-night Ritz dining room—came out into the courtyard and picked up the glassless frames. He examined them and, putting them in his pocket, moved off.

Floy went back to bed.

Max, hair still damp from his bath, looking like a young and not very reputable god, came into the bedroom. He tried the connecting doors to Curry's dressing room/bedroom to make certain they were locked and switched on the crystal chandelier, lighting up the room.

"I want to see you," he said, lying down next to her.

317

She could feel the strength, the desire, the tenderness coming from his body, awakening her own. "I want to remember everything about you," he said. And then he kissed her from her head to her toes with his corrupt cupid's lips, making love to her with his slow, sweet passion throughout what was left of the night.

In the morning Max rang for room service, and a young boy brought tiny cups of genuine coffee and a pack of Gitanes. They were old and stale but they were Gitanes, and Max lit one carefully, clamping it between his teeth, blowing out the blue-gray smoke, and sighing. It was, he said, time for the question, and so she asked it: "How did you know about Sacha?" It had never occurred to her, from the moment she heard his allegation, that he could be wrong. But she needed to know how Max knew.

"I suspected him when Louisianne was taken and no one else. It's obvious why, now: Louisianne couldn't go to London with him. She knew far too much. If he was going to successfully mislead and ultimately betray *Les Fleurs du Mal, les services,* Louisianne had to be gotten rid of. She was the only person who knew as much as he did about the Resistance."

"You know as much as they do. Did."

"But I am a mercenary. I am not going to England to have breakfast with De Gaulle. Besides, Sacha needed me. He couldn't just saunter across the border. It had to look as if he had made a daring escape through the *Zone Libre* into Spain, the Gestapo on his heels. That had to appear genuine.

"Toward the end he decided I was too dangerous. I was to be taken care of by Chambertin, and Cactus would get him over the Pyrenees. The Germans patrolling the mountains were alerted. That's why Cactus had so little interference on his most recent trips into Spain.

318

"Then, when we escaped from Chambertin, he decided to use me again. He had to get to Spain and soon."

"That was why Rivet called him a traitor," Floy said, remembering that scene in Mme. Rose's stable.

"And why he stepped so out of character—one he had taken years to build—and punched him. Rivet, of course, knew."

"He betrayed Billy as well."

"I think that was the most difficult betrayal. But Billy was too smart not to realize, once he knew there was a traitor, who it had to be. Sacha arranged for Billy's capture. I doubt very much if he arranged the way he died."

She wouldn't think of that photograph. Not now. Not again. "I still count him as the murderer."

"The Gestapo sent Sacha to Billy early on, when they realized what Billy was up to. In the early days Billy didn't bother to hide his tracks, and they were all keeping an eye on him, thanks to his activities in Spain. After Sacha turned Billy in, he took over.

"In the beginning, when I knew one of us was a traitor, I thought it was you, Floy. After all, you were Chambertin's mistress. You convinced me you weren't.

"Later I thought that it might be one of the Weinbergs, or both, that they weren't from Amsterdam but Berlin. I began to tighten up. But not enough.

"Sacha's nuns were taken and then Le Levandou and finally La Bégonia. Primrose, my Monte Carlo Russian count, is still free. So is Maude Hamilton and her little housekeeper, Madame Bertrand. Only people Sacha knew about were taken in this last series of *rafles*. No one else in the safe village. No one in Monte Carlo."

It occurred to her that perhaps Lousianne hadn't given in, given up, after all.

"Of course she didn't," Max said. "That was Chambertin twisting the knife. The man who was to get the pill to her was fingered, of course, by Sacha. God knows how he managed to get in touch with them. Possibly through the mayor of our safe village. She held out to the end and killed herself with a shard of glass.

"Chambertin was more frank with me. As he pried my toenails off, he told me how stupid we all were about poor old Sacha. He was delighted to tell me.

"He and Sacha knew each other from Heidelberg. I don't know who recruited whom, but they both believed in Hitler, heart and soul. In the New Europe. Sacha is a twentieth-century sort of monster."

"What will they do with him?"

"At this very moment they're checking his records as well as mine. After all, I am only a *passeur* working for money and not De Gaulle. Now that they know what to look for, it will soon be evident he's the traitor. It won't be difficult to substantiate the facts.

"They'll send him back to France with a great deal of misinformation. They'll continue to feed him more of it so he can pass it on to his pals in Germany. When he's no longer useful, either the Germans or *les services* will have him killed. It won't be a nice death, but few are, these days."

He put out his second Gitane and kissed the tears on her face.

"We all trusted him," she said. "Poor old Sacha." She looked up at Max. "Think of all the people we've trusted who have betrayed us."

He gave her the only solace he could. He made love to her.

They spent a full day in Barcelona, Max with the Englishman, repeating his accusations, offering proof.

"The Englishman," he said afterward, "was as *snob* as ever; but he took notes. He listened."

He brought back a letter of credit, a Clipper reservation from Lisbon to New York, and long letters from her mother and from the aunties, loaded with unanswerable questions.

"They don't know about Curry," Floy said. She told him why she had left America, about the aborted abortion.

"They'll have a surprise."

"I'm not going to think about it now. In the meantime, we're relatively rich with your money and mine. All we have to do is bribe someone to get you a Clipper reservation, and we'll be all set."

"For what?" Max asked, kissing her, taking her in his muscled arms, not letting her answer.

And then Curry came in wearing the new and sad little blue suit she had found for him—Spanish shops were nearly as empty as French ones—and said he was hungry again.

They looked in at the long, formal Ritz dining room. There were three waiters for every table, and a man in a white suit played "Tea for Two" on a white grand piano.

The _maître d'hôtel_ tried to catch Max's eye, but Max was a master at avoiding _maître d'hôtel's_ eyes.

He took both of them by the hand and led them to a sprawling café on the Ramblas where the special of the day was spaghetti à la Bolognese. It was also the only dish of the day. They all ordered it.

"You seem different this afternoon," Floy said, fearful for no reason she could come up with. In the merciless Spanish October sunlight, with his lashes against his cheek as, head bent, he concentrated on his spaghetti, Max looked more eighteen than twenty-eight. But there was a melancholy air about him. He seemed vulnerable, a boy going away to school for the first time.

"Curry," Max said, reaching over, touching Curry's hand. "I left my cigarettes in the hotel. Would you go into the café and buy me a pack?"

"No Gitanes," Curry said, coming back after a moment. "Only El Toro." He pointed to a cigarette poster in the café window, where a huge black bull threatened to come charging off the paper at them.

"I am afraid it will have to be El Toro," Max said, giving Curry money, watching as the boy headed into the glassed-in café and talked to the cashier.

And suddenly, overwhelmingly, Floy knew. "You're not coming with us, are you? You're going back."

"They've asked me. Someone has to warn Les Fleurs du Mal before Colonel Violet returns. The various groups have to be reorganized, renamed, supplied with money, new transmitting keys, safe houses . . ."

"You're going to take Louisianne's place, aren't you?"

He looked at her and then at what was left of the spaghetti à la Bolognese. "Yes."

She looked back at the café. Curry was involved with the cashier, who was trying to find the cigarettes. She suddenly felt a terrible anger.

"What about the money?" she asked. "I thought you were doing it only for the money. I thought you didn't care about France or Germany. That's what you said, what you told me.

"You wanted to start a new life. They killed your wife and lied to you for years about your son and you're going back . . ." She heard the hysteria in her voice and stopped.

"I have to take care of Madame Rose and Diderot, if he's still alive, and Hibiscus, the butcher's wife in Châteldon. And all the others. There's no one else. You wouldn't want me to let them be caught, would you? I have to take care of them."

"Who's going to take care of me?" she asked, and turned her head from him because she had begun to cry again. Auntie Ida would say she wasn't the sort of girl who cried in open cafés, but she didn't care. "There's no one else left but you, Max."

"You'll take care of you, Floy," he said, putting his arms around her, holding her. "Until it's over."

"It's never going to be over. It's going to be like the Hundred Years' War. It will go on forever."

"It won't, Floy. I promise you."

"I love you so much, Max."

"You wouldn't love me if I left Madame Rose to the Gestapo. You wouldn't love me when I started hating myself."

"They know what you look like now. They . . ."

"No, they don't. Chambertin's dead. Sacha knows but he won't last very long. They still don't know who I am."

It occurred to her, inconsequentially, that she didn't know his real name. It seemed important to know it.

"Maximilien Edouard de Saint-Vincent. Winterhagen was my wife's mother's name. I've taken it for the war."

"It's a very good name for the war," she said, and thought her heart was breaking, literally, down the center.

Curry came out of the café with cigarettes, and Max said he wanted to take a little walk with him, just the two of them.

Floy watched as they moved hand in hand down the crowded Ramblas toward the port and found herself taking, lighting, smoking, the terrible and unnecessary El Toro cigarettes.

Smoking and crying, she thought, in public, in a café in Barcelona, Spain. Oh, I've come a long way from Philadelphia. I've shot a man and I've escaped across two borders, if you count the *Zone Libre*, which no one much does, and I'm going home with my illegitimate son. I suppose it's all right if I cry and smoke in public.

And then Max came back with Curry. An Austin Princess had pulled up to the curb. Floy thought she saw the smooth blond hair of the Englishman in the back of it.

Max stood up, and so did she. She put her arms around him.

"I'm not going to let you go," she said. "I won't. You'll have to strike me, and they have laws against that sort of thing in Spain." She felt his smooth cheek next to hers and could feel his muscles through the thin cotton shirt. "You're not going." She held him as tight as she could, but after a few moments let him go.

"We'll come with you," she said, but no one believed that.

"How will you go back?" she asked. A chauffeur had gotten out of the Austin Princess and opened the rear door. They were impatient, waiting for him.

"Not in the Hispano-Suiza," he said, trying for a joke, but she couldn't smile. She wanted to smile. She wanted him to remember her smiling but she couldn't.

"Wait a few days. Let's have a week. Just a week. It's not such a very long time and . . ."

"There is no time, Floy," he said and gently, too gently, he took her in his arms, kissed her once more with those spoiled, corrupt cupid's lips and moved off, without looking back, toward the waiting Austin Princess.

"No," Floy cried much too loudly as the car moved off, leaving her alone in the foreign outdoor café. "Don't leave me, Max. Don't leave me alone."

"You're not alone, Mama," Curry said, smiling at her through his own tears, taking her hand. "You've got me. Max said you were to be in my charge for the duration."

She put her arms around him and said, "Yes, I have you. And you, Curry, you have me." She looked up just in time to see the car disappear up the Ramblas and then she put some money on the table.

"First thing we have to do," she said, leading him in the opposite direction, aware of the interested stares of the other diners at the café, "is to buy us some underwear, if possible, and . . ."

But she couldn't go on. She was crying again in public places and she didn't seem able to stop.

If Spain was comfortable after France, Lisbon was luxurious. The hotels and bars were filled with salon spies, mostly Germans, fat men with decorated buttonholes.

Floy spent days in the American consulate, pleading and begging, and finally, at the end of October, she managed to get her Clipper reservation honored. Curry would sit on her lap.

They began their flight on a gray, humid day. The Clipper was filled with sad, thin people. They all seemed resigned. Their first stop was Portuguese Guinea, where there was no public bathroom and no one spoke English to alert them to that fact.

They went on to Fisherman's Lake, Liberia, where American hot dogs, long past their first and possibly second freshness. were served with pork and beans.

That night they flew across the South Atlantic to Brazil, where the Clipper broke down for the foreseeable future. Floy and Curry spent a hot, nasty, fly-ridden week in a guest house in downtown Rio. After some maneuvering, Floy managed to get them on a plane to Trinidad and then on one to Puerto Rico, which went instead to Bermuda.

They arrived at La Guardia field on Thanksgiving Day, 1942.

Her mother and the aunties were there, looking exactly as they had when she left centuries ago. There were also news cameramen who had been told a French movie star—a bombshell—had escaped from the Nazis and was landing.

The cameras clicked away—it was a slow week for war news—while Charlotte and Rose and Ida hugged her. They all cried just a little.

325

Floy touched the emerald Louisianne had given her and which she still miraculously had, and looked at her aunties and her mother, powdering their noses from gold compacts.

"What is that?" Auntie Rose asked, snapping her compact shut, causing a little pink cloud of dust to escape, pointing at Curry, who had taken his mother's hand.

She took up her lorgnette and looked at him closely and knew. "You didn't. You promised. He couldn't be . . ."

"But he is," Ida said, resolutely taking Curry by the other hand, leading them all off the field away from the cameramen, accepting the situation with rare grace.

"What will we tell everyone?" Rose wanted to know.

"We're going to say he's a little souvenir Floy brought back from France. And let *everyone* make of that what they will."

Floy hurried after her mother, the aunties, her son, this new life she would have to learn to live without Max.

Paris, 1945

Après la Guerre

It wasn't until the spring of 1945, just after FDR died, that Floy was able to convince Washington and Warner Brothers that she had serious business in France. And then they let her go finally only because she agreed to entertain the restless American troops still stationed there.

"'Entertaining the troops.' Terrible phrase," Chantil said.

Floy had written to Chantil at the Central Park West hotel where her parents were taking comfortable refuge from the war, mourning Ilone and monitoring Chantil's every movement. "It was no fun, I can tell you." Chantil hadn't written back. She had simply appeared, her hair newly dyed a truly terrible red, her plump little size-twelve body squeezed into a size nine dress. "I've come to help," she said.

And she did. She took care of the house and the revolving maids and cooks and answered the phone and bossed the secretary and mothered Curry when Floy was at the studio. She also made judgments about everything, including that offensive phrase, "entertaining the troops."

"It makes you sound like a *fille de joie*, a camp follower."

"I don't care what it makes me sound like," Floy said, "as long as I get to go."

"As long as *we* get to go." Chantil put her fat little hand on Floy's forehead, checking for fever. It was a gesture that both irritated and comforted Floy, and she held her friend's warm hand for a moment in agreement.

"As long as *we* get to go," Floy amended.

They traveled aboard a transport ship along with a dozen actors and actresses—Chantil called them the never-would-bes—who had decided to "help our boys" to cash in on the publicity. Pathé sent a cameraman and that made everyone feel better.

The crossing was rough, the weather terrible, and the Hollywood troupe was, excepting Floy, seasick to a man. All confined themselves to their staterooms, pleading with God to help them or put them out of their misery.

Curry and Chantil, surprisingly, were also victims, both reverting to French in their agony, both becoming very small children. Floy and the stewards did what they could, but mostly Curry and Chantil wanted to be left alone.

Floy sat by herself in the first-class salon. It had been pretty well demolished by the officers who had been transported to and from Europe during the war years. The ship had once been a passenger liner, catering to Junior Leaguers "doing Europe" for the first time. The gay murals on the walls had been disfigured by initials, pornographic cartoons, and variations on the Kilroy Was Here theme.

Floy rather liked the seediness, the mended upholstery, and the cracked mirror behind the bar. She drank Scotch and tried not to think, but that, as usual, was impossible. This voyage reminded her of that other sad voyage to Europe, when she was pregnant and alone and, hating herself, mourning the death of her cousin's husband, her child's father.

"Do you think we'll find Max?" Curry asked, during one of his periodic phases of feeling as if the world had righted itself.

"I don't know," Floy said, blotting the perspiration from that reminiscent forehead.

But when Chantil asked if she thought Max was still alive, Floy answered definitely, "No."

"Then why are we going back?"

"To see what's left of Paris. To have a holiday. Perhaps to live."

She hadn't told Chantil about the package and the letter she had received the day they sailed. They were from Diderot and had been mailed a month before, in answer to a letter of her own.

Diderot had written that Max had died in the winter of 1944 from "complications" in Ravensbruck, that concentration camp located in the terrible marshes between Berlin and Stettin. His body hadn't been recognizable, but his single possession had.

Floy had torn open the package. Diderot must have polished the silver case. It shone as if it were alive. Inside, the snapshot of his wife and child had company: a much-reduced old glossy of Floy in one of her early films.

I'm not going back to Paris to find Max, Floy thought. I'm going back to mourn him.

Floy thought of telling Chantil about the letter and the case, but at that moment the ship crested the peak of an enormous wave, and Chantil turned a deeper shade of green.

"If you're really my friend, Floy, you will leave me alone in what I hope and pray is my final hour. I feel like a very sick and beached whale, and you needn't tell me what I look like. Shut the door, Floy, on your way out."

Floy looked in on Curry, who voiced similar sentiments. She kissed his sweaty face and made her way back to the first-class salon, where the bartender poured her a tumbler filled with Chivas.

Where the Chivas came from was a mystery to Floy. But Hollywood had been drowning in it for the past three years, so it was a mystery, Floy thought, that a good many people had the answer to.

She carried the tumbler to the half-circle of blue leather banquette, faded and stained, that had become her favorite drinking place and took a long pull at the Scotch. She looked at the bartender, who was looking at her, and then she closed her remarkable green eyes, touched the emerald Louisianne had given her, and thought about the endless, past three years in Hollywood. Hoo-ray for Hollywood, she thought.

She and Curry had been in Philadelphia for a week when she realized they were not going to be able to stay. Everyone she knew—and a good many she didn't—were aware that Curry was illegitimate, cousin Gloria's dead husband's son by Floy. That did not make even small social gatherings possible, let alone family gatherings.

Gloria had called and had insisted on coming to the house and was being very grand and forgiving and gracious. And then Curry had come into the room. Gloria took one look at him and fainted. It wasn't easy getting her to her car. She hadn't lost weight during the intervening years. *Au contraire*, Auntie Ida said.

Charlotte spent her time memorizing Charlie Knickerbocker's society column and wondering if there were any way she could get into New York for Jay Thorpe's holiday hat sale.

The aunties were being kind, but not overly so, dropping in at odd hours with a list of suggestions for Curry's immediate improvement and Americanization.

Then the immigration people, who seemed to have nothing better to do, came around and made vague threats. Curry had been born in France in Louisianne's apartment. He had never traveled out of France before. He had no papers, no passport, and did not, according to Miss Brumgart of the Philadelphia Bureau of Immigration, legally exist.

"How do we even know he's your child?" Miss Brumgart began.

"And not Adolf Hitler's," Floy ended, annoyed by the steam heat and the flowered drapes in Miss Brumgart's office, incensed nearly to fury by the way Miss Brumgart gazed rapturously at a photograph of Franklin Delano Roosevelt while she spoke. "What would you like me to do?" Floy asked. "Ship him back to France?"

When Miss Brumgart lowered her eyes and began talking about the Displaced Children's Center near Camp Kilmer in the Watchung Mountains of New Jersey, Floy became genuinely frightened and stopped making wisecracks.

Auntie Ida, coming through as usual, called the family lawyer, who gave her a list of people Floy had to go and see in Washington. Auntie Ida called them first to prepare them, to find out if the trip was absolutely necessary. It seemed it was, and so Floy went to Washington.

Getting to Washington in December of 1942 was neither pleasant nor easy, but Floy managed. She didn't seem to have a choice. She queued up for days, getting papers stamped, baring her soul and personal life to congressional aides' secretaries' assistants. She shared a room in the old Willard Hotel with a woman who snapped Dentyne relentlessly.

She didn't sleep at night, that terrible ache for Max creating a blue void in her body and mind.

Then, just as she had all the papers gathered and signed and notarized and had delivered them to an office on the first floor in the State Department (why an office in the State Department was concerned with the fate of a five-year-old boy was a question never to be properly answered), she ran into Christian Régent. He was the half-French, half-Hungarian actor who always had trouble not laughing at his lines in the studio on the Boulevard Richard Lenoir. He had emigrated to the United States just before France fell.

He was lean and tall and had smooth blond hair, melancholy eyes. He took her to a black-market restaurant where, surrounded by Europeans, they ate *choucroute garni*. They reminisced about Billy, and he asked unanswerable questions ("Whatever became of poor old Sacha?") and told her he was "starring" in a series of US government training films.

"You should come to Hollywood," he said, when dessert, a *pêche Melba*, came. "You would be a 'hot ticket,'" he went on, spooning vanilla ice cream into his mouth. "French actresses have suddenly become big box-office."

"I'm not a French actress."

He looked into her green eyes, and his fingers touched hers, as if by accident. She moved her hand. He smiled at her. "Who would know that, *chérie?*"

She wrote to René Clair who said, yes, he remembered her, and he was making a film with a part in it for her. He wanted her to come out and test for it. All expenses, his extravagant telegram read, would be paid.

She didn't, as Auntie Rose said, think twice. She packed for Curry and herself, and her mother and the aunties drove her to the Thirtieth Street Station, using up their fuel ration and reminding her of it.

The station was crowded with soldiers milling about under the statues of Icarus and Daedalus. The aunties kissed her. Rose said she was doing the wise thing. Charlotte, without thinking, said, "Bring me a souvenir from Hollywood."

Auntie Rose said, "Bite your tongue, Charlotte," and looked at Curry. Charlotte blushed, and no one except Auntie Ida was amused.

Floy never did work for René Clair, but Warner Brothers put her under contract, bleached her hair to a shade their cosmeticians called French Blond, and put her in a series of spy chasers. She played the girl tied up and left in the closet by the Germans.

In 1944 they let her hair return to its natural color

when she got what was considered her big break, a co-starring role with Bob Hope.

Floy played a spy pursued by Nazi agents, and Hope was his usual wisecracking dope. The film made money, and she went on to play opposite Jack Benny in one that didn't.

Still, she was considered "a solid property" by the studio.

"No Crawford in the hysterical acting department, but she's got class and she can walk across a room on schedule. The ladies love her eyes, the guys drool over her legs." This was said repeatedly by her agent, the most cordially disliked man in Hollywood.

She had miraculously found a cottage in Brentwood early on, even before that all-important Warner Brothers contract. Because he wanted to train to be a soldier, she sent Curry to a nearby military academy, where he thrilled Hollywood brats with only slightly embroidered tales of real-life exploits. Chantil, self-invited and more than welcome, joined them and took over.

"Now all you need is a man," Christian Régent said to her at one of those French colony dinners, taking her hand. But she took it back, saying she had a man.

"I'm going to wait for him, Christian."

"It might be a long wait," he said, smiling gently, but she told him she was prepared.

"It might be forever."

"I'm prepared for that too."

She heard from Max three times.

Once, a German-Jewish refugee—a young doctor with a profoundly scarred face—who had been hiding in Morocco, arrived in Hollywood with a letter. Two pages. One for Floy; one for Curry. They had been written in pencil and were barely decipherable, but still, they were from him. It meant he was alive.

That letter came just after their first Easter. There was another, one page this time, slipped under the door of that Brentwood cottage the following fall. More a note than a letter, it said he loved and missed them.

And then a dubious Englishwoman, a character actress Laughton was said to be sponsoring, said that Max sent his love, this at a dinner party for nearly everyone in Beverly Hills in 1944. When Floy called the next day, the lady had disappeared. Laughton said he had never heard of her.

Floy continued to make A-minus films while Chantil ran the house and her life. She felt about her work as she had felt about it in Paris: that she was marking time. Curry went to school in the same way. He did well in some subjects—English was not among them—and excelled in sports, spending weekends playing lacrosse at friends' houses in Bel-Air.

They listened to Gabriel Heatter every night and read newspaper accounts of the war and went to newsreels twice a week. The three of them followed the war as well as they could from Hollywood.

"I feel so cut off," Chantil complained. She wished she had not listened to Ilone, that she had stayed to help.

She mourned Ilone while Floy mourned Louisianne. Both knew they wouldn't be able to stop mourning until the war was over. Floy continued to wonder if it ever would be over.

There was no question—Floy never let it enter her mind, awake or sleeping—of mourning for Max. She carried on as if she believed he was still alive.

Then the war was over, and that letter from Diderot arrived, and there didn't seem to be any reason for doing anything. All she wanted to do was get to Paris.

Maude Hamilton was waiting at Bordeaux, blonder, pinker, and more exasperated than ever. She put one hefty arm around Floy and one around Curry and made Chantil walk ahead with Peter. Single-handedly, she shepherded them through a maze of men in and out of uniform, all asking questions, demanding papers.

"It doesn't seem to change much, no matter who's in charge," Floy said, handing over passports and visas and medical documents.

The rest of the troupe from Hollywood were being taken to Paris to stay at the Meurice. It wasn't until they were halfway there in the khaki bus provided by the US Army Air Force that anyone realized Floy was not among them.

"I'm back in my house in Paris," Maude said, sniffing into her blue lace handkerchief, mixing a Whiskey Sour on the pink-mirrored bar in the back of the Cadillac limousine. "Or what the Germans left of it. What on earth do you think they wanted with Peter's mother's portrait?" She sniffed again.

"Coming down with a cold, darling?" Peter Hamilton asked. He was thinner and more translucent but the same Peter Hamilton.

"I'm overcome with emotion," Maude said, giving her button nose a vigorous honk. "Floy is back."

"My dear," Peter said in sympathy. He had survived detention and a number of other indignities, never to be spoken of, at the hands of the Germans. He had been waiting for her at the house when Maude arrived, moments after De Gaulle entered Paris.

Her Italian friend—General Macaroni, as she referred to him in private chats with Floy—had disappeared with the liberation of the Riviera.

"I put up those little cards everywhere," Maude said as the huge car glided slowly into a gray Paris, "in all the detention centers and DP camps. Just as you said."

It had begun to rain. "I ran a daily ad in our poor little one-page *Le Figaro*—paper is at a premium—since day one of publication. I put one in the Recherche section of *Le Monde*."

The Arc de Triomphe emerged, gray and insistently

reminiscent. "I've had tea with the American head of the Red Cross, who said she would do what she could. Peter is on a first-name basis with the Ambassador and the men who count at Army HQ and he's been quite persistent, haven't you, Peter?"

"Yes, my dear."

Curry and Chantil sat in front on the opposite side of a thick glass window, chatting away in French with the driver. Beyond them Floy could see the Champs Elysées, still, disappointingly, unlit. Like paper, food, and fuel, electricity was at a premium in postwar France.

Floy opened the window closest to her. The Rond Point smelled of flowers, of clean air. Billy had liked to say that "the Rond Point is the best point in Paris."

"The truth is," Maude was saying in her this-has-to-be-said voice, "that there isn't a trace of him after Ravensbruck."

Floy hadn't told her about Diderot's letter, about the silver case. She put her hand in her jacket pocket and touched it for a moment.

"But one mustn't lose hope. There are so many refugees. That's the difficult part to take in. Thousands of nameless men without papers or memories—just yet—keep pouring out of the woodwork."

"Until recently," Peter said, "nearly a twentieth of the French population were still prisoners in Germany."

The Place de la Concorde was also still dark. Floy wished they would turn on the lights for only a moment. It seemed so much larger in the dark than she remembered it. The wooden bridge the Germans had built so that they could cross to their headquarters at the Crillon more easily had been taken down.

Beyond was the Louvre and the Rue de Rivoli, the Seine. All unlit, like back sets in a B movie, *The Phantom of Paris*.

It looked as it had while under occupation. The street lights dead, gray rain, *pissoirs* rising out of the pavement like little phallic castles.

Floy nearly said she had always wanted to see the inside of a *pissoir*, but she was afraid they would think she was frivolous. She didn't want to hear Maude's report. It didn't matter. Max was dead. They could stop looking.

"There are still bands of Resistance workers," Maude went on relentlessly. "They're holed up in some of the obscurer places and they don't think the war has ended. Max might have escaped from Ravensbruck. He might be with one of those bands right now. De Gaulle's people have been, if not enthusiastic, at least interested. Max Winterhagen is a hero in their somewhat calloused eyes. Still, no one seems to know what's happened to him."

Peter coughed apologetically. He said he had been able to find out a bit more about Max. He had been captured early in 1943 and escaped a month later from Fresnes prison.

The Germans hadn't known who he was, or he wouldn't have been allowed to live that long. He had been retaken, recognized, and sent to Ravensbruck. A final train, moving the prisoners west, had been bombed en route to Berlin. "He might have escaped then," Peter Hamilton said.

"If only there were a photograph of him," Maude said, "we could send . . ."

"He's dead," Floy whispered. And then she said it louder. "He's dead. He died in Ravensbruck."

She held out the silver case. "You can stop looking. You've been wonderful, but he's dead. Stop looking, please."

The car pulled into the Hamiltons' courtyard, and Peter got out. The butler came from the house to help the chauffeur with the luggage.

Chantil asked where the nearest bathroom was. "I've been holding it in for hours." Curry wondered if there wasn't another bathroom, and Peter showed them both the way.

Maude and Floy sat in the back of that over-upholstered car Peter's influence and money had secured. Maude put her hand on Floy's arm.

"I'm sorry," she said. "I thought you had come back to find him."

Floy put her hand on Maude's. "I didn't come back to find him, Maude. I came back to remember him."

The next morning she told the man from Warner Brothers that she wasn't going to sing the Hawaiian medley at the camp show that night, wearing a grass skirt and a rainbow-colored rayon bra. She told him that she wasn't going to appear at all.

"You lied," he said. "You got us to *schlep* you and that brat and that tons-of-fun secretary across the Atlantic Ocean under false pretenses. You could be prosecuted. You lied to us. To me."

She nearly laughed. He looked genuinely put out, as if he had never been lied to before, as if false pretenses were not an integral part of his life.

"You'll never work in Hollywood again, kid," he threatened, and though Floy knew he didn't have anywhere near that sort of power, she tried to look properly abashed as she stood up and said, "Promise?"

She left him and walked along the old and familiar streets aimlessly, thinking not much had changed since the Germans had left. Only the flags and the swastikas were gone.

Posters were plastered on every building, on every conceivable surface. One repeatedly. It featured De Gaulle's Lorraine Cross made out of twisted barbed wire.

The French were now fighting among themselves. That hadn't changed much either. She supposed it was

340

a Communist poster, depicting De Gaulle's France as just another prison camp. It depressed her.

At the cafés, coffee made of burned barley was being served. She wondered if it tasted better than coffee made of acorns.

The winter had been difficult. Coal and wood couldn't be had for any amount of money. Even Maude's house sported new sawdust-burning stoves; but there had been, Maude complained, no gas to start the stoves. There were no buses or even velo-taxies. Everyone except Maude and her circle traveled by metro, which ran on a sporadic schedule.

But there were plenty of promises. And the chestnut trees in the Jardin des Tuileries had blossomed with white, reminiscent flowers. Chevalier was singing at the ABC Club and Piaf was at Ciro's. Paris would go on.

She walked up the Champs. A man wearing smoked glasses, holding a cigarette, looked at her from behind a café window. For a moment the horror came back.

But these smoked glasses were green, and the man wasn't smoking an Abdullah but a Lucky Strike, and Chambertin wasn't sitting in a café, drinking Coca-Cola, because he was dead. She had killed him herself.

She tried to keep the ghosts away as she walked up the Champs. She touched the silver case in her pocket. But she realized the ghosts had defeated her long before she turned into Rue Balny d'Avricourt and stopped in front of number 33.

I could turn away, she thought. I could go join Maude, Chantil, and Curry for lunch at Fouquette's. I probably should. There's not much sense in opening wounds that have only just begun to heal.

Disregarding her own advice, Floy stepped in to number 33 and stopped short. She nearly rubbed her eyes like a cartoon character not believing what she saw, like Olive Oyl discovering Popeye still alive after his boat had exploded.

For there in its usual place was the black oilcloth shopping bag. And in her usual place, knitting, talking to herself, looking exactly as she had four years before, was DeFarge.

Floy ran into that evil-smelling little loge and threw her arms around that shriveled body.

DeFarge put her knitting down carefully and stood up with some trouble, returning Floy's embrace, tears coming into her wise, sad, old eyes.

"You've survived," Floy said, amazed that anyone had.

DeFarge managed a grim smile, hunting in the pockets of her apron for a handkerchief, finding one, dabbing with a curious dainty gesture at her tears.

"Of course. A lot of us survived, one way or another." She looked at Floy appraisingly. "You look rich and well fed and not too happy. Well, no one is. Your aunt's apartment is waiting for you. The *sales Boches*," DeFarge said, spitting on the floor, "did some damage but not much. The lawyers keep coming around, looking for you. I told them you'd turn up sooner or later. I've told that to everyone." DeFarge returned to her knitting. "In the meantime, *ma petite*, business as usual."

Business as usual, Floy thought, as she climbed the tiled stairs to the second floor. She had the feeling she was going to grow as tired of that slogan as she had of that other one, *courage*.

She let herself into Louisianne's apartment. It smelled clean and unused. Someone, DeFarge, of course, had been keeping it up. The salon looked as it had the last time she had seen it, filled with the absurdly upholstered chairs and sofas Louisianne's *lapins* had given her. She avoided the leopardskin chaise and the thought of Billy reclining on it, Sacha standing behind him at the pink marble mantel.

She wandered through the dark rooms—there was still blue paint on the windows—thinking that she could smell traces of Molyneux Number 5, Louisianne's favorite scent.

Any moment, Floy thought, Louisianne will come out of the bedroom in her silk wrapper, her head held high, ready for the day. She put her hand to her neck and touched the emerald she always wore, and waited.

She didn't want to remember that safe village and Louisianne coming out of the mayor's brick house with her bandaged, bloodied hands. Or Billy, who had loved a traitor and had had his head chopped off by the maniacs in Germany and then displayed in a terrible cheap photograph in the evening *Le Matin*. She only wanted Louisianne to come back, to put her thin arms around her, to make her feel loved again.

She forced herself to move on, to concentrate on Louisianne in life. She came full circle and found herself back in the salon. She sat in the same monkey-fur upholstered chair she had sat in when she had been a frightened, jilted, pregnant eighteen-year-old girl, and Billy and then Louisianne had talked "plain horse sense" to her. So she talked plain horse sense to herself now.

Max was dead, and later she would learn to face that. In the meantime she would live at number 33 again with Curry and Chantil. She would, she knew, work again. As much as she disliked making films in Hollywood, she felt that she would enjoy making them again in Paris. She and Curry and Chantil would have a life.

That resolved, she stood up, intending to go back to Maude's, gather up Curry and Chantil and their belongings, and move in as soon as possible.

She stood looking up at the portrait of a very young Louisianne which hung over the mantel, wondering if she had ever thanked Louisianne for all that she had given her.

"If I didn't then, I thank you now, Auntie."

On her way out, she caught sight of an enameled frame that sat on a low shelf of Lousianne's etagere. She picked it up and looked at a photograph of Sacha. It had been taken when he was young, his chestnut-colored hair falling across his forehead. He had been smiling. It was that surprising sweet smile Billy had been too fond of.

He had been killed near the end of the war by the partisans in the clean-up operation De Gaulle named "*Epuration.*" He had had a German lover, and they had been found in a house outside Paris. Maude said they had used an axe on Sacha and his friend, and that seemed appropriate.

She began to replace the frame but stopped and took the photograph out of it. She walked across the salon into that room Louisianne had called her office. She went to the blued window, and when it wouldn't open, took off her shoe and broke one of the panes. Thin sunlight came into the office. Carefully Floy ripped the photograph of Sacha into as many pieces as she could and then, remembering how she had thrown Chambertin's glasses into the Ritz courtyard, she let the pieces of the photograph float out onto the Rue Balny d'Avricourt.

That futile gesture seemed to help.

She left Louisianne's apartment and walked down the steps into the courtyard.

A man was standing at the far side of that patch of sunshine Curry and Max had both liked. He wore a dark suit of some heavy wool and a black turtleneck sweater. He had a Gitane clamped between his teeth and a half-smile on his corrupt cupid's mouth.

There were new, indelible lines on his face and new pain in his black eyes. He was very thin and very hard.

Yet as she looked at him, he seemed softer, more vulnerable. A little damaged but not beyond repair.

She went to him and held out the silver cigarette case. He took it and slid it into his pocket, as if it didn't matter very much.

"Someone at Ravensbruck stole it from me," he said, looking at her. "I hope it brought him more luck than it brought me."

"I thought you were dead," she said, reaching up, putting her arms around him, holding him to her as tightly as she could.

"I thought I was too," he said, putting his arms around her, resting his head against hers. They stood that way for some time.

"I've been waiting for you," he said later, as they still clung to each other. "I've been waiting such a long time. I didn't tell anyone I was back. I needed time. To recover. To forget. To stop thinking.

"During the worst of it I made up a fantasy, a dream that kept me going. After the war we would marry. We would make new, brilliant, realistic movies together. We would be rich with Hispano-Suizas and houses in the Midi. We would be happy. We would forget the horror. Curry would grow up and have children, and we would sit in our retirement village near Monte Carlo, growing old gracefully.

"When I didn't think I was going to have a life—when I didn't want to have one—I invented ours."

"Stop," she said, burying her face in his neck, holding on to him with all of her strength. "Please stop, Max."

"Why?" he asked, kissing her ear, the top of her head, content to be there in that patch of sunshine in Louisianne's courtyard, holding on to her.

"Because you're making me cry so dreadfully. I don't want to cry anymore, Max."

She pulled away for a moment to dry her eyes, to get —as Louisianne would have said—a hold of herself.

"I need you so badly, Floy." He pulled her back to him as if he couldn't bear not to be touching her. He kissed her with his spoiled, corrupt cupid's lips and she could taste the salt of their tears.

About the Author

DAVID A. KAUFELT is the author of the novels *Six Months with an Older Woman, Midnight Movies,* and *Silver Rose.* Currently he divides his time between homes in Sag Harbor, Long Island, and Key West, Florida.